LESSONS
Lee Zacharias

FAWCETT CREST • NEW YORK

FOR MY MOTHER
with thanks to Michael and Debby

Acknowledgments

The author would like to express her appreciation to the National Endowment for the Arts and the University of North Carolina at Greensboro for grants that aided in the completion of this manuscript, to Roman Lavore, and to the Eastern Music Festival.

Prologue

*M*y mother told me I would cut off my nose to spite my face, and, when I was thirty-three, to prove it she died.

It was August. I had taken two antihistamines to combat an allergy attack and was lying on my bed in a haze, feeling the parts of my body—my knee, my arm, my heart, my brain—wink off and then on in a contrapuntal rhythm that refused to release me to sleep. In the deep comfort of pillowed space I lost twenty-four years and a thousand miles, and I was nine again, lying on the bed in my old room, breathing through a handkerchief to filter the pollen from the air. The handkerchief was a map of South Dakota, souvenir from a friend's vacation, and the scalloped edge blurred the bottom of my vision with red. Through my window I saw the pale evening sky. In the next room my father was dying. In the living room my mother and brother were watching TV. Its drone mixed with the buzz of a lawn mower next door, the smack of a basketball on a sidewalk, the bark of a dog down the street, and the sounds confused themselves with the stickiness of my sweat on the sheets and the cool feel of the northern state printed on the cotton that covered the lower half of my face.

I was not especially unhappy, and there was nothing in the stew that near-sleep stirs from the senses which seemed out of place. My father had been sick a very long time. I was impatient for my life to begin. Sleepless and too weak not to sleep, I was feeling the precarious drained calm that follows a storm of sneezes and confuses the hysteria of membranes with a hysteria of mind. I sat up, and a jumble of antennas, rooftops, and wires rose beyond the windowpane. My brother was sixteen. He had a girlfriend and a job after school to pay for his brand-new used car. Any minute now, I thought, he would turn off the TV; he would drive beyond the bounds of rooftops and wires to where mountain ranges rolled into their miraculous place beneath distant cloudbanks of iridescent pastel hues. Any minute now, I thought, picking up the handkerchief, which had floated to the floor, he will knock to ask if I want to go, too. Pierre, the capital of South Dakota, was a black star on the cloth, and I had populated the Badlands with nosebleeds, a gaudy splotch of cities that wouldn't wash out. If my brother had knocked that night to say "Well, Janie, where will it be?" my poor imagination would have carried me no farther than to the state of Wounded Knee. We might have gone together to live in the cities I had settled by an accident of blood, but he was still watching TV when I fell asleep in Hammond, Indiana, where we had been stranded by the accident of our family. *Any minute now*, I remember thinking just before I fell asleep, but when I woke, it was already the next day. The first thing I saw as I rolled into my mother's arms was a blade of sunlight on the crumpled handkerchief. Her arms were there because she was shaking me. It was time to get up. My father had died.

It was a coincidence she should have chosen that afternoon twenty-four years later, when the accident of allergy and antihistamine had taken me home, to begin her own journey to the afterlife, which is no life at all, as far as I'm concerned. I had not seen my mother in more than fourteen years, and in many ways she was already dead to me.

I was the musician I had left home to be, principal clarinet with the Aspen Festival Orchestra and the Richmond Symphony. I had won an international competition, made a solo recording, and signed a contract for one more, but my mother had not heard me play since Memorial Day in 1963, when I marched up Hohman Avenue with the Hammond High School Band, playing "The Stars and Stripes Forever" in a repeat rendition I had named "Forever and a Day." Afterward, when I wadded my clip-on black tie and, with a jingle of medals, tore off the sweaty wool jacket to my uniform, she took both, smoothing them across her arm with annoyance so routine, it promised that she would never die. I had not graduated from high school, but I did not plan to go back, and my mother's habit of preserving what I had discarded irritated me. I was on my way out of Hammond to a world where the imagination could soar, although, now that I have flown, I see—and it seems sad—the ongoing trivia of exasperations she called love are the sine qua non of mortality. But I wanted to be immortal, and, as I watched my mother's fingertips work against the wrinkles I had put in those scraps of cloth, I persisted in believing that she would never have anything to teach me.

I hung up the phone. In the next room my husband was practicing a Chopin Nocturne, sweating at the keyboard in his baggy white boxer shorts.

"My mother died," I told him.

"That's too bad." The Nocturne rippled on.

"This afternoon," I said. "My sister-in-law called."

Abruptly the notes broke off, and he looked up. "You know, I think there should be a decrescendo right there." He frowned, and, with the pencil he stored above his ear, he marked one on the score. Fourteen years ago, when I was eighteen and he forty, I had married him because he played Beethoven so beautifully for me. "How's your hay fever?" he asked.

"I would have gone to see her. She didn't want to see me."

"Janie, if you work yourself up, you're going to have another attack." He crossed the room to hold me. Our skin was limp and damp as cotton clothes at the end of a hot day, but we were stiff beneath it. I didn't love him, and he hated me. It was my fault. He was a gifted pianist, but he couldn't play in public. I could. "I'm sorry that your mother died."

3

I wiped a wet spot beneath my eye. "I don't know what I feel."

"Why should you feel anything?" The balloon seat of his boxer shorts was flaccid, although he'd always been pudgy and now he was fat. "You never did before."

"I wanted to love her," I said and stopped before I added *I wanted to love you*.

"Well, you didn't." He dropped his arms. "You were too ambitious to love anyone."

I thought my heart had just been sounded, and, as I'd always expected, there was nothing inside. My mother had warned me, and now she'd come back to life just to die without forgiving me. "Ben," I said and stared, and, when the floor fell away, I found the wall. The air was too heavy, and the liquid of my own lenses was sliding all over my eyes. "Please," I gasped, "please," and they locked into focus. My mother was sitting across our old kitchen table. There was still time to take it back.

"I told you," my husband said. "I'll get you another pill."

And for a minute I was still angry. "Mama," I yelled, "you hear?" Then I was ashamed. To be hollering into that afterlife, where she ought to be free. The only eternity I believe in is music, a place where the heartstrings have no meaning but sound. The space between the wall and the floor was one long, clean measure. *Soon*, I thought as I fell through it, *I'll be punished. Any minute now.*

Part I

1

*M*y mother was worried about my social development. The previous year I had found a sack of rubber horses and a scarred set of Lincoln Logs left behind by my brother when he ran away to get married. With a girl-friend named Beverly I built fences and cabins, and on my basement floor we settled the West together for hours every day during the month of August, when the ragweed was ripe and my hay fever kept me inside. If Beverly thought her ranch the better, she never let on; she was a tolerant play-mate who sweetly forgave my firecracker temper and inflated ambitions. She grew up to have rather thick calves and ankles, but, according to her mother, who came to my mother's funeral last year, she is now married and has a baby; whereas I have very nice legs and no children.

Years later, at college, I roomed with a girl who had been, at twelve, equally enchanted with miniature chargers. Her father got her off the floor by buying a real horse. But we lived in the city. My mother enrolled me in band.

So, at the beginning of sixth grade, with a rented metal instrument, I took my place as last-chair clarinet in the Wood-row Wilson Elementary School Band, which met in a green cinder-block room at the end of the new seventh- and eighth-grade addition. During the first practice my clarinet lay in my lap; that afternoon in Mr. Pelfry's office I had my first individual lesson. I hooked my thumb under the rest, put toothmarks on the mouthpiece, and blew out my cheeks till I was dizzy, tasting the bamboo reed as though I were a patient expected to make my clarinet sigh "ah"; it sputtered a series of squeaks so astonishing that for a minute I thought it had played by itself. Mr. Pelfry corrected my bite; I huffed less and blew my first open G. By the end of the week I could run up a quarter-note scale, and my mother had to nag me to pick up the ranch I'd left sprawled on the basement floor.

My brother, who had brought his baby back home to live when his wife left them both, bought me a folding music stand and set it up in a corner of my room with a kitchen chair that had been vacant since my father's death from lung cancer three years before. He worked the afternoon shift at Inland Steel, and I got home from school each day just as he left for work. It was my responsibility to watch my nephew until six, when my mother returned from her job as a cashier at Kroger's. Supper was no trouble; usually my mother and I shared sandwiches and soup. After I did the few dishes, I was free to practice, and I left my mother goo-gooing at her grandson while I hunched in my corner and put the battered clarinet through its paces, until Dickie's howls banished me to the basement, where I huddled in a heavy gray sweater of my brother's for hours, improving my fingering and tone, picking out tunes I made up as I went.

I moved up two chairs and exchanged my silver clarinet for a black hard-rubber Bundy with worn-out pads. It had a fake-leather case with threadbare satin lining and my rental number stamped on the outside. The first-chair clarinet was a busty eighth-grader who sometimes strolled around to hear the back sections, leaning over us and tootling our part while we froze and only pretended to play. Sandy, my stand partner, a notoriously fast seventh-grader who had been demoted from the second section for laziness, muttered curses as soon as Norma returned to first chair. I thought Norma was wonderful. She wore T-strap flats and nylon stockings. Her boyfriend was a saxophonist, and after practice they snapped their instruments into velvet-lined cases and held hands. Norma's case was real leather, trimmed with saddle stitching, a scrolled Schaeffer-Buffet trademark, and a red plastic punch-tape with her name. I resolved to play well enough to make second chair so that Norma and I could sit next to each other and be friends, and I reminded Sandy that Norma was only trying to help us.

"She can help me all she wants," Sandy said. "I just wish she'd quit dragging her tits in my ear."

In a way, I thought Sandy was wonderful, too.

I couldn't wait to change classes every hour, like Sandy and Norma. I was stuck in a single classroom with greasy walls, motley chalkboards, and dingy, round lights that dangled from a high ceiling the dusty color of Necco Wafers. The paint on the windowsills was breaking up like ice on the scummy Little Calumet River. Excused for practice and my lessons, I dawdled in the bright, efficient light of the bandroom, rubbing my fingers over the satin veneer of the blond cubbyholes where we stored our instruments. I was putting off crossing the playground of vicious black cinders to the four-room brick schoolhouse with the smelly girls' bathroom in the basement, where you could hear the boilers groaning and pounding as if they would blow you to smithereens as soon as you sat on the pot. That building has since burned down and been planted over with grass; even the gingko tree that scraped branches across the window near my desk in the fall and stank up the classroom when it mated in the spring (if that isn't something, trees stinking like people when they pair!) is gone, and I'm sorry a little because it was the only green thing to be seen from my seat, since in 1957, with the shiny new school already overcrowded, the fifth and sixth grades had to meet in the old one.

At home my progress was applauded, but overshadowed by Dickie's progress in learning to stand and to walk. I couldn't see what the fuss was about. Everybody learned how to walk; not everybody learned how to play the clarinet.

At school I was promoted to the second section. Sandy sucked a chipped, carmine-stained reed and nodded a congratulation. "You'll be back," she predicted, "when you start dating and quit practicing. Why don't you come to my party on Friday?"

I said I'd ask my mother, and took my place next to my new stand partner, Arthur, a seventh-grader with a head so narrow, it looked as though it had been laid on a plank and trimmed. His eyes were squinched too close together, his nose too thin to have been much use in keeping them apart. He owned a Selmer, but I wasn't jealous because it was secondhand.

My ambition was to play as well as Norma DiLuccio, and lessons in Mr. Pelfry's office, with the tick of the metronome counterpointing the squeaks and burps from the practice rooms, grew dreary as I learned at official speed, so many lessons per week and no more. From my baby-sitting money I bought the second part of the *Belwin Band Builder* and secretly worked my way through, hoping to dazzle Mr. Pelfry with sixty-fourth notes when all he expected was a few piddly eighths.

"Norma D'Luccio takes private lessons," I informed my mother that night over a bowl of Campbell's vegetable beef.

"Open," my mother ordered Dickie.

"I don't see why I can't take private lessons," I argued, while most of Dickie's strained peas drizzled down my mother's uniform.

"Janie, would you wipe the floor before his mess gets tracked through the house?"

I wet a rag and continued loudly. "Norma takes private lessons, and she's first chair. I'll never get to be second chair if I don't take lessons."

"Janie, if you loved me, you wouldn't ask," my mother scolded. The brutal kitchen light made her look tired. "Frankly, I'm beginning to wonder if band was such a good idea. Beverly was over here twice last week while you were practicing. Surely you don't need to take it so seriously."

"I do," I insisted, hanging the rag on the faucet.

"Did you just put the rag you wiped the floor with in the sink?"

"And anyway"—I retrieved the rag—"I have lots of new

friends in band. Only they won't be my friends very long if I don't get to take private lessons."

"Don't be silly," my mother said. "If they're any kind of friends, they like you for yourself."

I made a face. Actually, I didn't have any new friends in band, except maybe Sandy, who certainly didn't care how well I played and probably didn't like me for myself either, and Arthur, who had offered to put my clarinet away for me if I was in a hurry. "You wouldn't have to pay for them. Norma takes lessons with Mr. Schunk, who used to teach at the Chicago Conservatory, and he played in the Chicago Symphony."

My mother's mouth tightened. "Has Dick been paying you for watching Dickie?" I toyed with my unused fork, rubbing my fingerprints into a patina. "Answer me."

I nodded and waited to get yelled at, although it was all her fault, because she gave me only fifteen cents allowance when most kids that I knew got fifty cents or a dollar.

"Well, if he wants to give you money, I can't stop him. Irregardless, if you loved me, you wouldn't take it. I mean—" she said, and I winced because, when she got to the *irregardless's* and *I mean's*, what she meant was if I loved her I would never do anything. "I warned him. A mother knows these things." She exhaled a long, sorrowful breath. "I'm not saying he didn't do wrong, but he's a good worker, and what kind of appreciation did he get?"

"I appreciate it," I promised. "So please?"

"I didn't mean you," my mother snapped, and the subject was closed, because my mother had forbidden the name of Dick's ex-wife to be brought up in our house, just as she wouldn't let us swear or smoke, for, though it would be years until the surgeon general released his report, my mother knew as surely as she'd always known Carole was no good that my father had been killed by Lucky Strikes.

On Saturday morning my brother drove me to Mr. Schunk's. I loved to ride in his car, a powder-blue '53 Chrysler with maroon plaid seat covers and a pair of fuzzy dice dangling from the rearview mirror, the radio blaring and Dick punching out the beat on the steering wheel at stop lights while I hoped the whole world wheeled by and took him for my date. Girls who had been to my house and who noticed those things told me what a cute brother I had. At first I hadn't seen it. In his steel-toed boots and Penney's work pants, he looked like my father had; oh not exactly, not bald, not even tired, but the gray twill seemed to cast its shadow up, hollowing his flesh like ground into which his features would someday have to settle like old houses. On his days off he looked more appealing, dressed in chinos with a light blue shirt open at the neck. My mother ironed his shirts, and, though he wouldn't say so, he thought she was sloppy with the collars—he was fussy, but, no matter how often he scrubbed, his fingernails were dirty, his knuckles stained black in the fissures.

We were both short and slender, but his face was one of those nasty tricks of nature that give a boy long lashes and skin as smooth and semisheer as Lenox, then stick his sister with stubs and splatter her with freckles. We had our father's gray eyes and hair the color of just-turned winter-wheat, not dishwater blond, as some folks are mean enough to describe it. He was cute instead of handsome only because a sliver of space was lodged between his front incisors, and he had a habit, which I share, of tucking his top lip across them when he smiled. When I caught a rerun of *Rebel Without a Cause* at a campus theater years later, I was shocked to see how much he had resembled James Dean. It made me sad. I considered my brother's life a cause without a rebel.

"That's some music, Sissy," he said when Elvis wailed "I'm All Shook Up." "Makes me feel old. Me and Carole had to dance the Tennessee Waltz." He idled the car in front of a white frame bungalow. "This must be it."

"Maybe it's the wrong house." I frowned. "I can't go in there. He teaches *Norma*."

"Aw, come on. You're as good as her."

"How do you know? You haven't ever heard her." I picked at a fingernail. "Anyway, Mom doesn't want me to take lessons. She doesn't even want me to be in band."

"Sure she does. She just worries about you. You know mothers. Shoot, she worries about me."

"That's because your life is ruined."

He laughed. "You believe that?"

"I guess so. Mom says so. I don't know."

He poked at one of the dice. We both watched it swing. "Carole wasn't so bad," he said. "Anyway, people don't wreck their lives that easy. So I had a little trouble. I got a good kid. Hell, I'm only nineteen. I mean, my life's not over." He squeezed my knee through my corduroy skirt. "Well, play your heart out, kid. Get your money's worth."

"I can't," I said. "I'm scared."

"Aw." He punched me lightly on the chin. "You'll knock him dead."

"Yeah? What do you know?" I said after I'd slammed the car door and watched him peel out. He never drove like that when I was with him. I scuffed my white bucks up Mr. Schunk's paintless front steps. A torn piece of paper was taped to the door: BELL DOES NOT WORK NOW DAYS. I knocked.

The door opened a crack, and two sunken brown eyes with dark half-moons underneath focused on my clarinet case. "Please, one minute." I heard the rasp of a night chain. "Abraham Schunk." A large-boned man who wore his drooping yellow flesh like loose clothing, he held out a trembling hand for my navy blue blazer. A copper bracelet protruded below the rolled sleeve of his beige cardigan sweater. "Arthritis," he explained. "Myself I cannot play so much now." He smiled, baring wet brown teeth. "I give you good lessons though."

In the living room he laid my blazer on a single bed covered with a plaid bedspread from the Sears catalogue. The room was the same no-color as my sixth-grade classroom, which might have been meant as blue or gray, with pipes painted to match climbing the walls to a high, water-stained ceiling. A line-up of unmatched dressers and knickknack tables hugged the walls, and I had to be careful not to trip over several oscillating fans feathered with strands of greasy dust. It was horribly disappointing.

As he walked, Mr. Schunk hunched forward, his leather house slippers flapping against the flowered rug. Pointing out another fan, he cautioned me to watch my step. "In the summer," he said, seating himself before the piano, "I suffer

13

from the heat but more the damp," but he didn't explain why the fans were still out and the filthy lace curtains tied back in October. "Next year I will move to Arizona." I left my clarinet case on the bed and assembled my instrument, sitting on a kitchen chair and placing *Band Builders* on the claw-foot music stand. He played a few bars on the piano and looked up. "Do you recognize?" I shook my head. " 'Ferryboat Serenade,' " he said. "A favorite of my wife." He nodded at a framed photo on top of the piano.

I thought his wife looked like Kate Smith.

"Dead," he moaned, "these fifteen years. She liked symphonies but also popular music. My children"—he nodded at another picture—"are gone. My daughter lives in Bloomington. Her husband is professor of music. His children like the song of the 'Hound Dog.' "

I giggled. "You mean Elvis Presley?"

"You like?" He shook his head. "It is different generation. But you like the symphonies also?"

As far as I knew we did not play symphonies at Woodrow Wilson. I nodded anyway.

"Good," he said. "I would like to live near my grand-children, but the doctor says Arizona." He coughed as if to prove his point and opened my book to the first page. "Play please."

Well, any idiot could have seen the big red check that proved I had passed it, so I began to turn the pages, but Mr. Schunk flipped them back, firmly tapped the music stand, and repeated, "Play please," then found fault with my first note. Prodding my back to straighten my posture and poking my puffed cheeks, he loosened my grip and tilted my head up. "Like so. Flatten the chin; arch the fingers. Yes, so." I blew an E, and he shook his head. "Flat." We tuned with the piano, and he shook it again. "Thin." He took my clarinet, wiped the reed, and, to my horror, put it in his mouth. The instrument sobbed a rich, woody C. After running up and down the scale, he gave it back. "Tone is not so good."

"Do you think I need a new clarinet?" I swabbed at the reed with the sleeve of my white blouse. I don't know what I was afraid that I might catch. Not arthritis. Whatever was contained in the slight smell of mildew that came from his house and his clothes and perhaps, I thought, his flesh.

He shook his head again. "For the student player the student clarinet. Later maybe you become accomplished player and get the Paris Selmer." He turned to the back of the book and asked me to play "Faith of Our Fathers." I touched my lips to the mouthpiece tentatively, but it had the familiar taste of wood and plastic and my own saliva. There were certain things about music I was learning to accept: the sight of the brass draining spit from their valves, the damp stink of the chamois when I cleaned my clarinet. I thought my mother would make me quit if she knew what it really took to play. She was always yelling at me for dipping into the sugar bowl with a spoon I had licked, and when she kissed me good night, she brushed dry lips across my cheek.

"No, no." He stopped me. "Maestoso, maestoso! Like so." He threw back his head and puffed his chest. I bit the reed to keep from laughing. Halfway through the "Oompha Boogie," he stopped me again. "Do not tap the foot. You must hear the rhythm in your head. The tonguing—lightly, lightly. Lu-lu-lu-lu-lu. No ta-ta-ta-ta-ta." He smiled. "Otherwise you are making the tongue say *achtung*." I did not get his joke. Taking my clarinet again, he showed me how to tongue without spitting. His house might be shabby and his marbles loose, but right away I heard the improvement. By the end of the lesson I had learned that without craft there is no art, although, of course, I did not think it in those terms. What I thought was simply this: I would come back next week and every week and for the rest of my life I would do whatever I had to do to become a musician.

When Dick honked, I blushed and spilled money from my pocket. Mr. Schunk licked his fingers and ruffled the edges of the bills while he counted. Then he handed me a slip of paper on which he had written *Rubank Method/Intermediate*, and I snatched my clarinet case with pleasure, having bidden good-bye to those green and white Belwin books for good.

In band I mentioned to Arthur that I was taking private lessons, and he invited me to the junior high sock hop. Since it was a school activity in the afternoon, my mother said that I could go, providing I promised to come right home. "And that means no stopping for Cokes or anything else, Janie." I treated the whole sixth grade to the news. "So what?" said Antoinette Cooley, but she was just jealous. Dick bought me a circle skirt printed with palm trees and monkeys and a banana-colored sweater that came from Rosalee's instead of Penney's.

"You're spoiling her," my mother complained as I peeled the tissue. Whenever Dick bought me a present, he had it wrapped, my birthday, Christmas, or not.

"It's her first date," Dick argued. 'She'll want to look special."

"It's just Arthur," I pointed out, twirling through the living room in my skirt.

My mother was still frowning. "I don't know that yellow is her color."

"I think she looks pretty," Dick said, and I swooned into his startled arms.

We met outside the gym after school, and Arthur took my hand to lead me inside, where I saw Norma hanging her arms around her saxophonist, her head resting on his shoulder as they shuffled back and forth while the school hi-fi spun "Love Me Tender." Arthur's hand was cold. I whispered to him about Mr. Schunk and the song of the "Hound Dog," and he laughed loudly. With stiff, small steps and Arthur's hand clenched at my waist, we danced a slow number. When it was over, I steered us toward Norma.

"I'm taking lessons with Mr. Schunk now," I told her. "I'm going to get my own clarinet soon too."

"Oh, that's nice," Norma said and leaned toward me to whisper "Don't you think he's just P.U. ?" She wrinkled her nose.

"I don't know," I said, because his faint scent of must and cabbage reminded me of how my father, twenty years older than my mother and wasted down to eighty pounds, had begun to smell before he died. I had assumed that people stank at a certain age, like meat left out on a counter, and the only thing to do was pretend you didn't notice. The hi-fi began "Poor Little Fool," and Norma swung to the dance floor with Tim.

Since Arthur couldn't dance fast, we went to the cafeteria for a Coke. He had squeezed a whitehead, leaving a grooved red welt beside his nose. For a few minutes we talked about band, and then there didn't seem to be anything left to say. On our way back to the gym, I excused myself to the bathroom.

Sandy was leaning across a sink, applying Hazel Bishop to her thin lips, but she didn't see me. A girl I didn't know combed her hair at the next sink.

"I saw your friend Norma," the girl was saying. "She's in the gym falling all over Tim Chudy. Do you think she puts out?"

Sandy snorted and tried to rub the lipstick off her teeth with a finger. "I *know* she puts out. How do you think her tits got so big?"

"What do you mean?"

"You let your boyfriend play with your tits and they get bigger."

I crossed my eyes at my chest as I flushed the commode, wondering if it would be worth it to let Arthur play with my tits. It didn't look as if I'd ever need a bra otherwise. I washed my hands at the sink next to Sandy, who plunged her hand into her inkpocked purse and brought up a gold tube. "Fire Engine. You want to use it?" Like my brother, I was cute, and I've never outgrown it. Not beautiful, not striking, not elegant, just a plain old freckle-flécked, pug-nosed puss who looks like a coloring book in makeup, I thought the new me in the mirror looked stunning.

"Tough," Sandy marveled. "Hey, you should have come to my party last week. I'm going to have another next month. I'll introduce you to some cool guys from Tech."

I licked the red slick from my teeth, thinking roses would taste like that if you ate them and that was probably why you didn't. "Are they here?"

"Nah, they're not interested in a *junior* high dance. Hey, maybe I'll come dance with you one of the fast songs."

"Okay," I agreed, but I sat them all out because she must have forgotten.

17

Every Saturday morning Dick drove me to my lesson, and, though Mr. Schunk picked at nearly every note, we worked my way through the *Rubank Method*. In band I passed Arthur, who hadn't even tried to kiss me that time after the dance, and after I passed him he didn't ask me to another.

Mr. Schunk told me about his wife, who had died of cancer, too. "They removed her breasts, and they took out her insides." I was horrified. "And anyway she died. That is what they do when you are sick—they take out the sick parts. How a person is to live without insides I do not know." He stared at his hands while I thought about my father, who had been opened and closed on the operating table like a book whose first page proves too difficult. "Six months," the doctors had said to my mother. "A year at the longest." He fooled them and lingered over two. "I suffer from arthritis, but they do not chop off my hands. A man can live without hands, but not without insides." Mr. Schunk shook his head. "Now I cannot play, with hands, without hands. Why should I want to live?" He coughed. "I suffer from the damp, and the doctor says go to Arizona. So next year I move to Arizona, but my children stay." He coughed again and wiped at the purple crescents beneath his eyes. "I am Jew. Because of Hitler I come to this country. Now I am sick. Always I am moving. What for?" He shrugged. "I cannot make music. It is horrible life wherever I am."

I dabbed at my own eyes.

"I am sorry." He patted my shoulder. "I do not want to make you unhappy. You are young girl, no reason for crying."

"Well, maybe your hands will get better in Arizona." He shook his head. "Well, then I'll play for you. I'll come to Arizona, and you can listen to me."

"You are nice girl, Janie."

"I'll learn to play as good as Norma DiLuccio."

"Ah, Norma." He nodded. "She is nice girl also. Nice." He cupped his hands in front of his chest, and I laughed. "Norma is practicing hard—it is important to practice." He dropped his hands. "But she has no talent."

"Norma?" I felt my eye sockets enlarge. "Norma DiLuccio is first chair."

"Practice." He nodded. "In the first gymnasium—in the grammar school—first chair. The fingering, the tonguing—yes, good, very good. But she does not hear the music." He tapped his head and gave me a stern look. "You understand? You practice, first chair. In the grammar school, and in the symphony orchestra."

"Me?" My voice squeaked like an excited woodwind.

He smiled. "You have not played long. You make mistakes. But you hear the music." He looked severe. "It is important to practice also." He looked mean. "It is important to practice without the red stain on the reed."

I was nodding and laughing. "I'll practice. No more lipstick, okay." I thumped myself on the flat chest. "Me—I practice. In the symphony orchestra first chair."

2

On a Friday night in November Sandy had another party, and she invited me to spend the night afterward. My mother didn't like it, but when Sandy promised that her mother would drive me to Mr. Schunk's the next morning, she reluctantly approved.

Dick bought me a baby-blue taffeta dress with a velvet collar and a stiff crinoline trimmed with blue ribbons. "You're spoiling her," my mother protested again, but Dick insisted that a girl who was going to parties had to have a party dress, and my mother admitted I would be needing a fancy dress for the Christmas band concert, anyway. I wore it with my first nylon stockings, held up by an embroidered garter belt that looked delicate and lacy but felt like a western harness, and a pair of black-suede low-heeled pumps purchased by my mother, who said they were for the concert, then added it wouldn't do to wear such a pretty dress with bobby socks. I took a bath and jitterbugged before the mirror in my finery, packed my flannel pajamas in a cardboard case once used to store my ballerina doll's tutus, and, because my mother did not drive, rode with a friend of my brother's to Sandy's.

I was early. Sandy and her mother were eating bologna

sandwiches in the kitchen. Her father wasn't there, and, though she'd never told me so, I knew he did not live with them. I thought Sandy and I might be friends in a way that Beverly and I had failed to be ever since the day I had ridden my brother's old bike around the block and waited on her front steps while her father bent to fix the chain on her green Schwinn. A few feet away, the sun gilded his bald pate, a dome that seemed as official and remote to me as any government that might be housed beneath. "Okay, Snooks," he said, giving her rear fender a swat, "let's see you tear off this one," and I looked up the street, embarrassed by her intimacy with this dull old man. I felt sorry for her, I felt unreasonably hurt, and I pedaled viciously. All afternoon I made her whimper, "Janie, c'mon, Janie, *wait* for me."

Now I said, "How do you do, Mrs. Gitzke," and spread my stiff skirt over the kitchen chair Sandy offered. Sandy was wearing tight black Capri pants with a cardigan the color of Campbell's tomato soup buttoned up the back. Neither of them noticed my new dress. Mrs. Gitzke gave me a vague smile, dripped ketchup on her pink nylon robe, and muttered, "Shit." After a few minutes, she began to list Sandy's responsibilities. "I'll be home around three," Mrs. Gitzke promised, "and I'd better find the place clean and you asleep." I certainly hoped my mother wouldn't discover that Sandy's party had been unchaperoned.

The first guest was a girl I recognized from Wilson, Vaneita Spisak. The others came soon afterward, one more girl and six boys, who were, I guessed, Sandy's cool friends from Tech. Vaneita was wearing a tight tweed skirt and a turquoise sweater; the other girl wore Capri pants and a blouse with a safety pin through one buttonhole. Nobody mentioned my dress, and right away my new stockings caught on a chair and ran. I fixed myself a Coke and sat next to Vaneita on the sway-backed sofa in the basement. The overhead light had been turned out. "Do you know these boys?" I whispered.

Vaneita shrugged. "They're Sandy's friends." She wasn't bad-looking, but possibly because she had red hair or because she lived in Columbia Center, the government housing project across the street from Wilson School, she wasn't popular.

21

There were two classes at Wilson, those whose fathers worked shifts in the refineries and mills, and those who lived off the dole. As early as first grade, we had known the distinction, giggling in line outside the gym, where the school nurse was checking scalps, because *we* didn't need any purple light to tell where the cooties would be found. All up and down my block the neighbors worried that one day the government would integrate the Center. My mother fretted too, although she taught me that everyone was equal, no matter if Polacks were dumb and Mexicans dirty and the colored, *well*. First of all, nobody could help being born colored, and it wasn't nice to say "nigger" or "chocolate drop." I should always be nice to the colored, but the day they moved to South Hammond was the day we were moving out.

"See that guy?" Vaneita asked. "The tall one with the cigarette? At Sandy's last party he stuck his hand up my sweater."

I remembered what Sandy had said that time in the bathroom and glanced at Vaneita to see if she looked as if she'd grown a lot lately. If she had, I couldn't tell; so I guessed maybe it took more than one time. "What did you do?"

"I slapped his face and told him I didn't do dirty things like Sandy. Now he pretends like he doesn't know me."

The boy had asked Sandy to dance, and they waltzed to the Platters, his cigarette a firefly at her shoulder. The rest of the boys surrounded the record player, mumbling to "The Great Pretender." "Your dress is so cute," Vaneita whispered, and I thanked her, crossing my legs to conceal the ladder in my stocking, but none of them asked us to dance.

When the record rejected, Sandy disappeared and came back with a bottle of aspirins. "I don't have a headache," I said as she passed them to me.

Vaneita laughed. "Goof. Take a whole bunch and drink some Coke."

"Get you high," Sandy explained, wiggling her backside to Jerry Lee Lewis. "I took twenty at school last week and puked all over the bathroom."

Sandy decided that we should play spin-the-bottle so that Vaneita and I could meet the guys. Sandy went first. She and her partner sashayed behind a clothesline hung with old quilts and drapes to the darker half of the basement, and after a minute the boys nudged one another. "Come on, Tony. I want a turn." Everyone giggled as I gave the bottle a twist to decide who the first boy I ever kissed would be.

Actually, he wouldn't be the first boy to kiss me. There had been a smarty-pants named Roger Greene in fifth grade. He had brown curls that drooped over his ears because his father drank the haircut money, and, though he lived in Columbia Center, I guess I thought he was cute. Every morning I recited perfectly while Roger's spitballs pasted me in the back of the head; every recess I beat him up. Though I was smaller, I always won. Anything went—kicking, biting, pinching, scratching—and we spent every recess on the field out behind the playground to avoid scraping ourselves in the cinders. As we rolled through the weeds, grasshoppers sprang into my crinolines, and for the rest of each day I had to squirm in my seat while they plopped from between my knees, pelting the classroom floor like the storm of locusts that had dropped on the banks of Plum Creek in one of my books. Our classmates circled us, the boys cheering for Roger, the girls for me, always warning us a few seconds before the first bell so that we could be in our seats by the second.

One day, busy raking Roger's face with my nails, I jumped up only when the second bell shrilled. By the time we slipped through the door, Miss Lowry was asking Bobby Mulvihill to name the capital of Idaho. Miss Lowry looked a hundred years old. She had come out of retirement to take our class because of the teacher shortage, and maybe she was afraid we would try to take advantage or something, because she kept a paddle that said IT IS MORE BLESSED TO GIVE THAN TO RECEIVE out on her desk where we all could see it, although the only ones who ever received were the boys. So she motioned me to sit, but asked Roger to bend over, and one of the boys hollered it wasn't fair on account of Roger would never've been late if I hadn't creamed him. I studied the inky pencil trough on my desk, trying to look as though I were merely passing time until I was asked to rattle off the capitals of all forty-eight states. "Creamed you, eh?" Miss Lowry scanned

23

the beads of dried blood strung across Roger's cheek. "Too bad she didn't churn you to butter." And Miss Lowry went on walloping her way into heaven.

After that we stopped fighting and stood around on the cinders at recess again, but just before school got out for Christmas, Roger grabbed me from behind and wrenched me to the slag. While the boys formed a company around us, Roger waved a flag of mistletoe. With his other hand he held both my wrists, and he must have finally come into his strength, because I wiggled and writhed and only got cinders up my butt. His mouth sat like a cannonball on mine for a long time before he rolled off. I started to chase him, but he didn't run, and what's the fun in that? My face flaming, I slunk to the bathroom and tried to scrub the cinder smear off the back of my dress. And that was the end of it, because over vacation Roger moved to West Virginia, which was just a bigger Columbia Center, according to my mother.

Now, of course, I know more, and I'd like to take this moment to say hi, Roger, wherever you are, sorry you blew town while I was still too dumb to know a good relationship when I had one. Even eleven months later, playing spin-the-bottle in Sandy's basement, you didn't count. I was ready for something more adult.

The bottle rattled toward a boy with slumped shoulders, who followed me behind the curtain. We stumbled into the hot-water heater in the dark. He kept his hands at his sides and pecked me on the mouth. "My name's Janie," I whispered as he felt the curtain for the opening. "Glad to meetcha, Janie," he said without looking back. The couples became slower to return. I spun Tony. "She's too little," he said. "I pass."

"I'll kiss her." The voice snapped like rubber bands. I liked the voice, but it belonged to the boy Sandy had danced with, the one who had stuck his hand inside Vaneita's sweater. Behind the curtain, he put his hands on my shoulders and slobbered all over my mouth. His breath smelled like smoking leaves, and I turned my head to wipe my chin. "Open your mouth, little girl." "I'm not a little girl," I said, and his tongue shoved its way between my teeth like a slimy piece of meat with the taste chewed out. I couldn't breathe, and my lips were smashed. I wondered if, when he ever stopped kissing me, I'd be able to play the clarinet. "You're cute," he said. "I like little girls."

"I'm not a little girl." I pawed the curtain, but he tackled me from behind, burying his face in my neck.

"Come on with me," he said. "There's a chair back here somewhere." He tripped and pulled me into his lap. "That's better. How tall are you anyway?"

"Four feet ten, which is nearly five feet. My name's Janie."

"That so? Well, Janie, I'm six feet. That makes you a little girl."

That also made it different, and, besides, he said I was cute, and, even if it was dark, I didn't care. "What's your name?" I asked, sitting on the edge of his lap ready to jump off if his hand slipped down my dress and oblivious of the difficulty its Peter Pan neckline would cause.

"Paul. Why don't you relax, Janie? The game's not going to go another round." He lifted one buttock from the armchair, pulling a bottle from his back pocket, then tipped it to his mouth.

A couple staggered into us. "Taken," the boy muttered, and Sandy whined, "I told you he'd have the chair."

"Drink?" Paul asked.

"Don't you leave that bottle where my mother can find it," Sandy threatened and snatched it. "O-oh," she gasped and sputtered until I thumped her on the back.

Paul laughed. "Go on back and take some more aspirin and Coke, little girl."

"Why don't you come back to the party?" Sandy asked him.

"Janie?" He held the bottle out to me.

"I don't drink," I said, shocked. "I don't take aspirin either."

"Listen to Miss Priss, who's been back here making out for half an hour." Sandy pulled Paul's sleeve. "I wish you'd come back to the party."

"I have not."

25

"We've invented a new game called rotation," she promised Paul.

"I haven't either been making out."

"We don't want to play," Paul said, and she flounced through the curtain, insisting, "Well, I wouldn't want to play with you anyway."

"Maybe we ought to go back," I whispered.

"You want to rotate, go ahead." I didn't leave. "Sit down, Janie, I want to kiss you." I didn't know what I wanted, so I sat on Paul's lap again, and he kissed me. "What's your last name, Janie?"

"Hurdle."

"Well, Janie Hurdle, maybe I'll call you sometime. You aren't related to Dick Hurdle, are you?"

"Do you know my brother?" First he had chosen to stay with me, and now he knew Dick. I imagined us together at the next sock hop and wondered if he would give me his ring so that I could wear it on a chain around my neck.

"Not really. His girlfriend used to be a friend of my sister's before he knocked her up. I heard she ran off with a guy from East Chicago after she had the kid." Paul took another drink. "Sure you don't want any?"

"I don't drink I said." I guessed we wouldn't go steady after all.

"You're a nice girl, aren't you, Janie?" I couldn't tell if he was making fun of me or not. "I heard your brother was a nice guy too. Nice enough to marry her, and look what she does to him. Nice guys finish last, Janie, do you know that?"

He wasn't making fun. "I don't know."

"Well, they do. I'd like to be a nice guy, too, but I can't afford to." He drained the bottle. Then he nuzzled my neck. I wriggled away, and he threw back his arms and laughed. "Okay, Janie, no hands." He kissed me without touching me anywhere except the mouth. "On account of you're a nice girl who's got a nice brother."

I guessed I wasn't really mad. Because I liked him and he made me laugh. "I think you're nice."

Shifting me in his lap, he scooped his hand over the side of the chair, and the bottle rang against the cement. "Janie, sweet Janie, know what?"

"What?" He liked me, that was what.

"I'm drunk." He gagged. "I am really really drunk."

"Uh-oh." I hopped up. His vomit splattered over the side of the chair as I turned my head and swallowed hard. He collapsed against the back, moaning an apology while I held my breath and touched my hand to his clammy forehead. "I'll bring you some water," I promised.

As I tripped on the steps, Sandy sat up on the couch. "Who's that?"

"Janie. I'm going upstairs for a towel. Paul's sick."

"Jeez-O-Pete," Sandy said, and stood.

I found a grimy dishrag near the kitchen sink. The counter was littered with dishes, and I opened three cabinets before I found a clean glass. When I went downstairs, the overhead light was on. Sandy's boyfriend was sitting on the couch, hanging his hands between his knees and studying the floor. The other couples were blinking, their faces pale beneath a sheen of sweat. Sandy stood over Paul.

"You know where the bathroom is—you don't have to puke all over my floor. And you better get it cleaned up before my mother gets home."

"Leave me alone, creep."

His face was the color of cold grease in a skillet, flecked with freckles, and the lipstick I'd borrowed from Sandy was smeared like strawberry Kool-Aid down his chin. I couldn't think of a single movie star who had red hair, yet there it was, dragging a damp kiss curl and doing a sodden float on top of his head.

"I'll leave you alone. Just you remember my mother's coming home at three." Sandy swished through the curtain. Four buttons on the back of her sweater were undone.

I scrunched down to clean up his mess, averting my head and wiping blindly. There was a spot of vomit on my shoe.

"Thanks," Paul said. "I'm going to clear out in a minute. Can I give you a ride home?"

"I'm spending the night." I hadn't thought he was old enough to have a car.

"You a good friend of Sandy's?"

"We're in band together. I sit in front of her."

"So you're really a good friend of Sandy's? Tell each other secrets and all that?"

"I don't have any secrets," I said. "She used to sit in front of me, but I passed her. I take lessons with Mr. Schunk. You could drive by my house sometime if you want."

Paul was laughing, and he looked much better, his face warming and two dimples appearing. "How old are you, Janie?"

"Twelve," I said sadly, "but I'll be thirteen next summer. How old are you?"

"Seventeen, and I'm going to tell you something. Sandy has these parties all the time, and I don't ever want to see you at another one."

"What do you mean?" I demanded. "You won't even be invited."

Paul lurched to his feet as Sandy punched through the curtain. "Thanks for the lovely party."

"Go to hell," Sandy said, and he laughed. Halfway upstairs he looked down. "And scrub that shit off your face, little girl."

I was struggling up from under the mistletoe again, and I didn't understand why it always had to be that way. I rubbed my hand across my mouth. "You're not either nice," I yelled. "I'm sorry I said you were, and I'm glad you got sick."

He laughed all the way to the top of the stairs, and I hated him, but I kind of liked the way he strutted when he walked.

Upstairs, Vaneita sat beside me on the sectional sofa while she waited for her new boyfriend to go to the bathroom. Sandy and one last boy were still in the basement.

"His name's Larry. He's going to take me bowling tomorrow," Vaneita whispered. "He's really sweet. I told him I didn't do any dirty stuff like Sandy, and he didn't even care." She picked fuzz balls off the waistband of her sweater. "You should've played rotation, and you might of met somebody too. How come you spent so long with that creep?"

"His name's Paul," I said. "He thinks I like him, but I don't."

Vaneita shrugged and got up to leave. "Well, see ya at school."

There was a whimper as they opened the door, and Larry handed in a tiny, shivering white poodle with brown gunk running from its eyes. "This belong in here?"

"It's Sandy's." A bedraggled blue bow hanging from each ear, the dog was shaved pink except for its pom-poms. When I patted it on the head, it snarled.

I pried a half-empty cup from the cover of *Photoplay* to skim an article about Piper Laurie, then fanned through the pictures.

"Hi." Sandy looked over my shoulder. "Eddie just left. I think that one's so tough." She pointed to a picture of Elvis. "Do you think Eddie looks like him?"

"Maybe." I checked my Timex. "Your mother's going to be home soon."

"Who cares?" Sandy glanced at the poodle curled in one of the chairs. "Who let the dog in? Come on, Pierre." Pierre didn't move as Sandy clicked her fingers. "Okay, you little bastard." She tossed it in one of the bedrooms, but it ran out between her legs, squealing and snapping at her hand as she grabbed it by a back muff and slammed it into the room again. "It's my mother's dog," she explained.

"He's very cute."

"He's a creepy little turd that shits all over the floor."

I put the magazine aside. "What's Paul's last name?"

"Nolta. Do you think he kisses good?"

"Does he go to Tech?" All the dummies went to Hammond Technical-Vocational High School. And the hoods. My brother had gone there, though he was not a hood and my mother said he was smart in his way. His way wasn't school, and he had quit to feed the mill furnaces while Carole watched TV and grew Dickie inside her. I thought it never would have happened if he'd gone to Hammond High, and already I was afraid that if Paul went to Tech, we could never like each other.

She jabbed me in the ribs. "Anyway, I think he kisses good. I used to date him."

When we finished picking up, we closed her bedroom door behind us. Sandy stripped off her slacks and asked me to unbutton her sweater. She had refastened the buttons that had been undone before. When she unhooked her bra and flung it in a corner, I turned away, although I really wanted to look.

"I think middle-sized boobies are the best, don't you?"

While she posed before the mirror, I peeked at her reflection. Thirteen or fourteen, she had real breasts with fat brown nipples. It didn't make any difference to me that I was only twelve; my own breasts had just started to grow, and they weren't much bigger than they had been when I first discovered the lima bean-sized lump and panicked. I had cancer. I knew all about cancer because of my father and because my mother read *Reader's Digest*. Now that I knew my disease was my breasts, I kept my back turned and hurried into my pajamas, dropping a puddle of clothes at my feet. "I bet Norma's sag." Sandy kept chattering as I got very depressed, thinking what was a whole breast to me would be just a pimple to her, and her middle-sized boobies bobbled as she searched the floor of her closet for a nightgown.

"Have you ever been hypnotized?" she asked, slithering into a beige nylon gown that gaped at the neck. She decided to hypnotize me, so I perched on the edge of her bed while Sandy wagged an aurora borealis pendant before my eyes. "You are going to sleep. You are very sleepy." My ear began to itch. "Put my sweater away," she commanded, and I scooped it into a drawer, wondering if the game was just a trick to make me clean her room. "Pick your nose."

"What for?"

She sighed. "Because I told you to." And when I jabbed a forefinger up my nostril, she said, "Janie picks her nose."

I dropped my hand. "I do not."

"You can't talk unless I ask you a question. Do you menstruate?"

"I do not either pick my nose."

She sighed again. "You've just been faking. You're not even hypnotized." She had dropped one hand inside her gown and was scratching at a nipple. "Let me see your titties."

"No." I wished that I were home. "What do you have to ask me to do all these weird things for?"

"Forget it then if you think they're weird. You're not hypnotized anyway." I didn't like this game, but I'd agreed to play it. "I am so," I swore and ripped off my Donald Duck pajama shirt.

"Boy, you haven't got anything on top."

I jammed my arms back into the sleeves, sniffling with rage.

-"I was just kidding," she apologized. She had retrieved her hand from her gown and was massaging the froth of nylon on her chest. I was fascinated by the way her breasts moved around, first one and then the other, like ice cream scoops in a root beer float. "You know what?" Her chin nudged my shoulder.

"What?" I asked. "You better not tell me anything that's dirty."

"I haven't even got to the dirty stuff. You sound like Vaneita," she added, standing and shaking her hair. It was long, the ends packed into a tight sausage that curled around her back and shoulders. Oddly, I remember too the way her neck twisted, long and graceful as the throat of a great white heron suddenly unfolding. "Are you hypnotized or not?"

"Not."

"Ha-ha-ha-ha-ha, then you pick your nose."

I'd had enough of the adult world. It was boring.

"Did you let him feel you up?" she said.

I would have thought it was my own private business if there had been anything to mean business, but instead I was shocked as she parted my hair above my ear and whispered, "Paul." I snapped my head away.

"I let him feel me up," she said. "Right in my basement."

"I don't care," I said. "I don't even like him."

She was walking around the room, shifting piles of dirty clothes from one surface to another. "You better not, 'cause he likes me." She thrust her face down close to mine. "He likes my titties, and you don't even have 'em."

I turned away. "He does not."

I looked back as she flicked her tongue across her lip. "He took his thing out and made me kiss it."

"*He never did*. Nobody would do that."

I had begun to cry, and Sandy looked ashamed as she sat beside me and put her hand on my shoulder. "Okay, Janie, we won't talk about it. I didn't know you liked him that much."

3

$\mathcal{S}$crunched in a single bed with Sandy, who kept flinging her arm across my face and rolling in the covers, I slept poorly and woke even before the sun stained the window shade yellow. My toothbrush lay on the bottom of my case, along with an old satin ballerina doll shoe, but I'd forgotten toothpaste and couldn't find any in the bathroom. I settled for brushing with water, swabbing my face with a sour pink washcloth I found wadded on the side of the tub. It made my skin smell like must, and as soon as I spit, my mouth was as dry as a birdcage again.

Sandy was still asleep, my pillow smooshed over her head. There was no use looking in my case. I hadn't brought anything to wear to my lesson, and my stockings were so laced with runs that I jammed my bare feet into my pumps. Paul's vomit had dried to a nickel-sized sheen on the suede. I caught my zipper and left blue taffeta wings flapping at my shoulders.

Wondering why no one but me seemed to hear Pierre yapping in Mrs. Gitzke's bedroom, I settled on the couch with a Nancy Drew book I found in a pile of movie magazines on the coffee table. Just when I got to the place where the house Nancy was sleuthing in slid off a cliff into the sea, the pages were stuck together with gum. I didn't care. I knew she got rescued. She always got rescued; that's the way her life was. In twenty-seven years of courtship, Ned Nickerson had never made her kiss his thing. Sandy was lying.

I woke her. "You said your mother would drive me to my lesson. I have to stop at my house and get my clarinet."

"Huh?" Sandy sat and hitched up her nightgown.

"I have to go to my lesson."

Padding into the living room, she shook a cigarette from a pack on the coffee table and dipped her face over the gas stove. "Want some coffee?" She yawned. "I must have caught cold last night in the basement. Shit." Sandy sniffed and wiped her nose on the shoulder of her nightgown.

"There's a spot on your dress."

"I'm going to change it," I said as Sandy rinsed two cups and poured the coffee. "Do you think your mother's getting up soon? I promised my mother I wouldn't miss my lesson."

"My mother likes to sleep late on Saturdays." Sandy was drawing faces in the sugar I'd spilled across the table. "Do you think Eddie looks like Elvis? I do." She rubbed out one of the faces, and after a minute she said, "I'm not allowed to go in my mother's room when there's a man in there."

"You mean your dad?" I asked, surprised.

Sandy sniffed loudly and scraped at her nose with her palm. "I must've caught cold." She wiped out all the sugar faces; then she looked up. "My mother only closes her door when she brings a man home from a bar."

"Oh." A nerve was jumping at one corner of her mouth, and I tried to smile as if my own mother brought men home from bars all the time, but Sandy had already looked away. "You said your mother would drive me to my lesson."

Sandy was shoveling her fingers through the tangles in her hair. "I love Paul Nolta," she said dully. "I love him, and I want you to leave him alone."

"Sandra." Mrs. Gitzke appeared in the archway, wearing the top to a pair of shorty pajamas. Pierre nipped at her ankles. "Will you shut the hell up? And you better clean this kitchen before Fred gets up and I bust your goddamn ass."

The half-moons of Mrs. Gitzke's bottom quivered through the living room, and the bathroom door banged.

"Maybe I could take the bus," I said. "Go away," Sandy growled at Pierre.

"The only thing is, I don't have any money." I opened the back door. "Com'ere, dog." As Sandy dabbed a finger below her eye, I closed the door, surprised to see a tear glistening on her knuckle. I would have crossed to her side to—well, I don't know—but she left the room. Then she came back with her mother's purse and looked up, dry-eyed. "How much is it?"

"Fifteen cents. But I don't have my clarinet."

She slumped over the kitchen table. "I like my mother," she mumbled, without looking up. "Me and my mother are pals." I took the money and walked six blocks to the bus.

Mr. Schunk met me at the door. "You are late." He cocked his head. "Without an instrument the lesson will be difficult."

I sniffled.

"Today you are not happy."

"I forgot my clarinet." I sobbed.

"It is not so terrible," Mr. Schunk said doubtfully. "Although."

I wiped my face. "Could I use your phone? I'll call my brother. He'll come get me."

"I have called your house. They are not home. Your mother or your father."

"My father's dead."

"I am sorry."

"He was old," I said, feeling nasty. "He had cancer."

Mr. Schunk nodded. "My wife."

"They said he went to Heaven." I had never talked about my father's death. Dick had tried to draw me out, but I was mad at him for bringing Carole to the funeral, and afterward I saw him kissing her as if nothing had happened. My mother went on about life everlasting, but if she was so hot about Heaven, how come she never went to church? "I don't believe that stuff," I said. "I don't believe in Heaven, and I don't believe in Jesus, and I don't believe in God unless he's a mean old man that likes to do people in.''

Mr. Schunk frowned.

"And I don't even miss my father." I clapped my hand to my mouth. I'd meant never to tell anyone.

"You did not like your father?"

I looked away. "No. I liked him fine. He was just"—I shrugged—"always sick." I looked back, at the flesh that hung from Mr. Schunk's face like empty sacks. "Do you think people tell the truth?"

"About your father?"

"About anything," I said.

For a minute he sat without speaking. "Today you are going to a party?" he said at last.

"I went to a party last night." I had forgotten to take my garter belt off when I threw my stockings in the case. It was twisted around my waist, the garters flopping and biting my legs.

"For young people that is nice. For old man it is too loud. The phonograph player . . ." He drew circles in the air. "It is not music. Noise."

I smiled.

"You had a good time?"

"No." That wasn't true. I had had a wonderful time at the party.

"The music is too loud?" I shook my head. "Why?"

"I stayed all night at my girlfriend's. She promised her mother would drive me, but her mother wouldn't get up, and she brought a man home from a bar, and now I don't even have my clarinet." I couldn't explain the rest.

"It is not so terrible," he assured me. "You would like something to eat maybe?"

I nodded, and Mr. Schunk fetched a plate of crackers and gave me a glass of milk. The crackers were dry and flat, and I watched as he chewed one with his mouth open; then I washed mine down with my milk. "Thank you," I said as I set my empty glass on the floor.

"Please." He gestured toward the plate. "Matzo. They are

for Passover but also good any time." He smiled. "Very good with beer. I take them to the ball park with me."

"They're delicious," I said as they grew in my mouth.

"In my country beer is better, but they do not play baseball. You like baseball?"

I nodded vigorously, speaking through a mouthful of paste. "My brother took me to a game last summer at Comiskey Park."

"It was good?"

"It was great! Minnie Minoso got hit in the head by a ball at the plate, and Landis ran into the wall chasing a home run."

"My son-in-law in Bloomington is big fan. When my daughter visits me, we go. He is a fan of Chicago Cubs."

"Boy," I said, "I feel sorry for him."

Mr. Schunk was delighted. "My son-in-law is American. He is not so smart in baseball? Eat," he added, pointing to the matzo mountain on the plate.

I shoved another cracker in my mouth. "The Cubs stink. Next year my brother says the White Sox are going to wipe up the field with the Yankees."

"Hah! I will tell my son-in-law." Mr. Schunk bobbed his head. "He is professor of music. Very good trumpet. Nice children." Mr. Schunk rolled his hand in the air. "But my daughter . . ."

"What does she play?"

Mr. Schunk shook his head. "She is graduate of University of Chicago in biology. She is here, in this country, before we come because"—he touched his hands to his chest—"the Nazis. I knew." He shook his head again. "I sent my children away. My son-in-law is student at Chicago Conservatory. He is friend to my daughter, and he helps to arrange teaching for me. Then she is married. No time for biology. It is waste."

"You mean you think she got married just because her husband helped you?"

He shrugged. "In Deutschland my daughter studied violin. I make her unhappy, she says. I do not insist that my children are musicians, but I have daughters, no sons. They must be—biologists then.'' He leaned forward and tapped a finger against his breastbone. '' She is proud person, my daughter.''

I stuffed my mouth with crackers and mumbled, ''Um-um.''

''Today the arthritis is not so bad.'' He held out his hands, which looked as knotted and shaky as always. ''I will play you a lesson. Wait here.'' He disappeared, and I heard the hiss of a toothbrush. I thought guiltily of all the times I'd drooled cookie crumbs into my clarinet and failed to clean the crust of saliva out with the chamois. Once Mr. Schunk had caught me storing my mouthpiece with the ligature still clamped around the reed, spit drying between them like mortar. He had not said a word, but at the next lesson he'd scraped my reed with a razor blade, saying, ''You must learn to do this anyhow, but especially if they are going to sleep in the same bed.'' I'd blushed and promised that I would give mouthpiece and reed separate bunks from now on. And I had, when he was looking.

He stood while he played, his back rising with the music, his mouth tucked around a crystal mouthpiece so neatly, it looked as if he were sucking instead of blowing, drinking notes from what to anyone else would have been plain air. Like the one dancer in a thousand whose brilliance is implied by a particular coil of muscle, Mr. Schunk promised music, as though that word meant something I had not yet dreamed, from his stance. The instrument whined and trembled, grew full and emptied, swilling sound like a cask of well-aged bourbon, letting it trickle now, and then making it pour. At least the effect is much the same as I hear him again in retrospect; his playing makes me dizzy, and the music makes me drunk.

Very carefully, he laid the clarinet on the piano bench and sat on the bed. ''That is the lesson.'' He smiled. ''You will never have a better one.''

''It was beautiful.'' I was too stunned to speak, and so I breathed words. ''I never heard anything like it.''

''No, you have not.'' His smile widened to a grin. ''I am not modest. I will not argue whatever you say.''

''I'm going to learn to play like that,'' I promised.

His smile disappeared. "You will never play like that. I"—he touched his finger to his chest—"play like that." Then he looked at his hand. "I *played* like that." I didn't appreciate the distinction, having failed to notice what an effort he made at tenses and how often his past spoke as present. He was sixty-seven; I could not comprehend the years beyond fifty-nine, which was my father's age when he died. Mr. Schunk rose with slow dignity. "You are right. There is no God."

I felt terrible. I thought Mr. Schunk must have gone through his whole life believing, and it was my fault he'd stopped believing now. Just when his playing had made me wonder if there was something to faith after all. Who knew? One guess was as good as another, and if they had choirs in Heaven, they might just have a band.

He reappeared as I set the cracker plate on the piano.

"You are not hungry?"

I shook my head.

"I am ashamed," he said and sat. "It is Stravinsky, what you heard. Modern music." He smiled. "I am old man believing in young sound. You must believe also. You must learn everything. You must learn Mozart, and you must learn Schönberg. You must learn to play in symphony, from the conductor, and you must learn to play solo, from"—he tapped his temple.

"I will," I promised, but he shook his head as if no promise would be enough.

"I do not like to give lessons, but I am teaching you. I will teach you the best, and I will teach you for no charge."

"You don't have to do that," I protested, humiliated that he should think I was poor. I wanted to explain to him about Columbia Center and about Sandy's house and how much nicer mine was.

He didn't look at me. "I would like still to be playing. In the symphony are many old men, but no crippled hands. In my day, the clarinet must play with the orchestra, but, with Chicago Symphony, I play the *Première rapsodie* of Debussy before I retire, and there are many ovations. Now there is much music. The clarinet will, more and more, play alone. From inspiration, no conductor, no violins to count coming in. It is different. Now you understand."

"Sure," I said, completely bewildered.

"You are not paying because you will play solo for me."

"But I forgot my clarinet," I reminded him, thinking surely he could not mean I should use his.

His face folded. "Perhaps I do not explain well in English. I have not learned the language until nineteen thirty-six."

I was born in 1945; it seemed odd to think that he had been an American longer than I had.

"In Deutschland—it is Germany to you; to me it is the *Vaterland*." He smiled. "That is my sadness. I do not burden you. As a quintet playing Schönberg we are scandal. It is said that we play in the way of cats. I do not agree with Schönberg. Because of his music, he must fight. He is thinking, when time is too kind, it will be harder. To be unpopular, to fight. I think it is wonderful not to fight. I think it is wonderful to be clarinet now."

"Well, I thought about playing saxophone," I said, "but they didn't have any extras to rent, and my mother didn't want me to play drums."

"It is not ideal." He frowned. "I am maybe the best clarinet in the world. One or two as good. For the composer, arthritis does not matter. For Beethoven, even the bad ear. For the performer it is more important, and so now I am teaching you. To play solo—it is like the way of the composer. And you will be almost as good."

"I'll be better," I promised.

"You will never," he said. "It is my sadness you will have more music. You know Schönberg?"

I shook my head.

"Too bad. Schönberg is very important. The revolution for modern music, twelve *ton*. He is not appreciated in his lifetime." He paused. "Schönberg is Austrian and is Jew, but also he is musician, artist. You understand? I am German, and I am Jew, but I too am musician. Most important I am musician, but for the Nazi it is most important I am Jew." He brought his fist down on his knee. "For the Nazi it is most important Schönberg is Jew. Dismissed from the Prussian Academy. Nazis!" Mr. Schunk pounded his thigh and splattered the music stand with spit. "In the war Webern is shot. By an American soldier who is drunk, but I tell you, if it is not for Nazis, the American soldiers are not there. They are scum, the Nazis. My brother, my sisters—concentration camp, Treblinka, Dachau. I want them to come with me to this country, but they do not. When the war is over, my brother and one sister are dead, and my other sister is in Mülhausen. You know Mülhausen?"

I shook my head.

"It is in East Germany, and now she cannot come. Russians! Nazis!" He spit again. "It is horrible life." The dark cups beneath Mr. Schunk's eyes were damp.

"What happened to Mr. Shurenburger?" I asked. "Did he go to Mulehouse?"

"Mülhausen. No. To California. He is retired but gives lessons because there is no pension. He wants to move to New Zealand, but the money is too much." Mr. Schunk jabbed a finger at his eyes. "No time to write music. In Hollywood the cinema offers money, but Schönberg is artist, he cannot do that." He began taking his clarinet apart and swabbing with the chamois. "He is dead six years and does not finish *Moses und Aron*. My wife is dead fifteen years. My children move to other cities." Mr. Schunk snapped his case shut. "When I go to Arizona—is far." He shook his head as though it were too sad to speak of. You read Deutsch?"

"No."

"Schönberg wrote to me letters. Not too many, I am honest. Wait, I show you one."

He returned with a handful of paper, showing me first a blurred black and white photograph of an orchestra. A dark-haired clarinetist was taking a bow. "It is me," he said. A faint pink flushed his face. "By my daughter. When I am playing Debussy." He handed me a discolored newspaper clipping with an even more blurred photograph and his name underlined in red.

''You mean you played in front of all those people?'' I demanded.

He smiled and took a pair of rimless glasses from the pocket of his shirt, then unfolded a thin sheet of typescript. '' 'My dear Schunk,' '' he read, then looked over the lenses. ''Me. 'My illness has prevented me from replying to your letter sooner. My complaints are not major—unfortunately, since for those there is remedy. My doctor has recommended the glass of brandy, and, although it does not cure me, I have enjoyed it.

'' 'At any rate that and the fact that I have no suitable record player have prevented my hearing your record of my Wind Quintet until recently. But I am gratified now to hear that my music still speaks to true musicians. I really feel as though I have again been listening to your playing in Berlin: the rendering is so beautifully shaped. I wish that we were younger and could count on living to see full understanding, but, as you know, I have predicted many years ago that the second half of this century will spoil by overestimation whatever the first half's underestimation left unspoiled.

'' 'And in any case I shall follow the performances of the other members of the quintet with the closest of attention. My congratulations on the birth of your grandson. I remain . . .' '' Mr. Schunk looked up and smiled as he refolded the paper. ''To me from Arnold Schönberg, with others I do not read. I leave for you the understanding.'' He inspected the envelope for dust, then took it, the photograph, and the clipping to the back of the house.

The understanding was limited, but as I glanced around the shabby room, I no longer saw the mismatched furniture, the fans feathered with dust. I saw the temple he had built with his breath, and my own tract house, with its slipcovers and boxy little rooms, seemed as tacky as Sandy Gitzke's in comparison.

In a few minutes he shuffled from the back room to answer the door, and Norma followed him inside, her saddle-stitched case bouncing against her thigh.

''What a pretty dress,'' she said to me. ''Let me help you with the zipper.''

I took the cracker plate to the kitchen. When I returned, she was practicing intervals while Mr. Schunk hammered his hand on the edge of the stand. "No, no. For the upper register the embouchure must change—so." It was nothing he hadn't said to me, but now I felt sorry for her.

"Boy, it's about time," I said when Dick honked and leaned across the front seat to release the handle.

"Hiya, Sissy, sorry we're late. Dickie and me went uptown. How was the lesson?"

"I forgot my clarinet." I swiveled toward the back seat to give Dickie's fat leg a squeeze. "So Mr. Schunk played for me, and we talked, and he's going to give me lessons for free from now on. He used to be a friend of Arnold Shurenburger, and he played a solo with the Chicago Symphony. Hey, where are you going?" I hunched my shoulders to conceal the Coke stain on my dress with my coat. "I thought we'd go to Fat Boy's for lunch. How was the party?"

"It was okay."

"Well, you must of looked pretty in your new dress. Was your boyfriend there?"

He meant Arthur. "He's not my boyfriend," I said. "Hey, do you know a guy named Paul Nolta? His sister used to be a friend of Carole's."

"I don't think so."

I watched the cars go by on Indianapolis Boulevard as we walked through the parking lot, hoping that Paul Nolta had driven by and seen me getting out of Dick's car. Dick was carrying Dickie, who had started to bawl. As soon as we sat down in the big, circular gray booth up front, I shoved the rubber duck we kept to distract him across the table.

Dickie lobbed it to the aisle and howled, but as Dick leaned out for it, still balancing Dickie, the waitress arrived with a spindle-legged red plastic seat and set the duck on the table. "Aw, whatsa matter, little fellow?" she crooned and helped Dick steady the seat and strap Dickie in.

It was always that way. Wherever we went with the baby, everybody made a fuss—when he wasn't even that cute, what with some kind of food or slobber all over his face, and it didn't matter if we washed it either, hollering his head off for no good reason and making you feel it was your fault even though you hadn't done anything. "He won't tell you," I said.

They shut him up with a sucker, and we opened our menus. The waitress fluttered at our table, waiting for us to make up our minds and saying things to Dick like how cute Dickie was and was I his sister?

"Can I play the jukebox?" I asked, turning in my seat. When the Diamonds began bleating "Little Darlin'," Dickie bounced in his seat.

The waitress returned, bringing him some applesauce. She flitted back and forth from us to the table near the lighted pie case, where she sat with nothing to do. Did we want more water? Could she take the chill off Dickie's milk? "Look at that," Dick crowed. "My kid's going to be a rock-and-roll singer."

"How old is he?" She had long blond hair, but I just knew that she dyed it, and her butt was too big.

"Ten months."

"Ten months! Well, he's a big fellow, isn't he? I bet you'll be walking soon." She leaned across the table to slobber all over Dickie again.

"Paul Nolta kissed me," I announced.

She glanced at me. "I'll go see if your order is ready."

"Paul Nolta—he isn't Connie Nolta's brother, is he? Well, so he kissed you, huh?"

"Uh-huh," I answered, but the waitress was back, leaning between us with a clatter of plates and glasses that took her several minutes to arrange. She reclaimed Dickie's empty applesauce dish.

"Well, you eat good, don't you, little fellow? What's his name?"

"Richard Alvin Hurdle, Jr."

She smiled at Dick. "You're the senior? Aw, that's nice. It's nice for a little guy to be named for his daddy. Well." She hovered near the table, her tray hanging like a purse at her side. "Will there by anything else?"

"No thanks."

"More applesauce?"

"No, we're fine."

"Okay," she said. "Just call me if you need anything."

"He got sick all over the floor," I said. I could talk to Dick. It wasn't like talking to my mother, who would have said, "Janie, please. We're eating."

"Want a french fry, Dickie? Who did?"

"Paul Nolta." I was talking with my mouth full. "He's going to call me today."

"You sound pretty interested in Paul Nolta."

"I might be." I wiggled a french fry in the ketchup. "Sandy got mad and made him go home. She says really dirty things, and her dog pooped in the house, and her mother came home from a bar with a man, and I had to go to my lesson on the bus. I owe her fifteen cents," I added and dropped the last pickle into my mouth.

Dick frowned. " Sandy who?"

"Sandy my friend. It was her party. She said she'd introduce me to a bunch of cool guys from Tech."

"You're too young to be meeting guys from Tech," Dick said so softly I had to lean across the table to hear him. "I went to Tech, Janie; I know. And I'm not sure I want you staying overnight where somebody's mother is bringing pickups home from bars."

"I'm not either too young," I said. "I try to tell you something like you're my friend, and you act just like Mom. Well, if that's the way it is, where's my apple pie à la mode?"

Dick signaled the waitress and reached for my hand. I yanked it away. "Oh, come on, Janie. You know I'm your friend."

"Oh yeah? Then how come you're yelling at me?"

"I'm not yelling at you." He had the most beautiful, the most reasonable, the gentlest voice. I have spent my life among musicians, but have never known anyone who could sing a note as lovely as every word he said, though it's true that while he spoke I scarcely listened. "And I don't ever want you to be afraid to talk to me. But you have to remem-

45

ber that you're my little sister, and I can't let anything happen to you. It's just not a good idea to be staying where—well, where the adults do things you wouldn't want Mom to do.''

"I don't care what she does. Oh boy," I said as the waitress placed my pie before me.

The skin between his eyes relaxed. "Okay, Janie. I just want you to be careful, that's all."

"I don't want to be careful." I wasn't mad at Dick, and I didn't know why I kept trying to fight with everything he said. I finished my pie and stirred what was left of my milkshake with my straw until the paper got limp and wouldn't suck up the thick stuff.

The waitress came to ask if we wanted anything else, and she gave Dick another sucker to keep for Dickie. She hunched over the next table to add up the bill, which I grabbed the second she slid it on the table. "Boy, she didn't charge you anything for the suckers or the applesauce." I caught Dick inching a dollar bill under the edge of his plate. "What's that for?"

"It's the tip." Dick's whisper had a sandpaper edge, since he knew that I knew exactly what it was.

"How come it's so big?"

Dick flushed. "She's a good waitress. She was helpful, and she took an interest in Dickie. That's important when you go into a restaurant with a baby.

I tossed my head. "You mean she took an interest in you."

"Not so loud," Dick said between his teeth.

I flipped the check over and gave a disgusted snort. "It's been a pleasure serving you. Thank you for your patronage," I read. "Marie. Oh brother."

"Give me the bill, Janie."

"Marie," I said. "Hot diggety dog."

"Give me the bill."

I held it behind my shoulder.

"Marie," I whispered. "The dawn is breaking."

"Janie, in two seconds I'm going to smack you."

I passed him the paper and pushed my lower lip out. In my whole life Dick had never threatened to hit me, and it made no difference to me that I was acting ornery. I squinched up my face and tried to squeeze out some tears, but none came, so I scuffed and kicked my way to the cash register behind Dick, carrying Dickie's dopey duck.

The waitress flashed Dick a big smile. "Thanks," she said. "Come back."

"Oh brother," I muttered and stomped my way to the car.

"Well," Dick said cheerfully as he pulled into traffic on Indianapolis Boulevard. "What are you going to do this afternoon?"

"Nothing."

"Janie," he inquired after the light changed at 169th Street, "wouldn't you like to tell me about it?"

I didn't answer.

"Okay," he said and turned right at 173rd Street. No one said anything for a while. Dickie had fallen asleep in the back seat.

"You know what Paul Nolta said to me?" I asked. I wanted to stop acting bratty and make it up, but I didn't know how.

"What?" Dick sounded interested, although his eyes were fixed on the rearview mirror as he slowed down for the railroad track near Southeastern Avenue.

"He said you had to get married." Dick looked as though he'd been slapped. "He said everybody knew. He said you were a nice guy, and nice guys finish last."

"That's not true, Janie," Dick protested. "You mustn't ever believe that."

"What?"

"About nice guys."

"Oh. I thought you meant about getting married." I felt like biting my tongue as soon as I said it.

He seemed to grow smaller. "I did have to get married. You know that."

I felt terrible because I'd made him say it, but I felt mean and hurt, too, because he'd said he would hit me, as if he were a grownup and I was a kid. "Then you've got a lot of nerve telling me what I shouldn't do."

He didn't say another word. When we got home, I climbed the cement steps without looking back, but in my room I didn't feel like doing anything, not even practicing. I cut through the living room, where Dick was sitting in front of the Bears on TV, to get a glass of milk, and I slouched in the doorway, hoping he would say something. He looked up as if he wanted to, but he didn't. Maybe he didn't know how. I opened my mouth to patch it up.

"You think you're so smart," I heard myself say. "I bet you never even heard of Arnold Shurenburger."

4

Norma had a solo in a medley we were preparing for the Christmas concert. It wasn't a real solo, just four bars of diddling *"Gloria"* while the brass held half notes until the rest of the band came in for *"in excelsis deo."* My part was just a bunch of rests, and it doesn't take much practice not to flub a rest. For something to do, I learned Norma's part. All I intended was to perform it for Dick and my mother so that they could finally recognize a tune. I was as surprised as the rest of the band when Norma began botching her notes.

"Her boyfriend ditched her for somebody else that doesn't even have big whoozits," my stand partner explained when I saw Norma, eyes down, slowly twist her clarinet apart while Tim Chudy rushed past without speaking. When she rose, she looked awful, fur collar on crooked, her nose pink, her eyes mapped with red. In the next days her attention traveled from her score to the saxophone section beyond the tip of Mr. Pelfry's baton, which he kept rapping on his stand, making the other clarinets rest on while Norma went through her solo again.

A week before the concert he gave up and had the other

first clarinets try her part. Then he jerked his baton toward the seconds. All down the row I could feel the players tense as I touched my lips to my mouthpiece, the overhead lights rattling so loud I thought they were my teeth. When I finished, Mr. Pelfry motioned me to haul my chair to the front. No one spoke as I clanked into place, and before I was settled, Mr. Pelfry beat on his stand. "At sixteen again. A little louder, baritones." As soon as the bell rang, Norma dropped her clarinet and flew from the room.

"You better watch out." Sandy was grinning at me. We hadn't spoken since the morning her mother had failed to drive me to my lesson; she hadn't even said thank you when I'd returned her fifteen cents the next Monday in band. The other players were clicking the locks on their cases and scurrying toward the door. "Norma's going to nail your ass."

I shrugged, though I felt like a rat. I'd got what I wanted: I was sitting next to Norma, but it didn't much look as if we'd be friends. I was first chair, and everyone hated my guts.

That afternoon I dragged my feet down the sidewalk. If I was the best player, why shouldn't I be first? Didn't everyone want what was good for the band? Norma had had her chance. It wasn't my fault Tim had dumped her. So how come I didn't want to hear my mother gush about how proud she was? I cut through the vacant lot at my corner, toes stubbing yellow boogers of ice that had formed on the path. Ahead, a dirty old sheet of a sky had been thrown over the roof of the Woodmar Church of God, where Sunday mornings and Wednesday nights the holy rollers prayed to get into that pitiful heaven. A handful of starlings fell like ashes on a few bread crumbs near the alley. So this is success, I thought, hobbling toward home over the knobs of that frozen, knuckled field, this and nothing better. As the starlings swept over a tangle of rooftops and wires, those dumb-ass birds flying north instead of south, I understood that no matter what success was not, I would never give it up. It was the first time I knew that I hated my life.

Norma didn't speak to me the rest of the week, and her shoulders stiffened each time she turned the pages of our score. I was grateful when Arthur stopped in front of our stand to say hi.

I didn't even mind his pulling up a chair at lunchtime, while I was perfecting my lesson in one of the practice rooms. It wasn't his fault his nose looked as if someone had tried to seal the nostrils with staples. He wanted to rehearse his science report. "Sound," he began. Did I know there might not be sound if there was no one to hear? I frowned. Was he trying to tell me my clarinet wouldn't play if he wasn't there? No, because the waves would strike my ears, but what if a tree fell in a forest with no one around? "That can't be right," I insisted. "If a tree falls, it booms whether anybody hears it or not." How did I know, he challenged. What would I say if he told me the *World Book Encyclopedia* said I was wrong? I'd say, I informed him, that *World Book Encyclopedia* was full of shit. So we ended up arguing about whether a lady should use cuss words, but I didn't mind, because it was nice to have someone act, for a change, as though I weren't rotten to the core and contagious.

I hadn't mentioned my promotion to my mother or Dick, whom I had hardly seen in weeks. He was working overtime, going in early, and in the afternoons I picked up Dickie from the lady next door. By the time he got home from the mill, I was in bed, and the rest of the time he was out. He had a new girlfriend, my mother told me and sighed. She hoped he knew what he was doing. She was afraid he was getting serious, and she stewed on account of Dickie. The only person I told about being first chair was Mr. Schunk, who congratulated me in one breath and picked me apart in the next.

"Allegretto," he grumped, "not allegro. You are not a galloping horse. *Allegretto con anima*. Maybe trotting. The spirit must know the difference."

I said the spirit was going to have to because I didn't, and anyway I didn't see why composers couldn't write their instructions in English. He looked at me as if I were a Nazi.

"I am German," he said for the hundredth time. "When I come to America, I speak English. When I am at the ball park, I speak baseball. When I am playing music, I speak Italian."

"I don't know Italian."

"I do not know English. I have learned. Play the scale, please." I couldn't see what that had to do with learning to play allegretto, but, since Mr. Schunk had begun giving me free lessons, I felt obligated. "Play the scale from G."

"The scale starts at C."

He shook his head. "Today it will start at G."

"Okay," I said doubtfully, and played it twice, wincing on the seventh step. "Wait," I insisted and sharped the F.

"Very good. Now play the scale from D."

This time I listened for the wrong tone, then played it quickly and right. "How come I have to keep changing the notes?"

Reaching over my shoulder, he tapped the two sharps keyed on the staff of the étude I'd galloped through instead of trotting, and I groaned because one of my goofs had been playing a C-natural at the end of a line. To remind me, Mr. Pelfry always circled the notes that were keyed flat or sharp. "Signs with the notes are for the accidentals," Mr. Schunk huffed, but as far as I was concerned, all flats and sharps were accidental. "It is the key of D major. You have good ear, but you do not know the study of music."

"Well, I guess I know something," I said. "I passed Norma."

He laughed. "*Allegretto con anima* Janie."

"That's not even funny," I said, hurt. I had never expected Mr. Schunk would make fun of me.

"High spirit. You remind of my daughter."

"I don't remind of anybody," I muttered. "All I want to remind of is me."

"You remind of daughter," he repeated and blushed, waving his arm around the dusty room. "I am old man. My children are gone. Now you are here." I got ready to wipe my eyes, since we never had a lesson without tears. "In your home there is music? Your mother is listening to Bach, to Beethoven, to Brahms?"

"My mother works at Kroger's."

"Ah." He nodded as if he'd just heard my life story, and everything about me fitted into place. "You do not know the study of music because there is no one to teach you. I teach you." He flipped through my lesson book. "Here. Scale of G major. Scale of F major."

I took the book. "They're just regular old scales. Anyway, I want to learn about music. I don't care that much about scales."

He clutched at his chest. "Music is scale, scale, *scala.* Look." With a pencil he slashed a staff inside the cover and drew a chromatic scale. "One octave, twelve tones. You understand? Good. Later I will explain to you the twelve-*ton* music. Now. How many notes in the"—his lips twitched— "regular scale from C?"

"Eight," I mumbled. "Do you want me to play the next lesson?"

"No." He shoved the book at me. "Show the notes you are not playing, please." When I struck the flats and sharps, with his pencil he divided the scale into halves. "One octave, two tetrachords. Now you see."

"What?"

He groaned. "Play F-flat."

"There isn't one."

"It is E. Play B-sharp."

"I don't have one."

"C. Look." He drew a circle. "The circle of fifths. Listen." With a flourish, he seated himself at the piano and played scale after scale as proudly as he might have played the "Appassionata." "The pattern is the same."

"Scales are always the same."

He grunted. "For major modes. For minor they are different. For Dorian, for Mixolydian, for Phrygian, different, different, different."

Dick honked.

"You must understand," he said. "Without scale you do not know music."

"If I study the scales, will you come to Wilson's concert?"

"I do not drive."

"Would you come if my brother took you?"

"Very kind," he said. "For the next lesson you must come at nine, please, with music paper."

The day of the concert Arthur stopped by my stand to wish me luck. Though he meant well, he reminded me to be nervous. By dinner my nerves had shorted, and I blew my fuse at Dickie, who was dribbling pudding down the leg of his high chair. Dick was smacking his lips over the pineapple and marshmallow salad. My mother had cooked all my favorite food and didn't complain when I scraped my plate into the garbage, though I'd expected her to remind me about the starving children of China. Standing at the sink in her housecoat, she told me to go on and get dressed while she did the dishes. Dick patted my shoulder on his way out and said not to worry.

"Where are you going?" I demanded. "You have to drive Mr. Schunk."

"Relax. I'm just going to get the baby sitter."

"You're not even dressed yet. We'll be late."

"Janie, it's only six o'clock," my mother scolded. "Take it easy."

After I bathed, I snitched some of her Evening in Paris. My blue dress was laid out on my bed; the stain had come out at the cleaner's, and it looked just like new. By the time I pranced out, my mother was showing the old woman from Columbia Center where Dickie's diapers were kept, and Dick was splashing and singing "Round and Round" in the tub. My mother wrinkled her nose. "What's that smell? Janie, the idea of perfume is to use just a little."

"Be ready in a sec, Sissy." Dick popped around the doorway in his suit pants and socks, his hair damp around his forehead, a black knit tie in his hand. My mother almost bumped into him as she hurried from her bedroom to tell the baby sitter one last thing she'd forgotten. Then she had him crane his head up while she knotted his tie.

"Don't you look handsome?" she said. He did. "Look, Mrs. Watson, at what a fine pair of children I've got."

"Yeah, and you've got a grandson with a shitty diaper," I said, moving away from the playpen. "P.U."

The veins on my mother's temples trembled. "Jane Catherine, concert or no concert, you are going straight to bed if I hear that word again."

"All right already," I muttered, and Dick held the door for my mother, who looked pretty, with her dark hair fluffed around her face, in spite of her crappy wedgies.

"Are you sure this is the right house?" my mother asked when Dick pulled up in front of Mr. Schunk's. It was dark.

"Of course it's the right house," I said, wondering if Mr. Schunk could have fallen asleep and forgotten my concert.

"Well, I guess a Jew is a Jew," my mother murmured, which I thought was a whole lot worse than saying "shitty."

Already in his overcoat, Mr. Schunk opened the door before I knocked. "I have turned out the lights to be ready," he explained and followed me to the car, holding out his hand to my mother, who had to lean forward and shake it over the seat. "Very proud."

"Dick Hurdle," my brother said as he pumped Mr. Schunk's palm. "Janie's told us a lot about you."

"Very proud," Mr. Schunk said again.

I squeezed my crinolines next to my mother in the back seat to let Mr. Schunk have the leg room up front. While I concentrated on remembering the notes to my solo, Mr. Schunk apologized for putting Dick to trouble, praised my playing, and told my mother that she should be proud. My mother studied her fingernails.

"Aren't you coming?" I demanded when Dick dropped us.

"Of course. You think I'd miss it? Mom's going to go on in and get seats while I pick up my date."

"What does he have to bring a date for?" I said to my mother while Mr. Schunk held the school door.

"He's proud of you, honey. He wants to show you off to his girl."

"Oh brother."

"Your brother is very kind," Mr. Schunk said. "Also he looks well." In his tweed overcoat and burgundy tie Mr. Schunk looked well himself, would have looked distinguished if he hadn't been rolling his words from the air with his hands.

I left them at the entrance to the gym and walked to the bandroom. Clarinets were running up and down scales, the cornets were tuning, while the drummers kept dropping their sticks, and the flutes tweeted at the top of their register to show off. The fluorescence seemed icy with the windows dark, and we all looked too strange to one another, in our taffeta and net and new suits, to talk. "Psst." My mouthpiece bumped against my front teeth as a hand touched my shoulder. "Where's Norma?" The chair next to me was empty. I shrugged and skipped down the sixteenth notes to *"Gloria"* again. A ball of paper hit my music stand. "Open it," someone whispered.

Bending down, I glimpsed Arthur blushing. In my lap the paper burst like a bud, but it didn't turn into a very sweet posy. "It's snowing down south," I read as Mr. Pelfry cracked his baton. I dropped it, my face stinging as if I'd been slapped.

"Adcock."

"Here."

"Anderson." The litany faltered at DiLuccio. The chair beside me was still empty. "DiLuccio," Mr. Pelfry called once more. After Worocz, he instructed a drummer to remove Norma's seat from the stage, and, while we waited, he leaned toward the various sections with last-minute reminders of pianos and fortes. I wiggled in my chair, hoping to hike my slip up, until I heard Sandy whisper loudly, "Look at Hurdle. She's got ants in her pants." A hand brushed my neck, and the girl behind me said, "I just fixed your dress. The label was showing." I was ready to cry.

I couldn't look at the audience from the stage to see where my family and Mr. Schunk were sitting. My stomach felt like an enormous stone, and vinegar was already trickling down the walls of my mouth. I was going to throw up, and, even if I didn't, I knew my stockings had runs. No doubt Norma was sitting in the back of the gym waiting to boo through my solo. Mr. Schunk would rise to announce that the first-chair clarinet couldn't play the scale of G. The notes on my score drowned in a sea of lines as I put the instrument to my paralyzed lips and waited for the downbeat of "Good Christian Men Rejoice." You might think that, even after all these years, I could still hear my first public performance; at the very least that the many times I've sat on stage since would bring it back. Not so. Though I can still feel the nickel rims of the holes circling the balls of my cold fingers, can still taste the mixture of bamboo and sour spit, Arthur was right: I'm no longer there. Perhaps, if sound travels at something like the speed of light, one day on the other side of the Milky Way a very frightened clarinet will fall down a series of scales, and a bunch of spaceniks will turn to one another to say "*Gloria*. Praise God and great talent." Until then, there is only silence. No one booed; no one rose to make awful announcements. The audience clapped, Mr. Pelfry whispered we'd made him proud, and it was over. I hadn't thrown up. I had played a solo.

As we stood next to each other in the bandroom to take our clarinets apart, Arthur congratulated me. The sleeves of his gray suit crawled up his arms as he reached for his case. Clearing his throat, he asked if he could come by my house to visit me during Christmas vacation.

"Are you mad?" he asked when I didn't answer. "I didn't send that note. I just passed it."

"I don't care," I said.

"I thought maybe girls liked to know about things like that." In college some creep used the same excuse to tell me my breath smelled like onions.

"I mean I don't care if you visit me." I snapped the latches on my case and fled to the hall without waiting to see if I'd hurt his feelings.

Dick and my mother hugged me. Mr. Schunk took my hand. "As I have promised, you are playing solo. Also you are looking well." He dropped his eyes to my dress. "Very proud," he added.

Then Dick dropped behind them to pull his date forward. "Janie, this is Marie Souckova."

I should have known. It was the waitress from Fat Boy's, hiding her big butt in a red tweed coat, the yellow light of the hallway softening her brass-colored hair as she gushed. I turned my back to let my mother and Mr. Schunk fuss over me.

"You didn't tell us you'd be sitting up front," my mother said. "We kept looking for you in the middle."

"In the band first-chair clarinet is the concertmaster. Mistress," Mr. Schunk corrected.

"Say," Dick broke in, twirling a finger in Marie's hair, "we're all going back for cake and coffee. Would you like to come?"

My mother nodded. "We'd love to have you."

"Very kind," Mr. Schunk replied.

"Oh, Dick." My mother caught up to my brother and Marie, who were holding hands on their way to the car. "Isn't Walgreen's still open? I'd like to run by and pick up some film." She turned to Mr. Schunk. "It'll only take a minute, and I know Janie would love to have some pictures with you."

"I don't want any pictures," I said.

"Of course you do. You want to be able to look back and remember your concert."

I sighed. "It was just a dumb old school program."

"Well, I thought it was *nice*, and I'm sure Mr. Schunk did too." Oh brother. I couldn't look at the man whose picture had been in the paper after playing the *Première rapsodie* with the Chicago Symphony.

"Very nice," he agreed and patted my shoulder. "You are playing as true musician."

"Do you think I played as good as Norma?" I knew I shouldn't ask, but I couldn't help it.

"You are playing better," he said firmly, and I glowed.

In the car I wanted to ask Mr. Schunk more about my solo, but Marie kept him busy with questions about Germany. No one noticed I was sulking. I wanted to make it clear by stomping to my room the minute we got home, but Mrs. Watson met us at the door, and my mother had to invite her to stay for cake. So I had to help lay out plates and forks while my mother put the coffee on. Marie teetered into the kitchen on spike heels to ask if she could do anything, going on about what a lovely house we had and admiring our china, which was just a soapbox special and proved she didn't know shit.

"I think Janie and I have got it under control," my mother demurred. "In fact, while the coffee's brewing, I think I'll see if I can remember how to load the film in the camera. I want to get some pictures before we eat so Janie can take her dress off."

"It sure is a sweet dress," Marie murmured.

"Dick picked it out. He has nice taste for a man," my mother said.

"Yeah, in clothes," I sneered, but they didn't get it.

"When's the coffee going to be ready, girls?" Dick sniffed into the kitchen.

"Not for a few minutes," my mother said, but he didn't leave, putting his arm around Marie and beaming at me.

"Yes, sir," he said, "when I saw you sitting up front looking so pretty, I said to Marie, 'There's my little sister.' "

"He did," Marie agreed, "but I would of recognized you anyway from Fat Boy's. I guess it's a real honor to sit up front like that."

I shrugged.

Dick gave her shoulder a squeeze. "Isn't she something?" he said, and I waited for Marie to nod, until I realized he meant her. "I'll tell you, Dickie's just crazy about her."

They smiled at each other. "Well, I'm just crazy about him," she said. "He's my little sweetheart."

While my mother got the camera, we sat in the living room, which seemed tiny with all the people and the playpen. Mrs. Watson craned her neck to keep up with "Dragnet" as Dick settled into the chair nearest the TV.

"How long have you been in America?" Marie asked Mr. Schunk, but his answer was swallowed by sirens.

"Janie, turn that idiot box off," my mother said.

"I'm not the one that's watching it."

"I don't care."

"I have come from Germany twenty-one years," Mr. Schunk said. "I am American citizen for nine years."

Marie nodded. "My parents are from Czechoslovakia." She had a broad face, which might have seemed pretty with her brown eyes and blond hair, but now that I knew where to place it, I imagined her in a babushka, like the pictures of peasants from behind the Iron Curtain. We had learned about the Iron Curtain in school. My teacher was mad because while the United States was inventing Stripe toothpaste, the Soviet Union launched Sputnik. She seemed to think it was our fault. After we all flunked our math test, she said, "You'll be sorry when the Communists bury us." I gave Marie a suspicious glance. Even if she wasn't a Communist, *I* didn't like her.

"A beautiful country." Mr. Schunk smiled. "But not so beautiful as Deutschland. It is my homeland," he added by way of apology.

"Of course," Marie said.

"My son got killed by the krauts in the war," Mrs. Watson remarked, and my mother gasped.

"That's not Mr. Schunk's fault," I said. "He wasn't even there. And besides that, the Americans killed Rayburn."

"Webern," Mr. Schunk corrected. "It was an accident. However, Webern is all the same dead." His face sagged.

"A lot of men died," Marie murmured, as though it were a revelation. "From both sides. I hope we never have another war."

"We will," I said. "The Russians'll start it, and my teacher says they'll win."

"Don't be such a pessimist. There." My mother snapped the camera shut. "Dick, why don't you take a picture of Janie and Mr. Schunk?"

"You can just take it of him," I said.

"You must be in the picture also," he said. "Now you are real musician."

"Sure," Dick said. "It's your party."

"Don't be shy," Marie said.

So we sat on the couch, and Dick popped a bulb that made a dark spot in the center of my vision for several minutes. Twenty-two years later, now that my vision has cleared, I am still scowling from a page in my photograph album, eyes closed above the crinolines that pushed my skirt up to my chin, a ruffle-lined sousaphone blowing out some legs. Beside me, Mr. Schunk looks grim and dignified, although he has the red eyes of a rabbit.

"That should be a good one," Dick said.

"If it takes," my mother said.

"Let me do one of Dick and Janie," Marie suggested. Then she took one of me, Dick, and Mom; and Dick took one of Mom, me, and Marie; and Mom took one of me, Marie, and Dick; and everyone took a picture of someone, including one of Dick and Marie sitting so close they probably got prickly heat from the pressure. To be nice, my mom took one of Mrs. Watson, who drops out of my life as soon as the party is over, except that I've still got her picture in my album.

"I'll get the coffee," my mother said. "Janie, I want you to change your dress now. Marie, why don't you come cut the cake?"

"I don't want to change my dress."

"Janie, I don't want an argument."

"You're not changing *your* dress."

"I don't have to take my clothes to the cleaner's every time I wear them."

"I'm not taking off my dress," I insisted. "Dick bought it for me, and it's mine, and I can wear it whenever I want."

"Suit yourself," my mother said. "But if you spill anything, I'm not getting it cleaned for you." She offered to hang a dish towel from my neck, and, while everyone lined up to load his plate, I stalked into the living room.

"Let her go," my mother said to Dick. "She's been a grouch all day." I really loved it when she talked about me as if I weren't even there. So no one came back for me, no one begged me to have a slice of my very own cake, and in a minute they were on our couch and chairs, forks chattering against their plates while I pouted in the corner.

Mrs. Watson began an ode to the cake and added, "That little boy of yours was good as gold. I put him down at seven-thirty, and I haven't heard a peep out of him since."

" Stick around," I muttered, but they all ignored me.

"Isn't he sweet?" Marie gushed. "He's just as cute as a bug."

I rolled my eyes.

"It is wonderful cake," Mr. Schunk said to my mother. "You have a second son?"

"She got it at Kroger's," I said.

"He's Dick's son," my mother said. "My grandson."

"No!" Mr. Schunk turned to Marie. "And you are so young a mother."

My mother flinched as Marie said, "Dickie's not mine. I love him like he was, though." She looked around the room as if to make sure that we took note.

"My wife and I are separated," Dick said.

"I am sorry." Mr. Schunk blushed and dropped his fork, spilling his coffee as he bent to retrieve it. "I am sorry," he wailed, dabbing his dark sleeve at the liquid sopping into the rug.

My mother jumped up. "Don't bother. You'll ruin your suit."

"We don't care about the carpet," I said. "Dickie pees on it all the time."

"I'll get it." Marie was already back from the kitchen, waving a dishrag. "Shoot, when you work in a restaurant, a little old accident like this is nothing."

"Very kind," Mr. Schunk said passionately.

"How do you like America?" my brother asked while Marie finished wiping the rug and Mr. Schunk gave her a grateful smile, which she returned with such warmth you would have thought he was giving her free lessons.

"How do you like the United States?" my brother shouted, and I scowled. After all, Mr. Schunk wasn't deaf.

"Oh, very nice. It is full with many wonderful people like"—he smiled—"my hosts."

They all sighed with pleasure, but my mother caught me twisting my features and said, "Jane Catherine, if you can't straighten up, I want you to go to your room."

"It's my party."

"I'm warning you."

"I didn't spill anything."

"You heard me."

"*Okay*," I said, rising a second too late. The tears washed over before I reached the hallway. My door whacked in the awkward silence.

"She's all keyed up," I heard my mother say.

"Everybody's touchy when they're that age," Marie said.

"Mr. Schunk, do you have family? Will they be spending Christmas with you?"

"He's a Jew," I sobbed, face down on my bed. "He doesn't even have a Christmas, dummy." I sat up because I thought I heard Dick at my door, come to wheedle me back, but no one knocked, and after a while, I lay back down and covered my head with a pillow so that I wouldn't have to listen to Marie eating my cake and having a good time with my brother and my teacher at my party.

5

Arthur never showed up over Christmas vacation. I didn't really care, but if he didn't want to come, why did he ask? I hadn't seen Norma since the morning of the concert, and nobody in band knew if she'd been kicked out or had quit. It was Sandy who started blabbing what she'd heard from someone who'd heard it from Norma: real garbage-mouth stuff about the day my dress had been undone at Mr. Schunk's. I tried to explain about my zipper, but there was no use denying it to Sandy, who grinned all the while I sputtered because she knew it wasn't true—she just didn't care. She *said* she believed it, and I believed her. So all Christmas vacation I waited for Arthur, sure that he wouldn't come and then that he hadn't come because everyone in the world thought Norma's stinking gossip was true.

The weather was crummy. While Bing Crosby sang "White Christmas" on the radio, a cold wind blew a gray drizzle in from the lake, and muck slopped to the collar of my stadium boots before freezing one night into snot-colored ridges. I remembered the tree trimmings in the years we'd been a real family, when clean snow had drifted over the streets, and the living room, as cozy and bright as a paperweight dome, had smelled of balsam and vanilla. As soon as the tree stood crowned and shimmering, my mother had served cookies with hot chocolate. Then she wrapped the stand in a sheet, and I built the teeny village where sweatered rubber inchlings skated across a pocket mirror sprinkled with cellophane snow.

Now, as I wiped up the muddy water dripped by the pine boughs, I saw my father, a quiet man who smoked and dropped ashes on the armchair while the television talked. I didn't miss him very much. When someone's dead, he's gone; that's all. But at Christmas, things were different. I wanted my daddy to untangle our lights. I wanted to lie in bed and hear him curse the easy instructions for toys shipped unassembled, then pretend to believe that the presents had dropped down our chimney all put together, as easy as one-two-three. Without a mantel, my stocking had bounced on a rubber band from my doorknob, and I wasn't very old before I realized that anyone who came down our chimney would fall into our furnace. Still, I thought, if my father were there, I would believe. As soon as we got the tree up, Dickie reached for an angel I'd made from pipe cleaners and a clothespin. I suggested we keep Dickie in the playpen, but my mother insisted he was at a stage where he needed to walk, and decided to put the tree inside the playpen instead. Who wouldn't miss her father with her Christmas tree in jail?

So all that first weekend I played with Dickie on the living room floor, until he got me in trouble by swallowing a Monopoly house while I impersonated a boardful of players and banked all the money myself. My mother wouldn't even have known if it hadn't shown up in his diaper.

As soon as the rain quit, I left him to eat his own toys and took the bus downtown. I bought my mother a fancy bar of bath soap and a bottle of Black Cat bubble bath. For Dick I got a pair each of parrot-green and taxi-colored socks that I liked so much, I decided to go back to J. C. Penney's and get a red pair for Mr. Schunk. I didn't think he would mind getting a present for Christmas even if he was a Jew. At the dime store I bought a finger of green embroidery thread, intending to stitch eighth notes on the ankles. I didn't have to worry about my teacher, because my mother always took care of her, though I hoped she wouldn't make me give nylons. When I was in fourth grade she sent me to a birthday party with a box of underpants for the hostess, so I don't know how come she thought it was weird that I refused to believe she had ever been young. In the basement of W. T. Grant's, I picked out a turtle and then bought myself a box of Magic Rocks, guaranteed to grow into a fantastic multicolored city in a glass of ordinary tap water.

"A turtle?" my mother said when she cleaned my room. "I didn't know you wanted a turtle, Janie."

"Not so loud," I warned. "It's for Dickie."

"Honey, he can't take care of a turtle."

"I'm going to take care of it for him until he gets bigger."

My mother smiled. "Janie, those things don't live very long. That paint on their shells suffocates them."

"It does?" I gasped.

"Well, don't worry about it. But you'd better not give it to Dickie. He's liable to eat it."

So the turtle remained in the dish on my dresser, and actually thrived until the next summer, when I transported his tepid little ocean to the front steps to give him some sun and Dwayne Binton stepped on him. Shoebox funerals had begun to seem sort of silly, so I flushed poor little Ludwig, and I guess he finally got to the sea.

While I pricked my fingers and bled into Mr. Schunk's socks, my Magic Rocks did indeed grow into a fantastic multicolored city, though by the time school started, the water had evaporated and I was left with a glass of multicolored scum. Mr. Schunk was so pleased with the socks that he wiped his eyes, apologizing because he had nothing for me.

But I got what I'd asked for—my clarinet. While my mother piled a rainbow of wooden rings on Dickie's Rockastack, and Dick, who liked his socks so much that he tried on one of each color, whooped and sent balls of silver and gold paper rolling across the rug, I scooped into the playpen for the package that looked most likely. It was a case just like Norma's, and inside were the parts to my very own Schaeffer-Buffet. I was twisting them together before I noticed that the keys were as dull as the handlebars of my old bike. I closed the case and felt for the sticky strip where the punch-tape label had been.

"We could never have afforded a new one that good," my mother was explaining. "Here, Dickie." She handed him another ring as he grasped at her Christmas robe. "Mr. Schunk said we'd be better off investing in a good used one than putting the money in a piece of junk."

Dick sat on the sofa beside my mother, the hem of his flannel bathrobe dipping between his knees. "He's the one that found it for us, Sissy, and he checked it all out, so it must be okay."

"He said it had a specially sweet tone." My mother shrugged. "You couldn't prove it by me. No, Dickie. You put the big one on the bottom."

"Give him to me," Dick said. "Hey there, big feller." Dickie grabbed for my brother's nose. "You aren't disappointed it isn't a new one, are you?"

Listlessly, I picked among the unopened boxes. "I don't care. Thank you for the present."

"Well, Janie, you wouldn't of wanted us to get you a piece of junk, would you?" My mother reached for Dickie. "I wish you wouldn't roughhouse like that. You'll hurt him."

"I'm not going to hurt him," Dick said. "He likes it." Dickie jiggled with laughter as Dick put his dukes up.

"Well, I don't," my mother said, and Dick let her rescue Dickie, who started to bawl and throw his Christmas toys.

"Sissy, we got you what we thought you wanted. If it's not, I'm sure Mr. Schunk can get us our money back."

"I don't know about that," my mother protested. "It's not like buying something from a store."

"I said thank you," I mumbled. "I don't know why everybody has to make a big deal." I prodded a wad of green paper, not looking up because I knew, if I saw Dick, I'd cry.

"Well, you don't seem very excited."

"I'm excited." I cried anyway. "This is Norma's clarinet. How could you get me Norma's clarinet?"

"How could it be Norma's? Doesn't she want it herself?"

"We didn't know whose it was." Dick crouched to loop his arm around my shoulder. "Mr. Schunk handled the details."

He nudged me. "You should of heard Mom on the phone trying to talk to Mr. Schunk."

"You always said you wanted a clarinet like Norma's," my mother said.

"Well, I didn't want hers." I sobbed so loudly I woke up Dickie, who'd quit hollering and had fallen asleep.

"Did she get a better one?" Dick asked. "Is that why you're upset?"

"She's not in band anymore. She said—she got mad at me on account of I passed her and it wasn't even my fault, but she said . . ." I sniffled. "Bad things about me."

"Oh, honey. You have to learn to take things with a grain of salt." My mother shifted Dickie. "Dick, would you go in the refrigerator and get that jar of strained apricots? We're going to have to feed Dickie something or he's never going to quit."

"Dirty things," I persisted. "About me and Mr. Schunk, and everybody believed her, and I don't want her clarinet."

My mother frowned. "What sort of things?"

I snapped and unsnapped the locks on the clarinet case, looking away. "You know."

"They're on the second shelf," my mother yelled. The refrigerator door slammed. "Do you want me to talk to Mr. Schunk?" she asked finally.

"No," I screamed. "Don't call him. Norma's telling lies."

My mother frowned. "Is there anyone else in the house when you go for your lessons?"

"Mama, you can't call Mr. Schunk up on Christmas."

"What does he care about Christmas? He's a Jew."

"Why are we calling anyone on Christmas?" Dick asked.

My mother lowered her voice. "Apparently there's been some . . . ugly talk about Janie and . . . being alone at Mr. Schunk's. It's upset her, and, frankly, I don't much like it myself."

"You're not going to call him about it?" Dick didn't wait for her answer. "I don't think that's a good idea."

"Janie." My mother leaned forward as Dick began spooning apricots into Dickie's mouth. "Has Mr. Schunk ever done anything . . . funny while you were there?"

"Mom," Dick protested.

"Touched you anyplace he shouldn't? Touched himself anyplace he shouldn't?"

"Mother, for Christ's sake . . ."

Her mouth quivered. "Don't you swear at me. It's Christmas."

"I'm sorry," Dick said as I kept snapping and unsnapping the clarinet case, wishing I'd never even started to take band. "But you don't have to embarrass her. If there was anything wrong at Mr. Schunk's, Janie would of told you."

"I'm not embarrassed," I said in a voice that was hollow.

"How do I know?" my mother said. "She doesn't tell me anything."

"Look. Why don't we just finish opening our presents? Janie can decide what she wants to do about the clarinet tomorrow. No sense in ruining Christmas, is there, Sissy?" Dick knelt beside me, feeling underneath the playpen for the presents that hadn't fitted inside. "Hmm. Let's see what we have here.

My mother wiped Dickie's face with a diaper. "You needn't tell me how to run things. I was around when you were still messing your pants." But she didn't mean it.

"If he gives her a diamond ring, I'm leaving home," I grumbled to my mother as soon as Dick left for Christmas dinner at Marie's with a tiny box in his hand.

"Good heavens," my mother said. "Whatever gave you that idea? It's a necklace—and much too expensive. That boy thinks he's made out of money. Did you see the label on my robe? It's from Marshall Field's." Later she offered to pull the wishbone with me, but I wouldn't hear of it and insisted I be allowed to wait up for Dick, who tiptoed through the back door after midnight.

"Janie," he said as I popped off the couch, where I'd spent the time since my mother had gone to bed, humming carols and squinting at the Christmas tree lights in the dark. "What are you doing up?"

I thrust the wishbone at him, observing his rumpled suit. "Were you out parking with Marie?"

69

"Nah." Dick laughed. "It's too cold. Say, we must have forgotten to pull this before I left."

"I didn't forget."

"Well, make a wish, kiddo," Dick said, discarding his tie.

"I already did. You make one. What was it?" I asked as the bone snapped.

"If I tell I won't get it."

I waved the good half. "You aren't going to get it anyway. I bet I know what you wished. You wished you'll marry Marie." I didn't tell that I had wished he would not.

He excused himself to go to the bathroom. When he came back, he said, "What makes you think I want to marry Marie?"

"You do. You don't care about me."

"Silly." He sat next to me on the couch and let me cuddle against him. A flash at his wrist caught my eye.

"What's that?" I demanded, pulling his sleeve.

"My deluxe new timepiece." Dick held his wrist out and tweaked the expansion band.

"Is that what you got from Marie?" I guessed two pairs of socks couldn't seem like much of a present with a brand-new Bulova circling your wrist. "How come you have to marry her?"

Dick sighed and sank into the couch. "Janie, I want you to understand that I haven't even thought about marrying Marie, but what are you going to do if later I do think about her or somebody else? You wouldn't want me to be lonely all my life, and don't you think Dickie deserves a mother?"

"But you're not lonely, and me and Mom take good care of Dickie. Anyway, he's got a mother."

"A lot of good she does him. I hate to say it, but as far as Dickie is concerned, his mother is dead. Oh, I'm not going to lie to him. When the time comes, I'll tell him who his mother was, and then especially don't you think it'll be important for him to see that somebody loves him enough to keep him? You know . . ." Dick looked away, his eyes fixed on the three bars of dark glass in our front door. "A guy doesn't like to talk about this, but do you have any idea how much it hurts to have your wife take off and not just leave you but your kid?'' He fumbled in the pocket of his suit coat and pulled out a cigarette.

"Hey," I said. He might be nineteen, but if our mother saw him, she'd make him put it out. I couldn't remember her crying when my father died, only the white rim around her mouth as she broke every ashtray in the house. I watched the tip of his cigarette steam into the darkness.

"Get me a saucer from the kitchen, will you?" He hunched forward, inhaling very seriously. "That's what I can't forgive her for, not me—and oh man she hurt me plenty—but a three-month-old baby, that sweet little kid."

I didn't think he was that sweet, but I got Dick the saucer and kept my mouth shut.

"You know, Janie, I never told this to anyone because a guy doesn't like to admit he's been done dirt, but I come home from work, and my son's crying and hungry, and I think, well, maybe there's an emergency or something because why else would my wife go off and leave the kid? So I feed him and change him, and then I go next door to see if she's left a message because I'm trying to maybe buy a house someday, and I don't want to spend money on a phone. Well, there isn't any message and so I ask Mrs. Poulos if I can use her phone, but she's just mopped her kitchen floor, and I have to wait till it dries, sitting on her sofa and wondering where in hell my wife is while this lady in pincurls watches me count the feathers in her linoleum rug. So when I can finally walk in the kitchen she listens to me call Carole's folks, the hospital, the police station, and then she gets her husband out of bed, and he's got to take me out in the hallway so if I go crazy I don't wreck his place because his wife's known all the time I'm sitting, she's just afraid to tell me herself." He stubbed out the cigarette. "So now I got a kid who's going to want to know about his mother, and you want to do what's right, what's best for your son, and how do I tell him his mother left him with a load of crap in his diaper and walked away without even writing a note?"

"Well, maybe she'll come back," I said because I wanted to cheer him up.

"Oh Janie." He turned his face to me, luminescent in the

red and green and blue and gold light. "You really think I want to see her?"

"I don't know." I picked up the saucer.

"Oh, Jesus, why am I telling you this? You're too young to understand."

"No, I'm not. I know about things like that." I meant that I knew about love and sadness, but I felt silly as soon as I said it, because what were Paul Nolta and my piddly sadness compared to Dick's? But I think I went on anyway because I wanted to make my sorrows important by giving them a name. "Paul Nolta said nice guys finish last."

"I thought I told you not to believe that." Dick's voice was sharp. He lit another cigarette. "You believe that, it's just like giving up. I'm not saying she didn't have reasons, but we had some good times, it wasn't all no fun. I got memories."

"Well then how come you have to get married again?"

"You just don't understand," he said.

"Life looks different when you have a kid. At least it looked different to me—that's my mistake, I guess. I thought it looked different to everyone. Even when it happened the way it did. I didn't mind. I thought we'd be happy."

"I'm not going to get married," I said. "It just doesn't sound like anything I'd like."

"You'll change your mind."

"That's what you think. Hey." I scooped up the saucer and was surprised to see that he had been right after all: I didn't understand. Because I had to put his cigarette out and clutch him close while my big brother, who knew everything I didn't, cried into the flat front of my bathrobe.

6

With a throng of New Yorkers, Guy Lombardo, and a bowl of popcorn, my mother and I saw 1958 in together. When the ball dropped, I felt that my childhood had officially ended. I was a great believer in ritual, as perhaps only a child whose life has been conspicuously devoid of it can be. Unlike so many of the neighbor children, I made no first communion, I never said rosaries for the souls in Purgatory, and I had no grandparents whose deaths prompted ceremonial gatherings of the family clan—in fact, I had no clan.

No wonder I loved the pomp of the band. In high school I was the only player who never griped about the scratchy maroon and gray uniforms. When I tossed that jacket aside, it was because I was ready for the secret shiver of thrill I still feel when, zipped into a floor-length dress, I tune with the orchestra that rehearsed in jeans just that morning, a litter of instrument cases for an audience, pocketbooks spilling Kleenex and hanging by their straps from the chairs. I swear even the tuning sounds better in the ceremony of tails and long black skirts.

Once I asked my mother if I'd ever been baptized; it was

something, she said, they'd always meant to do but forgot. Religion to my mother was a lifelong, nondenominational lip service to Jesus, who went about his business without bothering us until an emergency called him on duty, something like the National Guard. My father was, from the time a nun cracked his hand with a metal-edged ruler, a renegade Catholic with few strong opinions save an abiding distaste for the church, and he died without forgiving the pope.

My mother refused to make New Year's resolutions. "Why bother? They only get broke." I sat before the Zenith with a Big Chief and pencil to think, but in the end I submitted the usual (be nicer to Mom, keep room clean, don't grumble about washing dishes). I didn't vow to practice harder, because that went without saying. For me, the spirit of the evening was more evolution than resolution. In August I would be thirteen. I thought that meant I would be from then on whatever I turned into tonight.

And I was only halfway wrong, for by the end of the year, my life had changed, though I still had a lot of time to mark before I went to college and could prove what I had known all along: that my mother was mistaken; I was not her daughter but my own. I wonder now why I did it. And how come, so many years after at five o'clock, I poured myself some sherry and pondered, as though that ball were still in its gravital trip, resolutions to begin my life? I regretted, but not enough, what my mother had predicted: that I turned out to be a fine musician and a rather poor person. By which she meant lousy at love.

On Valentine's Day, Arthur bought me a card that cost a dollar, embarrassing me by presenting it in band, and everyone watched while I unwrapped a froth of paper doilies spilling from a padded satin heart that said YOU'RE SWEET. I hid it in the bottom of my box of virginal Kotex for fear my mother or Dick would see it. Dick gave Marie a heart too, but hers had a diamond ring dangling from a red bow in its cleavage. I never saw the card, and I didn't see the diamond until Saturday, when Dick and Marie took me to Bowl-Era and she spread her left hand on the table while she penciled our names down the left side of the scorepad. It was a tiny solitaire that popped rainbow lights. I turned away. Maybe she'd spread her hand in hopes that I would notice, but Dick hadn't told me, and so I didn't offer my congratulations. Instead, I picked up my ball and sent it clacking down the gutter. When we finished the first game, I had rolled a twenty-seven.

"You'll get better—won't she?" Marie said. "You should have seen me my first time. I thought I was ready for a team when I broke forty."

Some comfort. She'd rolled a 109. I curtseyed into the alley with another gutter ball, stamping my foot and announcing I quit. "Don't be like that," Dick said and made me stand where I was while he paced my approach and guided my arm for a seven. " See?"

I flounced to my seat. "Shit," I said, sucking down my second Coke and polishing off a bag of potato chips. Two lanes down, I watched the rack descend over an empty frame and rise before ten new pins sprouted in the space. "All right, killer," a girl at the scoretable said, and the boy smirked and flexed his muscles before I realized he was Paul.

"Come on, Janie," Dick yelled, but what little game I had was gone as soon as I saw that the girl who'd sent a marbled turquoise ball whizzing for a split was Sandy. I was suddenly aware of my scuffed, tricolor rental shoes, and I tried to look inconspicuous as I slunk back to our table.

"Who cares?" I muttered. "Who even wants to be good at bowling?" The thunderclap of Sandy's second shot kept anyone from hearing, and I bowled the rest of the game half-blind with tears, escaping to the ladies' room the minute it was over. I intended to spend the rest of my life there, but Marie had to pee, and located my hideout before I'd spent five minutes.

"You're getting the knack," she said as she leaned over the sink to touch up her lipstick. "How about another game?"

"There's no point to it," I said.

"Well, nothing's fun if you take it too serious." She gave me a sympathetic smile, and rubbed a finger across her chin. "You have the prettiest complexion. Every time I get my period, my face breaks out in zits."

I pulled the door open, and the sound of the alley rolled in like surf. "Why don't you keep me company?" From the purse she had set on the vanity, she took a brush clotted with blond hair. "After all, Dick can't start without us."

I let the door go, and with a little whoosh it snapped shut. "My arm hurts," I said.

"Well, if your arm's really sore, we can always go." She licked the tip of a forefinger and slicked her eyebrows. "There." She turned on me so quickly, I had no time to look away. "Why don't you like me?"

I didn't answer.

"Is it just because of the bowling?" She rested against the counter and smiled. "Because if it is, I know how you feel. There's lots of things I'm not good at. I used to study my head off, and I never once got a good grade in school."

"I always make A's. Anyway, this was only my first time. Dick said I'd get better."

"You probably will, unless you quit playing. Then you'll stay lousy for sure."

"I'm not lousy." We sparred glances in the mirror.

"You're not real good," she said. She turned, and again we were face to face. I can't say that Marie was a beauty; her cheeks flattened and spread and swallowed her features before she was forty, but in 1958 the way to look was well fed and pleasant—the beanpoles wore flats and falsies, not the spike-heeled mules and frontless blouses they slink around in now. I've grown an inch since then and feel shorter than ever; by the time I grew tits, they were out of style. At five feet three, wide face above a busty Bishop Noll High School sweatshirt, Marie was a girl just right for her time. "Is it because I'm going to marry your brother? Because if it isn't"—she leaned toward me—"you don't have any reason. I've never done a mean thing to you."

I swallowed and toed a scab of black gum on the tile.

"I guess if I thought I was losing my brother I might feel like you do, but I wish you didn't 'cause it makes us feel bad." She paused. "Only we're going to get married anyway. Well"—she picked up her purse and smiled—"you ready?"

She'd won, and she hadn't made a single concession. I

should have been furious, but quite suddenly I admired her, and I didn't want to leave. "Do you know that guy out there? The one with the red hair that kept getting strikes?" I thought we must look like welfare cases with our beat-up Bowl-Era balls and shoes that smelled of all Hammond's feet, but I no longer minded, and I suspected that Sandy's sea-colored ball, like her dog and her loyalty, might belong to her mother; that she didn't, after all, have a thing more than I did; that in fact maybe I had more.

"I didn't notice."

I crossed to the mirror, brushing my bangs with my fingers. "His name's Paul. One time we were at a party and he kissed me. How come you went to Noll?" I knew why, but I was talking just to keep talking. "Are you going to make my brother turn Catholic?"

"Only if he wants to." She smiled. "He has lots of time to decide. We can't get married until he gets his divorce."

"Oh yeah." I'd forgotten about the legal restrictions. "My dad said that nuns are real mean."

She kept smiling. "All teachers are mean."

I smiled back. What I liked about her now was that I didn't have to say things the way I thought she wanted to hear them. I was sure I could say whatever I felt, and she would say whatever she felt, and it wouldn't matter if we felt completely different. It wasn't like talking to my mother, and it wasn't even like talking to Dick. "No, they're not." We were grinning. "Did you ever have another boyfriend?"

"Sure."

"Did you . . . ?" I wanted to ask if she put out for him, I wanted to ask if she put out for Dick, but I didn't know how to phrase it. My mother had said "have intercourse," but that sounded disgusting, like having an enema. Sandy said "get screwed," but I didn't want to be like Sandy anymore.

"Did I what?"

"Did you ever think about marrying him?"

"Maybe."

"How come you didn't?"

She shrugged. "Well, I wasn't out of school yet. And I

guess we didn't want the same things. And after a while we didn't love each other.''

I thought. "What if, after a while, you don't love my brother?''

She smiled again and tapped a finger against my shoulder. "I think Dick's real lucky to have a sister that wants to make sure he's happy.''

I blushed. "Hey,'' I said to distract her, "can I see your ring?''

She extended her hand, which was plump like Dickie's, with dimples where the knuckles should be and long fingernails polished the color of pearls.

"Ready?'' she asked. "Dick's going to think we fell in.''

I stalled, fixing my eyes on the drain in the floor while I said what I would have been ashamed not to say now. "I like you.''

When I looked up, she was smiling again. This time she really was pretty, and my image of her still, in spite of the weight and the years, is a teen-ager in bobby sox and bowling shoes, her future on her finger, no clouds on her face. She held the door.

I made a point of not avoiding Paul and Sandy, plunking myself in front of their table and introducing Marie as my brother's fiancée. Paul winked at me. He had a nice face, not handsome, kind of doggy and wicked, as though he were pleased with himself for peeing on the carpet. "We saw you rolling gutter balls,'' Sandy said.

Marie's teeth clicked as she put her arm around my shoulder. "That must of been me. Janie played a great game.''

We sat on the bench to change our shoes, and Marie nudged me to watch Sandy's beautiful ball go thumping down the gutter. The minute we got outside we looked at each other and giggled.

"You girls sure sound happy. How about a trip to Fat Boy's?'' Dick asked.

"You know what I think?'' Marie said as she let me slide to the middle of the front seat. "I think that boy likes you and his date is jealous.''

I snuggled between them. It was Saturday night, and they

didn't seem in any hurry to get rid of me. The crisp neon lights of Calumet Avenue winked under a moon that was fastened to the black sky like a big mother-of-pearl button. Paul remembered me. The radio crackled with the Everly Brothers. "Bye bye love," they sang, and I chimed in with gusto. "Bye bye happiness, hello emptiness," I chorused as though I were bidding goodbye to the measles and welcoming good health. I was glad that my brother would marry Marie.

But they didn't wed until August, and my wish for a blue chiffon dress and a nosegay of rosebuds never came true, because as far as Marie's priest was concerned, until Carole died, they wouldn't be married at all. They ended up eloping to Michigan City, and by November Marie was expecting Dickie's little brother, who never materialized because of some problem with her insides that sent her to Saint Margaret's in March to deliver a hunk of dead tissue clotted in blood. I was in college before she produced a healthy babe, and then not one, but a pair of identical girls. Marie was by then more a part of the family than I was, though at first my mother had been reluctant to hand Dickie over to a stranger, and Marie's parents were as wary of second-time husbands as some people are of used cars. Every other Sunday they had dinner at my house, and on the Thanksgiving of my freshman year in college, while helping my mother set the table, I had to ask Marie to find me a serving spoon, as though it were her table and her house, not mine. I liked her, but we had nothing in common. She and my mother had more to talk about. It was babies, curtains, and specials on pot roast till I thought I would scream.

But it wasn't their fault they didn't know what to say to me. I was strange to them, a girl who knew nothing about babies and less about boys; who, as far as they knew, never had a date before she came home a wife. "It can't be she isn't asked," I once heard Marie whisper to my mom. "If I'd of been that cute, I'd of had a date every night." By my thirteenth birthday I had put boys behind me as finally as I had once left my rubber horses strewn across the basement floor. I was every bit as odd as they thought I was, but there was one thing they didn't know, and that's this:

In late February, the Wilson band chartered a bus to Portage for my first district solo contest, where I scherzoed in C minor as I had the last five Saturdays at Mr. Schunk's to the tune of a gold medal clipped to a royal blue ribbon. By the end of high school I had nine more just like it, as well as enough city and state armor for a bulletproof vest.

Sandy played her "Mount Vernon Minuet," which is a real dipshit solo, badly, and walked to the bus empty-handed, loudly telling everyone that contests were a joke. A lot of the kids had come with their parents, and the bus was half-empty. Mr. Pelfry sat behind the driver and checked off names as those who were left got on. I chose a window seat in the back, where the tubas rested on their bells and cases cluttered the aisle. I was depressed and didn't know why; after all, I had won a gold medal, but Dick and my mother were working, and, though I knew they'd be thrilled when I got home, it wasn't the same as if they had come. When Mr. Pelfry got off to drive home and Sandy hopped over a tuba to sit beside me, I felt like moving, but I would have had to climb over her knees. As the bus pulled out of Portage, I stared through the window while she nudged and poked and tried to get me to talk. The world was going dark, a blue marshland floating buoys of lights. Everyone was sleepy; all up and down the aisle the kids nodded off.

"I didn't know your brother was getting married again." In the dusk her front teeth gleamed like a cannibal's. "I wouldn't want to marry a guy with a kid." She thumped the clarinet case I was hugging on my lap. "Pretty neat instrument, but you know what I heard? I heard it was Norma's." She undressed a stick of Juicy Fruit and doubled it into her mouth. "Want some gum?"

I shook my head and should have kept my mouth shut. "I don't chew gum. Mr. Schunk says the sugar gets in your spit and rots your pads out."

"Well, la-de-da," Sandy said, drumming her fingers on the seat. "Norma told me all about your boyfriend, Mr. Skunk, and you know who else told me *all* about your brother?"

"I'm not interested," I said, "I don't care who you talk to."

"Paul Nolta." Her tongue was covered with a torn membrane of gum. She wasn't sticking it out at me; that was just the way she chewed. "He told me *everything*. And you know what I think? I think your brother is dumb."

"I don't care what you think."

"You know why?" she continued as I pressed my nose to the cold window to get away from the rotten fruit of her breath. She put her mouth to my ear. "Because everybody knows if you pull it out before it squirts nothing'll happen."

My lip curled against the window. I waited out the little spasm of revulsion before I turned my head back. "I think you're disgusting," I said calmly.

She smirked. "I know someone you like who doesn't think so." I didn't ask, but she answered anyway. "Paul Nolta, that's who. I guess you'll be interested to know we're going steady."

"I don't believe you," I said. But he had taken her bowling and had told her about Dick.

"Oh no?" She punched me in the ribs. "Here's his ring." She dropped a piece of jewelry in the crevice between my clarinet case and my crotch. It was his ring, I knew it, and it had been sized to fit her finger with a dirty wad of wax.

"See this?" She arched her neck in my direction. "That's from Paul too."

"I don't see his name on it." It was too dark to see the hickey, but I knew it was there, and I knew he had left it.

"I got another one too, you know where? On my tit."

I flinched toward the window. My stomach hurt, and I was afraid I was going to throw up. "What's the matter with you?"

"Nothing. The matter's with you, you know why? 'Cause everybody in the whole world screws except you."

I closed my eyes and saw Mrs. Gitzke's bare bottom bouncing down the aisle of our bus. "Your mother screws. Your mother screws dirty men she picks up in bars. The only reason Paul even goes out with you is you put out, and my mother says boys don't respect that kind of girl."

Sandy hollered with laughter. "The only time your mother screwed was to get you, and she held her nose the whole time."

"I've got a brother."

"Twice." Sandy hooted. "She held her nose twice and got two kids who stink."

"You shut up," I yelled, mad because I suspected Sandy might be right. The way my mother said "intercourse"—I thought she and my father must have gone to a hospital and scrubbed down with alcohol first. My mother said you would have to be married before you could do anything that nasty. I thought you would at least have to be in love. How could Paul be in love with Sandy? "Everything you say is a lie, and I want you to shut up." I was screaming. The bus had begun shaking and groaning.

The mellophone player two seats in front of us leaned into the aisle. "You shut up," she said to me, and Sandy smirked.

"Paul's got a bi-ig wiener," she hissed at me, "and I squeeze it, and I li-ick it, and I rub it on my belly."

I clapped my hand to my mouth and choked. "You make me sick," I said as the bus shuddered to the shoulder.

"Shit," Sandy yelled as the driver got out. "The goddamn bus is broke, and I've got a date tonight. Hey, gang. Anybody wanna play rotation?" She stood. "See you later, alligator." In the window I watched her reflection while she whispered to two cornet players; when I turned my head, I saw her in person behind a whole factory of tubas. I wished I were home.

In the front of the bus they were singing "One Hundred Bottles of Beer on the Wall." One of the cornet players bumped a tuba and slid next to me. "You wanna play rotation?" he whispered.

"No." I clutched my clarinet and pressed my face against the smudged black glass. One faint light skimmed the horizon, a car on another road, a crashing plane, a flying saucer. I didn't look up. You never saw the stars around Hammond—the air was too dirty.

"Come on. Everybody else is."

My shoulders shook. Sandy popped over the next seat, and

her voice cut between us. "She doesn't wanna play, you know why? She's afraid you'll find out she doesn't have any tits and her little puss is as bald as a baby's butt."

I think he was shocked. He was a nice guy, really, if he's the one I think he was, second cornet with a crew cut, hardly taller than I, but already with a deep voice that squeaked as he said, "Huh," then bent toward me and whispered, "Everybody knows she's nasty."

"Don't come near me," I spat. "Don't you touch me."

"Rotate," Sandy yelled.

"I'm sorry," he said and slipped from my life and the seat.

I was bawling by the time the fluorescent white cuff, too long for its suit sleeve, brushed my knee.

"Arthur," I sobbed. "Did you come to rotate?"

He put his arm around my shoulder, and I flooded the front of his frayed shirt. Why Arthur? Because if there was a secret to life, he wouldn't know it either.

"Don't cry, Janie." His big knuckles tightened on my shoulder.

"I can't help it." I sniffed.

"Anyway," he said, "I think you're *neat*."

I set my clarinet on the floor and blew my nose on his father's tie. "Arthur, I am *not* a child."

"I'm not either," he said. "Want me to show you how to do it?"

So right there, on the sandy shoulder of U.S. 12, in the back of the dark band bus, Arthur reached under my skirt to pull down my Spanky pants, I heard his zipper scrape open, and then I learned what everyone else knew. *Why* did I do it? Because it was rotten and disgusting. Because I was *mad*. Because the only boy I'd ever liked had kissed me and then done it with Sandy. It was the kind of knowledge I *wanted* to hurt.

It did.

I still can't get over it. Gawky old Arthur—I mean, who would have expected *him?* . . . Well, never judge a book by its cover, as they say; a touch by its bony wrists or hangnails. Crowded between the backs of two seats and encumbered by winter-weight clothes, my initiation was not an easy task, but

Arthur knew what he was doing—suck, slurp, probe, push, pull, pinch—my God.

My head banged against the wall beneath the window; then he sighed and let me slide from his lap. I stammered a question. He hoped I didn't mind that he'd done it before. He had cousins.

No one noticed us. Sandy kept the back of the bus busy rotating, and the front had all it could do just to sing those bottles of beer off the wall. There was no chaperone, although Wilson never again chartered a bus without stationing several along the aisles. Apparently, mine was not the only pair of underpants left beneath a seat. Of course, I never claimed them, and when they didn't turn up in the wash, I told my mother they'd been stolen in gym. She shook her head. "I swear, those Center kids'll steal anything," she said.

We gathered our instruments and lined up in the aisle. My crotch throbbed; it felt as raw as if it had been scraped open on cinders, and the cold wind that whistled up my skirt burned as we changed buses. All the way home Arthur blew kisses in my hair, stroking my hands while I cried. His hangnails scratched against my skin.

As we rode through Gary, he planned our future. In three years he would be sixteen; he could get a summer job and buy me a diamond. When he was eighteen, we could get married, unless I wanted to wait until I graduated from high school. In the meantime, he figured, we were unofficially engaged. What could I say? After all, he was the man of the world, and even if his world consisted of cousins, some of whom were boys, by the way, at least his hot dog had been out wandering while my little puss stayed home. He knew everything, and it hadn't done him the least bit of good. Don't get me wrong. I liked him. I thought he was very nice for a nerd.

So I went home from my first solo contest bedecked, deflowered, betrothed, and depressed. "I'm proud of you," my mother confessed as she sorted laundry. "First place, Janie—you should be a happy girl tonight." I sighed. "I'm happy," I said, watching her fingers flick our clothes into piles of colors and whites. They worked so fast, they made me dizzy, and I imagined how they must have gathered speed over the years, sorting laundry, changing diapers, slicing onions, ringing up grocery totals, snapping out the folds of my father's flesh the way Arthur had tried to teach mine to do, growing more efficient with practice until the whorls of her fingerprints and the weave of the world wore slick from the friction, sliding off each other so cleanly they no longer lingered to feel. "Hand me that box of Tide, honey, would you?" The way the cardboard corners fitted into the ellipse of her palm made me sad. The resistance of surfaces was all in my mind.

"Mama . . ." I said.

"Umm?" She was measuring a cup of granules.

I shook my head. "I'm tired," I said finally. "I'm going to bed."

"Without your supper?" I nodded. "There's some canned spaghetti." She relented. "Well, it's been a big day—I don't wonder."

I closed the door to my room with relief, but my bed was no longer a sanctuary, invaded by dreams no doors could keep out. In the halls of Wilson, Arthur's hands popped out of lockers, each hangnail a penis poking my cheeks and my nose as it pushed at my mouth, and then his toes turned into organs, wiggling down the corridors and pulling pinkly at the hem of my dress. If the downstairs stuff had been all there was, I might have adjusted, but that upstairs business with my mouth was just yuk. Then we were at a concert, performing onstage while everyone watched, and when I turned around, Arthur was playing a red penis that writhed in his lap. That did it. When he called on Sunday, I made my mother tell him I was sick, and, though she threatened to tell him I was having a tantrum, I threw up so convincingly, she capitulated, making me Jell-O and writing a note so that I could stay home from school the next day. Later we opened the front door, and under a rock on the porch was a note in a get-well card signed with a ribbon of X's and O's. I tore it up without reading it, and on Tuesday at school I pretended I didn't hear him when he asked if I'd gotten his card. Though he followed me from the bandroom, those hangnails and hands jerking at my coat, I would not look at him, would not speak. It took a few days for the message to get through, but, in the year and a half he had left in the Wilson band, we never exchanged another word.

I began practicing five hours a day, taking lessons two and three times a week, declining to change teachers, even though Mr. Schunk, who became senile and impossible within a very few years, advised me to. I had decided on him as my only friend, and no failure of health could make me give in. I thought he was the one person who knew what my mother and all Hammond did not, that, finding the flesh a cramped and uncomfortable home, one could choose to live in the gracious house of the mind. When he threatened to move to Arizona, I told him he could not go, and one Saturday morning, after I'd played a particularly difficult passage of Prokofiev and he picked fault, though by then we both knew the fault was not there, he ordered me to leave his house and added I was not to come back. I lay down on the floor, screaming that even if he killed me my spirit would stay. He shook his head in one of the lucid moments my madnesses seemed to inspire. "You will find, as my brother found at Dachau, when the body dies, the imagination dies also. Get up please." I got up. "I don't believe you," I said, but it was on his advice and against my mother's wishes that I left high school and Hammond at the end of my junior year with a full scholarship to study music at Indiana University and every intention not to return.

There is a postscript. Last summer I ran into Paul Nolta at a bar in Calumet City, where I was drinking brandy Manhattans and feeling sorry for myself because I wanted to be anywhere but alone in a dark booth that looked out at State Line Avenue with all Hammond just across the street. Sorrier still because I couldn't think of where else I'd rather be or anyone I thought I would like to be with. Never mind that I was married. My mother's funeral had been that afternoon.

There was a buzz of laughter from the TV screen and a dull, steady knock of glasses against the bar. I recognized

Paul as he passed on the way to the men's room. Same red hair, curling down his neck now, a sheen of sweat across his forehead—wearing jeans and a dirty blue work shirt straining at the buttons, white cotton socks, and (my heart caught) steel-toed boots. I think that secretly I'd always believed he would rise from Sandy's bed to become someone. I plead no more than the death of a childhood fantasy, and yet, even before I asked him to sit down and saw the mill grit beneath his fingernails, I felt absurdly bereaved. Of course, I was more than halfway drunk.

He slid across from me and signaled the bartender, smiling like a fat, freckled springer spaniel.

"I'm not trying to pick you up," I said quickly.

"Too bad." He leaned back and looked me over. "So you know my name. Am I supposed to know yours?"

"Jane. I know *you* if you're the same Paul Nolta who used to know Sandy Gitzke."

His brow creased. "Ah, Sandy. There's a real blast from the past. I didn't meet you here, did I?" He raised himself from the booth to pry his wallet from his back pocket, giving me a wave of his hand as I reached for my purse. Crumpling the cellophane from his cigarettes, he extended the pack toward me.

I shook my head. "You went steady."

"Everybody went steady," he said, swiveling his head toward the jukebox.

"I didn't."

He blew smoke in my face and shrugged, and for a minute I thought he might leave. "What else is new?"

"Not much," I admitted, feeling foolish. One sip of my fourth drink, and my head was spinning.

He drummed his fingers on the table. After a minute he stretched his features into an unsettling imitation of a grin. "Well, what's on your mind, Miss Married Jane?"

I tucked my left hand under the table, saying, "I'm not very married"; then thinking only a real ass would say something like that.

"I'm not very divorced." His grin relaxed. "Look, I think you're real pretty, but I just don't remember you."

"It was more than twenty years ago."

"You were a friend of Sandy's." It was a question, although he didn't say it as one.

"I knew her. I met you at one of her parties. I was just a kid, but I had a terrible crush on you."

He snapped his fingers, bringing his hand down so that the forefinger pointed at me. "You had a brother." I nodded as he began snapping his fingers again. "You *were* a kid. You had on this *gross* party dress, and you looked so miserable, no one would kiss you."

"You did."

He laughed and crooked a finger. I leaned across the table to get kissed again, but, you know, things are never as good as the first time. His lips were wet, and the table cut into my ribs. Looking pleased with himself, he sat back. "Janie," he said.

"People call me Jane now."

"Jane." He ordered another beer and another drink and lit another cigarette, the smoke drifting between us. "So, how's your brother these days?"

But I was feeling the brandy, a pleasant rounding of the rough corners of consciousness, and it was a relief after the ordeal of the afternoon. Tonight I would sleep in my old bed in an empty house; tomorrow I would have to go through my mother's things. I didn't want to think about my brother until then. "By the way, whatever happened to Sandy?" He frowned. "Sandy Gitzke, remember? The girl you went steady with."

"I didn't."

"She said you did. Well, you were fucking her, anyway."

"That," he said, "I admit. Good old Sandy."

"What happened to her?" The rim of my mouth was sticky, and I had a comfortable warmth, as though I were a little girl home from school with a cold, propped up on pillows while my mother spooned me cough syrup. Another spoonful, another drink, and I'd be sick, but for now I floated. Who cared what happened to Sandy? It was enough not to have to think about what happened to me.

"I knocked her up."

My shoulders snapped against the back of the booth. "You *married* her?"

"Nah." His grin was slightly sheepish.

"Well, I think you should have."

His glass slapped the table, and he laughed. "Still a priss, eh, Jane?"

"I'm not." But I had been, and I sounded so prim that I said it again. This time I sounded playful. I hadn't meant that either, but so what? I decided to risk the other drink.

"No, you're not. You're a nice girl." He was fat, and I was foolish. I was the clarinetist Mr. Schunk had promised, but here I was in a scummy bar, with a millhand, on the flimsy excuse of a previous connection to avoid thinking that I'd muffed the connections that should count. "Getting a little old to be a nice girl, aren't you, Janie?"

"Jane." Morosely I circled the smudged rim of my glass. He leaned forward, no longer smiling. "There's no need to get holy about Sandy. So I was a bastard and didn't marry her. I gave her money, and I didn't have to do that. You only need six guys to testify—I could have found a dozen with no sweat."

"No doubt."

"You don't have to be snide. Her life was no bed of roses. Her old lady was a lush and one hell of a bitch. And I'll give her credit—she was a damn decent kid in her way."

Maybe, but all the same, Sandy had been awfully indecent to me. So why did I suddenly see her again, drawing faces in the spilled sugar on the morning after her party while Pierre yapped in her mother's bedroom? Why did Mrs. Gitzke's bare bum bounce before me? My conscience exploded in my stomach. "I'm going to be sick," I said. It passed, and I smiled. "No, I'm not." "You ought to slow up on that brandy." He watched me until he seemed satisfied that I was not going to throw up. "Well, no reason for you to get choked up about Sandy. After all, she hated you."

It shouldn't have been a surprise, but it was. "Why? I never did anything to her."

"For one thing, I liked you." The doggy grin again.

"And, for another, you were a snob. She might have acted tough, but she got hurt, just like everybody."

"I don't think I was a snob," I said. "Anyway, that was twenty years ago." After all, it wasn't as if Sandy was why I had left Hammond. Besides, if one thing doesn't point you on your way, you can always find excuse in another. One course taken, it is not easy to remember there were options. I was too old to let Paul and Sandy or even Dick and my mother close a circle, not all the Calumet Region with its mills and heavy winter skies. More likely, my first sight of the ivy scaling the limestone walls of the auditorium at Indiana University under a blue sky stretched so tight over heaven, I thought it might break and let Paradise fall at my feet. That and the first bittersweet note of Stravinsky Mr. Schunk had played. Poor, dead Mr. Schunk, who had said it was a horrible life but taught me that nothing could be horrible as long as you heard the music. The circle had closed inside my own ear.

For a moment I felt elated. How odd that I should have had so little irony about myself when the music I loved best . . . What had happened to music in the twentieth century, I thought, was irony. The ironic dissonance. When I looked up, I was so surprised to find myself still in the bar with Paul that I said, without thinking, "I'm leaving my husband."

He laughed, then tipped his head back and gave me the once-over. "Well, well, well. You're looking real good, Janie."

"So are you," I said and giggled. He looked *terrible*. My head was skidding all over the room. I had forgotten to call Ben.

"Where are you going?" Paul asked when I stood.

I was still giggling. "I have to call my husband."

"I thought you were leaving him."

"I am. I have to tell him."

"Look, Jane, you're pretty drunk. Maybe you ought to wait."

"I'm going to the ladies' room," I said.

"You feel okay?"

"I feel great."

He stared at my legs. "You look great," he said. It seemed to depress him.

When I came out, Paul's arms were spanning the jukebox. "This place is a dump, but it's got the world's greatest jukebox. Memory Lane. Well, what the hell? Let's celebrate you leaving your husband and dance to old times." The giddiness was gone. I had a headache and couldn't remember why I wanted to leave Ben. I didn't love him, but I never had. I wanted to go home. The machine whirred as Paul swept me into his arms, and we waltzed to "The Great Pretender."

He sang along with the Platters, a hum like a bit of fuzz in a speaker, holding me so close that I got a mouthful of stained work shirt when I said, "I'm not going to spend the night with you."

"I didn't ask you to." We kept turning the same tight circle between the bar and the booths. "You're still a snob," he said. When the dance was over, he dipped me back, and we sat at the table without speaking. I bit my lip.

"I'm sorry," I said.

"Forget it."

As I started not to, a muscle jerked at one corner of his mouth, and I stopped. He was right. I was a snob, and I realized that if he had asked me to, I would have slept with him to prove I was not, just as I had spent fourteen years married to a man I did not love to prove to my mother that I did. There was irony for you. What I had proved was exactly what she had known. I did not love anyone. I had resisted that old mortal passion. It hadn't been good enough for me. So here I was. The bar was dreary, and the drinks were lousy. The truth is, mine had too much bitters, but I am wary of making bad jokes. Life may be ironic, but it's not very funny. My glass slipped out of my hand. The ice cubes rattled and slid across the table on a wash of brandy and sweet vermouth. "Oh, for Christ's sake," he said as I dropped my face into the liquid and cried, but when I looked up, my cheek cold and wet, it occurred to me that he had been very nice not to leave.

"My mother died. I went to her funeral this afternoon."
My voice quivered. "I hadn't seen her for fourteen years."

He held out a napkin. "Where's your family? Come on."
He was on his feet, with his arm around my shoulder. "I'll
drive you home."

A shimmer of heat rose from the pavement. The August
night air was no fresher than the stale chill of the bar, as
cloying as damp sheets, with a faint hint of sulfur. He had to
lean across me to roll my window down, to remind me to
remind him when to turn. I was no longer drunk, only tired.
We had not come to terms, and yet there was something
sweet in his silence after the clamoring sorrow of the afternoon.
Perhaps no one ever came to terms. And, if some did, my
mother was dead. We would have no reckoning now, only a
sorting and dispersal. We had not done the best we could, but
we had done. I felt weightless, relieved of all burdens to
prove, uncertain of what I would carry instead, so numb that I
might have been asleep, had I not felt a sharp pain where the
key to my mother's house cut into my hand.

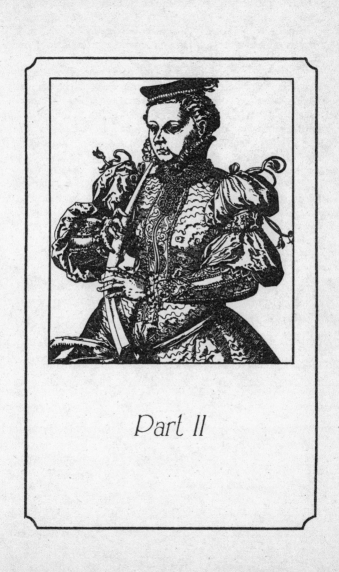

Part II

7

*M*r. Schunk died on the Tuesday of my music theory final my first semester at Indiana University. It was a day as dreary as the Friday, earlier in the semester, when John F. Kennedy was killed and I had sloshed to the Music Building to give the other members of the I.U. Philharmonic the news. It had been raining ever since, a wall of dirty clouds the apparent portal to Heaven.

Mr Schunk had never moved to Arizona, though every Wednesday and Saturday until I left for college I listened to him mourn his coming exile. He saw hardly anything save the milk of his cataracts, and when he grew temperamental, thumping a knotted finger against the music stand for sharps I had not missed, calling crescendos where there were none, my own temper rose. Yet for me he was the perfect maestro, with an ear so cantankerous that I learned to trust my own. Another teacher might have taught me to count more accurately, to play as I was told; he taught me to *imagine* the music, as passionately as if I had written it myself. I was the first freshman ever seated in the I.U. Philharmonic, but more than once in rehearsal the conductor glared me down to say "Miss Hurdle, may I remind you that there is an orchestra playing with you?'' More than once the conductor of the Richmond Symphony had to do the same. When Howard Feltner, my clarinet teacher at Indiana, first heard me play, he said, ''You've got a lot of style, and your tempo is eccentric but good, but you're too loud in the fortes and too soft in the pianissimos. Now I'm going to mark this up, and I want you to do it my way.'' I put down my Paris Selmer. From it I had coaxed a tone that ranged from the dark hues of the German to the brittle, chromatic tints of the French. ''I won't,'' I said and thought of Mr. Schunk. ''You're blind as a bat,'' I'd said to him once. ''You can't even read the notes.'' Mr. Schunk squared his shoulders. ''When the eye cannot see, the ear can hear. And when the ear is deaf, the heart will know.'' I picked up the clarinet and played the piece again, not exactly Feltner's way, but different, an improvement on my own.

But when the heart stops beating? Mr. Schunk's daughter called me. Her husband taught trumpet at Indiana, and from the day I'd arrived the Solomons had taken me in. She said, ''Jane, I thought you'd want to know that my father passed away in his sleep this morning.'' She grunted. ''Listen to me. We haven't even seen those funeral parasites yet, and already I'm speaking their language.''

''Oh, Ruth.'' I gasped, shocked because Mr. Schunk rose for me in that moment in a way that, living, he had not been able to do all fall. I hadn't written; over Christmas I'd found some excuse not to visit. Our temperaments had battled for so long that I was afraid he hated me, and I didn't want to admit I'd needed him. I heard him saying, ''When I come to America, I speak English. When I am at the ball park, I speak baseball. When I am playing music, I speak Italian.'' Now he was dead, and his daughter was speaking mortician.

''Now, Jane, don't be weepy. He didn't suffer.''

I sniffed back my tears. ''He was always suffering.''

''Isn't that the truth?'' Though I hadn't meant to be funny, Ruth laughed. ''Martin and I are driving to Hammond this afternoon. Sam and Jake will probably thumb up from Champaign. I've told them they'll be lucky not to be killed. 'You know what kind of people pick up hitchhikers,' I said. 'Your beautiful young bodies will be shot full of holes and tossed out in a ditch.' But they never listen to me. David doesn't know—he didn't come home last night. You know how he is when he's got his thing up a new skirt. Anyway, we'll have plenty of room if you want to come along."

"Good Lord," I said.

"I'm just being realistic." Big-boned like her father, Ruth too was an epic complainer, though no one took her grievances as seriously as I had once taken his. Her voice was brusque, and she had a brisk way of walking, as if life were nothing two rolled sleeves and a bottle of ammonia couldn't cure. She was proud of her boys' bodies because she refused to admit she was proud of them, and I never heard her say a sentimental word about any of her sons, three grown and the two under five who had slipped through a hole in her diaphragm, she claimed. "There's nothing more ridiculous than an old woman with a baby," she would say as she slung diapers from the kitchen counter to fix a martini. She was still nursing Michael, and she often stirred the pitcher with one enormous tit hanging out. They lived in a big, sloppy frame house filled with tattered wicker, Oriental rugs, cats, dying plants, students, and noise. "I can't keep up—I'm not Superman," Ruth was moaning when I first punched the doorbell that was as defunct as her father's, having been invited for dinner my first Sunday in Bloomington at his suggestion. She glared at a basket of philodendron with brown leaves folded and clinging like dead moths to the stems. Two of Martin's pupils were already sitting on a willow settee, and, in spite of her, we politely praised Ruth's plants, her cheese dip, her cats, and her kids. She brightened. Michael was a regular monkey in motor skills, and Joshua, her fourth-born, would have a big dong. "I swear the kid's an idiot," she said, "but he's hung." We smiled nervously in search of something neuter to praise. "Well," she pursued, "it certainly can't hurt him." It didn't take me long to understand that her complaints were really declarations of love.

"Well," she said now, "do you want a ride or not?"

"Of course," I said, and so I went home.

I hadn't planned to, though my finals were over and there were almost two weeks of empty days before second semester began. No, I had decided, when the bus taking me home for Christmas crossed the Kankakee River into the cocoon of soot spun by the mills, home was where the heart beat wings against the wall. The week before the Christmas recess, Dick lost his right index finger on a coil in the sheetmill. A wad of oozing gauze and adhesive tape hung from his hand. "My fault." He shrugged. "The mill's no place to be horsing around. You turn your back on those machines, you're lucky they don't cut you in half." We had Christmas dinner at his kitchen table, and he joked while I averted my eyes from the hand by his plate. "Never thought a fellow wore his nuts on his hand, but here I sit like a girl while my wife carves the turkey. What'll it be, Janie, light meat or dark?"

"I'm not hungry," I said. Dickie spilled his milk on my plate and made a pink swamp of my cranberry sauce. In the living room the television babbled; all morning the battery-run forklift my mother gave Dickie had lifted and lowered and lifted and whined. Everything depressed me: Marie's melon belly ripening under her maternity smock, new curtains, old platitudes, arguments, advice.

My mother wanted to know about my life, but dorm stories and gush about my classes bored her. She'd never had a roommate; she'd never taken theory. She had only worked in a cafeteria and got married. Oh, it wasn't that I didn't love them, though I wished they could talk about something besides labor pains and union dues; wished that my mother would remember I spent my time in the music library, not the *liberry*—I hadn't followed in her footsteps, and I didn't ring up fruit. "Well, what do you do if you don't go out?" she asked, and I told her about the Solomons. She frowned through my re-enactment of a particularly hilarious turn from our Sunday night charades, not waiting for the answer before she mused, "You know, your brother makes good money if they can just settle without a strike."

"I can't talk to you," I said. She shrugged. "I don't know why not. I never change." I packed for the few remaining weeks of first semester and explained I'd have to stay in Bloomington for break because the Phil was getting ready for a concert. "Suit yourself," she said.

At the bus station, which wore a tinsel garland above the ticket desk, Dick pinched my cheek with his left hand. "Don't be sad, Sissy." I stared at the rag claw he hadn't raised to touch me. He'd driven me to the station, and now I had to take leave of him alone. "Aw, come on, it isn't like I play the clarinet. For a man with a family, better a finger than your paycheck." I kept my eyes on his hand because I couldn't bear to look at his eyes. "I got a real family now."

"So, everyone's got family." I swooped to straighten the I.D. tag on my suitcase. "It's the universal misfortune.

"Hey." He stooped into an awkward hug. My mother usually shamed me into grudging manners; I treated him worse and loved him more because he never pouted, never ever shamed. "You calling me a misfortune? You're my family too."

"Well." I straightened. Why did I always want to hurt him? "Better your pay than a finger when it's time to diddle your wife.

He blushed. "Janie, those kind of things are private."

I grinned, but when he looked away, I was ashamed. "I didn't mean it. I was just *kidding*." My bus had pulled into the shed. He picked up my suitcase. "I'm sorry, I'm sorry," I begged, clutching at his sleeve as we moved forward in the crush of passengers. I wanted to say something and did not know what it was.

He patted my shoulder. "Well, kid, don't take any wooden nickels." It was the goodbye my father had always used, and it sounded as stupid as it always had.

I looked up. The golden wings of the Presley pompadour stretched beyond his temples in a parody of flight. College boys wore short hair. The edge of his eyetooth was dark with rot. "I'm not coming back." So that was what I wanted to say. "I hate it here. Next summer I'm going to Chautauqua or someplace and get a job." He had the most beautiful, clean gray eyes, but the color now reminded me of lead. I grabbed his coat and pressed my face to the wool. "I don't hate you, I don't hate you, you're the only one I'll never hate."

"Course not." He raised my head and took the ticket from

my hand. "Hey, you gotta get on the bus now. Take it easy. Why, when you get back to that college and start thinking about your good-looking brother, I bet you won't be able to wait to come home." The line of passengers was sidestepping us. "Besides, you can't tell me I went to all this trouble to make you an aunt again and you aren't even going to come see my kid." I stopped sniffling, and he bent to peck me.

As soon as I got to my seat, I opened my window. "Dick," I yelled, leaning into the damp, exhaust-fouled chill of the shed. He paused at the door to the station. "Write me a letter, okay? The only one who writes is Mom."

He smiled the saddest smile I've ever seen and held up his maimed right hand in reply. And I meant that to be my last memory of Hammond. But then Mr. Schunk died.

My mother was surprised to see me. It was her day off, and she was lounging on the sofa in a pink duster while a soap man threatened to leave his soap wife on TV. "I don't know why I watch," she apologized, flicking off the set. "Nothing ever happens." She put the coffeepot on, and we sat at the kitchen table. It was hard for me to believe that she was only four years older than Ruth, though her dark hair was just beginning to gray and Ruth's was steel-colored, pulled back into an untidy scouring-pad bun. Ruth would go slack-faced like her father; already her flesh had begun to sag. Save for a little crêpe under the eyes, my mother's had held tight for forty-nine years.

But Ruth was my friend, and my mother was my mother, and if she gave the same advice as my mother, at least Ruth gave it from the gut. And Ruth practiced what she preached, while my mother, nine years after my father died, still listed our phone in his name. In the car on the way up, Ruth lamented that her father had never remarried. "Life goes on," she said. "You may as well make up your mind to go with it, and it's a shame to die alone. That's just the way I feel." She'd been disgusted when she heard that I didn't date. "Now, you listen to me, Jane Hurdle. You're only a freshman, and already you've got a good reputation at the school. But music isn't everything. We didn't get those five kids with a trumpet."

I was willing to admit that Ruth had a point. So I'd had a bad experience when I was twelve—tough luck. I had used it as an excuse much too long. I wasn't twelve anymore, and it was no longer sex that put me off: it was hangnails, pimples, and bald spots on the grad students. The men I knew were brilliant but guilty of dead skin, pustules, or thinning hair.

And so, throughout first semester I was lonely when the dorm emptied on Saturday nights. Their faces knocked cockeyed, their blouses buttoned wrong, the girls in the hall jammed the elevator at 1:00 A.M., squealing and sighing. They *said* they were virgins, but I knew better. Sandy Gitzke had tipped me off: everyone did it, no matter what she said. A cute Beta in my comp class invited me to his pledge dance. I wanted to go, but I was embarrassed to tell him I couldn't do the leg, the mashed potatoes, or even the twist. Instead, I told him I didn't date. "Not ever?" He looked startled. "Not ever," I said. He had a beautiful blond bang and a stomach as lean and hard as a washboard. I imagined us in a dark room, Brahms on the stereo while that soft blond hair brushed my breast. But he didn't listen to Brahms, and I didn't dance. Sidney, my roommate, spent the nights between dances in the television room of the Lambda Chi house, where the only light was the gray snow of the screen, and the windows were painted black so that Lambda Chis could drink and screw their girlfriends in private. While she was out, I stood on a chair and looked myself over in the mirror. I'd barely hit five feet, but I had high, round tits like whole notes in my pockets. From hip to waist and back, I was a harmonic minor, ascending and descending. I was ready, but only if I could find someone as beautiful as that Beta willing to sit out the dances with me. I let Sidney fix me up.

His name was Eddie Ziegler, and he was drunk when he got there. While he crawled under coffee tables with a foot of garden hose, whining, "Friend or enema?," I spent the evening watching "Gunsmoke" with Sidney and her boyfriend. On the way home he snatched my wrap-around skirt and charged a Volkswagen on Third Street, screaming, "El toro, el fucking toro, mother," leaving me on the curb, sobbing and shivering in my lace-trimmed pettipants. I forgave Sidney, who swore it wasn't her fault and Eddie could be a riot when he wasn't stinko, but I didn't let her fix me up again.

Should I have explained all that to my mother as we sat at the kitchen table, drinking coffee, and she said, "When you said you were staying at school, I hoped it was maybe because you'd met somebody"?

Not on your life. Ruth had roared when I described my date with Eddie. My mother would have used it to teach me a lesson. What kind of friends was I making at that college? She wanted me to have a good time, but only on her terms.

She twisted her wedding ring and stared at her coffee. "How can you see with all that hair in your eyes?" I ducked my head as she reached to smooth back my bangs. "Well, I should of known you wouldn't bother to come home to see me. I suppose I ought to be glad you came home at all."

"That's a crummy thing to say."

"I didn't *mean* I was glad about Mr. Schunk. Although . . ." She had this way of beginning sentences with *though's*, as if everything she said had been preceded by a point she took exception to. "You have to look at it this way, Janie. His family must be relieved he went so fast." She shook her head. "You were too young to remember. It's terrible when they linger like your father." She looked out the window for a minute. "Ever since you went to college, we're not good enough for you."

"That's not so," I said, hating her for bringing it up and hating myself because, of course, it was true.

The light that came through the window behind her was gray. We hadn't turned on the fluorescent light—no sense in wasting electricity in the afternoon. The dim room was a memorial to my father's tight-fisted ghost. "I feel like I'm onstage," he had said once, when he came into my bedroom and found me, under overhead and Cinderella lamp, reading *The Bobbsey Twins and Baby May*. When he snapped off that silly dresser lamp, I stood on my bed and pummeled the front of his gray work shirt with my fists. "I'm reading," I shrieked. "My teacher says you have to have good light when you read." He'd shrugged me off. "Your teacher don't pay the bills." He died less than two years later, a gray man in work shoes and twills who'd allotted our lives in kilowatt hours. Now my mother's face was dreary with shadow. She rubbed a finger in a coffee stain till nothing was left but a wavy brown ring and her iridescent print. My heart constricted with family: my brother, those little evasive rubs. I jerked my hands from the table.

"Well, they say you always hurt the ones you love."

"Will you drop it?" Oh Lord, would I never be done with that noose they call kin? Why couldn't my mother, like Ruth, complain in an epic tradition? Why did she always bring up the tedious, small business of love? "I'm sorry if I hurt your feelings, but would you please, *please* just get to the point?"

"Never mind," she said in a voice as worn as the rubber heels on my loafers. "You're not interested." She took another sip of coffee. "Oh, honey, I *am* glad to see you. It's just that I worry about you, working so hard. Don't you ever feel like getting out?"

"You don't go out," I said.

"Me?" She looked surprised. "I'm an old grandmother."

"But you don't look like a grandmother, and you're prettier than Sidney's mother or Ruth, and they're not even as old as you."

She smiled and covered my hand with hers. Like mine, her fingernails were ragged. Weak nails, nice legs, a stubborn habit of solitude—they ran in the family, so what did she expect? "Do you think so? Why, Janie." I don't think I ever saw her look so pleased.

"Besides," I growled, embarrassed, "I tried to get out over Christmas. I wanted to go to the Chicago Symphony, but you didn't want me riding the South Shore that late, and Dick wouldn't take me because Marie had to go to some dumb shower."

"That shower meant a lot to her. After all, being a mother is the most important job in the world." My mother rose and dashed the dregs of her coffee into the sink. "You know yourself those trains don't run very often at night. Anyway, I didn't mean with your brother."

The phone rang.

She sighed. "Well, maybe you do get out and just don't tell me. You always were secretive."

"I'm not secretive."

"Answer the phone," she said. "You're closer."

It was Dickie. "Is my mom there?" he asked. "Who's this? Grandma?"

"It's Jane," I said.

"Aunt Jane," he whooped. "What a pickle." That was the advertising slogan for Aunt Jane's Polish Dills, and whenever I was crabby, he called me Aunt Dill. "Let me talk to Grandma."

So my mother forgot about my social life and hung up in a snit because Marie was missing. She had disappeared, it turned out, all the way next door, but my mother didn't feel the least bit foolish, because, as she said, "when a woman is due any minute, you want to know where she is." When I pointed out that she wasn't due for another three weeks, my mother added that I didn't know anything—the baby could decide to come any day.

And even though it would prove her right, I halfway hoped it would. After all, I would be its aunt. And something had to pass the time.

I saw the Solomons only at Mr. Schunk's funeral, which wasn't at the synagogue. Though the Solomons weren't observant, immediately after the burial, they honored Mr. Schunk his way by starting the traditional mourning period, staying at the house I had visited so often. There they received the rabbi and members of the congregation who came to say the prayer for the dead, as well as Dick and Marie and me, but all we did was sit. Hadn't I reminded Mr. Schunk of a daughter? But his daughter just sat, too. I wasn't so sure that was his way. He'd told me himself that he was a musician first and second a Jew. Martin and I were also musicians, but at the funeral all we could do was listen to some boring old man eulogize the goodness of the departed without mentioning the Chicago Symphony, while the vibrato of that goodness—those first notes of Stravinsky—rippled up and down my spine. Believing in nothing, I felt like nothing, too. The Jews said they were God's chosen people. So did Catholics, and my brother had turned Catholic when he married Marie. Everyone I knew seemed to be headed for a heaven where I would not be welcome. I banged my heel against the leg of my folding chair. If God existed, I didn't like him. Mr. Schunk had been an artist. What could he want with that pretentious mediocrity Yahweh, the old jaw-well, who kept time in a tedium of hour upon twenty-four hours while musicians worked with what was given and created counter-rhythm? Given a choice of life or art, I could not understand who would think life the superior invention.

I didn't see much of my brother either. He was working double shifts to put aside something extra in case he went out on strike that spring. His hand had healed, the bandage replaced by an angry stub of red flesh that would later whiten. He had transferred from the sheetmill back to open hearth. Mostly he talked baby, patting Marie's barrel of a belly.

Dickie took me to his room to show me the squeak-toy, a blue rubber baseball mitt he'd bought with his very own money to present to his new brother. "But, Dickie," I protested, even though at seven he was already insisting his name was Rick, "what if your new brother is a sister?" He widened the brown eyes he'd got from his mother. "Aunt Dill, if it's a girl, she won't be my brother, and if I don't get a brother, I'm going to give my *present*"—he said the word contemptuously, as if I'd tainted it—"to the orphans." "Don't you like girls?" I asked. He grinned. "Aunt Jane, would you loan me five dollars? 'Cause with five dollars I can buy a real one, and if I don't get a brother I can use it myself." "Dickie," I said sternly, "it's the thought that counts." He frowned. "But Aunt Jane, if I get a baseball glove, I won't care if I don't get a brother." How's that for thought? I gave him five dollars because I thought, never mind his mother's eyes, the little bastard takes after me.

But my generosity didn't buy me a baby, though, to prove my mother right, it did come early, choosing the day I was scheduled to leave. So, with my suitcase and a shopping bag full of books and scores in one hand and in the other the $700 Paris Selmer, which I had spent evenings after school and two summers spooning dead goldfish from a tank in the basement of W. T. Grant's to earn, I struggled up the steps of a city bus to get to the Greyhound station downtown. The Solomons were staying an extra day, doing whatever you did to begin settling an estate—call Goodwill, for all I knew, to haul away the rickety furniture and fans that were Mr. Schunk's wealth.

You wouldn't have caught my roommate on a city bus or a Greyhound either. Sidney had her own car, a 1962 Rambler she parked illegally behind the Lambda Chi house because freshmen weren't allowed to have wheels. Yesterday afternoon she would have driven from Greensburg to Bloomington to check her mailbox for sorority bids. She wouldn't move to the house till next fall, but all spring, I knew, she'd be busy with pledge dinners and mixers. Besides Ruth, she was my only real friend, and I felt I was losing her. "Another dinner with the big shots?" Sid had teased as I dressed for one of my evenings at the Solomons'. I shrugged. At the Music School, I hinted, all the students fraternized with profs, but in fact freshmen usually didn't. I was different: honors and in the Phil, almost a member of the Solomon family. Having nowhere else to go, I was grateful, though I sometimes felt like a mascot in my knee socks and pleated skirts. Still, I beat my piano teacher at charades; the grad students listened to my opinions. And, while I was short on experience, I was long on opinions. Martin was nice, though his idea of sparking conversation was to ask what you thought of your classes or the Cubs. He blushed at anything off-color, and, though he laughed when I thunked his head to act out "Night on Bald Mountain," he turned purple when I pantomimed "mount." If Ruth hadn't been there to direct him, I suspected he might have indeed tried to beget his get with a trumpet.

So what if I had my dinners? Without Sidney I would have no one to giggle with, and show me a girl who doesn't like to giggle, I'll show you a girl who is a freak. "There's nothing wrong with Janie," I'd overheard Dick insist to my mother. "She's just special." I was more hurt than mad to hear her reply, "Maybe that's her problem." Sidney made me feel normal. She borrowed my shampoo; she asked my advice as if boyfriends were something I would know about. Together we bitched about mystery-meat meals and after hours let down a basket on a rope for pizza. But next year she wouldn't be in our blue room on the third floor of the limestone castle that looked like a medieval fortress with real ivory towers. Of course, I might not either. We had heard rumors that Morrison would be converted to a classroom building, and any leftover maidens who didn't graduate or pledge or get married would be shipped off to the newer dorms on the fringes of campus.

But even a new dorm would be better than the sooty air of Hammond, which I was leaving like last year's skin, and I thought how glad I was to be going back as I walked the dead length of State Street to the bus station, past Goodwill and toward the burned-out strip of Calumet City, where a poster in front of a boarded-up burlesque invited you in to see Lottie the Fabulous Body, whose legs flapped in wet paper shreds from her fabulous hips. It was snowing, and tire treads cut through the street like pastry wheels, but the sky looked as if it had been rolled out of a tandem mill. In the station I slumped in a chair and picked enamel flakes from the painted canvas seat. I watched a student who sat on a plaid suitcase chatter with her girlfriend, whose Weejuns dripped dirty puddles around her feet. The girl with the Weejuns lived in Morrison; I'd seen her in the lobby. I supposed there was a bid waiting in her mailbox or maybe a proposal from a distant boyfriend. Behind them a Negro woman with a belly the size of Marie's slapped at a knock-kneed little girl, who screamed, "I be good, I be good. Just don't hit me again, nigger." In the alcove that had once been a concession stand, its dusty shelves now empty, the cash register flagged no-sale, drawer distended like an idiot mouth, a girl was weeping on her boyfriend's shoulder. Next to me a hand belonging to an old man who reeked of wool and perspiration throbbed beneath a newspaper. The bus would stop in Kentland and Lafayette before I changed coaches in Indianapolis (why, oh why, do they call them coaches?) to pick up a fresh supply of perverts, derelicts, and ex-cons. I got up to get a cup of coffee.

I'd been wrong about the failure of metamorphoses in Hammond; they happened every day, even if they happened backward. In the terminal restaurant I saw a man become a dog.

The waitress's powdered face had the texture of sandstone, and two glittering black eyes peered through clean little holes under painted-on brows. When Sidney asked what my father did, I'd been relieved to tell her my father was dead. Her father was a doctor. When her parents visited, they took us to the Fireside for lobster Newburg. The waiters wore red jackets and bow ties. I wouldn't have wanted to confess that my father had shoveled coal in a mill or that, when you ate on us, you went to Fat Boy's, where my sister-in-law, who wore a big button that said TRY OUR FRESH STRAWBERRY PIE, instead of a Kappa key or Pi Phi arrow, had wiped tables.

At the counter a man in an oversized gray loden coat trailing threads of lining ordered water and handed her the menu. Her eye holes slit, and he cackled. She folded her arms and watched until his laughter shook him loose and he clutched at the counter, fingers slipping over the edge and disappearing into the crumple of his coat as the stool toppled and rang. She picked up a rag and began polishing the counter. "Bitch," he yelled, rearing his head from the tatters. He began crawling, tangling arms and legs in the coat before her wadded rag hit his neck and his limbs buckled. I stood, no longer thirsty. He threw his head back again. "I ain't dirt . . . can't treat me . . . call my lawyer . . . ." As she howled with laughter, he bayed at a peel of paint hanging from the tin ceiling, then lunged at the wet hem of my slacks and barked up my leg.

"Stop it," I begged, scooping up my books and thumping my suitcase. "Go away."

He bit my ankle. The waitress was bleating with laughter. For a moment I simply did not believe it. There was no rocket of pain through the corduroy and sweat sock. Nevertheless the son-of-a-bitch had sunk his teeth in my pant leg.

"Your lawyer, my ass," the waitress hollered, bowing her head to the counter and wiping her eyes. "What you need is a rabies shot."

"Lady, I need a dime." I shook my foot, and he fell back.

"Aw, go on, get out of here before I sweep you up with the trash," the waitress said.

He raised his head. "Lady, I ain't askin' for the Purple Heart, just a thin silver medallion." He rose to his knees and clasped one of mine. "You don't even have to hang it on a ribbon. Just 'In God we trust' and, when you turn it over, 'E pluribus unum.' A dime, lady. You gotta have a medal to make a fuckin' phone call." He howled a crescendo, throwing himself forward so hard, his chin cracked on the tile.

"He's dead," I guessed, looking up at the stony bluff of the waitress's face.

"I should be so lucky." She sat across from me and put her hands on the table, her fingers smelling faintly of disinfectant. "The jackass comes in once a week and writes filth on the menus, but this is the first time I ever seen him bite a customer."

I struggled upstairs to the ladies' room and dredged my purse for a dime. I didn't have one, and the free stall was filled with mops, buckets, and spare rolls. No wonder the hall stank of urine. When the two girls from downstairs came in, I waited for one to finish so that I could sneak in without paying. "Look at it this way," Plaid Suitcase called to the Weejuns. "If you don't get your B.A., you'll get your M.R.S." They laughed. I pulled up my pant leg and peeked down my sock, disappointed that there was no mark on my ankle, something to prove Hammond to Sid. When they flushed, I jumped for a door. In case you've never noticed, only middle-aged women pass on pay toilets.

By the time I clumped downstairs, the loudspeaker was gargling my bus call. The station had jammed with people in a hurry to leave Hammond, and I was lucky to get a place by the window. There was nothing I wanted to see, but I spread my luggage and tried to look mean in hopes of hogging the seat. Just as the bus began wheezing and revving, the girl who had wept on her boyfriend's shoulder puffed down the aisle, sniffling while I took back my clarinet and shopping bag to let her sit. She leaned across my lap and beat on the window, waving to the boy, who grew smaller in the shed as we pulled into State Street. She sobbed all the way to Kentland. In the parking lot of the Post House she looked up. "I won't see him till February." She whimpered, her swollen face working. "And what if he meets somebody?" "Oh, damnit," I said, "turn off that faucet," and she sniveled into her coat sleeve all the way to Indianapolis, where I caught the night coach to Bloomington.

"Hurdle!" When I kicked our door open, Sidney was sitting cross-legged on her bed, half-slip hanging from her armpits over bra and panties, the uniform for lounging that year in the dorm. "I thought you were staying here for break. Kent's not back yet, and I'm going crazy."

"Well," I said, nudging my suitcase toward my desk and dropping the rest on my bed, "don't keep me in suspense. Kappa or Pi Phi?"

"Kappa." She watched me shrug my coat to the floor. "I know, I know. But the Kappa house is closer to the Lambie Pies, and my mother would have shit if I'd turned down her legacy."

"Closer by a block," I said, stripping off my sweater and slacks and pillaging my suitcase for my muumuu. "Jesus, Sid," I added through a mouthful of flowered cotton. "What do you have legs for?"

She stared at her slippers, two red sheepdogs sleeping on our rug. "Hurdle, I'm so depressed."

In fact, Sidney was never depressed; she just thought she was. Her two passions at school were, in order, her diet and her boyfriend. She couldn't stick to either, and she fretted over both. A premed with a photographic memory and straight A's, she was also a wonderful actress who had perfected the role of a dolt. I'd been amazed when she came back from her first classes, put her glasses on, and sat at her desk without shifting for three hours while she underlined chemistry formulas in four colors. But her imagination belonged at home, to an Arabian stallion named King of the Wind from a book we had both loved as children. She had wanted to go to an equestrian school, but her father sent her to the university to become a doctor. She didn't mind, she said, though if she had to go to college, she would rather have gone to the veterinary school at Purdue. I suspect I was the only person who knew she was really not very happy, and I felt sorry for her because there was no place I would rather have been than Indiana.

"I know." I crashed on my mattress. "The Pi Phis have all the queens, but the Kappas have the brains. Tough decision."

"Don't be mean." Reaching for a cigarette, she knocked over a bottle of nail polish. She painted her toenails every night, only to stuff them into socks. It was her peculiar vanity to hide her vanities. Her frosted toes snuggled into Adlers, she let her fingernails go bare. While I spent hours trying to decide which of my four skirts to top with which of my four blouses, she jerked the same pair of white Levi's from her closet full of clothes, and she wore her thick silver-blond mane in braids whenever the humidity frizzed it. She had a slightly addled look, and when her amber eyes widened, they reminded me of eggs over light, but she also had smooth, honey-colored skin and a glorious smile. It was the sort of face that always gets elected high school queen, though none of the generations that follow will ever fathom why from the picture. "Oh shit," she yelped and dabbed at the crimson clot with a Kleenex. "Look, Dumbo, we're still going to be friends, and you know my mother'd never speak to me again if I didn't pledge. Besides, you know I know it's all bullshit. We all went over to the house this afternoon, and get this." She jumped up and turned her back to me, wiggling her bottom inside her slip. "Kappas are never seen on campus without girdles." She flopped again. "Sheeit. The only time Kappas don't wear girdles is when they're on their backs beneath the Sigma Nus."

I laughed. "Guess what. A man *bit* me at the bus station. Hammond—yuk." I thought of my mother's shadowed face, and shuddered. You came away to school to escape your family—what did Sid want with sisters? "Oh, Siddie, did you mean it, about us always being friends?"

She looked at her red toenails. I'd embarrassed her. "Of course I did, Dumbo. Who else could a creep like me be friends with? How come you went home?"

"Mr. Schunk died."

The fire doors to our end of third whacked against the wall. "Oh, it's beer beer beer that makes you want to cheer!"

"Christ," I moaned, slapping my hands to my ears. "The nerds are back." I pounded my face into the pillow. "The nerds."

"In the halls, in the halls, in the halls, in the halls."

"Oh, it's wine wine wine that turns you to a swine," Sid sang lustily, kicking our door shut and adding, "Shut up, finks." She sat at her desk. "I'm sorry, Hurdle. I know you really loved him."

I shrugged. "Well, I've been to funerals before."

She was nodding, her eyes soft as chick fuzz, and I felt like slapping myself. Why didn't I tell her the real reason I hated to go home? Why did I play on my half-orphanhood for all it was worth, more than it had ever been to me? Because the real reason wasn't good enough, and I knew it. I was ashamed to belong to them and even more ashamed to be hamming it for Sid.

"How come you're depressed?" I asked.

She dropped her chin to her hands. "Oh, God. Do you know that jerk Kent only called me once over vacation? So I was feeling lonely, and Suzy Pollert and I drove over to this bar in Cincinnati, and we met these guys, and, well, anyway, what did I think Kent was doing? Running around with God-knows-who up in Muncie. So we went to this party, and the guy I was with—his name is Riggs, he's in law school in Columbus—turns out to be crazy about horses. His uncle raises Arabians in Colorado."

"Yeah?"

"So we wound up"—she dropped her voice—"making out in the bedroom."

"That's it?"

"But, Hurdle, you know what Kent was doing? The poor baby called last night, and his mouth was so sore he could hardly talk. He was getting his wisdom teeth pulled."

"So?"

"So? It hurts."

"Yeah, well, we all hurt," I said.

"I'm so ashamed. Besides, he wants to drive down to see me, and obviously I can't go out with him, but . . . ."

"No."

"No, what?"

"Don't you want me to go out with him?"

"Are you crazy? Just because I can't doesn't mean I'll give him to you. I really like this guy."

"Oh." I fiddled with a concert program that was hanging from my bulletin board. "Well, this semester I'm going out. I decided."

"Great, but you'll have to find your own men. Come in," she yelled as a knock set our door chattering on its hinges.

The girl from the Hammond bus station peeked in. "Hi. I'm Betty Ingram, up on fourth?" She'd changed her wet Weejuns for fuzzy turquoise slippers. It was the year you walked on impossible animals instead of feet. Though I hadn't asked her, she sat on my bed. "Would either of you want a date tonight?" Talk about timing. I winked at Sid.

Sidney smiled at Betty, her top lip tight across her teeth. "Not me. I've got the clap, and my roommate's a recluse." Socking her hand in her mouth, she giggled out her nose.

Betty's face gave an angry twitch, and she paled. "I get it." She rose.

"Well, wait a minute," I said. "I'm not doing anything."

"I thought you had to practice," Sid said.

"Huh?" I'd never thought Sidney would try to shut me out. She picked up a book and pretended to study while Betty paused in the doorway. I smiled. "You say this guy's a friend of yours?"

"Well, not exactly." She took a step back into the room. "He's a Phi Delt. One of his brothers fixed us up to go out drinking, but now I've got the cramps." As if to prove it, she clutched her stomach. Sid turned a page. "I'd call him, but it's getting kind of late."

Sid turned another page. No one read that fast. I gave Betty the once-over. She had squirrel-brown hair staggering toward the collar of her bathrobe. I thought I remembered she had a flat ass and chunky thighs. Her teeth were tiny, like an animal's, and when she smiled, her gums showed. That moment, when the elevator doors parted like curtains and a girl was onstage, couldn't be any more disappointing to the boy on the lobby sofa with me than with her.

"I'd have asked somebody I knew, but they all had dates."

So I was a lousy judge of Bettys. I'd thought she was coming back to get bids and proposals when all she got was cramps.

"I'll go."

Sid looked up.

"Thanks," Betty said. "There's just one thing—the guy that fixed us up is really going to be pissed if he hears I punked out, so could you do me a favor and give him my name?"

"Why not?"

"Hurdle," Sid said.

Betty Ingram, marketing major from Whiting."

"Hurdle," Sid repeated.

"What's his name?" I asked.

"Kelly McCullehey. He's a junior." Groaning, she rubbed her stomach. "Maybe I can do you a favor sometime."

"Did you say *Kelly McCullehey?*" Sid rounded the corner of her desk, but Betty was gone.

I stood before my closet. "Well, say, what should I wear to go drink with the Irish?"

"Damn you."

"Something green, don't you think?" I avoided looking at her until she slammed my closet door and backed against it.

"I can't believe you're doing this. *Why* are you doing this?"

"Why not?" I shrugged gaily. "It's my chance to be a rose by any other. By the way, I thought you were rude. Can I wear your new cardigan?"

"You spend a whole semester turning down every man who calls you, and now you have to rush off with the first guy that somebody you don't even know drags in." She marched to her desk for a cigarette. "Boy, Hurdle, you make a lot of sense."

She had a point. But I sat on my bed to put on my knee socks. "Can I borrow your sweater?"

"It's three sizes too big for you." She yanked out a drawer and threw the sweater at me.

"I'll roll the sleeves up." I stood to button myself into it. "You know what I think? I think you're just mad because you're depressed and you don't want anyone else to have a good time."

"You know, you really come up with a lot of crap, but that's about the shittiest thing I've heard yet. Hurdle, you don't know this guy."

I opened the door to the little closet that housed the sink and telephone we shared with the room next door. "Well, you know the Greeks. Just one big happy family," I said with my toothbrush in my mouth.

"Oh, cut it out. With your grades and looks you could have pledged any house on campus."

"I didn't want to," I said, as I always did, instead of admitting that I couldn't afford to or that I had resolved to go out because I was afraid to be more lonely than ever now that Sid had sisters and I wasn't one.

"Okay, I give up. Have a great time." She was reading at her desk when I came back and scooped my coat off the floor.

"I will." I lingered in the doorway. "Hey, when I get back, you want to order out for pizza?" She didn't answer. "Well, see you later."

Her amber eyes weren't eggs; they were bullets. "There's just one thing I want you to know, Smarty. Betty Ingram's a slut, and Kelly McCullehey is pinned to a Kappa."

8

*P*arked in a beat up Plymouth the color of a bloated tick, we spent the evening sinking to our hubs in the muddy shore of Griffey Reservoir and drinking Colt 45 from the can. Rain sluiced down the windshield. "Cold?" Kelly asked and turned on the engine. A burned smell made me inch toward my door and crack the window. A chill mist blew in, and I breathed deeply. I wasn't taking any chances with leaky floorboards and carbon monoxide.

He finished his first Colt and opened another, leaning forward to puncture the top with the church key he wore on a chain around his neck. He wore a medal on the same chain, and it clinked against the can. I wanted to ask if he was Catholic, but that seemed nosy. *Teen Talk*, the "frank discussion of the traumas and triumphs of the twelve-to-twenty set, including 'Can I Be Date Bait?' and 'How Far Is Too Far?' " which my mother had given me for Christmas the year I was fourteen, said: "Ask about his interests. Does he collect stamps or operate a ham radio? He's probably dying to explain the carburetor (that's under the hood of his car, gals). Get him to talk about sports." Nothing doing. My brother had already explained the carburetor, and any date who pulled that ho-hum number was going to get a key-by-key description of the Boehm-system clarinet in return. One went to class to get educated, on a date to get laid. I just wanted to be a good enough conversationalist to have him fall in love with me first. "Ready for another?" he asked. I shook my head. The malt liquor had a stale, sweaty taste. "Rotten night," he observed, and I shriveled into my coat. He *meant* the weather. Still. "I hate rain," I said, circling the rim of my cold can with my finger, then giggled. What kind of conversation was that going to start? I love snow, loathe fog, and am dying to hear your position on hail?

"What's so funny?"

"Nothing." The defroster had blown a bar of windshield clear, but all I could see beyond were the torrents tinted green by a street light downshore. In the bilious light I could make out only shadows of features. He was tall, handsome in an ordinary way, dark Princeton haircut, eyes, nose, and mouth in a harmony without melodic line. In the 1:00 A.M. smooch under the yellow lights of the Morrison lobby, the girls on my floor would flick their eyes in our direction and remember that Jane Hurdle had been out with cool. If she survived the evening, if she didn't bore him so bad he took her in at ten. He was wearing a leather and wool high school jacket with a gold letter nesting near his heart. "Oh hell," I said, gulping the Colt and holding out my empty can. "Are you interested in sports?"

He laughed, twisting toward the cooler on the floor of the back seat. "I'm on the swim team. I'm training for the Olympics."

"Oh. Neat." Either I'd hit bingo, or he thought I was incredibly naïve. I sipped the overflow and wiped a dribble from my chin. "I can't swim." *Don't be afraid of sounding dumb, gals, Teen Talk advised. Be a good listener, and he won't care if you don't know a touchdown from offsides.* Did that include not knowing an Olympic swimmer from a champion lie? "But I'm not *against* it," I added.

"You're weird," he said, though I seemed to amuse him. "Well, Betty Ingram, what are you for?"

"Music," I said automatically, then smushed the tips of my fingers against my mouth. "My major's marketing."

"So you said."

"Did I?" I tried to think of something interesting to say about marketing. What was it anyway? Four years of college for a degree in squeezing grapefruit and sniffing melons? In that case—"Yeah, my mother's in marketing." My mind wheeled down the odd aisles of my experience. It wasn't exactly a supermarket; more a cramped specialty shop. Last semester, when Sid and I went to the bookstore to get our supplies, I had lingered at a display of green canvas book bags, thinking, with clarinet in one hand, I could sling my books and scores over my back. Sid circled from a shelf of mugs crested with the *Indianensis Universitatus Sigillum.* "Hurdle, you can't"—she grasped my arm and led me away— "buy one of those." "Why not?" I'd protested. "They look kind of handy." Sid groaned. "Because everyone would think you were a green-bagger." And what was a green-bagger? "An intellectual," she whispered, "a weirdo, a freak." "Oh." I'd given a wistful glance back at the counter. Sid was busy inspecting a small, leather-look notebook *sigillumed* in gold. That, she explained, was what I wanted, and when I met somebody, I could slap his Greek decal just under the crest. I should have known my Latin logo would go lonely. A green-bagger was undoubtedly all the educated daughter of a brown-bagger could hope to be. "Sort of. She works at Kroger's I mean."

"You're weird," he said again.

Another impasse, another aisle. In my theory class, Christy Ahern had complained that writing harmony was hard. Dr. Gabriel shook his head. "Christy, do you have any idea how many times Edison went over that bulb before he got it?" She flunked her first theory test. "Who cares?" she huffed on her way out of class. "There's not one person in my ensemble that gives a hoot if I know theory." I folded my perfect paper into my notebook. "What kind of ensemble?" "Christian," she said. "You know, the music comes from the Lord." I shrugged. "Too bad the answers didn't come from the Lord." *If you can't say something nice, don't say anything,* my mother always told me. It was good advice, I realized as Christy backed from me, her eyes bright with tears, but for me it was always the other way around: if I couldn't say something nasty, I couldn't think of anything to say.

No wonder I couldn't talk to Kelly. I was an *awful* person. And I would rather have been any old Betty.

Moreover, the only thing I knew a thing about was music. I transposed. "Last semester we had these problems in marketing, and some of the kids were complaining they were hard. So you know what the prof said? He said, 'Listen, do you have any idea how many times Edison went over that bulb before he got it?' It was funny," I added.

Kelly dropped his empty can and wiped the shining rim of his mouth. "Betty, my legs are kind of cramped. Would you mind if we moved to the back seat?"

"Most cars have more leg room in the front."

"I know," he murmured, lips grazing in my hair. "But it's really much more comfortable in back." When he finished nibbling at my scalp, he began rooting at my throat.

"Do you plan to go to grad school?" I asked. "When you graduate, I mean."

"Law school." He had backed me into my door, and the handle was digging into my spine. The car was getting steamy.

"Do you have a carburetor?" I gasped as he lapped at my chin. "I'm dying to know how it works." His tongue missed my mouth and licked my nose. "No? How about a stamp collection then?"

"Betty, you're so sweet, so sweet. It makes me feel bad to think that you don't trust me." I turned my head, and the tongue slid in my ear. Actually, I wouldn't have minded nuzzling in the back seat no matter who he thought I was, but once I slipped my hand under his school jacket to feel for Phi Delt gold, I'd have to fondle whatever I found. And I didn't suppose I could just ask if he was pinned. "Tell me what I have to do to make you trust me."

I bucked him away, sitting up straight and rolling my eyes. "I don't trust you worth a damn, and if I did, it would mean I thought you were queer or ugly."

His head bounced against the seat cover as he laughed.

"Betty. I like you." He dipped in his jacket for the church key. "How about another brew to you?"

"I still have some." I patted the floor for my can. "Oh-oh." It had spilled, and I wiped gritty fingers on my coat. The car reeked of hops and aftershave. He reached into the back seat to get me another, and we were back where we started: he was on his side, watching the rain slide down the window, while I clutched a cold can and discarded impossible topics of conversation.

His major was history. I said, "Do you think Oswald acted alone?"

He gave me an odd look. "Where do you get these questions, anyway?"

"What's wrong with them?" He caught me with my mouth open, and I dropped the Colt, splattering us both. "Goddamn it," he said, without really removing his lips, "put it *down*." "It *is* down," I said with a mouthful of his tongue. It was the kind of kiss that torpedoes right to your torso, hits that wishbone of nerves, and breaks at your crotch. I didn't know that few men can kiss like that. With a little energy and interest, most men can fake it at fucking; men who can kiss have the burden of talent, and they'd better not fake anything else. But, with my *Teen Talk* and clarinet and not a boyfriend to my credit, I thought he was average, remembering the girls on the elevator with their faces gone ga-ga. Wow, I thought, no wonder. When I'd picked my way through the clenched couples in the Morrison lobby, I'd had no idea how they were wired. I stiffened lest I overcharge. "Well, I, um, my goodness." I giggled and exhaled words like smoke. "Do you have any hobbies?"

"Jesus Christ." He sat up. "Would you shut up for five minutes?"

"I'm just trying to let you talk about your interests."

"I'm interested," he said slowly and pointedly, "in kissing you."

So we grappled and did it again, his hand crawling around my armpit until it found my breast. There were a fiber-fill bra (I didn't really need the filling, but now I know why all good girls wore them then), a blouse, Sid's sweater, and a fleece-lined corduroy coat between us. The little quickening I felt deep in my belly must have come strictly from the idea.

"Betty," he murmured, "let's get in the back seat." I was slipping below him. He kissed me some more. "Please, Honey, I can't come in you right with the gearshift stabbing me in the back."

"What do you want to do that for?" My voice was tiny. His other hand was tunneling between buttons, tangling in my skirt.

"Betty, I want you. Feel."

I stiff-armed him, clapping my thighs shut. I had gotten twisted; my shoulders rose against the dash, and my bottom began sinking in the space between it and the seat. "Help." He hauled me up with one hand, examining the other, which had been caught in the vice of my thighs, as though it were crushed.

"What the hell did you do that for?" He took a drink.

"My name's not Betty," I said. "Say, do you have another one of those?"

He opened a can and muttered, "*Try* not to spill it. Look, honey, I'm sorry. I'm a real jerk when it comes to names."

I had an idea. Though I'd had a vague plan of doing my duty by Betty until he liked *me* well enough that I could become Jane, I had no idea how I'd intended to bring off the transformation. But now that he was apologizing, I could tell him who I was, and he'd think that's who I'd been all along.

"My name's Jane."

"Betty Jane?"

If I had known then that relationships are mostly politics, I might have kept my advantage. "Nope. Just Jane. Betty's someone else. A well-known slut, in fact. Say, I've never seen a Phi Delt pin up close. Why don't you show me yours?"

"It's at the jeweler's." He frowned. "I broke the clasp."

"Liar," I said, and here's where I made my big mistake. "By the way, my roommate's a Kappa."

He slid across the seat and rolled down his window, tossing the empty cans out. "Hurry up with that brew, will you? And mop up the floor if you can. I get a D.W.I., I'm off the team."

"Litterer." I took a long sip. "You *lied* to me."

"At least I gave you my right name."

"But that's the only thing I lied about." I took another sip. "Well, my major's really music. I made it up, about marketing."

"I don't care what your major is. Just hurry up, would you, Mata Hari?"

"My name's Jane," I screamed. "It's Jane Hurdle, and you take me home." I threw my can at his head, but he caught it, though not before the contents splashed the seat.

He wiped his leather sleeve. "I don't give a damn what your name is." He shifted into reverse and stamped the accelerator. There was a sucking sound as the car shimmied, then settled into place. He put his head on the steering wheel and swore.

"You're stuck," I said. I leaned forward. "Hey, it's quit raining. Turn your wipers off, huh?" He gave me a murderous look and turned off the engine. I felt sorry, in a way. "It was a coincidence. My roommate being a Kappa, I mean." No answer. "Well, I'm sorry I spilled beer on your car."

He turned the engine on, but as the wheels spun, we squished deeper. He opened the door.

"You aren't going to leave me here?" I said.

He sighed. "I'm going to push while you hit the gas and steer."

"I can't drive."

He let loose another series of oaths. "You're a real winner in every respect, aren't you?"

I tried to see things from his point of view. They didn't look too good for me. "I guess not," I said, and here's what I liked about Kelly: he laughed.

"I guess it's been a real drag, huh, Jane?" His voice was kinder. Without waiting for an answer, he added, "Well, look, I've got some studying to do. It's in gear. All you have to do is pump the gas when I tell you to."

Now that we were friends again, I was in no hurry. "What if I goof it up?"

"You won't," he promised, but I did, racing the engine so long that I couldn't hear when he yelled, and nearly knocking him down as we slid back into place. "Hold it," he shouted as the car finally careened backward onto the road. It took me a moment to find the brake, and the car lurched to a stop, then stalled with the rear wheels hanging onto the shoulder on the other side. He didn't speak when he finally got in and we climbed the hill to the wooded suburbs that overlooked the reservoir. My music lit professor had held the last class of first semester in his limestone and glass retreat on that hill, and after listening to an excerpt from the *Magnus Liber Organi*, we had made an enthusiastic expedition, only to find an overflowing septic tank and half-finished subdivision in his front-yard valley. "One of my profs lives out here," I said as I tried to pick his house from the waterfall of lights. Kelly didn't answer. We whizzed under the blinker at Kerr Road and the by-pass. "Boy, you didn't even look. You don't have to be in that big a hurry." As we passed the new dorms on Fee Lane, blocks and blocks of lights without a single tree, I shuddered. "I sure hope they don't make me live here next year." We turned left at the stadium on Tenth Street, right on Jordan, then glided along the avenue of Greek castles, plantations, and chateaus. "Show me the Phi Delt house."

"We don't go by it."

"Oh. Well, I'm sorry I asked all those dumb questions." He turned right again on Third Street. There was a single intersection left between us and Wells Quad, and I was sorry about that too, as words suddenly bloomed in my mouth. "I always talk too much. When I was a kid, my mother used to tell me to shut up a hundred times a day." *Janie, please,* she begged, *your father's not feeling well,* while on the living room floor I chattered, I sang, I told my paper dolls stories, the midgets who lived in my dollhouse shouted room to room. *Janie, I'm warning you.* My father had rehearsed for lung cancer with emphysema. Almost all I could remember of his life was his death. And no matter how much noise I make, I can still hear the rattle and hum in his chest, each breath a last bubble slurped through a straw. Kelly parked his car in the circular drive in front of the quad. "I'm sorry I spoiled everything."

The engine was idling. "So it didn't work out. Big deal."

He was right. Bumbled blind date? Have a laugh with your roommate. Don't fret, no sweat, kiddo, forget it. But now that it was over, I wanted it not to be, without knowing why. I didn't like him, although I didn't really dislike him either. I didn't know him. Ask every question in *Teen Talk*, I never would. The point of listening is hardly to learn, gals; it's to show off as good listeners. Blind dates are mirrors, testing the familiar image, just as the unexpected glass in restaurants and bars startles the face with new light.

Was this me? Stripped of name, family, and my meager fortune of friends, I had wanted to woo myself with my ability to woo him. Instead, I saw a nervous schoolgirl, pretty but unpolished, running off at the mouth, no more attractive than the image contained in the faces at home. Was I really the nasty girl my mother saw? Or my brother, who viewed me more kindly; but, even so, how could he see what I was, blurred as his vision was by what I had been? On the day when and if I finally took principal chair in the New York Philharmonic, my mother would remember the day I'd come home from grade school crying because I'd wet my pants.

Kelly had not turned off the ignition. "Uh, look, would you mind if I didn't walk you to the door? I've got a cramp in my leg."

"You've got a cramp in your brain if you think I believe that," I snapped and slammed the car door behind me.

Sid was just coming in the door at a quarter past one when the phone rang. "I got a goddamn pink slip," she bitched, flinging her coat on the armchair. "That's the third one, and now J-board's going to ground me."

"Dumb-ass. Why don't you leave the Lambda Chi house before the clock chimes?" I had folded Sid's sweater in her drawer and changed to my pj's, rolling the legs to my knees while I swabbed my calves with Jergens.

One of our suitemates banged the door between our room

and the half-bath that connected ours to theirs. "Jane, telephone."

I picked the receiver out of the sink. It was Kelly. "How's your leg?" I asked, closing the doors to both rooms and settling on the floor. Someone's towels had soured.

"I was a turd not to walk you to your dorm. I apologize."

"It's okay." I rose to my knees to press my nose to the towels. Sid's were damp, scented slightly with Chanel. It figured. The stench came from the blue polka-dotted irregulars I'd left over break. "I had a close call when this guy tried to rape me, but—a girl out by herself after dark—what do I expect?"

"I said I was sorry. I just didn't want your roommate to see me."

"She wasn't there. She was late."

"Is she there now?"

"In the next room." I peeked through the crack. Sid was crying face down on her bed. "Hey, I have to go now."

"Well, wait a second. I called because I got to thinking. Maybe it would work out if we gave it another chance?"

I frowned. After all, there was no doubt that he was pinned.

"Tomorrow night?"

On the other hand, maybe he and his girlfriend were breaking up.

"I wouldn't even have called, but—this is crazy—I think I like you."

"I don't know," I said.

"Well, damn it." He hung up, leaving a faint hum on the line.

Sid had moved from her bed to her desk, her hand hissing against the paper as she wrote in her diary.

"Sid?" Her horn-rimmed reading glasses magnified her eyes. She wouldn't wear them on dates because they made her look froggy. She was funny about things like that, the sort of woman who wouldn't wear frosted eye shadow even on New Year's and wouldn't feed the horses without spraying her armpits and shaving her legs. She'd never forget her towels over vacation. "Is anything wrong?"

125

She folded her glasses. "That your mother?"

"Unh-uh."

"Then guess what. Your sister-in-law had twins. Girls. Your mother called while you were out."

"Are you kidding?" I fell back on my bed. "My brother had twins?" I tried to imagine him pacing the hall of Saint Margaret's until the nurse appeared with a pink bundle in each arm. That was as far as I could go. I didn't know anything about having babies, and the more babies Dick had, the less I knew him. For a minute I was hurt. How come he had to go and have two? And why hadn't he called me himself?

Sid moved to her bed and began slicking her legs with Aquamarine. "They're naming them Marie Dawn and Dawn Marie."

I sat up. "Boy, what tacky names."

"I think they're cute. At least they won't get mail addressed to *Mr.* Sidney Engel." She sighed. "I wish I had a niece or a nephew."

"You've got a whole houseful of sisters," I said.

"What if they can't tell them apart?" She replaced the lotion on our bureau. "Anyway, lay off about the Kappas. How was your date with Kelly McCullehey?"

"Okay."

She leaned across the clutter of bottles toward the mirror. "Oh God, look at my hair. What do you mean, okay?"

I picked up my alarm clock as she took a ruffled bag of rollers from her desk. "What time do you want to get up?"

"Damnit," she said, winding her hair furiously. "Can't you wait until I finish?"

I put the clock down and went to brush my teeth.

When I returned, wiping Crest from the corner of my mouth, she was sitting on her bed with a roller in her hand. "It must be weird, having twins," she said. For no reason, she burst into tears and let the roller roll across the rug.

"Sid, what's the matter?"

"Nothing."

"I can't believe anybody could make such a stupid fuss about a pink slip." I poised at the light switch. "You ready?"

Still weeping, she flapped a wing of hair.

"Then hurry up." But she burrowed into her pillow. "Did you have a fight with Kent?"

"Well, then, are you mad because I wouldn't tell you about my date?" Her sobs sounded like a steam engine, a sort of chugging snuffle. "Nothing happened. We had an argument, and he brought me home." I thought it over. "He's a liar, like you said. He told me his pin was at the jeweler's and said he was going to be in the Olympics."

"He probably is." She sniffled. "We've got a great swimming team, and he's one of the stars."

"We do? I didn't even know we had one. He called me back to ask me out."

"Good," she said and kept crying.

"Huh? I'm going to bed. If you want to finish your hair, use the john." I darkened the room and slid between my sheets. There was no moon, just a faint wrinkle of silver clouds beyond the treetops. Sid was still whimpering. "I was just kidding. You can turn the light on if you want to." When she didn't answer, I crossed the room and touched her shoulder. "Siddie?"

She flung her arms around me. "Oh Hurdle, I'm not a virgin."

"Well." I disengaged myself and sat on the edge of her bed, wondering if it would make her feel better to know that I wasn't either. "For God's sake, Sid, you're pinned, hell, you're almost engaged. I *assumed* . . ."

But it wasn't Kent," she bawled. "It was Riggs."

"Who?"

"The guy from Columbus." She clutched the shoulder of my pajamas. "Do you think I ought to hurry up and do it with Kent? And then if I'm pregnant he'll think it's his."

"I think that's the dumbest idea I ever heard."

"What's my father going to say when I have to quit school?" She pitched herself into her pillow. "I'm too young to be a mother."

"No, you're not," I said. "I read in the paper about this girl that had a baby and she was only nine. I didn't even have a period till I was almost thirteen."

"I wish I'd never had one. I wish I were a nun."

I patted her back. What kind of freak was I, to have said something like that? If you can't express your feelings, can you be sure you really feel? Oh, we were silly schoolgirls fretting over things that make us snicker now, but, though the reasons grow, I think the same old worries never do: am I the fat lady, the thin man, a chicken with two heads, a daughter-sister-friend without a heart? The parts aren't parceled equal; there's no guarantee I got my share. "Anyway, you probably aren't. But the first thing to do is to break up with Kent."

Sid propped herself on an elbow, sniffing. "I know. I *betrayed* him."

"Sidney, Kent is a jerk."

"Oh no. I'm the crud that stabbed him in the back."

"Then let me put it this way. Are you in love with him?"

"I guess not," she said finally. "But, honestly, he can be really sweet."

"That's not the point."

"I suppose." She began to sniffle again. "What is the point?"

"How should I know?" I stood and leaned on the slate sill, pressing my face to the cold casement window. Clouds were creased around the moon, which had finally appeared, like the pale flesh of an old man's belly. I wondered if anyone was watching the same moon in Hammond. I supposed not. It was after 2:00 A.M. "I don t know what the point of anything is."

She sat up. "You're right. I just didn't want to admit it, because the thing is, I ought to love him."

"You ought to love your family. Anyone else you get to pick." Though the radiator under the window seared my thigh, I shivered. Failing to love my family well, could I pick? I curled into the valley in my bed and bunched the spread at my cheek. "Don't worry," I said. "Well, good night." I closed my eyes, remembering how I had crossed my mother's back yard last night before it snowed, the roof of my house black against a charcoal sky, tinsel in the grass where my brother had dragged our Christmas tree to the alley. My teeth chattering as I ran because it was too much bother to put on a coat just to carry out the garbage.

"Hurdle?"

"Um?"

"I feel better. Thanks for talking to me."

"Go to sleep," I said, following again the glittered path to the warm block of light in my mother's back door. I dreamed that my yard was a litter of stars. They burned my fingers as I tried to pick their points from the grass. In their bed beneath that frozen plot, my father's bones rattled. He was cold. *Give me back my blanket of stars.* But I went on stealing, and when I had them all, I took them to my room and closed the door. I turned the heat as high as it would go and spread them across my bed, as though they were paper dolls and I was a little girl, only playing. It didn't make sense. My father is taking his eternal snooze at the Woodlawn Cemetery, and the only thing under my mother's yard is the trashfill that Hammond is built on. I had no reason to dream anything so crazy. Because it was the night before I fell in love, and if you had asked me that crazy spring, I would have insisted that until then I had not had enough imagination to dream.

9

When the phone rang, I was sitting in nylons and pettipants on the blue velvet cushions of our armchair. Sid had left an hour ago with Kent, and, though I had no date and no hope, I had spent the two hours since dinner not wrinkling my skirt, which was spread on my bed like the arms that I wished were waiting to hold me.

I felt as uncomfortable as if I were seated in someone else's body, like a guest abandoned by a host who has been summoned from the room by an important call. But it was my room, and the phone was for me. I had a caller. I slid my skirt over my head and turned off Sid's stereo. In honor of Mr. Schunk I was still trying to like Schönberg, and while I had waited, the twelve tones of *Variationen für Orchester* fought among themselves like the twelve tribes of Israel.

I'd first heard twelve-tone music at Ruth and Martin's. The Hammond Public Library owned no Schönberg, and Mr. Schunk had not had a record player. "I am like Beethoven," he'd said. "I hear with the heart, not with the ear. I do not like the clicking when the music is finished." They played his own recording of the Wind Quintet. "Nice," I murmured, because I supposed I ought to murmur something, though I have since learned—with the exception of *Pierrôt Lunaire*, whose moon-drunk *Sprechstimme* singsongs with more dissonance than any of the twelve-tone pieces—to like, if not love, Schönberg. He had been so proud of this performance. The composer himself had praised it in the letter Mr. Schunk once read to me.

"Schönberg is your favorite composer?" Martin asked.

"Well, not my absolute favorite," I admitted.

"She likes those atonal nuts because they remind her of life," Ruth said. "Incomprehensible. Amoral."

"Pantonal," Martin corrected. "Who is your absolute favorite then?"

"Oh." So this was what it was like to spend an evening with professors. I could follow what they said; I'd read *Modern Music*—I'd underlined it. But I couldn't tell if Martin liked Schönberg or not, and the notes seemed to wander in search of a home that my reading assured me those orphaned tones would not find. "I don't know. Brahms, I guess. And Beethoven. Well, I like Rachmaninoff a lot too. Ravel. Debussy. Well, and Mozart and Chopin and Tchaikovsky and . . ."

They laughed.

"Anyway, I don't think music ought to imitate life. The whole principle of art is structure." For a minute I felt superior to Schönberg and Schunk. "Besides, I don't think life is so confusing." I folded my hands in my lap, waiting for the Solomons to see that I was no dummy.

"Give it time," Ruth said. "You will."

Martin rose. "How about some structure, Malcuzynski, and Brahms's First Piano Concerto then?"

I leaned forward. "What was Schönberg like? It must be exciting to know a composer."

"I never met him," Ruth said. "But I suppose he was like all other revolutionaries and artistes."

"How's that?"

Ruth shrugged. "A snob, a bore."

"Not true," Martin said. "He loved to play tennis, was a brilliant teacher, and absolutely charming. At any rate, Jane, if you'd like to meet a composer, I'll introduce you to Karl Winkler. You should take his composition course."

I shook my head. I didn't think my imagination would work if it wasn't first given a score. Like Mr. Schunk, I was awed by the idea of Schönberg, no matter what I thought of the sound.

And if his sound had been a disappointment, at least I'd been right, or so I told myself on the way to the elevator. Just when life seemed most confusing, it suddenly made as much sense as art, on its level of course, but still. Without prospects, I'd dressed for a date, and now, sure enough, I had one.

The lobby was empty. I peeked into the room where our mailboxes lined the wall. "You can come out. There's no one here to see you."

"Aw, Jane," he said, falling in step beside me. "You're kind of mean."

"Perceptive's the word. And you're kind of sneaky." We paused to look each other over. Had the lobby been full, I might not have known him, though I would have recognized the jacket, blue wool and cream leather, CAPTAIN KELLY appliquéd across one arm. His face was less handsome than sensuous, I realized, with large, lazy features and blunt bones. His eyes were the color of summer. I think they were the most beautiful eyes I have ever seen, and also the cruelest. What it was about his eyes, I decided months later, was that when you looked into the shadows of those dense tangles of lashes, expecting mysterious green depths, you found instead the aquamarine of sunlight on suburban swimming pools. To talk to him, I had to tip my head up. "To say nothing of the fact that you've got a bad temper. You hung up on me."

"What did you expect?" he said. "How come you're so dressed up? You have a date tonight?"

"With you."

"I wouldn't have known it." He held the door open. The moon was a Cheshire grin and the breeze faintly balmy. Every winter in Bloomington there is a two- or three-day spring, a premature warmth that penetrates the earth and loosens a damp fragrance of loam. Scarlett O'Hara didn't know what she was missing, with her crummy handful of red

132

clay. Dirt doesn't mean anything held in your hands; sucked into your lungs, it's next to your heart. "I just dropped by to see if you'd changed your mind."

"I guess I did." Although he was tall, I walked easily beside him. "Where are we going?" We were on the asphalt path midway between Morrison and Memorial; above us, bare branches of elm webbed the sky. He placed both hands on my shoulders and kissed me.

"Well." Giddy, I backed off. "So that's where we're headed." We climbed the stairs to the archway and the horseshoe drive beyond. "Where's your girlfriend?" I asked as he helped me into his car.

"The Phi Delts have a cabin out in Brown County," he said as we turned onto Third Street. "I thought maybe we could go out there. I don't know what you like to drink, but I brought some wine."

"I like wine." As we drove into the country, we filled each other in. His father was a professor of business administration at the University of Michigan, but he'd come to Indiana on a swimming scholarship, because, though Michigan had a good team, frankly, he thought Indiana's was better, and since he'd always had the Olympics in mind, would have gone four years ago if he hadn't clutched at the try-outs, he figured the best place for him was where all the superstars came.

"I'm on scholarship too," I said. "I got a clarinet scholarship and didn't even finish high school."

His stroke, he said, was the butterfly. He liked the slap of the water, the smell of the chlorine, the splash of sound from the crowd. He made, he said, no bones about it. What he liked was to win.

"I like to win, too," I said, thinking how strange that water should sing in anyone's ears. To graduate from Hammond High one had to swim five lengths of its pool. I was lucky I'd won a scholarship; I might still be dog-paddling toward my diploma. With the clarinet I could float, I could stroke, I could flutter. With water I was sure I could only drown. "I won a first in the state solo contest three years in a row."

''Congratulations.''

''Oh, well.'' Now what had I said a dumb thing like that for? ''You're a funny kid, you know that?'' His voice had picked up speed since last night. Now that he was interested in talking, it clipped along like the allegretto horses Mr. Schunk had bade me imagine *con anima*. ''You like sports?''

I had always been sadly unathletic, the last girl chosen for a gym class softball team, and a White Sox game with my brother seven years ago had been my solo stunt as a fan. ''Well.'' I paused and shook my head. ''No. Do you like music?''

''No,'' he admitted. ''So much for that. You mind?''

''I don't know.''

''Hey,'' he said, ''how come you're so indecisive? You've got to take the bull by the horns, you know?''

I thought of my mother's voice, which always seemed weighted with some sorrow, of my brother's, always faint with reason and concern. He was kind, and his voice was lovely, but had he ever taken the bull by the horns? Had my mother, my poor old passive mother, who mouthed what she believed in a voice so tired I thought that her beliefs must be exhausted, too? *Your brother is a hard worker*, she would say, as if working hard were his only reason to be. She was too, but, oddly, work had stripped their words of muscle and filled them out with flab. What it was about Kelly's voice—I should have known from its difference that night, that night from many nights—it was energetic, it was cheery, I might even say *indicative*. He was not in an iffy mood.

I fell in love with his voice, and, oh, it made me like him. ''I don't mind at all.'' I looked out my window. We were somewhere in the country, and the landscape was lit only by the unmistakable flicker of a TV screen, a gleam in the dark eye of the night. I took a breath. ''About that cabin. Is there a party out there?''

He glanced at me. ''Does it matter?''

''No,'' I said. ''Yes.'' He slowed the car and bumped to the shoulder. ''What are you doing?''

''Turning around.''

I reached across the seat to put my hand on his arm, but

didn't, shy. "Well, wait a minute." I didn't know if he meant to take me home or to a movie, the fraternity house, the Commons for a Coke. "Would you take your girlfriend out there, or is it just someplace you'd go with Betty Ingram?"

"I like *you,*," he said. "I wasn't even going to come over tonight, but I'm glad I did, and I thought you were too."

"I'm glad," I said.

"I'll take you back to town if you're afraid."

"Oh, no." I was terrified, but if I let him take me back, I knew I'd never see him again.

He smiled. "I promise I won't do anything you don't want me to." He released the brake. "I won't even ask you to slide over. But if you're going to sit there, do me a favor and lock the door. I don't want you to fall out on a curve."

I blushed and slid over.

The cabin was a tarpaper shack at the end of a dirt road that ran out in a clearing. He had me hold a flashlight while he found a broom and swept the rubble of beer cans from the stretch of floor between the sofa and hearth. Then he settled me on the prickly couch with the wine while he carried wood and wadded papers. In a few minutes the smell of dank cigarettes and beer burned away. He dropped his jacket to the floor and sat beside me.

"Warm enough?"

I nodded, and he kissed me, uncurling my fingers from my Dixie cup and setting us both on the floor. He had already spread a blanket.

"A fire and a pretty girl. What more could a guy want?"

"Some wine?" I suggested, and he poured himself a cup.

"You from a big family?" he asked.

I shook my head. "My father's dead. My mother works in a grocery store. My brother's divorced, except he remarried. Last night his wife—that's my sister-in-law—had a baby, and guess what she had. Twins."

"That's great. Your brother sounds like a great guy."

I laughed. "But I haven't told you anything about him."

"He had twins, didn't he?" The way he said it made it sound like a superhuman feat.

"Yeah," I said and laughed again.

135

"I've got four brothers and six sisters." He went on about his family, naming every sibling, every nephew, every niece, while the fire did a foxtrot on his face. As I listened, it seemed as if the flame were inside me, a pirouette above the warm hearth of my heart, touching his skin with soft light, twirling as far as my own family. "You like music," he said. "I'll tell you a story. My old man's an alcoholic, and he loves Frank Sinatra. He used to listen to the stereo for hours, getting drunk as a skunk, sitting in his Lazy Boy and slopping bourbon out of the baby's training cup, and my mother was about ready to throw him out, but this one Christmas Eve when he's really gone he says, 'Well, let's just call Old Blue Eyes and spread some Christmas cheer.' So I dial up this buddy who gets his singers crossed and croons 'White Christmas' in the old man's ear. And just like that my father pours his bourbon down the sink and says, 'That son-of-a-bitch is so soused he sounds like Bing.' He hasn't touched a drop or bought a record in at least two years." Kelly laughed and wiped his eyes. "So I guess you'd say it's music that keeps my old man straight."

I thought it was the most marvelous story I had ever heard, nothing like my family's tales, which all began, "That's nothing. When *I* went to the dentist . . ." and went downhill from there. He slipped my flats off and brushed my toes with his lips. "How'd you get to be so tiny?" he whispered. I just hoped my feet didn't smell. He lay down beside me. Underneath my turtleneck, my heart began to bang.

I sat up. "You said you wouldn't hurt me."

"I won't." He eased me back. "I won't do a thing that you don't want me to." Was I supposed to tell him what? This but not that, here but not there? Hadn't I agreed to everything already? It was much too late to post my property now.

"What do you want to do?" I squeaked.

He laughed and got up to drink, standing over me like a tree, rooted near my cheek by a pair of Weejuns and blue heather socks. "I think, for a minute anyway, I'd just like to stand here and watch you look scared." He knelt beside me.

136

"I'm not making fun of you. I think you're charming. You're a virgin, aren't you?"

"No."

A log popped. He blinked. Then he raised me by the shoulders. "I think I'd like to make love to you." Oh, in the long run, it wasn't a storybook romance, but just for a minute it was the way storybooks make you think it should be. Head bowed before my flesh, prayerful, parted lips. Corny, except when the communion cup happens to be you.

And I thought, why not? Remembering that winter night six years before, speeding down Calumet Avenue between Dick and Marie, the Everly Brothers singing "Bye bye love, bye bye happiness, hello emptiness" in voices that implied losses were fun. And, as I'd already admitted, it wasn't as if I had it to lose. By bye emptiness, hello happiness. I raised my arms and closed my eyes, expecting, when I opened them, to have ascended into Heaven. But my turtleneck got stuck on my head, my garters bit my legs, my pettipants tangled on my heels. He salvaged the solemnity with a little intake of breath when I lay beside him in nothing but a flamestitch of shadow. When he began to unbutton his shirt I touched my hand to his. "Wait. I want to do you." And followed up with the same comedy of clothing. Still, when he was stripped to his Saint Christopher's, stretched beside me in all the muscle it takes to butterfly through a pool, the funny biz was finished.

No, it wasn't a storybook romance, and in many respects Kelly was a son-of-a-bitch. I try to make my memory pause with the tableau of that first night, but it is instead only part of the pageant in which, six weeks later, he sat on that same sofa, cock drooping into the cushions, medal dangling against the damp cleft of his chest. Moments before I had saddled him and straddled him and ridden his horn. "But *why?*" I sobbed, shivering at my end of the couch, Kelly not asking if I was, why I was, cold. The horn had played its finale, sad jazz in an empty room of full ashtrays, stained glasses, a lone woman waltzing, one trumpet whining, because her lover's gone home and he's not coming back. "Janie," he said. In the six weeks of our grasping and grappling, he'd grown fond enough for nicknames, and the sweet edge he gave mine broke my heart. "Have you ever considered that maybe I'm just a bastard?"

"All men are bastards," I raged later that night while Sid studied, and she looked over her horn-rims from her desk to my bed. *She* could afford to. She was two months pregnant and ready to wed. "If you say so. But some of them are winning, you've got to admit." Nothing would do until she quit studying and helped me clear my bulletin board of program notes to make room for a bastard list, a piece of white poster board cleft into two columns: winning and losing, which I proposed we fill out with the names of every man we had met. Riggs was winning; she couldn't commit herself to another contribution. I added Kent to the losing list, and she shrugged. Kent was behind her; so, really, were college and the Kappas, though she would finish the year because she loved me and Riggs would wait. She didn't care if she bulged beneath her gown. Oh, we pretended the real reason she waited was to be that much ahead. The baby would have a sitter. While Riggs finished law school, she'd transfer to Ohio State. But in her heart she must have known they'd never do it. He didn't finish; she never transferred. Still, they have a stable of Arabians; they have each other; they have their son. ("Jesus, Hurdle," she said the last time I saw her, though my name hadn't been Hurdle for years. "You screw once, and your lousy body does you in. Then you spend the rest of your life screwing, and all the temperature charts, shots, and consultations can't get your body to do it even once again.") She stayed because she was afraid I would ruin my life by running off with Kelly if she left me on my own. "You know where I'd put Kelly," she said, but I'd bathed my swollen eyes to pretend I hadn't been crying, so I wrote his name below Riggs's with Magic Marker. A winner after all.

He was one hell of a lover. Of course, I'd had no other; Arthur was the fence post by which I'd been deflowered. I had no one to compare him to, but he carried me places I've hardly been since; he moved me in ways no one else has; and if we took a while to get all the mechanical bugs out, anyone who's ever diddled herself knows what a pale thrill that technical triumph is without the humping and heaving, that intake of breath, the whisper of name. A slow swimmer at love, he stroked and he glided, he fluttered and surged. Neck arched, as though to keep his head above water, he never closed his eyes—only last week I heard a song that made me think of Kelly: "Your sweet and shiny eyes are like the stars above Laredo." (Unfortunately the next line made me think of my husband: "Like meat and potatoes to-o-o me-e-e-e." I'm unkind to my husband, and he doesn't deserve it. It's not his fault I prefer plums and petits fours; not his fault that long before the state joined us I had married both water and fire.) In my craziest fantasy I'd like to conduct a survey to see if swimmers all make better lovers. They have the most beautiful bodies; they have the stamina, the rhythm, the distance, the drive. I'm being silly, of course, but I did look over the team on TV the next fall, when Kelly swam in Tokyo for bronze, and ever since, though Kelly is no longer swimming. (Where is he now, and what is he doing? I want to say hi. You-know-what to yours, Lady Jane to John Thomas, perhaps even still one missed heartbeat and sigh.)

And, though I cannot go back to that, I have been back to Bloomington. The university took Morrison. They sealed off the third-floor lounge with its french doors to the sundeck; they cut up the leaded-glass bays of the dining hall for labs. They lowered the ceilings and installed fluorescent lighting. In my old room and on all the third floor they do genetics research. In the hall, my lungs filled with animals and shit. I took the elevator to fourth. The doors parted, and I was left in a hallway, locked out at the entrance to the Kinsey Institute for Sex Research. (I once met a girl who had lived as a child in an apartment downstairs from Alfred Kinsey. While her mother stood at the sink, he lowered an apple on a string outside their kitchen window. He mowed the lawn in his jockstrap. She couldn't remember another thing to tell me, but that was enough. Ever since, I've been charmed to know that his interest wasn't *just* for the betterment of mankind.) Before I left Bloomington, I applied for a job at the institute, nothing important, class two typist and clerk. I didn't get it because I hadn't finished high school, and I blushed through the interview because, though I wanted so badly to work in

Morrison, I was sure the director suspected I wanted to work in sex. In retrospect I see my priorities were backward. If I couldn't work in music, I should have worked in mating. I've spent my life thinking about rhythm.

Every stab he made, I felt in cadence, and, though he never seemed to stop, we couldn't wait to begin. Maybe it's true, what he said, our minds never met; it was still a crime against nature to uncouple those magnets of flesh. Fatal lust, he called it, terminal tension. What did I care, I sniffed. For a disease like that I was ready to die.

I try to think of Kelly, but memory provides another detail about Sex Research. In my freshman year we received a number of obscene phone calls, those heavy breathers all posing as Kinsey staff. They took surveys. Naïve as I was, I heard the first questions out. Silly stuff, I don't know—Do you do it on your feet, do you do it sitting down? Do you do it wrong side up, do you do it in the round? Do you have to have a ring, or would you do it like a slut? Do you take it in your mouth, and how about your butt? Well, I cracked, you never know until you try. And though I meant to be wise, I wasn't so smart. Fool that I was, I took it in the heart.

A didactic word about being in love: there are some people who deserve it (my husband for instance). They might get it more often if they'd take it where it came, but, deserving, they feel it should come on demand, as if love is a dividend that wise investment returns. Reasons don't count when you're taking that tumble. Because love, I think—and that's what I mean, though I say mostly sex—is a grand act of the imagination, and if you try to control that, you won't imagine much. After all, it's imagination that hears the music—and it doesn't matter what kind, as long as you dance. Oh yes, he was a bastard. He was *winning* simply because I fell in love.

When? I don't know. Somewhere between his voice and his touch, for that first night when we finished and I lay between him and the fire, I was whimpering, my vocal cords rippling like overtones from the notes that he'd struck. While he kneaded my shoulder, I touched his face and traced the silver path of his chain.

"It's time to go," he said.

"No." I sat up and shook my head slowly.

"We have to." He investigated the clot of clothing. "Yours, I believe."

I took my pettipants, examining them with wonder, as if I'd never seen them before. "This comes later. I have to have some other things first."

"What do you need?" He held up a clump of white cotton. "Mine."

"I need . . ." Should I have said *underpants* or *panties*, *garter belt* or *dohickey?* I wonder now how I could have been embarrassed in those days when we asked for stockings instead of pantyhose, but the names seemed so deflating, I found the stupid things myself. ". . . you." I giggled, not at all embarrassed to stand before him while I hooked my bra and he looked me up and down.

"You have a lovely body. I didn't hurt you, did I?"

I sat down hard. "Oh, Kelly, let's phone in sick."

"No way." He bent to give me a perfunctory peck. "They'd string me up for corrupting you. Come on." He slapped my thigh, and his zipper growled.

I stood, one stocking gripped in front and sagging in the back. "You didn't corrupt me. Do you want to hear about my first love affair?"

"Not especially." He doused the fire, but paused when we reached the doorway, holding my shoulders and bending to look me in the eyes. "Jane, that was fine. Very, very fine, and I thank you.

"Well, it's okay," I said. "Any time." And snuggled beneath his arm all the way back to Bloomington, chattering all through my first lesson in love: what a man has, he gives in that spurt. There's nothing left over, not a word, not a kiss, not even a light in the eye. He parked the Plymouth in the circle.

"I'd like to see you," he said, "tomorrow night."

"I have rehearsal."

"Can't you skip it?" He didn't ask what I rehearsed for, didn't ask if he could come listen in.

"I shouldn't." But I did. "What about your girlfriend?" I

141

asked as we began our walk to the dorm. "Are you breaking up or what?"

He smiled. "Could be."

"What's her name?"

He frowned. "Why do you want to know that?" Though we walked side by side, he didn't take my hand.

"I just do."

He shook his head as he opened the oak door. The lobby was jammed, and Blackmon, the old bat of a counselor, was flitting between bodies and shouting, "Three minutes. Three minutes." Blackmon was the sort of woman who makes teen-age girls think over-twenty-one is the same as sixty-five. She wore Hush Puppies to her seminars in educational psych, she never shaved her legs, she carried a briefcase, she used a toothpick—there were a thousand reasons, but the one that just slayed us was her frizz of little curls, those absurd infractions of a head as sensible and sexless as her shoes.

"Well, what's she going to say if we go out tomorrow night?"

He was still holding the door, but I didn't go in. I clung to him. He kissed me. "Go on. It's a mob scene. We can talk tomorrow night."

As a couple brushed by us, I clenched his jacket. "Not until you tell me if you're pinned, like Sidney says."

"Two minutes."

"Go on now," Kelly urged. "Before they throw me out."

"No." I held tighter.

"Go upstairs like a good girl."

"I'm not a good girl, I'm a nice girl," I said, referring to that classic distinction: a good girl goes on a date, goes home, and goes to bed; a nice girl goes on a date, goes to bed, and goes home. Either way, home seemed to be the inevitable end.

"One minute."

"Tell me."

He peeled my fingers from his snaps. "Jane . . ."

"Out. Out. All men out."

We flattened against the door as the men funneled through. He was backing. The clock began bonging.

"Give me your jacket," I said.

"What?"

"Give me your jacket. I want something too."

"Out." From behind a hand snatched my collar, and the V-neck of my coat rose like a noose as Blackmon jerked me in.

He grinned and tossed it to me just before the door shut in his face. I pressed my own face to the nubs of the letter and caressed the cold dangle of creased leather sleeves. When I looked up, I smiled, breathing deep, as though by inhaling that dust scent of wool I'd taken in Kelly all over again.

If Blackmon's shoes looked like boats, her face was a storm. "I am giving you a pink slip."

I wrapped myself in the jacket, still warm inside. The knit cuffs of the sleeves hung way past my hands, and the waistband nipped my pleats at the thigh. "I was here."

"You had one foot outside the door."

I admired myself and skipped to her office.

"I'm surprised at you," she said. "Of all people I certainly thought *you* would have more sense."

From that scold of a face you'd have thought I'd stayed out all night and come home to spread syphilis through her hall by sitting on toilets. A thorn like her would rather see the bud of a late bloomer rot than flower. "Well, I don't."

"You know, I could confiscate that coat," she said. "You did obtain it illegally."

I clapped my hands around my shoulders to protect it from attack. "What do you mean?"

"It was handed in after hours."

I took a step back. "It's my property."

"Not by residence authority rules." I took another step back as she advanced and held out my pink slip. "I wish you could see yourself. Have you been drinking?"

I took a step to the side. Slowly we were doing a dance around her office.

"You might ask yourself who you think you are. Because you are a *minor* coed who lives on state property and must follow rules." Her chin rose in triumph. "It is illegal in this state for a person under twenty-one years of age to consume an alcoholic beverage.''

"Get fucked,'' I said.

Her eyes flashed. "Give me the coat.''

I took two more steps to the side. "It's a jacket.''

"Give it to me.''

"No." Another step, and I was crowding the glass doors of a bookcase full of catalogues and notebooks. She moved toward me. I closed my eyes, and glass shattered. I heard the flap and sputter of flying looseleafs as the icy rain began, and nails nicked my neck, stripping Kelly's shape and scent from my back. I screamed. There was a thump-thump of notebooks, the clap of a chair overturned, and the siren in my throat shut off. "Take your hands off me,'' I said, panting.

"I haven't touched you.''

I opened my eyes. Glass intact, catalogues and notebooks lined on the shelves, Blackmon looking down her white nose and blinking. Everything in humiliating and deadly gray order. She stepped to her desk and made a notation. "I'm having you appear before the J-board. They can decide what disciplinary action to take.''

"What for?''

"Lateness, drunkenness, profanity in public.''

"I'm not drunk, and this place isn't public.'' My voice rose again. "With you in charge, it's the fucking Gestapo.''

She was smiling. "You're free of course to tell that to the J-board.''

I stalked out, embracing myself in case she still wanted the jacket. I suspected an obscene plan to sneak it to her room and spend the night sniffing Kelly. At eighteen you have hard notions about twenty-seven-year-old-maids.

Sid was boo-hooing into the bedclothes. When I came in, she sat up. "It's all over. I gave him back his pin, and whoever would have thought he'd take it so hard? Oh, Hurdle, he loved me.'' She stared as I sat on my bed, stroking my cream-colored sleeves and smiling. "What's that?''

The phone rang. I jumped. "I'll get it. It's Kelly.''

It wasn't. It was Ruth—they were back and wanted me to come next Saturday for dinner.

"What do you want with a high school jacket?" Sid asked when I returned. "And where in hell have you been?" The phone rang again.

I leaped. "Let me."

It was Kent. While Sid was talking I spread Kelly's jacket across my pillow and rubbed my cheek against it.

"He wants me to give him another chance." Once more, the phone rang. "You get it. If I have to listen to him cry, I'll kill myself, and then everybody'll be happy."

"Don't be an ass," I said and picked up the phone.

"Hey." I slid down the wall to the floor, my eyes as dazed by the clash of Sid's pink towels, my blue ones, and our suitemate's green stripes as if I were looking at Kelly's face in firelight. "How do you feel?" he asked.

"I got a pink slip," I replied.

"I'm sorry. Jane . . ." He paused. "Tonight was so fine, and, you know, I couldn't stop thinking about you, and . . . well, I called because I didn't want you to think I was, um, trying to get out of telling you about something I understand your wanting to know about."

"I didn't think that," I said.

"And I didn't want you to think that I was just out, uh, screwing around and would, you know, try to lie to you."

"I didn't think that," I said.

"I mean, I suppose I should have laid my cards out, but, well, when we got out to Brown County, I just, uh, wanted you."

"I wanted you too," I whispered.

"I just want you to trust me till tomorrow night, and, Jane . . ."

"Umhm?"

"I really like you."

I floated to my bed.

"I said," Sid said.

"Hmm?" I looked up.

"My God," she said. "Didn't you hear me?"

"Hmm?"

"Jesus." She lit a cigarette. "I'm only in the middle of my

life's biggest crisis. I come home to talk it over with my roommate, and you're not even here."

"I've got a life too," I reminded her.

"I'm warning you, Hurdle. Don't you dare get a crush on Kelly McCullehey."

I closed my eyes. "I haven't got a crush."

"Well, you've got a goony look."

I opened them. "I'm in love."

"Oh shit." She stood over me, arms folded, smoke rising from her shoulder. "That's the worst thing anyone can do to herself."

I sighed, I smiled, I hugged my jacket.

10

I called Ruth back to ask if I could bring a guest to dinner. Could I bring a guest? They'd love to have a guest. Said guest wouldn't happen to be a man, would he?

Well.

In that case, there'd be steaks, and maybe seviche, the kids early to bed, and David would just have to turn down that crap he called music, the silver, the Meissen if Josh didn't break it before she could wash it, her best lead crystal, champagne (well, why not?), and luckily Martin had just received for review Toscanini's recording of Schubert's *Great* Symphony—did said guest like Schubert?—which was absolutely exquisite, a Soria Series. I'd heard the Heifetz-Piatigorsky, hadn't I?

I had, but I didn't know, I said, that said guest liked Schubert, and, please, nothing too fancy, he was after all just a guy that I knew, I wouldn't want him to think I was trying to impress him, though steaks sounded neat, even champagne and crystal, but Martin wouldn't look him over too closely, would he, and . . .

"Why?" she asked. "What's wrong with him?"

147

Nothing, I said; I just didn't want him to get the wrong idea. " Ruth, you won't say anything vulgar, will you?"

"Vulgar?" Her voice wilted. "When did I ever say anything vulgar?"

"Oh." Now I'd done it—I'd hurt her, and she and Martin had been so wonderful to me. Besides, I thought she was funny, didn't I? "I didn't mean *nasty*, I mean maybe *vulgar* is too strong a word, but you won't mention the kids', um, privates, will you? I just wouldn't want him to be embarrassed."

"*Jane*. You're not bringing Ben Gabriel to dinner?"

"Of course not." Why would she think I'd bring my theory teacher to dinner?

"Well, he's the biggest prude I know, and he's always going on to Martin about how much he thinks of you."

"Oh, he just likes me 'cause I know all the answers. You wouldn't believe how dumb some of the kids in that class are."

I couldn't imagine why she would think Dr. Gabriel a prude—in class he was crazy. "You don't know what *parlando espress* means?" he said. "Then don't sing for me because I'll have to take my Alka-Seltzer and lie down." When I waved my hand, he winked. "In a speaking manner—good, Jane. Christy, how do you sing in a speaking manner?" Christy didn't know. He banged a chord on the piano. "Theory at eight-thirty." Bang. "Darn that class." Bang. "But alas." Bang. "I'll never pass. Get it?" We got it, and I giggled, but he never joked around with students in the hall. Ruth was wrong. He didn't even know me.

"Anyway, it's just a guy. No one you would know."

"Are you screwing this guy?"

"Ruth," I protested. Honestly, she had no sense of what was somebody else's own business. I began to regret that I had called, but after all, the Solomons were my friends. Wouldn't Kelly want to know my friends? Who knows, he might even escort me to a recital. I was planning to attend every swim meet from now on.

"You don't have to simper. I'm not one of those ninnies in your dorm who's going to have you saying Hail Marys for each stinky finger, and you can just look at you and see that

148

your mother never told you anything—now did she?—and if you are, *somebody* ought to make sure you get to a doctor.''

''Don't be silly. I'm not even Catholic.'' So that's the way it was. You went out in the woods just once and wound up before the J-board *and* the A.M.A. Oh God.

''So I'm a Jew,'' she said. ''What do I know about Christians?''

''Please,'' I begged, ''he's just a guy I know. You won't say anything, will you?''

''Besides birth control, there's venereal disease. Did you know it's on the rise now that people are taking the pill? And not just between the legs, either. Jane, if you put it in your mouth, use Listerine.''

''Ruth,'' I sobbed. ''We're just friends.''

''Oh,'' she said. ''In that case we'll have hamburgers.''

I could have and should have left it at that, but it was a dinner for Kelly. Also, Ruth was my next-to-best friend. Never mind that she was almost as old as my mother—she wasn't my mother. ''We could have steaks,'' I conceded.

''I thought so,'' she said. ''Now I want you to promise me you'll make an appointment with Doc McQuisten.''

So I promised, but, of course, I didn't do it. Still, I had some panics, and in them I cursed myself for getting only as far as a phone booth in the Union. I had to ask for change at the activities desk from a boy in my theory class, and, though I was sure he couldn't hear me, I leaned out of the booth to make sure he didn't watch. The desk was in a stone hallway with a ceiling as high as the roof of a cathedral, lit by a pale shaft that fell from the arched foyer windows to the slate floor. Across from the desk was the Memorial Room, a shrine to the honor and courage contained in the names that were writ in the golden book under glass. It was the record of the men and women of the university who had served in the wars of the Republic, and every day a hostess unlocked the display case to turn another page. Stained-glass windows dappled light across the bronze plaque on the floor. I knew by heart the pamphlet that explained why old glass does not cast a colored image. Without faith or patriotism, I believed that ''there is fitness and meaning in the fact that the grave and solemn loveliness of the stained glass, which is a treasured relic of our civilization's antiquity, should admit the light over our memorials, giving us a perspective in time and beauty." You see, I wanted my name writ in a golden book of beauty too.

It was a bad choice of phone booths. So near lofty list and hallowed hall, I ought to have been calling a king about a kingdom, not a gynecologist about my gonads. I have never been on a more impressive campus—gothic halls and green hills, everywhere you look grandeur and tradition. Above the entrance to the old graduate library, stone letters spell A GOOD BOOK IS THE PRECIOUS LIFEBLOOD OF A MASTER SPIRIT; above the windows of the old Music Building, the names of Bach, et al. Set into the walls of Recital Hall are the stone curls of Beethoven, Mendelssohn, Chopin, Tchaikovsky, Wagner, and Mozart. In bas relief on the side of Ballantine Hall, two nudes touch hands across the sun. *Veritas filia temporis*—in other words, naked time will get you naked truth. Nowhere is there a monument to fucking in the woods, though if numbers name the soul of an institution, it seemed to me that the walls of its public privies wrote more truth than all its carved stone. But never mind that I had numbers on my side. It was an institution of *higher* learning, and those rock walls, the ivy, the names beneath glass, the seals that couldn't be stepped on, and those goddamn stone mascots, who never had to go to a gynecologist in all the ages it took for *veritas* to get to be *filia temporis*, made me feel filthy. The receptionist answered. I heard Musak. I hung up.

The boy at the activities desk waved as I went by. He had often taken my requests for records to be played in the South Lounge, where, all winter, flames licked the limestone fireplace while students kicked off their loafers to curl into comfy leather sofas and study to Rachmaninoff, and the balding heads of our master spirits bowed before the chessboard. "Hey," he called. "We just got the Scarlatti Gabriel was telling us about. I'll put it on." "Some other time," I said and hurried.

No doubt about it, doctors were out. I would just have to bring up the subject with Kelly, which might be hard since what he mostly brought up with me was his wong. He hadn't even mentioned Saturday night, and already it was Thursday. We'd been out every evening, and each time we came in he asked what I was doing tomorrow. "But that's Thursday," I'd said at the door last night. "Thursday nights I have a practice room." "I want to see you," he said. Okay, he could see me. I'd be through at nine-thirty; if he met me on the third floor of the Music Annex we could leave right away. "That doesn't give us much time," he complained. Well, I didn't like it either—cut short at the climax, no drifting dénouement. "All right, all right," he said. "Is it that big round building over by the Ed School?"

He couldn't find me. Little wonder. The corridors formed concentric circles connected by halls that cut the musical pie into quarters. No matter where you stood, before you were two or three closed doors and a curve of ceramic tile topped by a band of perforated wood. Kelly got lost in the outer circle, while in a wedge off the inner I tootled and retootled a fancy run, fanfare for the moment he would darken the square of light that came through my door. Instead, a Japanese violinist pounded and shouted, "Time is up. It is my turn." I stowed my clarinet in my locker and circled to find Kelly.

"Let's get out of here," he said. "This place makes me dizzy."

"So?" I said as we walked around the building. I couldn't say a swimming pool made me feel right at home—I played with that, as we'd played all week with our lack of mutual interests, charming each other with the thought that we had something even more sympathetic than shared minds, and tugged his arm to hurry us to the car. The air was still warm, and a tremble of aria and scale floated from the open windows of the old Music Building. Kelly was wearing a red nylon jacket that said I.U. SWIMMING; its sleeves whistled while he walked. His pinwoman, Sidney said, had his college letter jacket. I didn't care. I liked his nylon music, and the high school letter I now wore made me feel that I came first.

A few minutes later we were parking on the shoulder of a country road. "Hope you don't mind," he said, already beginning to unbutton and unzip. "It's too late to hit the cabin." I didn't complain. I was ready to take him wherever I could get him, even on his lap in the back seat, with the base of my neck snapping the elastic of the front seat cover loose. Only when we were slippery and limp did I speak. I asked if he would come to dinner at the Solomons'.

He shoved me. "Get your clothes on. I don't want a cop to see that pretty bottom." He tossed my underpants, inspecting his own for the two holes that matched. He couldn't find one sock, and he stooped to sweep one hand along the floor. "Saturday night," he said, and I waited while he flicked the overhead to turn his T-shirt wrong side in. A bloom of prickly heat had opened on his chest. Without looking at me, he dashed us into darkness. He didn't know, he said. As a matter of fact, he'd been thinking about staying in to study.

"Bullshit," I said, scrambling the car's width away. His scent came after me: sweat, sex, and aftershave. Even in the dark, I could see his surprise, a slight start in the nostrils. "My roommate told me why you've had so much time to spend with me. Your girlfriend had her appendix out over semester break, but now she's coming back, I bet, and . . ." Sid had told me what she thought I needed to know, but she knew too much, and I wouldn't tell her this. I couldn't stalk our room, snarling and hissing, then purr when Kelly called. I had to purr for Sid and snarl at Kelly. She had had her own boyfriend; I was borrowing one, and if I wasn't careful, she'd figure out what the difference was.

"Jane." It was that damn kind voice again, and I began to wonder if that wasn't the tone that made me maddest. I could deal with the shades of liar and cheat.

"You're not going to study. You only go out with me 'cause I'm an easy lay."

"Maybe." He found my hand and squeezed it. "But I also like you, stupid."

"Do you sleep with her?"

He shook his head. "She wants to wait until we're married."

"Oh." My voice was faint; it was sorry I had asked.

He laughed, but his voice softened. "Jane, I haven't been honest with you, I admit, but I haven't exactly lied. I am pinned—you knew that. I went out with you because I needed to get laid—you're a smart girl, you ought to know that too."

"Are you going to marry her, then?"

"I don't know." He was looking out the window while I lay my head against his shoulder. "She expects me to." He brushed his fingers through my bangs. "Look, honey, I'm going to go to law school. I don't even want to think about getting married for years." He rolled his window down. "Damn, it's nice out."

"Do you love her?"

"Maybe." He sighed. "I thought I did. Hey—you cold?" He rolled his window up.

"No." I sat up, still shivering, and he handed me his jacket. "My roommate got depinned this week."

"Obviously that's an option. I know I don't want to stop seeing you." He drummed his hand on the dashboard. "Did I tell you we've got a meet with Michigan a week from Saturday? I want to be up for it mentally."

"Is it a big one?" I didn't care if a world cup would be the outcome, not while my flesh still rose in bumps of fear, as if my skin were too thin a coat.

"The biggest. We're defending champs—undefeated since 'fifty-nine. Michigan figures we're ripe to get our ass kicked."

"I didn't know you were champions."

"Who does?" His face livened. "All anybody cares about is basketball and that lousy football team that hasn't done a thing since nineteen forty-five." He patted my knee. "So what I'm saying is—and maybe it sounds selfish, but—I just don't want to complicate my life right now." He tipped my chin up. "Hey. Don't look so sad, huh?"

I forced a smile.

"You haven't said what you want."

Was he asking? How much did I dare demand? I took a guess. "I want you to beat Michigan."

His smile was dazzling. I closed my eyes for him to kiss me. "Give me a week," he whispered. "I'll call you when I get back from Ann Arbor." We had begun pecking and cheeping. I thrust my throat up. We fell upon each other like buzzards on meat.

*   *   *

I asked Sid to tell me his girlfriend's name.

She looked over her horn-rims. "Nothing doing." Pens flew at her as she yanked out her desk drawer. "Damnit. Where is my meal ticket?" She flung the drawer on her bed and plunged into that coffin of empty matchbooks, old love letters, and confetti-edged notebook paper headed "Dear Mom and Dad" and footed short with commas. And, though I teased and pleaded, she refused to give in. After raining paper rubble over her shoulders, she threw the drawer on top of her desk and stripped the bed.

"Well, then what about meeting her in the Commons for a Coke?"

"Just when I'm in a hurry. I wanted to eat dinner early and be back before Riggs gets here." I jumped aside as she attacked the bureau. "Hurdle, is this your idea of a joke?"

"Me? What are you blaming me for?" I sat at my desk and picked up the album cover to *Eine Kleine Nachtmusik,* wishing I could be the one to find the lost minuet between the Allegro and the Romanze. I wished I could find anything instead of always losing. I read the jacket notes out loud: " 'The outer movements are in ABA design, with the increased harmonic interest lying somewhere after the development begins. Interestingly, Mozart has superimposed a kind of ABA over the more confining identity in the fourth movement.' Interesting, huh?" I set the jacket aside. Christ, even though that's all it's made of, I hate to hear music reduced to ABC's. "You wouldn't have to introduce me. I wouldn't sit down or even say hi. You could act like you didn't know me."

"Damnit." She sat on her naked mattress and looked up with a face gone wild. "I had it at lunch. Now where is it?"

I wrote Kelly's name on my blotter, then scribbled through it. "You're a Kappa, and you ought to get to know your sisters. Just ask her to meet you. All I want to do is walk through and get a look."

"Oh no!" She dropped her face to her hands. "You know where it is? In my notebook."

I jumped up. "Great. Let's go eat—though you may be

sorry. They're having tuna coronado.'' I swirled my wrap-around skirt—the same skirt Eddie Ziegler had used to flag down a Volkswagen—over my cut-offs. They wouldn't let you eat shit without a skirt, and if you wore one, that's exactly what you ate.

"I loaned it to Sharon Goldman so she could copy the notes she missed in chem."

"Is that Kelly's girl? You can meet her for a Coke and get them back."

Sid stared at me. "Are you crazy?"

I shrugged.

"Well, damnit, Riggs'll just have to take me out for pizza." She flopped full length on the mattress. "Screw my diet. You're a witness—I tried."

I sat on my own bed. "I'll give you a character reference when they haul you off to the fat-farm."

"That's not very funny, Hurdle."

"If you don't want to meet her, just tell me one thing: is she pretty?" I hoped she was a hunchback with cross-eyes and a face mined with acne. Except, what did that say for Kelly? Better a beauty with a fatal flaw like her brain. Maybe she would say something dumb tonight, and when she laughed, her mouth would creak open like the door to an empty closet. Maybe he would call me the minute he took her in.

Sid rose on an elbow. "Are you sleeping with Kelly?"

"Oh." I looked at the wall. "What makes you ask that?"

"Because if you are, you're asking for trouble."

"Is she?"

"What?"

"*Pretty.*"

Sid sat up. "Why are you picking on me?

"Who's picking on you?"

"I have problems " she said. "I can't go to dinner, and I'm starving. I'm fat and I'm going to have to eat pizza. I haven't done my laundry, and I don't have any clean underwear. The whole Lambda Chi house hates me because I'm a rat. And to top it all off, I'm pregnant.''

"Well, maybe you aren't," I said, knowing as well as Sid did that, although she would have to wait two more weeks for a test, she was. I didn't want to think about it. Because if I thought about Sid, I would have to think about—maybe I should have bottomed-up for Doc McQuisten. But he'd make me take my clothes off. "So?" Ruth had said when she described the dismal doings. "He's a doctor—he's seen thousands of women." That was supposed to be a comfort? I thought I'd feel better if he'd never seen one before. Maybe I'm the only woman who still wonders, when her doctor says to the nurse who doles out the diaphragms, "Let's try a seventy," if that's as good as 38-22-38, or if the last woman who went through took a sixty-nine. *Oh no.* That business was for other ladies. I was a serious student. I took the intellectual approach to birth control: I thought about it.

"Yeah," Sid said. "And maybe I am."

"Well, if you are, you might as well eat pizza." My hand closed on the doorknob. "Want me to bring you some tuna?"

"Yuk." She was mad, and she hollered after me as I went out the door, "Her name's Marianne Sauder, and you can look her up in last year's yearbook."

I went straight to the library. If she had a flaw, the *Arbutus* didn't show it. As a freshman she'd been Tyronian queen. I hoped that her appendix had pained her greatly. I went by myself to the Solomons' on Saturday night.

Ruth met me at the door. She was wearing a gray wool dress that matched the paint peeling off the floorboards of the porch and trailed threads from its crooked hem. Once I was inside, she poked her head out the screen door, which still bore the initial B from the two sons-of she said had sold Martin the house. "Where is he?" she asked, as if I might have hidden him under a board on that tedium-hued piazza.

I pushed a paper sack at her. "Here. My roommate's boyfriend went to Strong's." It was a bottle of Mateus rosé.

"Thank you," she said. "Where is he?"

I peeked into the living room. The Playskool plastics had been picked up, and the rug bore wheeltracks from the vacuum. Martin had his back to us as he poked the fire. I said I was sorry I hadn't called.

No problem, Ruth said—one thing about steaks, you could always throw them in the freezer. "Where is he?"

I shrugged. "Oh, he had a swim meet."

Ruth held my bottle up for Martin. "Look what Jane brought us."

"How thoughtful. Ruth, did you know that wood David stacked is green? Listen to it hissing."

I followed Martin to the living room and sat on the edge of the green wicker sofa. Ruth had placed a basket of pine cones on a hole in the Oriental rug. The room was as neat as I had ever seen it, though I could hear the kids thumping upstairs.

"Well," he said, "what can I get you to drink? I was just about to mix up a pitcher of martinis."

I said I'd try one, and he bumped into Ruth on her way back from the kitchen. She exhaled herself into a wicker rocker. "Did you call Doc McQuisten?"

I had.

"Did he put you on the pill? It's the best thing that ever happened to me."

Through the arch to the dining room I saw the mahogany table set with four places, a gleam of silver from the center, a patina on the chairs. "Everything looks so nice. Is that a new philodendron?"

It was a finger aralia, and she'd had it two years. Philodendron was the only plant I knew, so I figured I'd come close. It wasn't as if I'd asked if it were a new Airedale. "He didn't give you a diaphragm, did he? You know what I've got to show for one of those."

I shook my head.

She leaned forward in the rocker. "This friend of yours—he's a swimmer?" She set the martini Martin gave her on a nearby bookcase.

I took a sip of mine. It tasted exactly as I imagine a glass of rubbing alcohol with a shot of motor oil might.

"Well." Martin selected an old Morris recliner near the fireplace. "Not a bad fire for new wood, is it? Although I distinctly told David not to bring up that hickory." I hid a smile. I was *fond* of Martin. So were his sons, none of whom but David would have bothered to bring up any wood at all,

157

and I knew Martin would have told David so distinctly and so often that David would have been unable to resist. I knew because it was exactly what I would have done. David and I shared a perverse imp, though his had better humor, the difference being that his did and mine just thought. Ruth knew all about it. She was smiling too. "Jane, how are your classes this semester?"

"Fine." I'd dropped piano because—had they heard?—I'd passed my keyboard, and added psych. This was my science, which was a requirement, and every morning I had to shiver through the dark to class and watch Dr. Macht reduce me to the giant O between his Stimulus and Response. This was the alphabet of behavior, and I resented it, much preferring to his predictable $S \rightarrow O \rightarrow R$ the unexpected fancy flights inspired by the circle of lettered fifths.

"Jane's young man won't be joining us," Ruth said. "He had a swim meet."

Martin's brow creased. Last fall he had sat before the television in a Chicago Cubs cap, cursing Don Drysdale so loudly that his youngest son cried. He knew, he said, nothing about swimming, but his sympathies were obviously with a man who missed dinner to make a meet. "Who is it with?"

"Michigan, and they figure we're ripe to get our ass kicked." Did they know that Indiana was undefeated? And not only that, but Big Ten champ? That as soon as the NCAA probation was lifted, we'd be a shoo-in for the national title? Or that Doc—Doc Counsilman, who coached via microphone through an underwater window, wasn't that neat?—was slated to train the U.S. Olympic team? That our very own swimmers would be its backbone? Including, by the way, my friend.

They hadn't known that.

"Who does?" I said. "All you ever hear about is basketball and that lousy football team that hasn't done a thing since nineteen forty-five."

"You should have called and told us you wanted to go to the meet," Ruth said. "We can have dinner any time."

"Maybe it makes him nervous to have Jane watch him," Martin suggested. "Anyway, I imagine it's over by now. We can call the radio station and find out who won."

"Actually," I admitted, "the meet's not till next week." Ruth gave me a suspicious look. "But it's important to be up for it, you know, mentally."

"You mean to tell me," Ruth said while little hairs began to sprout along the gray slope to her bun, "this boyfriend of yours is staying home to *think* about swimming?"

I nodded.

Martin gave me a conspiratorial smile. He had a thin face with a nose as sharp as a dinner knife and very little lip around his mouth. He was the nicest man, but he had no sense of humor, and the least hint of a smile turned serious on his face. "Now Ruth, you know at least half of sports is attitude."

"So a steak dinner with fresh cream of spinach soup, potatoes Anna, and a fennel and endive salad is going to ruin his attitude? To say nothing of cherries jubilee." She picked up her martini and gulped. "Ugh, Martin—too much vermouth."

I glanced at my own glass. "Oh, so that's what's wrong with it."

Martin's mouth drooped. "You think so?" He stood. "Well, I'll make you another. Jane?"

"Oh, it's fine," I said.

Ruth handed him her glass. "Don't dump it, honey. Just slop in some more gin. And get Jane another drink. She doesn't like martinis."

"Sure I do," I said.

"Fiddlesticks." She rocked toward me. "When you don't like something, say so. Now tell me just what's going on with this fellow, what's-his-name? He thinks we're old fuddy-duddies?"

I laughed. "I don't think *anybody* thinks you're a fuddy-duddy."

"Busybody?" She pursed her lips. "Well?"

I didn't answer.

"You don't want to tell me anything, then tell me to mind my own business. Does your mother let you get away with being so mealy-mouthed?"

"Most of the time my mother wishes I'd keep my smart mouth shut."

"Phooey. That's no way to raise a kid." She sat back and folded her arms across her massive bosom. "You had a fight, is that it?"

I shook my head, afraid my voice would quaver, then bit my lip and studied the rug until I whispered, "He has another girlfriend."

She gave me a pat and sat beside me. "I'd like to shoot your mother or whoever it was that made you such a worrywart. It's a rotten world—so have another drink and toughen up. Speaking of which"—she rolled her head toward the archway—"where's Martin?"

"Coming," he said and handed me a glass that floated moons of orange and lemon above a reef of maraschino cherries. If he could have found one, I believe he might have tossed in a flower, and never mentioned that he'd thrown a perfectly good martini down the drain. "Why don't I put on the Schubert?" He knelt before a bookcase full of records.

"It's too bad David had a date tonight." Ruth rose. "I'm going to call Ben Gabriel."

"What for?" Martin asked.

"We have four beautiful T-bones. I had Hayes cut them myself. There's no sense in letting one go to waste."

"I'll be glad to eat it." Martin blew dust from the Schubert, though I knew there couldn't possibly be any.

"Please. He's my teacher. I wouldn't want . . ." I didn't know which was more mortifying—Ruth's trying to fix me up with Dr. Gabriel or with her son.

"We also have a bottle of Moët."

Martin placed the record on the turntable without dropping the needle. "Well, I've never met three people yet who couldn't kill one bottle of champagne. And how is Ben going to feel being called at the last minute?"

"A whole lot better than if he's not called at all. He's probably sitting right now in that filthy apartment, boiling hot dogs, while Carla feeds those kids of theirs lobster." She fixed her eyes on me. "My own kids eat hot dogs and like it."

"Oh, he's married," I said, relieved.

"Divorced," Martin said. "Well, Ruth . . ."

"You're always saying yourself we should have him over more often. I don't know why I never think of it in time. Now that I have, I say let's give the poor dog a T-bone."

"I wouldn't put it that way. Ben's a fine fellow."

"He's a stuffed shirt. Every time he opens his mouth I want to scream. But what do you think?"

"Oh, he's a very good teacher," I said quickly, feeling as awful as if I'd stumbled into a bathroom where Dr. Gabriel was taking a dump.

"I think it's indecent for you to be making matches between Ben and a student. The man has enough problems as it is."

"Phooey. I'm talking about asking him to dinner."

Martin conceded. "If Jane doesn't mind, it's all right with me."

"Of course she doesn't mind." Ruth looked at me. "Do you?"

"No," I said miserably and spilled my new drink. Martin leaped to mop it, and for a minute I thought we were all going to cry.

"Oh, go ahead and call him," Martin said, irritation flushing his voice.

"Really," I echoed, "I don't mind if he comes."

Ruth stood, her voice inflated. "Well, I will then."

Martin studied his album. "Shall I put on the Schubert while I go make you a new drink?"

I nodded, and the horn called, the strings plucked, the orchestra replied.

Ruth returned. "He's coming. He was delighted."

We listened to three movements before she glanced out the window, muttering, "Fool. He's just standing there. How many times has he ever been here when the doorbell worked?"

She let him in, taking his trench coat, hat, and a paper bag from which she pulled a bottle of Mateus. He raised his hands in a flutter of applause as he walked in. "The *Great* Symphony—I salute you." His face wore a sheen from the shower, his sandy curls a dark slick. I bent toward my drink.

"Ruth, don't you look lovely? As always, I might add. So sweet of you to call me. Martin." They shook hands as my finger slowly circled the lip of my glass. I dipped to nudge an orange seed around an island of ice, my hair falling like a bridal gauze before my face. Through that modest cataract I saw tweed blisters at his knees. The corner of the cocktail table lanced them as he said, "Jane! How *nice* to see you." I raised my head through arcs of pain. He was wearing a suit, and from the rough skin of herringbone a scrubbed pinkness climbed into my vision, as innocent and indecent as the cheeks of a baby's privacy.

"Dr. Gabriel," I meant, I tried, to say. I giggled and gushed tears.

He sat beside me. "Fine, thanks, and you?"

And that's how I happened to marry Ben.

11

Or at least that's what I told Ruth when she protested. "It's *your* fault," I insisted, already acknowledging it was a matter for blame. "You invited him to dinner."

"I asked him to eat," she said. "I didn't say anything about marriage."

"Well, you know how one thing leads to another." But she expected better of me. A few months earlier, I had expected better of myself.

That night, when I stood to announce it would soon be hours, time for a Cinderella like me to slip off lest the wicked dorm mother note my absence and add it to the pending charges, Dr. Gabriel offered to drive me. I said I could walk; he said I shouldn't. It was a ritual exchange, but usually I had it with Martin.

I wasn't afraid to walk the streets of Bloomington at night. It was a small town, settled from the hills of Kentucky and Tennessee, and the townies (stonies, we called them because so many of them cut limestone in the quarries nearby), who lived on the west side of Bloomington, the far side, and to the rolling east in towns like Beanblossom, Gnaw Bone, and

Stony Lonesome, spoke with a Southern mountain twang. I made fun of their accent, just as students from anywhere but Lake County made fun of mine. "Haa-ammond," they said I said; "da-a-amnit, Ga-a-ary." They laughed and called me a hood from "da Region." You could spot a boy from da Region by the drooping white socks he wore with black shoes, a girl by the flakes of old Clearasil caked in her pores. Where was my switchblade? they teased me, and, though I protested, God knows I wouldn't have walked the streets of Hammond at night. *I* lived on the wrong side there. Here, I was as privileged and safe as I had always believed the daughters of da Region steel executives were.

"It's no trouble." Dr. Gabriel yawned. "I don't want to keep these good people up all night."

The ride was, he said, a pleasant end to a pleasant evening, most pleasant of all the surprise of seeing me. We'd eaten with a clatter of conversation about people and places I didn't know. At eleven, David came in, opened a beer, and sat next to me. "You want to come upstairs and listen to records?" he asked. "I was just asking your father to play the *Great* Symphony," Dr. Gabriel interrupted. "I came in at the end, and I haven't heard the Toscanini recording." "No thanks," David said and cocked his head at me.

"David," Martin said, "we are going to play the Schubert, and if you go upstairs to play rock and roll, I want the volume kept on low." "Go ahead," Ruth whispered to me. "You've already heard the symphony." "Oh, I'm sure Jane would like to hear it again," Dr. Gabriel said quickly, crossing his legs so tightly that his trousers crawled up his calf, and I agreed, not wanting a teacher to think one hearing was enough for a dedicated student like me.

I gave David an apologetic smile. The nicest Saturday I had spent last fall had been with him and Sam, who had done the dozens on each other while we hiked through Brown County until I laughed so hard I hurt, but when David suggested we drop Sam off and take in a movie, I declined, and declined again when he called to ask me out. He had a wonderfully wicked sense of humor, but he also had terrible taste in music, a bad complexion, and kinky hair, and I wouldn't have gone out with one of Ruth's sons for all the fun in the world. She was so nosey. But he continued to tease me, saving us both from embarrassment. He shook his head at Dr. Gabriel just for me to see as he went upstairs, and we listened again to the Schubert, the faint beat of "Let's Twist Again" pounding into the pianissimos. We said our thanks in the hall while Martin held my coat. Dr. Gabriel filled the six blocks to Wells Quad with his list of *pleasant's* and complaints about the calligraphy he got from our class. "Are they supposed to be notes or lollipops?" he asked, excepting mine for praise as he parked his Volkswagen in the circle.

"Oh, you don't have to walk me," I said. "Martin never does."

"My pleasure," he insisted, extending a stubby arm to assist me from the car. My skirt twisted, and his eyes congealed on a scab of red nail polish that contained a run inside my thigh. In my effort to conceal it, we grappled, but he was as serious about his manners as David Niven, and I had to float to the front steps on his arm as if he didn't really remind me of Inspector Clouseau. "Jane, it's been delightful."

He came toward me so quickly, I barely had time to glance his lips off my cheek. He was my teacher. He was my teacher, and he'd tried to kiss me. Oh mercy.

A black plush Cossack cap sat on his head like an unlucky cat. I had no idea how old he was, but I was eighteen, and underneath that stupid hat, his hair was wearing thin. Kelly wore his suit of muscles as casually as his letter jacket and jeans, but Dr. Gabriel's apron of fat fitted him poorly, bunching inside his belt and ballooning against his shirt, leaving him tugging at his balls when he sat and wiping sweat above his collar. It made me pull at my own clothes just to watch him.

"Well, good night." His wingtips shuffled on the steps.

"Good night." He was short, and from the step above I had to commit the agony of looking into his eyes. His face was wide, features clustered around his nose like trees around a farmhouse on an expanse of Illinois prairie. Hair grew like grass inside his nostrils. Still, he was a very good teacher, and at least one girl in my class had a crush on him. For his sake, I wished he had tried to kiss her instead of me.

"It's been such a lovely evening. I'm so grateful to Ruth for this opportunity to see you"—he blushed and licked his lips—"romantically."

What had I *done?*

"You're so bright. When I see you sitting in that third row in the mornings, your face is like a star."

I felt faint. "Fourth." Why hadn't I gone up to listen to records with David, who suddenly seemed incredibly appealing and would, if I could find an excuse to call him, make Dr. Gabriel seem funny?

"So charming, so . . ."

I'd never call David. He was ugly, and he'd know I'd noticed, and Kelly didn't care, and nothing was funny anyway. "Well, and of course I had good lessons. Did I tell you Ruth's father was my teacher? He died." I watched a girl whose boyfriend was smearing her with kisses. What was I talking about?

"I know. I was sorry. Ruth's a stout soul, entertaining so soon."

"She messes in my business." I turned my head back. He was watching too. Around us couples were flying like moths for the lights of the lobby. Sid and Riggs swept by us. Riggs had his arm around her. He wore black-rimmed glasses; he looked sincere and studious, not her type. But she was in love; you could see it. I turned my head again to follow them. "I loved her father. They're blinking the lights. I have to go."

He took a step forward. He was my teacher. How could he be such a fool? "Well, life is for the living, don't you agree?"

"I'll get a pink slip."

He took another step, his eyes shifting to the place beyond my shoulder where Sid and Riggs were nuzzling their good nights. "And here we are among the living." He licked his lips again, and the nastiness that was flapping around inside me flew out.

"That's my roommate. She's pregnant," I said flatly, then

lowered my head, ashamed. I hadn't meant to betray her. I had meant only to tell him that I saw.

"Pregnant?" he said, savoring the word like a succulent treat, and this time he caught me, his lips tasting of coffee and as lifeless as a doll's. When I opened my eyes, his were still fixed on Sid. I wiped my mouth.

The phone was ringing as I came around the corner to third short, and I left my key in the open door as I dashed to pick it up.

"I've missed you. Where have you been?" Kelly said.

"At dinner." Though Sid wasn't up yet, I closed myself into the half-bath and dropped my coat.

All night? I wanted to see you."

"I wanted to see you too." I slid down the wall to the heap of my coat. "I *asked* you to go."

"I've been trying to call you. I want to see you." My ears began to ring with the refrain.

"It's hours," I said, "but I really am glad you called."

"You could sneak out."

"No, I couldn't."

"Where have you been?"

"At dinner. I *told* you." The overhead glared off the enameled yellow walls, so I stared at the muted plaid of my skirt. "You wouldn't go."

"Well, I wanted to see you."

For two days I had awaited this call, not sure that I would ever hear from him again. Now that I had, I forgot how willing, how eager to please I had felt. "Are you drunk? I didn't think athletes were allowed . . ."

"How come you had to eat dinner all night?"

"It was a party. We sat around." I rolled my pleats between my fingers. "My theory teacher drove me home."

"Are you intimate with him?"

"What do you mean?" I jabbed at an exasperated tear. "How can you even ask me something like that?"

"How am I supposed to know who you sleep with?"

Joined to another person by a telephone line, I have always felt strangely depressed by my intimacy with the scene I can see, as though my inability to ignore the heat of the room, a loose thread in my skirt, or needing to pee were the one thing that prevented a perfect union of minds. The faucet was dripping, and my stomach was sour. I'd had too much coffee and too many citrus fruits with my gin. I was tired. "I don't sleep with anybody, and you know it."

"Yeah, well you told me yourself I wasn't the first."

"Oh God." I was rubbing my hand raw on the wool. "I was twelve years old, and I did it once in the back of a bus."

"Keep talking, Jane. That's really great news. There's nothing I like hearing about more than my girl and other guys."

The elevator doors rolled open, releasing a burst of laughter and screams. It was hopeless. In a million worlds Kelly and I could have never reasoned with words. "I'm not even your girl."

"Oh no? I've got a friend here who says you are."

"Who?" It was no one I knew; that was sure.

"Don't be dense. Okay, look, I know I've been a jerk, but when I called to make it up, where were you? On your back with a grade book stuffed up your cunt."

"I don't have to screw my teachers for grades." My voice was dry ice. "Because, for your information, Mr. Son-of-a-Bitch, I'm smart. And furthermore, I haven't done one goddamn fucking thing wrong, except be rude to my theory teacher, who happens to be one hell of a lot nicer than you."

"That's real pretty, Jane. You've got a nice way with words."

The door opened. "Sorry," Sid said. "Did you know you left your keys in the door? Oh, Hurdle." She sighed her review of the night.

"Go to hell," I said to Kelly, and Sid closed the door. For a minute we both listened while neither one of us hung up.

"I'll get a motel room," he promised.

"I *can't*."

"I *need* you," he said.

"I need you too," I admitted. "Will you come over tomorrow?"

Sid pounded on the door. "Hurdle, hurry up. Riggs is going to call."

"Jane, I took my pin back. If you want it, I'll give it to you tonight."

If I wanted it. All last semester Sid had worn Kent's crescent and Greek letters to bed. If I had his pin, I wouldn't have to sneak out. "I'll get caught."

"You won't." I didn't answer. "Please?" he whispered. I didn't answer. "Janie, I love you."

"Oh," I said and gave in, agreeing to meet him in fifteen minutes in the parking lot behind the dorm. I put my coat on and slipped my toothbrush into my pocket.

"Hurdle!" Sid banged the door again. "Riggs has to go back to Columbus tomorrow."

"All right already. I'm off—if the phone rings, you'll hear it." I combed my hair and stared at the mirror. Maybe not a Tyronian queen—but still. I took the toothbrush from my pocket. The phone rang. Sid yanked the door open, and we collided at the sink.

"Hello?" she breathed as I ducked beneath her arm and wiped a froth of toothpaste from my chin. "It's for you," she said, scowling. "A guy. Just don't be all night."

"Kelly?" I said, unbuttoning my coat.

"Jane? This is Ben Gabriel. I know it's late, but I hope you weren't asleep. I was afraid I might have said something to upset you this evening."

I swallowed the rest of the toothpaste.

"I didn't realize your father's not living. And I give you my deepest apologies if I made a thoughtless remark."

"Huh?"

"When we were talking about Ruth's father. I could see you were distressed. Did he die recently?"

"Who?" I said, fingering the wet bristles I'd put back in my pocket. I meant to tell him my roommate needed the phone, but my tongue wouldn't work.

"Your father. I called Martin. He told me your father had passed on. Of course, I understand if it's too painful for you to talk about."

I sagged against the wall.

169

''But if you do want to talk . . .''

I started to cry.

''Oh, I'm sorry, I'm so dreadfully sorry,'' he sputtered. ''Forgive me. Oh, please, my dear, don't cry. I only want to help. I am very, ah, sensitive in these matters because I do, you know, have children myself. I don't know if you knew, but I am divorced. Jane?''

I nodded.

''Their mother has custody. So you see? You've lost a parent and I've lost my children. Jane, are you all right?''

''I'm fine,'' I whispered, hating him for making me a hypocrite. I didn't care about my father, and what I needed was not comfort, but to be downstairs when Kelly arrived.

''Well, there is another, ah, reason I called.''

'' Hurdle!'' Sid screamed.

I snapped up. ''Oh, hey. My roommate needs the phone.''

''Could I call you again then? I—to tell you the truth, I've been thinking about calling for some time, and I would have, but—well, I wished you would sign up for another section this term. This is awkward.'' His laugh was a cackle. ''I've never dated a student before.'' My senses scrambled. I *heard* him blush. ''Do you know that I looked up your number months ago? I hope you don't think I'm silly.''

I did.

''And then, when I saw you tonight—you don't mind, do you? You're so lovely, so talented. So *young*.''

''Uh-huh. Look, I better go. My roommate's mad.''

''I'll call you tomorrow then. I thought we might take in the Budapest.''

''I have a boyfriend,'' I said.

He paused. ''Oh, I see. Well, in that case, I'll just say good night.''

Sid was smoking a cigarette and pacing. ''It's about time.'' She gave me an odd look. ''I wouldn't have been such a bitch, but you know I won't see Riggs all week.'' She frowned. ''Aren't you hot? Why don't you take off your coat?''

''Oh. Sure,'' I said, still standing in the middle of the room. I let it fall.

She narrowed her eyes. "What's the matter with you?"

"Nothing." I began a slow shuffle toward the door.

"Hey, if you're going to get ice, would you bring me some? Riggs gave us a present." She opened her desk drawer with a flourish and held up a half-pint of sloe gin. She set the bottle on her desk. "Where *are* you going?"

"To get pinned," I said and whisked out the door.

The corridor was empty, but at the other end of third I could hear the pock-pock of a popcorn popper, and the scent of melting butter mingled with the smell of stale vegetables that persistently rose from the kitchen of the quad dining hall. Laughter trailed from an open door into the stairwell. Morrison straddled a hill, and, though I lived on the third floor, I had to descend five dimly lit flights to the rear exit. The door to the dining hall was chained. In my stealth I felt like a belated and irrelevant shadow to a picture from the *Arbutus:* roommates in bathrobes and curlers tiptoeing down for a midnight snack. At the end of the decade I thought of that picture again, when I saw those cute coeds camped in the administration building, raising their fists on "The Huntley-Brinkley Report." They were shouting: "One, two, three, four—we don't want your—bleep—war." I wondered whether the camaraderie it takes to giggle your way down to the dining hall would have propelled me all the way to the president's office, whether I might have been part of my generation had I not crashed the bars that left me outside that night. I doubted it. While their giggles thickened to a guttural chant, my own desperation thinned. Boredom was what was left after that. I stirred the white sauce while Ben caught the weather and scores. The kids went to jail. We unfolded our napkins and ate.

I wouldn't have thought it would come to that. Not while I paused on the bottom step, so young that I could wonder if all it took to be like everyone else was to be pinned. The Coke machine hummed, and I found a dime in my pocket.

I guided the door back to make sure the lock didn't catch. Not that I expected anything to go wrong—but she was wise, I thought, who left latches open. I darted across the short limestone court to Sycamore Hall, Coke sloshing down my arm, the cup already melting in my hand. By daylight I had crossed that court dozens of times to use the washers and driers in the basement of Sycamore, but none of us did laundry after dark because last fall a girl from my dorm had met up with a flasher.

It was a clear night, and the air had grown cold. The street light down the drive had the crisp look of an acrylic moon painted on velvet. The asphalt shone with the light like a river. Kelly wasn't there yet. The silhouette of a safety man floated into the light pool, and I crouched behind a bush that had lost its leaves for the winter, raising my head to peep over the wall between me and the small lot where the kitchen staff parked. Except for an old black Ford, it was empty. The cop was coming up the drive. I scraped the limp cup on the stone as I crept around the corner of the wall and crawled under the car, chin to the cold pavement while I watched his oxfords tramp by. He was humming "Heartaches by the Number."

The humming stopped. The exhaust pipe crowded my shoulder, and I felt a powder of rust on my face. His flashlight bobbed on the building. I took a breath, expecting to smell gasoline, but all I inhaled was a shiver of night air. My teeth began to chatter, and I pressed my cheek to the tire, watching the pale asphalt wash down the hill to the point where light dipped to dark. My back hurt, my bones were cold, and my knees smarted. The underbelly of the auto was sinking, I knew it. In a minute I'd be bearing the weight of the Ford.

The humming resumed midphrase, then faded around the corner of the building. Where was Kelly? Oh, I'd expected to turn my tit up to take the sword and shield of Phi Delta Theta, not to drag it across the blacktop. "Appendix," I whimpered. "Everybody has their appendix out." There was probably, I assured myself, some very good explanation, though at the moment I couldn't think of one plausible point on Kelly's behalf. My tensed thighs were shaking as I climbed out from under the car. I listened so hard I thought I heard the traffic light change at an intersection blocks away. Then I remembered one teeny, obvious fact.

I have always had a superb sense of direction and absolutely no sense of time.

How long had Dr. Gabriel kept me on the phone?

Oh, but only a bastard would come and just go. Kelly couldn't—he wouldn't. Yet I knew as surely as Sid knew she was knocked up that he had. For a moment I was more disappointed than angry. I wanted to see him. I saw now that our quarrel had been a mere ritual of foreplay to the inevitability of my giving in. Then I was depressed because I thought I knew exactly what love meant: I was horny. Love was an irresistible demand of the body, and to get it I would give and give and give in.

The back door was locked. So much for the legend of incompetence that surrounds the campus police. I thought about creeping around the side to call up to Sidney, but if she didn't hear me, someone else would. If only she'd ordered out for pizza. I could drop a message in the basket she let down with money. Once we'd had a bed-check with pizza midway up the building. Sid had snuffed the lights, and we faked sleep, my head anchoring the rope that ran from my pillow. We mumbled our *here's*, and that was all there was to it: no flashlights in our faces, no pinches to prove us. A bed-check like that was a cinch to wad clothes for, but I hadn't even thought to do that, and tonight the dummy was out in the cold, hoping that her mother would be more understanding than she had ever imagined when she came home expelled and put away her clarinet to sell goldfish until she retired.

I did the only thing I could do: I set out for the Solomons'.

Watching over my shoulder for cops, I slipped through the quad, then sprinted for Third Street, pausing once to retrieve a shoe I'd outrun. I glanced back at the faint light in the Music Building stairwell; then the bushes sprouted hands that took my elbows, and, though the touch was gentle, I started. Flashers were supposed to be all show and no contact. Obviously I was in the grip of something else, and every girl alive has been warned what that is. My heart was weighted with wooden shoes, clopping in my chest like a frightened Dutch girl. Two hulks rose behind the hands, and a third hand clapped my mouth, though it needn't have bothered. On the lam from the law, I was too scared to scream. But I was also pissed off, so mad at Kelly that I tossed my head, and the palm drew back from my mouth. ''Shit,'' I said. ''I've been screwed, now I'm raped. What's the difference?''

They laughed, and as we moved into the green stream of mercury vapor that marked the boundary between campus and town, I sucked in my breath. They were in blackface, and their pale eyes drank the queer light, turning the color of gin.

''Jesus Christ,'' one said. ''What happened to you?''

I looked down. My sweater was smeared with grease, my skirt was twisted, my knees were bleeding, and my nylons were shredded. One of my flats was dragging its bow. ''I fell.''

''You ought to be more careful, girl.'' I twitched my eyes from one to the other. In their crew cuts, car coats, and khakis they had to be students instead of psychopaths. They should have been stuffing phone booths instead of carrying off coeds. ''After dark, life be dangerous.'' The arm bit my throat, and I choked.

''Hey.'' I coughed as he released me. ''Take it easy. You could hurt a girl that way.''

They rolled their eyes at each other. ''You be wanting to hurt her, or you be wanting me to hurt her?''

''You guys think you're Amos and Andy or something?'' I stepped from the curb, but a hand dug into my shoulder.

''Why you think we be white boys? Baby, we be mean colored boys, and you out awful late.''

''Oh, cut it out,'' I said, trying to shoulder free and adding, ''You aren't even colored, so there.''

''Oh, baby, you so smart. Dat right. We be *niggers*, and we habn't decided who get to hurt you yet.'' I flailed a fury of elbows and gagged as the wind was squeezed from my throat.

They meant business now, and so did the blade, beaded with light, at my chin. I began to cry as the one loosened his grip on my neck and I beheld those twin villains from a nightmare so absurd that I knew I'd never wake up. I tried to think of something cheerful, remembering the girl from Wells

Quad who'd seen what the exhibitionist had to show. "No sweat," she'd said. "I just looked at it and laughed." I kept my eyes fixed on the knife. "Ha-ha," I began, but the rest of my words could not seem to climb the mountain in my throat. I tried again. "Okay." I threw my arms out. "You can have me. I won't struggle, I won't even scream. But, well, I think I should warn you—I mean . . ." I kept, goddamnit, crying. "Nothing serious, of course. Just a little, uh, social disease." Their make-up was impassive, and I was no longer sure they had faces beneath. "So rape at your own risk, only"—my voice broke in the tremble of my mouth—"could you do me a favor and not kill me? I've got an important concert coming up." Big giraffe tears rolled down my face, and I asked, "Are you really going to hurt me?"

"I done tole you, girl. We habn't decided yet." They found my elbows and began pumping me up Third Street, half-dragging me to the sidewalk before Myers Hall.

"What are you going to do to me?" I cried. I'd never been in the anatomy building, but I'd heard there was a basement museum where pickled people floated in formaldehyde. Sid said there was a man cut in rings like a tree. I went slack. "No, please."

We didn't descend to the disgusting aquarium. Knees to my back, they kept nudging me up, and when the stairs ran out, I heard a jingle of keys. "Relax," said the one who gripped my arm as the other unlocked the door, and he prodded me into the dark mouth, which opened, with a flip of switches, to a long, buff-colored lab, the tables laid with dishes for dozens, covered with stainless steel domes. Overhead the fluorescents buzzed like flies at a picnic. "Go on." And I was shoved to where his friend was lifting the mummy-shaped lid to, my God, what meat.

"You okay?" He caught me as I fell back. The room reeked of formaldehyde. It was the smell, and not the sight, that had spun me into his arms.

The ceiling reeled. I had almost, but not quite, fainted. Now I straightened, stepping closer. "I'm fine." Never mind my father and the death that reek brought back. So these jokers were sickos even sicker than the obscene callers—not

175

enough for them, the outraged hum of wires. They were premed students who had, for the first time, dissected someone, and they meant for someone else to see.

I knew nothing about doctors, having lived all my life on the wrong side of Hammond's railroad tracks. I didn't see them socially, and since my seventh year, when I'd had rheumatic fever and dropped out of school, I had not needed their professional advice. I was a healthy kid, a complete recovery whose heart had refused to be done in. And my father, well, he lived and he died. I'd been too young to have much truck with the middleman, though I remembered the smell or maybe not even that one, just an antiseptic clog in the lungs that killed everything human, even the rot. What I thought about doctors was that they had a nice life: Cadillacs in the driveway, country clubs down the street. Doctors were crooks who ripped you off, and anyway you died. Their kids wore John Meyer of Norwich, Capezios, and Gant; they snubbed you in high school and screwed you for grades, then slammed the door to the dissecting lab, where they honed their hearts into scalpels and learned to be doctors themselves. Yet these boys, with their pallid streaks of skin behind their greasy masks, looked more pathetic than steeled.

I lowered my eyes and bowed my head before the beast.

It was a woman. You could hardly tell, really. It was last Thanksgiving's carcass, human-size, what skin there was left a brittle oven-brown, the flesh hollowed from the feast, a few stringy sinews left clinging to the bone. Gutted and carved, plucked and picked, it was served to me with hands, feet, and face left on the plate, a refuse of inedibles and hide. If it had had a soul, that was gone now. What was left was just everything we can know about what we are.

"Her name's Minnie. Isn't she cute?" So I was wrong and they were savages. It didn't matter. I'd seen the instrument opened; I'd seen the hamstrings inside. And, though it's true of revelations—that they never seem to reveal as much in daylight as they do in darker hours—this one's stood me well because I maintain that I was right: in the face of our own trash, there was still a moment of wonder, and anything that came after was only the blush and gather of clothes.

I gave Minnie a last look and backed from the table. "I think I've seen what you wanted to show me."

"You've seen the works." One of the blackfaces winked. "The way out's the way you came in."

I walked down three flights of stone stairs into a cold I never felt all the way to the Solomons, who flashed their hall light as they answered the door, blinking and babbling, wrapping kimonos around their bare calves (so people slept naked at their age), demanding what was wrong, where was Ben, what had happened.

Nothing, I assured them; I just needed a bed. I was, yawning, so-o-o sleepy, too tired to talk, I could even sleep on the floor if they had, please, an extra pillow. It was, by the way, a beautiful night out. The stars were as crisp as new Christmas gifts, and . . .

"Where's your coat?" Ruth demanded.

"Ben called." Martin looked down, at my sweater, my skewed skirt, my had-been stockings. "What did he do?"

I yawned. "Nothing. He kissed me."

"I'll have a word with him," Martin promised, wagging his head at the damage.

"For a kiss?" Ruth shoved me into the dark living room, where the embers in the fireplace had not yet cooled to ash. "I'll have a word with Jane."

But I wouldn't talk, and in the end she had to give up, going upstairs to get me a pillow, grumbling that for once the beds were full, imagine, five kids at home, oh mercy upon her, she didn't know how long she could take it, the mess, the noise, that rock-and-roll music, and anyway I needn't sleep on the floor, the wicker settee was really a daybed, but I'd better be ready to hop in the A.M. because when those kids came down, no one could sleep through them.

I said I was ready to hop whenever they were, I thanked them. I bade them good night, I yawned. And thought, so what if life is nothing but a symphony of hamstrings? There has to be a muse to make the music go. In the grate the coals undulated like a gaudy coral reef seen through a wavy sea. So it all came together, water and fire, and as for earth and air . . . I peeled clothes with one last, drowsy thought of Kelly.

In a world where all the elements could marry, our meeting still seemed possible. I fell asleep as soon as I touched the pillow. I dreamed the sweetest dreams of the cunt and the spirit. And, while those are not exactly the same, there are times when they seem to be.

12

On May 11, "for conduct unbecoming a female student at this university," I was expelled. More than three months had passed since the five Solomon sons lined up on the porch to wave me off as I set out for the dorm, as light as a balloon bobbing toward the bright blue horizon and whatever miracles might meet me beyond.

I had forgotten my crime during the merry chaos of breakfast, when, through the window, which laid a gold trapezoid on the table, I thought I saw my future shining before me like a road. Hammond was two hundred flat miles to the north. I was in love and in school, and those were the only places I had ever wanted to be. Remembering the scrape of silverware and ticking silence of breakfasts at home, I smiled when, before disappearing into the sports section, Martin announced, "We try to make breakfast here a quiet affair. The children are instructed to keep their noise to a dull roar." Michael beat a spoon on his high chair while Martin cursed whoever had smeared jelly on the basketball results. When he poured coffee on his cornflakes, Jake and David winked at each other and David gave me a nudge. I giggled. The toaster bucked.

"Martin," Ruth said. Plaid flannel bosom brushing her

plate, she leaned across the table to read Mary Worth. "Did you hear me? I said when are we going to get that blamed toaster fixed?"

Jake hunched around the crossword puzzle. "What's a five-letter word for the sound of dawn? Goddamnit, move your mitts," he said to David. "You're getting gook all over it."

"Crack. And nineteen down is tart. Why didn't you tell me you were moving in?" David whispered to me. "You could've shared my room."

Ruth finished the comics and brushed toast crumbs from her tits. "Who has Ann Landers?"

"I've got the front page if anyone wants it." Martin looked up.

"What about a kennel sound?"

"Arf-arf," I suggested.

"Bow-wow," Josh shrieked. "Bow-wow-wow-wow-wow."

"What I want," Ruth said, "is to know what Jane was doing here at three A.M. with her clothes on cockeyed and dirt smeared on her face."

David whistled. "Who were *you* with?"

"Wolf," I offered. "R-r-ruff, gr-r-ruff."

"Ben Gabriel," Ruth said. "Did he attack you or didn't he?"

David's mouth dropped. "That dirty old man?"

"Meow."

"I'm sorry." David looked unhappy. "You *like* him?"

"I wasn't *with* him, and he didn't attack me. Why does everybody always have to inquire into my private life?"

"Morning. Hey, Pop, who won?" Sam stood in baggy pajama bottoms, scratching white lines across his belly.

"We got company," David said. "Tuck your dong in, jerk-off."

Martin rattled the paper. "The Hoosiers lost in overtime, but the Van Arsdales got forty-seven points."

Ruth poured herself another cup of coffee. "David, don't inquire into Jane's private life. If she wants to explain how she managed to turn up at three A.M. with her clothes on cockeyed, she will. If she doesn't, we'll all just sit here and pretend that we don't want to know." Without a glance at Sam, she added, "Don't you ever get dressed?"

"Hey, Jane." Sam took a slurp from Josh's glass and straddled a chair. "Who's private life are we discussing?"

"Well?" Ruth glared at me.

"Do you like him?" David whispered. " Squeak, I'll never bother you again if you just tell me that you do."

Never bother me again?

"I don't like him," I admitted. "Not like that, anyway."

"Samuel Solomon, get your own milk," Ruth ordered. "Oh, shit, Michael, you've got cereal in your hair." She glared around the table. "Jacob, I want you to finish that puzzle and give me Ann Landers *now*. David, will you please quit trying to look up Jane's skirt?"

"I wasn't." David gave me a naughty grin. "But I will if you want me to."

"And all of you shut up."

"Son-of-a-bitch," Martin said into the ripple of Debussy that terminated the kennel of sound, and I realized that the Gieseking Preludes had been playing quietly in the living room all along. "One of the children has poured coffee in my cereal."

As we laughed, I thought again of my mother. Why hadn't we ever worked crosswords at breakfast together? She read Ann Landers, but not because she thought it was funny, and the occasional poem-to-live-by she clipped to send me advised that life was not a laughing matter. It was from my mother that I learned life must have purpose to have meaning, but her purposes were all so humorless ("to live my life with dignity, Janie") or banal ("to replace those faded drapes as soon as Goldblatt's has a sale"), conceived, I suppose, with passion but rarely brought to term, that I wondered if she had any sense of life at all. The bare branches of an overgrown forsythia outside the window threw a web of shadow across my arm, and I stroked it. "I love it here," I said, and Ruth's eyes crossed with irony.

* * *

When I reached my room, Sid's mood was serious. "Blackmon wants to see you," she said. My legs, which had grown heavy as cement just around the first corner, where the university had rushed toward me, buckled.

I sat on my bed. "You mean?"

She nodded. "Damnit, Hurdle, why did you do it?" I shrugged and stared at the rug. "Well. Did you get pinned?" I shook my head. "I knew it." She sat on her own bed. "I told you Kelly was a turd. When are you going to learn?"

"Did he call?"

"No."

"Are you sure?"

She rolled her eyes. "Hurdle," she said as I rummaged through the heap of clothes on our chair, "what are you doing?"

I waved the campus phone book.

She shook her head. "If Kelly wanted to talk to you, he'd call."

"Well, maybe he had an accident. Anyway, I want to talk to him."

She shook her head again. "No, you don't. It's a game, dope. If you want to win, use your noggin."

"Is that what you did with Riggs?" I was furious with the old suspicion that the world was a conspiracy of secrets. Name a tune from the top forty; everyone else had heard it. Pick a dance; they all put their feet down right. Where did they learn? Who taught them? Why was I never informed?

"That's different. We're in love."

"Yeah, well maybe we're in love too." Pouting, I dumped a drawer to find a clean pair of underpants to wear to my interview with Blackmon, though I don't know why I expected my snow-white dainties to impress her. "Are your panties fresh?" my mother had asked every time I left the house. In case of an accident she wanted the undertaker to know I'd been raised right. No wonder I always expect the worst.

"*You're* in love, you mean. Besides, Riggs and I are practically parents, and what my father is going to have to say about that . . ." She shuddered.

I pressed my clean pants to my eyes. "He said he loves me."

"Oh Jesus. I wish he did. Come on," she added after a minute, "quit crying. Blackmon's waiting. I told her you were spending the night with a friend in Smithwood or Towers and must have forgot to sign out."

"Oh wow." I dropped the panties. "Sid, you're a genius. I stayed at the Solomons'."

"Unh-uh. It's against rules to spend the night off-campus within a fifty-mile radius of Bloomington. Can't you call a friend in the dorms?"

"I don't have any." I changed my clothes and combed my hair. "But, look, I didn't know, and if I forgot to sign out, I couldn't find out. They'll slap my hands and tell me never to do it again."

Sid shook her head. "Don't forget your pink slip. Blackmon's got it in for you."

"Oh, piss on her. So they'll give me a social." I pirouetted in front of the mirror. "Well, wish me luck. If Kelly calls . . ."

"He won't. And try not to look so damn cheerful in front of Blackmon."

I didn't by the time I reached the lobby, where a loop of girls in wool suits and high heels was unwinding down the stairs toward Sunday dinner. My future had lost its luster. So I couldn't be young and in love forever—for the nonce I would have settled to be sure I would stay in school, to be in line in my navy blue jumper with nothing more to worry about than the menu and the dress code.

Blackmon's face was granite. "You're to appear before the center judicial board in my office this Thursday at seven P.M."

"I'm really sorry," I said, stalling as I scanned her parlor for a sympathetic object—a stray roller, a half-eaten cookie, a dogeared copy of *The Group*. But it was an extremely anonymous little room, furnished in the somber colors of the forties, a framed print of a Turner landscape hanging from a molding hook above the brown sofa. Not even an illegal pat of masking tape. Her open briefcase rested against a table leg. The book on her desk had the gray hardcover of an education textbook. "I don't know why I forgot to sign out."

She stepped forward, as though the quota of space between us would propel me to the door, but I skirted her. "See, I had dinner with my friends—they live on University—and their car was broken and they didn't want me to walk back alone—you know, after dark. Anyway, I'm sorry I caused so much confusion." My laugh was porous.

"The judicial board will hear your case on Thursday night." She angled behind me, and I was dismissed, without punishment or forgiveness, just as I would be by the center J-board, who referred me to the higher authority of the Inter-Residence Halls Association, who in turn sent me on to the Dean of Student Life, who was out of town when the Dean of the Music School presented my petition and so his secretary misplaced it. And, even so, I might have stayed in school if I hadn't violated the terms of my probation and grown so tired of eating humble pie with my excuse, which was a half-truth about staying with the Solomons, that I told the whole truth about sneaking out to meet Kelly and breaking into the cadaver lab, adding a few opinions on women's hours, dormitory counselors, and the sort of person who would sit on a student court. On the last subject, I became quite articulate, though not, I confess, very original, and the Dean of Student Life seemed to be most moved by my choice of words. He was a rather awesome figure, and I paid tribute to his power by terminating what he called "our little talk" with a suggestion that the entire university could fit up his ass.

What else can I say? Except that I have to hand it to Blackmon, who did not, as I suspected, badmouth me up the pyramid of powers. (Nor, of course, did she come forward on my behalf.) She was, in the end, an excellent judge of character, smart enough to presume that, given enough rope, I, who am no judge of character at all, would manage to put it to the proverbial use.

But I wasn't handing anything to Blackmon that day, as I stood outside her white cross and Bible door, thinking that her dismissing me had been a most un-Christian act, for, although I've never had a speck of religion and told my husband more than once, as he set the alarm to accompany his children to church, that in my opinion Christians were all cannibals (after all, it's flesh and blood every Sunday), I will say this much for the faith: it doesn't leave you rattling the deadbolts of Limbo, which, I considered, was exactly what Blackmon had done to me.

I sometimes wonder what might have happened if I'd married Kelly—oh, it wouldn't have worked, I know. But even though he was passed-out drunk that Saturday night, didn't call me till Tuesday, and then could not remember demanding I sneak out, I could have, you see, and that's good enough cause to reflect. Why do I think of this now? Because it's easier than conjugating the verbs whose futures have slipped into past.

I imagine us raising our passel of noisy little Catholics (because, of course, I would have had to convert). They would have inherited the best of both of us, belief and body and bravado, none of our weaknesses, none of my doubts. Corny, isn't it, but never mind that. We would have sent them to confession. (Did my brother go to confession? Was he filled with faith and saved? I never asked.) Let a priest see to what I could not: aim again and again up the gold road to heaven, which ran out for me like a dead end.

"Do you go to confession?" I once asked Kelly—after we'd gotten together again since he'd left me forever in March. It was the evening after the Little 500 bicycle race, and, with four other Phi Delts and their dates, we had hiked from the cars along an overgrown railroad track to spend Saturday night of the world's greatest college weekend (that's what it's called, and I had no idea that it was going to be my last college weekend) roasting steaks on the cliffs above an abandoned, spring-filled quarry. My appeal had been ignored for so long that I'd begun to think I could finish college without its ever having been decided, and that was fine with me, as long as I got to finish. We found a narrow ledge below the others to make love, and then Kelly grasped an old tire hanging from a tree at the edge and swung out, pounding his chest and screaming like Tarzan as he dropped fifty feet and splashed. My heart stalled. Above me, his buddy Morgan thrust his head into the late light. "That son-of-a-bitch is crazy. If you don't watch it, Squirt, you'll be a widow before you're wed." I retreated from the edge. Heights left me dizzy—fear of falling compounded by the delirious desire to jump.

A few minutes later Kelly was dripping beside me, swearing that if I just weren't so scared, he could teach me to swim. Now he was putting on his pants as he asked, "Want a beer?"

"Sure. How come you always avoid the subject of religion?"

He climbed to the cooler, and when he came down, his Saint Christopher's clinked against my can. He had a Dixie cup of Hawaiian Punch for himself, having suspended drinking until after the Olympics next fall. "How come you always bring it up?"

"I don't," I said, "do I? Anyhow, do you confess?"

"I'm a Catholic." He brought his bare right foot above his knee and bent to inspect it. "You don't have a Band-Aid, do you? I cut my heel on some broken glass."

"I didn't bring my purse. Is it bleeding?"

"Nah, it's okay." He settled against the rocks and made a hollow with his arm, where I nestled and sipped at my beer. It was early May, but already the evening air was buzzing. It had a damp, indistinct smell, the fresh loam scent of March not yet replaced by the honeyed weight of summer. "Oh man, can I taste that suds. First thing I do when I win the gold medal. I'm not even going to wait for the national anthem."

"Have some of mine," I said, tracing my finger along two names painted on the rock. "Surely one beer couldn't hurt." He shook his head. "Do you confess what we do?"

He shifted, and I clutched his arm. "Take it easy," he said. "It's only water down there. How do you like your steak? Morgan's getting ready to build the fire."

"Rare. I'm just asking."

"Hey, Morganit! My lady wants hers rare."

"I bet she does." There was a burst of laughter above us. "McCullehey, you decent? Get your bods up here; there's a party going on.

"Otherwise we might think you're antisocial." It was the sticky voice of Morgan's girlfriend, which always reminded me of pink sugar icing squeezed from a tube to make rosettes. A platinum-haired Pi Phi, she had a knack for speaking just to Kelly while addressing both of us. In high school she had been Marianne's best friend, and in the weeks since March, when Kelly had briefly gone back to Marianne—who had finally let him have her cherry because, I presumed, she knew that he'd had mine—Patti's voice hardened with hatred whenever she spoke to me.

"All right, Morgan, all right. I see your fat face every day. You can expect us when those steaks start to sizzle." Kelly smacked his lips as the heads disappeared.

"Do you?" I insisted "You know, confess what we do?"

He sighed. "You accusing me of kiss and tell?"

"Of course not " I studied his profile, though I must have known every bump, every pore. The sun had faded his hair to the color of caramels, but the dusk was turning it dark again. "I was just thinking, that's all. If you confess it, you must think it's a sin."

His shoulder stiffened. "Look, if we're going to fight again, let's just go up right now."

"But why would you think it's a sin?"

"Because it's a mortal sin." He sat up. "Get your clothes on."

"I'm not fighting."

"Get your clothes on anyway. Morgan and that bitch of his are liable to come charging down here any minute."

I wriggled into my cut-offs. "Anyway, all sins are mortal. You know, the price of being."

"Very funny."

"Well, what other kind are there?" In the failing light I buttoned my blouse wrong.

"Venial, dimwit. You do a little time in Purg. I thought you told me your brother was Catholic.

"He is." I nudged him with my shoulder, and he relaxed against the rock wall. "But we don't ever talk about that. We don't ever talk about anything, if you want to know the

187

truth.'' He shrugged, and I moved with him, looking frantically at the edge again. "I know. You think families should be close. Well, mine isn't. It's my fault. I'm a cold person. I'd like to be different, but I don't know how.''

"You're not a cold person." He turned his head to gaze over the abyss to where trees spread against a slate and pink sky, the colors of a '57 Ford gone to heaven. I shivered. "Cold?" I shook my head. "You don't think anything's a sin, do you?"

" Sure I do." I rubbed my finger against the painted names again. "Being mean's a sin. I want to know where it stands."

"It's not even on the roster." He smiled. "Anyway, you're not mean. Mortal sins are the ones you burn in Hell for."

"Hmm." I gave him a playful pinch. "You'd think we'd be venial. It sounds dirtier, you know?" I slapped at my ankle. "Hey. First mosquito of the season. I bet it's really vile out here on summer nights." He didn't comment. "Do you really think you'll go to Hell? I'm serious."

"So am I. But you only go to Hell if you're not absolved."

I wriggled closer. "Boy, you better not go diving off any more cliffs."

"I wish you'd quit making jokes about my religion." His face was beautiful, the way it held the last dull light, or maybe it was faith that made it so solemn, that could chisel flesh as fine as marble, no quiver in the curves. Mine, I knew, was not like that, always twitching, impatient to turn each moment into next.

"I'm not. It's just that it doesn't make sense to ask forgiveness for something you're going to do again."

"I promise not to."

"Ha," I said. "Then you're the one who's making jokes."

"But I mean it when I promise."

And I meant not to be so nasty. I would have liked to have his faith. "Oh, well. No wonder we're so fucked up."

"You've got a foul mouth, you know that? I don't like that in a woman." He turned his head back, and his voice was sad. "You're everything I never wanted."

Mine was just as sad. "Except in the hay." He didn't

smile. "I love you," I said, surprised by the sound of the words in my mouth. I had never told him, had never told anyone, and now, when it seemed so natural to say so to Kelly, I was sorry I'd never told my brother too. I had been too embarrassed, I supposed, imagining Dick and Marie as they smacked lips before bed, repeating like robots, "I you, me too, cheep-cheep, sweet sleep, night-night, sleep tight, tomorrow I'll tell you again." Now it seemed possible that the message had fallen with as much grace between them as it had between us.

"I love you too," Kelly said, but instead of kissing me, he lit the one cigarette he allowed himself each day while in training and wrapped me in a white veil of smoke. We sat, watching the ember travel toward his hand as warily as if, when it got there it would burn us both for our risk of verbs.

He put it out. "Do you want to get married?"

I was so used to living in Limbo that I spilled my beer and busied myself mopping my legs with his shirt. "You mean when we finish school?" I asked finally.

"No, I mean now."

"Now," I repeated, as though, if I heard everything twice, the sense would sink in.

"Why not?"

I picked at the soft fringe of my cut-offs.

"McCullehey!"

"Oh shit." He leaned forward to look up the wall.

"Man, does it take you all night to come?" Cork Canada was clambering down the rocks to crouch beside us.

"Later, Cork," Kelly said. "I'm trying to talk to my girl."

"Hey, man." Cork was drunk. He'd spilled bourbon on me at the race and come back from the victory pool with the wet T-shirt of an enraged Alpha Phi. I was surprised to see him still conscious. "Didn't your daddy ever talk to you? You gotta gun your rod to get her going."

Kelly frowned. "I don't like that kind of talk in front of Jane, you know?"

"Okay, okay, man, don't get touchy." Barely balanced,

Cork tried to back off while still squatting, upsetting Kelly's Dixie cup and sitting in Hawaiian Punch. He felt his haunches and sniffed his finger. "Drinking Kool-Aid these days, McCullehey?"

"Never mind," I whispered, trying not to giggle at Cork as Kelly's muscles tensed.

"You're turning into a faggot, man. What's the matter? Won't she give you any?"

"Kelly, don't be dumb." The words arced too late, and for a moment I was agog with the grace of his spring, then aghast with its extravagance. I closed my eyes, babbling caution and panic, barely relieved when I opened them again and saw that the tussle was really more menace than contact. The accidents that befell drunks at the quarries were legendary. Kelly had dragged Cork to his feet and was leaning into his face, punching out words. "Man, I don't stand for anyone insulting my girl."

"I don't mind," I said, but they weren't listening, and anyway it seemed to me that Kelly was the wounded and I the superfluous party. Cork had ruined everything. I pulled at Kelly's arm. "But where would we live? What would we live on?"

"Take it easy, man. Shit." Cork detached himself and collapsed. When he glanced to the side, he almost fell. "Jesus H. Christ!" He inched inward, looking sad. "Goddamn Suzy's gone up to the car to sulk on account of I embarrassed her at the race. Shit. It's Five Hundred weekend, man, time to bust loose and tip a few brews, have a blast and let's get it on with our girls. Shit. We got the rest of our life to be sober."

Kelly helped him up.

"Maybe you could go talk to Suzy." Cork looped an unsteady arm around Kelly's shoulder. "The bitch won't listen to me. Oh, shit, man, look." He stopped to rub his bottom, and for a minute I thought he might cry. "I got Kool-Aid on my pants."

"Ah, it's dark. Who cares? I'll be back," Kelly promised, disappearing up the cliff with Cork and leaving me in a fury of frustration at this baffling fraternity of man-man-man.

But Kelly was back before I expected, carrying two steaks on a limp paper plate. "Here." He handed me a beer and a clump of paper napkins. "Those assholes forgot the forks. Well, come on. You'd better eat while it's hot."

"I'm not hungry."

"Damnit, it's not my fault Cork blew the moment." Swallowing, he wiped juice from his chin. "Look, I'm sorry. Eat your dinner and we'll talk."

"You eat it."

"I don't want it." He put the meat down and touched a greasy hand to my sleeve. "Honey, I'm sorry. If I'd planned this, I'd have given you a dozen roses and a bottle of champagne. I will, I promise, on Monday morning. I don't have enough cash to get you a ring." He waited for a minute, perhaps hoping I would say that my objections were all to the method and not the madness. "We can get you one later—as big as you want."

"I don't need a ring." He'd given me his pin early in April, and I wore it as confidently as I might have carried a charge card in my wallet. But now he'd caught me short like a creditor, demanding the balance when I had only an installment.

I loved him, and if it seems odd now that I didn't tell him so when he had clasped his shield on my breast, it was only because I had felt so official that passion seemed almost irrelevant. I wanted to pay. I was willing to plight my troth, but I couldn't deliver.

"I can't quit school," I said.

"For a year. If I go to summer session next year I'll be finished."

"What about law school?"

"Maybe I won't go. Shit, I've been in the pool six hours a day this whole semester. I may not even have the grades to get in."

"But you'd have to leave the house. I don't know how to cook. We don't have any money. You don't care about music."

He held my face between his hands. "What I care about, dummy, is you."

"I care about you too."

The future, which had always seemed so liquid, now rose like a continent from the gorge of space between us. Its shape was Walnut Grove, the university-owned trailer court. They looked so hot and tiny, those tin shacks, more confining than my brother's slab house, where the buggy was parked before the sofa as if it might do double duty as a coffee table. "But why do we have to get married?"

"Because I'm going to Tokyo in October, and I want to be in a good frame of mind. I can't concentrate. Every week it's the same damn story—run to the priest and swear off you, then back to the house and pace around, and before you know it I'm right back inside your pretty puss."

"You don't have to swear off me." I poked at the rock. "It just seems so stupid.

"Is that what bothers you?" He kissed me, his mouth tasting like steak. "I don't care if you're not Catholic."

"But why can't we just be pinned?"

"Because I want to be married."

"Well, so do I. Just not yet." I thought of how many times I'd seen his face close with anger and now it was too dark to see if hurt might open it. "I can't quit school." I heard echoes of other conversations: I can't understand, I can't believe, I can't sneak out. I can't cut practice. I can't, I can't, and yet I always did. The rhythm was the same; only the subject changed, or maybe it hadn't. Perhaps we had always pitter-patted around one thing:

I can't marry you.

Even though I love you enough to think I'll die.

I felt sick to my stomach. I wasn't going to marry him ever.

"Why not?"

"Because." I bent my knuckles back.

"Because why?"

I kept fiddling with my fingers. "Because nobody in my whole family ever did anything but get married. I want to do something else."

"You mean better?" His voice was as flat as my mother's. They made it seem less impossible than not worthwhile.

I bit my lip. "It's not like you think—not because I want to be better than they are, or maybe I do. I don't know. It's just that when my father died—well, he died, that's all, and he never did anything, and nobody remembers him. At least I don't." I looked away.

He held me. "Everybody dies, sweetheart."

"That's okay for you to say—you're going to Heaven. You don't even have to be good to get in."

He picked up his shirt to wipe my face. "Well, if we get married, I'll get a family plan. Here. Eat your dinner."

I shook my head. "I can't quit school."

He set the shirt aside and sighed, saying what—I had to give him credit—he'd hoped I wouldn't make him say. We'd been through it. It was his fault, I said. He was sorry, he said, and he quit drinking, and there was nothing else to be said. "Jane, they are *kicking* you out."

"I *want* to get married," I said. "I never thought I did, but now I do, and I want to marry you, and I love you, and we can have a family and everything, but I have to finish school first." And after that, I knew, it would be grad school and then my career.

He sat up. "You don't want to quit because you're a cunt—you'd rather make it in the back seat than in your own bedroom."

"That's not true. And anyway they can't kick me out. Martin won't let them."

A tiny muscle gave an angry twitch beside his mouth. "Look, I asked you to marry me. If you don't want to, that's fine."

"But I do. I do, I do, I do." It was the same old burst of useless grief and rage. I have never been big enough to hold my emotions, and it has nothing to do with being short.

"Lower your voice, would you?"

"I do," I whispered, and he reached for my hand. "I just don't see why we can't wait, that's all."

His hand brushed my leg as it fell, and I shivered. "Sure. If that's the way you want it. I'm going up and check on Cork—the poor fucker passed out on top."

"Wait." I scrambled after him, clutching at his belt. "Kelly, I love you, I do, I really do, I . . ."

His face was so cold, his lips barely moved. "Well, baby, that's your tough luck."

I take it back, Sid. He wasn't a bastard, only another poor fucker, and when you get right down to it, aren't we all? We don't choose whom we fall in love with. We don't choose how we deal with the pain. (In that sense, it was an accident.) We don't choose to be grown up or just kids when it happens, and I suppose we were, as Ben Gabriel dismissed us, mere pups in puppy heat. Well, life is long, and love is short. We get over it and don't choose even that, any more than we choose how to wear the scars. My father died when I was nine years old. I loved him. I loved my brother, I loved my mother. I didn't choose not to tell them so. And I wish that I could say this now to my mother: we don't choose and don't choose and don't choose, and yet, if we beg excuses, what we live is only an atrophy of life. I want to understand her static sorrow so that I can choose not to make it mine. I do not consent to be a victim. I do not consent to die. I *chose* not to marry Kelly.

(But it was an accident, it was an accident. I do not, I did not, the bag of bones that is left after that old failure of passion does not assent . . .) I looked up and saw his silhouette move into the gray haze of smoke that hovered where there had been fire. Someone had started singing, and I threw myself off the cliff.

13

*B*ut I was a June bride after all, for in my despair, I became so confused that I dove off the wrong side. Pain screamed along my nerves like bad brakes, and I came to a stop in a tangle of brush and barbed wire. I had tumbled ten feet to a lower cliff, and I must have put my arm out. It slammed into my face like a wall.

Morgan drove me back to town. Kelly didn't come, and I saw him only twice again, once on television the next fall (I cried when the barest fraction of a second turned his gold hopes bronze) and two years later on Indiana Avenue, in front of the Law School, across from a hamburger joint where we'd once been so silly we'd sipped one Coke with two straws. He was pushing a stroller, and I don't know why, but it was his daughter's white bonnet that broke my heart. We nodded as we passed and said hi.

So it was Morgan who held my hand at the infirmary, where we waited for a doctor to stitch my chin and set my broken arm. It was Morgan who kissed me goodbye at the Solomons'.

I'd missed my curfew while we waited, and I was afraid to go in late to the dorm. It was just as well. Painted in iodine from head to toe, patched together with adhesive and gauze, I didn't much feel like talking to Sid, who was marrying Riggs the day after her last final exam and passing her engagement clipping recipes. I didn't really want to talk to Ruth either, but I had nowhere else to go.

I had spent more time with the Solomons that spring, afternoons when Kelly was in the pool and I couldn't get a practice room, evenings when I accompanied them to recitals and Kelly studied, picking me up afterward, and stopping in for a while. They liked him, and that made me proud, though I feigned nonchalance. "What a body," Ruth said once as we sipped gin and tonics on her front porch and watched him pass a football to David. "I bet he's a real tiger in bed."

"I wouldn't know," I said primly, and she laughed.

"What's so funny, ladies?" he asked when David left, but Joshua appeared, and he spent the rest of the afternoon teaching the baby to throw. "You ought to marry that boy," Ruth said, and I touched a finger to his pin. I wasn't really surprised that she liked him, but I hadn't expected him to fit in so easily. Which just goes to show how dumb I can be, for there was nothing that impressed Kelly more than a family— all those brothers and sisters of his own and he was so proud of the dullest details about every one that I sometimes wondered how anyone could make such an artless production of love. Although, in a way, I suppose I envied him.

"Are you going to be okay?" Morgan asked as he walked me up Ruth's front steps. He pressed the bell. " Hey, everybody has fights, you know?"

"It doesn't work," I said, my chin straining to split open again.

He knocked. "Do you want me to talk to him?"

I shook my head.

There was a flurry of noise in the hall. "Well, take it easy, Squirt." He brushed my cheek with his lips. "Just don't go jumping off any more cliffs." He had the grace to pretend he was teasing—in the dark I had supposedly slipped on a beer can—and I would have been grateful if I hadn't been so wretched.

"Gone," I announced tragically when Ruth opened the

door and said, "You look nice tonight. Where's Kelly?" She didn't press it. I stayed at the Solomons' until Tuesday, but only David could get me to talk.

"What happened?" he asked as we sat at a picnic table behind the Dairy Queen, where he'd bought me a banana split to cheer me up, although I insisted I didn't want anything.

"I fell in love," I admitted.

"You must have fallen pretty hard. It ought to be against the law to be that handsome and that talented. Was he rich?"

I wiped at my eyes. "No."

"Well, there you go. He was a nice guy, but he didn't have everything. Hey, I'm sorry." He touched my shoulder. "Could you get back together?" I shook my head. "You want me to beat him up?"

I sobbed a laugh. "No."

"I probably would have got the worst of it, anyway." He watched me dribble tears and syrup down my sling. "Yeah, I fell in love too. It's a real bitch, isn't it? She's got a couple of kids. Boy, I've only even known her three weeks." He shook his head slowly. "How many banana splits do you think you can eat?"

I started to say "I'm not really hungry," but he was trying so hard that I was touched. "A lot." So we complained until we laughed and ate ice cream until we got sick.

On Tuesday I was officially expelled. "But what about my petition?" I demanded. "You can't just—I'm second clarinet in the Philharmonic—we've got a concert—they're counting on me."

The Dean of Student Life sighed. "Mrs. Inge," he said through the doorway. "Have we received a petition for Jane Hurdle?"

I sat back while we waited. "Well, it's nice weather we've been having," I said when the silence grew thin. The secretary put the paper on his desk. I leaned forward.

"Thank you," he said and scanned it. After a minute he made a notation and set it aside. "Denied. I'll have Mrs. Inge notify your parents."

"Mother," I said in a fatigued and far-off voice. "My father's dead."

He didn't look up. "Your legal guardian. Whoever is listed on your matriculation form."

"But what about the concert? Who's going to play my part?" I looked down at my broken arm, realizing for the first time that I couldn't play anyway, and something burst inside my chest. "You can take your fucking school and stuff it up your ass."

"Anything else, Miss Hurdle?"

"Yeah," I said, trying not to let my voice tremble as I waited to see what it was. I gazed out the window behind him, where the green umbrellas of Bryan Woods departed like a bunch of concertgoers in the rain. "You can kiss my rose-pink cunt before I'll cry in front of you."

He opened a drawer and placed a box of Kleenex on his desk.

"You didn't," Sid said. "You told the dean that?"

I nodded as another tear licked at my nose. I was lying on my bed. She had just come in from the sundeck, and the aroma of coconut oil made me feel as purposeless as I had been the day after school let out each summer, lying in the sand at Marquette Park while the rest of the Hammond High band sported in the Lake Michigan surf.

"Have you told Kelly?" I shook my head. "I didn't think so. Jim Morgan called me, you know."

"Oh? What did he want?"

"He wanted to know if you were all right." She stepped out of her bathing suit bottom, leaving a red crease where the elastic had cut into the bowl her belly made. She had already shed her top, and her nipples stuck out like the necks of two rubber funnels. As her body changed, she made a point not to hide it, and I couldn't help noticing how her areolas had darkened and spread as her waist thickened. I would have forgiven her a sudden modesty, though I understood why she didn't claim it—it was no longer her body. She rubbed her neck with a towel. "You know, I haven't even mentioned how you go out on a Saturday night and don't come back until Tuesday. I wouldn't do that to you. The least you could have done was call."

"I was at Ruth's."

"Yeah, well I guess I had to figure you were somewhere. Did it ever occur to you that I might be worried? Did it ever occur to you this whole bloody spring that I was concerned?"

I touched my good hand to the cool, gritty plaster. "What for? I was happy . . . most of the time."

"That's just it." She wrapped herself in a bathrobe. "I *worry* about you unless you're depressed."

"In that case, boy, have I got good news for you." She sat on the edge of my bed, and I sat up. "Would you mind moving? You smell like the whole goddamn state of Hawaii."

"What have you got against Hawaii?"

"Nothing. I'm sure it's a wonderful place to go when you graduate. Maybe you and Riggs can go there on your *honeymoon*."

She stood. "In case you've forgotten, I *have* to get married."

"Yeah. I don't have to do anything."

"Does your arm hurt?"

"Not too bad," I said. "Not as bad as my heart."

"Well, I'm going to take a shower. I feel like a greased pig. Do you know I gained six pounds last month?" I didn't answer. "Hurdle, I'm sorry it happened, but it's not the end of the world. Don't you have any idea what you'll do?"

My mother had used the very same words over spring vacation when she inquired precisely what career I was being prepared for. "I'm going to be a musician," I'd said, impatient because I had been lying on my bed then too, listening to the last movement of Brahms's Fourth Symphony bom-ba in my head. It seemed urgent to keep my heart filled with bombast because Kelly had ditched me and not yet come back.

"Can you live off of that?"

"I don't know," I'd answered. "What do you care? Anyway, I'm going to go to grad school when I get out."

"Oh, I see. How long does that take?"

"As long as I want it to." One bar was repeating like a scratched record. Why didn't my mother go away so that I could send the symphony on?

"Well." She seemed doubtful. "I suppose your scholarship pays for that."

"Nope. You don't have to panic. I'll get a T.A."

"A T.A.?"

"Teaching assistantship," I said.

"Oh." She seemed relieved as she sat on the edge of my bed and picked at the chenille. "So you are thinking about teaching. You know, I was just thinking how nice it would be if you could teach at Wilson or, well, wherever the schools had an opening. This is a big house, and . . ."

"It's a little tiny house," I said.

"It's a big house just for one person, and there must be a lot of schools in Hammond that have bands. We could work out whatever you thought was fair for room and board."

"Are you kidding? I'm not directing any grade school band." I sat up, appalled to realize that not only did my mother think I should major in music ed like the dummies; she had given up on my social prospects and was already planning our shared spinsterhood.

"High school, then. I don't know what you want."

"Well, I don't want to direct a dinkshit kiddie band." I sighed and lay back down. "What I want is to get out of this place and not come back." She winced. "Mama, I just don't want to live in Hammond. It's so ugly."

She rose slowly, as if she had to collect the parts of her body. "Well, it was good enough for me. I just thought you might want to work where you got your start. After all, that band at Wilson meant a lot to you."

"It doesn't anymore. Mama, don't you see? I'm better than that. I'm *good*."

"Of course I do. You and Dick both did well at everything you tried.

"And when I give my senior recital, I want you to come down and hear it." It was useless. When the time came—*if*, and my stomach lurched, the time came—I might miss every note, and she'd think I'd done just fine.

"This boy who's coming to see you tomorrow . . ." I jumped because I thought she had gone. "Do his parents live around here?"

"He's not a boy, I told you."

"Well, Dick is off tomorrow. Marie said you could invite him for dinner if you want."

"I don't want. It's not a date, I told you. He's my theory professor at school, and he's practically an old man, and he was going up to Chicago anyway to hear the Symphony, so he said I could come along."

"Well, that's nice," she said, as if I hadn't told her the same thing already twice before.

And I had to tell it again that evening for Marie as we sat in the living room. Dick was working second shift, and she had come over with Dickie and the twins, who also did well at everything they tried. They could wave their arms and shit, guzzle milk and sleep sitting up.

"What does that say?" Marie asked, squinting through her new glasses at the crest on Kelly's Phi Delt sweatshirt, which trailed threads from its cut-off arms. "It's Greek," I said. "It belongs to my roommate." I had not told them about Kelly because once you start talking, you never know how much they'll make you tell. "You have so many pretty things," my mother said. "Why would you want to borrow something like that?" Dickie was sitting two feet from the TV, watching "Rawhide," while Marie ironed a knee patch on a faded pair of pants. My mother looked up from the button she was sewing on a blouse that I had torn one night in Kelly's Plymouth when it wouldn't come undone fast enough. "Tomorrow, as long as you're here, Janie, you ought to go ahead and call up Grant's."

"What for?" I looked up from my book.

"To make sure you can have your summer job back. Ouch." She squeezed a drop of blood from a finger.

"I don't want to work there."

"Well, you know, sometimes you have to take what you can get, jobs don't grow on trees."

"I'm going to get a job in Central City, where they have the opera house." I knew a girl in my music lit class who had all the information on applying, but I'd put off writing because I hadn't been able to make up my mind to leave Kelly, who would stay in Bloomington all summer to train at Royer

Pool. Now, I told myself, I would. First thing when I got back to school next week.

Marie folded Dickie's pants and flattened one of Dick's twill work shirts on the board. "Oh, that's nice. You'll get to play your clarinet."

"Well, I'm not going to be in the company. I'm just going to wait tables in one of the restaurants."

My mother's fingers worked the thread in a hood of lamplight. They seemed to have gathered folds around the knuckles since I'd last been home. "Where?"

"Colorado."

Marie set the iron down. "What would you want to go all the way out there to sling hash for? You can do that right here at home."

I closed Sid's copy of *The Great Gatsby*, which I had been trying to read between remarks, in disgust. My mother said it was rude to read in front of company, although doing the daily chores or watching TV seemed to be just fine. "What's the matter with you people? Don't you understand anything?" I looked at the television so that I wouldn't have to look at Marie.

"Well, excuse *us*," my mother said, and I reopened my book.

"Hurdle, you haven't even moved," Sid said, and I woke from March and Hammond to May and the drip of my roommate's just-washed hair. All spring, with the threat of this moment fogging the future, I'd had trouble with my sense of time, dozing from one world into another until I had lost nearly all sense of which was now. Only my affair with Kelly had kept me going forward, but now—and now was now and it was over—I slipped into a stupor in which the past and present interchanged themselves and the future had no place. "Don't you think you ought to call your mother?"

"Huh?"

"Call your mother and tell her." She was toweling off her hair. She had just come back from the shower, or was it the sundeck? Or maybe I had slept for twenty years and this wasn't even Sid. "You act like you're dead. Hurdle, I'm

202

worried about you.'' She began to roll her hair. ''Have you thought at all about what you're going to do?''

''Umhm.'' I nodded. ''I think . . .'' Slowly I slid my legs over the side of my bed. ''I think I'm going to take a shower.''

Afterward, I went to the Music Building to get my clarinet, though I didn't know what I meant to do with it. Instrument case in my good hand, I leaned my cheek against the cold locker door until it began to feel warm. The bandage on my chin was a soggy gray ball, and my stitches itched. I walked from the dim corridor of the old Music Building into the fluorescent circle of the Annex, feeling as if I were listing to one side as I slogged my way around it. The perforations in the acoustic paneling seemed to separate in rows that could be counted, but the circle turned back on itself, and I had no idea where I had started. Three men in suits came around the bend and went into the lounge. Change clinked in the coin return as I read a cartoon taped on a door. The coffee machine revved and splashed out the dull hum of conversation.

''. . . Copland, but surely you'd agree that *Gebrauchmusik* cannot . . .''

''. . . say what you will about Cage, his work has imagination.''

I stepped up my pace as the voices grew louder.

''Well, it may be innovative to clamp the piano strings with clothespins, but I certainly prefer to hear a Bach Invention.''

''Jane. Jane Hurdle.''

I turned around. One of the men was Ben Gabriel, the last person I wanted to see, one more reminder of the botch I had made of everything.

''Good heavens,'' he said. ''What happened?''

''I had an accident.'' I scuffed at the red tile floor with a rubber flip-flop.

''I should say you must have. Is that arm broken?''

I nodded, then lifted my chin to show the wet bandage, feeling the tape curl along my jaw. ''Stitches.''

''Were you driving?'' one of the men asked, while the other—it was Ghent, the bearded cellist—gave me a look that said "Kids!" and tapped Ben's arm. "Will you be at the committee meeting tomorrow? We need to vote on the proposal."

"No, I wasn't in a car," I said, thinking for a moment that they were planning to propose that I be reinstated.

"Four o'clock?" Ben eyed me. "We're planning a course in contemporary composers. If it goes through, you'll have to take it. Have you met Stan Leggett and Peter Ghent? Jane Hurdle."

I nodded at them, but Ghent was already out of sight around the circle.

"Jane's one of our star undergraduates."

Stan Leggett smiled. "I bet it only hurts when you laugh."

"Would you like a cup of coffee?" Ben asked, his hand tinkling in his pocket.

"No thanks."

Leggett looked at his watch. "Well, my son has Little League tonight. It was nice meeting you, Jane. Howard Feltner raves about you."

Ben took my clarinet. "Where's your locker?" He accompanied me to the second floor of the old building. "I'd open it, but I don't know your secret code." He looked me up and down. "You certainly have banged yourself up. I knew something must have happened when you weren't in class today."

"I'm not coming back to class," I said.

"Why not? You're not seriously injured?"

I shook my head. He was fiddling with my combination. "I just got it out," I said.

He gave the case an odd look. "Well, you're not going to practice now. One-handed?" Now that we were alone, he seemed disconcerted. I couldn't blame him. I hadn't treated him very nicely. "Have you had dinner?"

I shook my head again. "I'll get some when I go back to the dorm."

"Why don't you get some with me? If there's anything a lonely bachelor hates, it's a chicken pot pie for one. Come on." He touched my sling. "You aren't in pain, are you? I want to hear about this accident."

One of my feet had slipped off the side of my rubber

sandal, and the floor felt cold against my heel. I opened my locker. Ben shoved the clarinet in and slammed it. Backed against the bank of lockers, I raised my eyes from the floor to his face, watching the blue cord cuffs of his trousers, the little bulge of shirt above his buckle, and the diagonal stripes of his blue and yellow tie travel past until I stopped at his eyes. "It wasn't an accident."

He opened his mouth but didn't speak. The glaze of teeth between his lips looked like a stripe of icing. His features seemed to separate in the batter of his flesh, but it was only one of those illusions you have when you stare too hard at anything—like rolling a familiar word on your tongue until the syllables come apart and the only sense left is sound. He was staring, too.

"I've been expelled."

"Oh, my poor little girl," he whispered, and I felt myself folded into the crisp arms of a man's summer suit.

14

*I*t was not our first date, not the first time we'd sat in the bar of the Fireside, pleating the checked tablecloth between our fingers and watching the candle flicker behind its mesh sleeve. He had been very sweet to me, and, no matter how badly I treated him, I was glad to know that he was still my friend, even touched when I returned from the ladies' room, where I'd fled the instant we arrived, and saw a daiquiri in front of my chair. He would not make a fuss about having ordered it, though I was certain that he remembered the night we sat with the Solomons on the other side of the same room, having drinks after the opera. They had martinis; I showed my I.D., and the waiter brought me Coke.

The girl in the ladies' room mirror was a mess, in wrinkled yellow Bermuda shorts and a stained sling, a map of scratches on her legs and other arm. Peeling the wattle of wet gauze from my chin, I nearly cried when I saw the seam. My mother always matched her thread to the fabric. Why did they have to use black to sew up my face?

"That cut looks pretty nasty," he said as I sat down again.

"It itches."

"Don't scratch it."

"I wasn't."

He fiddled with his napkin, dipping his face so his threadbare scalp showed. His skin was baby-smooth across his cheeks, but a gray crust of soap extended the length of a razor nick from the place where his right sideburn was just starting to curl. There were creases of fatigue underneath his eyes. He had celebrated his fortieth birthday that spring.

Holding his martini aloft, he suggested a toast.

"To what?" I asked as his glass clinked against mine.

"To you." He smiled. "Your future is undoubtedly brighter than you think."

"I don't think I have one," I said, for what had been my future until today now seemed only a slight variation on our immediate past, tacked on like a coda, after which all I could see was THE END. We'd been through this.

Early in March he had asked me to go for coffee after class. We hadn't spoken since his phone call, but I knew what this was about. The Friday before, I had been suspended, and Dr. Gabriel was about to tell me I was no longer welcome in his class, which I had continued to attend on the theory that, if I refused to acknowledge it, it wouldn't be true.

We crossed the street to the Chatterbox, the dismal hangout for the Music School. Its cinder-block walls and wooden booths were painted beige, its hamburgers cooked gray. But it was cheap, and it was close, crowded, as always at 10:00 A.M. Cigarette smoke lay over the room like a plague. "I've received a notice that you've withdrawn from school."

"That's a polite way to put it. Hi." I nodded as three members of the Phil passed our booth. "Hey, Margie."

"Does it have anything to do with your father?"

I waved to a boy from music lit. "My father's been dead for nine years. They're kicking me out."

"But you're my best student." He drained his cup.

"It's not academic." I wiped coffee from the corner of my mouth, turning my head to look for someone else to greet so that he wouldn't see how much it mattered. "Disciplinary." When I looked back, his face wore a question mark. "I got caught staying out all night."

"What are you going to do?" he said, and I burst into tears.

Keeping a discreet silence, he was impersonal enough not to pass me a handkerchief, and when I at last snuffled to a stop, his tone was no different from before. "Does Martin Solomon know about this?"

"I didn't tell him." He was being so nice, I felt guilty. "About that night—when I was caught? I was staying at the Solomons'. I mean . . ." I looked down.

"I understand."

"It just happens to be against rules." I looked up. "I wasn't staying with my boyfriend."

It was his turn to look down. "You didn't have to tell me that."

It was the polite thing to say, and only after we were married did I realize he'd said it because he believed it was true.

So he told Martin, and Martin told the Dean of Music, who offered to draft an appeal, and before my mother could be notified, I was readmitted on probation. I was grateful, and neither Dr. Gabriel nor I had a nine-thirty class.

Well, I liked to go for coffee, and I always had with one or more members of the Phil, who joined us on occasion, and Dr. Gabriel never seemed to mind. It wasn't like that night on the steps of my dorm. A star student with a friendly teacher, I felt as if we were all posing for a picture in next year's college catalogue.

He was careful. He didn't praise me unduly, didn't ask me out. After a week I thought I must have been mistaken. His interest in me really was professional. "But how do you *know* that Sessions is a minor composer? Look what happened to Telemann and Bach." The grad student with the thick glasses turned his palm up for emphasis as one of the Singing Hoosiers bumped our table and Dr. Gabriel's gaze lingered on her. "Hi, Dr. Gabriel, Kurt—Jane. Didn't I see you at the She-Delt dance on Friday? That guy you were with is some *hunk*." I nodded at her, fingering Kelly's ΦΔΘ on my notebook while Dr. Gabriel explained to Kurt why Roger Sessions was not now nor would ever be in Johann Sebastian's class. This was exactly what I had always hoped college would be like.

So we talked about music, but not just that, and isn't it funny how I can remember those morning conversations so clearly yet cannot recall what we ever filled fourteen years of evenings with? (Practice, concerts, records, but what was it that we *said?*) I remember, too, how he always arranged to sit facing the door so that he could watch the girls as they came in; I noticed but didn't mind, because he was my teacher and you can forgive a great teacher nearly anything except yourself. He wanted to know about my other classes; he wanted to know about my life. His was sad. His wife had divorced him recently with no reason. He missed his children, whom he saw twice a week. His daughter Bridget was sixteen. He produced their pictures from his wallet, and I showed him a snapshot of the twins my mother had sent. I had one of Kelly, too, but I didn't show him that. What I did in the back seat was my business. We were friends, not confidants.

So I was never able to ask him if it was just coincidence when he invited me to hear Zino Francescatti, the violinist, the morning after Kelly and I broke up. On Saturday we accompanied the Solomons to the opera, and for the week until I rode the bus to Hammond for spring break, he took me to dinner every night. I was not to worry about my probation, he insisted, and each time I gave the same glum nod. I wasn't thinking about my probation. It was Kelly who kept those evenings grim, Kelly and Dr. Gabriel's good-night kiss. If it hadn't been for that peck (which is all I see of passion when I try to remember rhapsodic moments now, the trees beginning to feather just beyond his left shoulder as his mouth slowly swims toward mine), I might have at least enjoyed the steaks, filling up my body while my spirit drained. Dating was something kids did; so was love and so was lust. Dr. Gabriel was old enough to be my father. Never mind that my own father had been old enough to be my mama's daddy; she had never been young enough for that to matter, and, oh, it mattered terribly to me as I shivered on the front steps and waited for those limp lips to brush mine. There was something dirty about it, and when I saw his mouth move with words in class (''You hear any little noodling in that piece? No! She wrote it as a chorale. Play that again, Jane''), I bit my lip as if to bleed it clean.

Perhaps that's why our dates seemed strained. Looking back, I see that I've mixed metaphors: he's a bird, he's a fish—he's never human; that's the thing. He was a teacher, and I couldn't see him as anything else until he melted his eyes on my shoulders in the Van Ormand Suburban Inn the chilly night of our honeymoon (beyond the drip of the air conditioner, Bloomington was stinking; in our apartment the roaches were hatching and scheming) and I faced his raised red weapon, astonished that I had married a man.

And so I presented him as my teacher when he came to Dick's house for dinner over spring break. My mother invited him when he called to say what time he'd pick me up for the Symphony. I asked her not to do it, but it wasn't as bad as I'd expected. It was worse.

My brother lived on a block of asbestos-shingled houses built on concrete slabs, and, though he had improved his with aluminum siding, he couldn't make it taller—like the others, it crouched too close to the ground, as if the dirty sky had weighed it down. In my mother's neighborhood the house trim was kept painted, the sidewalks edged. It was like a room full of small but neatly wrapped boxes. Window frames rotting, storm doors hanging loose, tricycles and balls littering the yards, my brother's neighborhood looked more like the paper rubble with the presents gone. The living room was too small for the three-piece sectional sofa, and the rug was mined with toys. Instead of smelling like dinner, the house reeked of baby, that distinctive combination of sour milk and weak pee.

I didn't know if I was ashamed of my family for looking shabby or Ben for looking overdressed. Beside my brother, whose stomach was still tight as a drumhead beneath his twill shirt, Ben seemed pudgy. He would impress them, I told myself. After all, he too worked with his hands, but later, when I saw them on the table, next to my brother's scuffed and stained knuckles, next to that dead-end stump, his fingers were a sick, magnolia-white. He was wearing a gray herringbone suit, a white shirt, a Princeton tie. Once we were in the city, I knew he'd look fine. I looked sweet, Marie said. I was wearing my Sunday jumper and a pair of cultured-pearl earrings that pinched my earlobes. I felt like a kid in dress-ups, and Ben looked much too old. He was only nine years younger than my mother, who had called him "this boy" until the moment he arrived, after which she called him "Mr. Gabriel." To her, the only doctors were M.D.'s, and his eyebrows lifted when I introduced him as one, although I had called him "Doctor" myself until he told me firmly that his name was Ben, and after that I hadn't called him anything.

Marie appeared in a sheen of kitchen sweat and wiped her hands on her apron when he rose to present her with a bottle of wine. Since the birth of the twins, she had put on weight, and, as if it were part of the family conspiracy, my mother too had begun to broaden. She had had her hair cut short, against the curl, that morning, and it hugged her head like a rubber bathing cap.

"Reba did a good job, didn't she?" Marie asked me, indicating my mother's haircut and leaving Ben standing while she fussed at Dick about the twins. "Watch her neck," she said. Dick was jiggling Dawn while my mother gave a bottle to Baby Marie.

"She's okay."

"She's not going to be okay if you keep snapping her neck around like that," my mother said.

"Hey, Mister." Dickie shoved his face in Ben's stomach. "Do you play the guitar?"

"Dr. Gabriel is a pianist," I said.

Dickie's face wrinkled. "What does that mean?"

"He plays the piano," Marie said. "Like my grandpa. He could play polkas and everything, you name it. Oops." She dashed for the kitchen as the timer began dinging, and Ben was finally able to sit down.

He tapped my knee. "Hi," he whispered.

Dick cleared his throat. "Sissy says you teach theory, Mr. Gabriel. What kind of theories do you have?"

"Well, I play the guitar," Dickie announced and picked out a shaky "Red River Valley" on his plastic mandolin.

"Isn't that something?" my mother asked. "Seven years old."

Ben agreed that it was something, and Dick said, "Play 'Oh, Susannah,' Dickie."

"I can't."

"Sure you can." My brother seized the instruction book, holding it in one hand while he continued to jiggle Dawn.

"Dick, her *neck*," my mother said.

"Actually it's a study of the principles of music. Theory," Ben added as everyone looked blank. Whenever my family asked you a question, by the time you had a chance to answer, they'd forgotten what they asked.

"Well, that's nice." My mother smiled. "We appreciate you taking Janie into Chicago, Mr. Gabriel. She doesn't get out much."

I excused myself to the bathroom as Dick said, "No, yellow string, Dickie, yellow—like the sun," and Ben said, "I don't know why. She's a lovely girl."

I rested my head on the edge of the sink. "Yellow," I said to the stopper. "Yellow, like baby shit." And, sure enough, as I returned when I heard Marie sing out, "Okay, everybody— time to chow down," my mother was holding Baby Marie up by the feet, displaying her smeared bottom while Ben slipped a diaper beneath her and the air thickened with the stink until my stomach met it in my throat.

I groaned.

"She's never liked to be around young people," my mother was saying. "I don't know what's wrong. She's always done well in school."

We ate in the kitchen, squeezed around the Formica table. Ben's back was against the oven door, and we bumped elbows when we passed Marie's Tupperware. Dickie was mushing his meat loaf into his peas on the other side of the plastic floral arrangement. I couldn't bear it after facing Ben off over the Solomons' silver candlesticks. No one offered him a drink, and only when we finished our fruit cocktail did Marie remember Ben's wine. He had to pry the cork out with a paring knife, and she served him in a jelly glass with the Flintstones circling the side. Neither my mother nor Marie drank, though they had no objection to Dick's occasional beer.

"I'll have some," I said.

"It's okay," my mother agreed, and I was so thoroughly humiliated that I thought Dick meant me when he said to Ben, "You're real good with children."

"I have three myself," Ben replied.

Marie began clearing the table. "Well, I guess they're the light of your life then. I know ours . . ."

"Dickie, don't talk with your mouth full," I said when he asked if he could have some ice cream.

"Why? My daddy does."

My mother's face had turned pink. "Mr. Gabriel, I hope you didn't think your wife wasn't welcome . . ."

"Your daddy doesn't know everything," I said. Ben was stirring sugar into his coffee. "Dr. Gabriel's divorced. I'd like another glass of wine, please." At the end of the table my brother looked down. Although he took it black, he was stirring his coffee too.

"Janie, I think you've had enough."

"I've had one."

"I said I think you've had enough."

"Oh brother." Now my brother was sipping his coffee, lips pursed, eyes focused somewhere around the knob of the back door. "I've had one glass, and you think I'm drunk."

Ben tapped my wrist. "The concert starts at eight."

Marie gave him a grateful look and jumped up as a baby screamed.

"I'm ready," I said. "I don't want any ice cream."

Dick looked up. I had never noticed how the weight of his jaw had begun to draw his mouth down. "It's chocolate."

"Let's go!" I said.

Marie joined us at the door with Dawn. "Well, it was awful nice to meet you, Mr. Gabriel."

"It was a pleasure meeting you." Ben's smile panned the room to include all of them. "That was a delicious meal."

"What kind of car do you drive?" Marie squinted through the storm door at Ben's Volkswagen. No doubt she asked because she thought Dick had forgotten to, but he came only as far as the doorway between the kitchen and living room, his coffee cup in hand, and I knew that he wished we would go, just as I knew that if she should later remark on how quiet he had been, it would be with the same innocence. In my way I knew him better than she ever would, for when his answer came, she would be surprised. "But that's silly," she would say. "He puts his pants on just like you." He would wait a long time to speak, and then he would repeat, "I never met a professor before." I didn't know who embarrassed me more: Dick for being cowed, or her for not.

"Oh," she said. "One of those foreign ones. It's cute."

Dickie pushed between. "My daddy says foreign cars are nothing but tin and safety pins."

Marie smiled an apology. "My husband works at Inland. You can't get much closer to Detroit."

Or maybe Ben. Dick was my brother, and I was ashamed to be ashamed. "Foreign cars are better," I was surprised to hear myself say. "You think everything has to be from here to be good, but I'd like to know where you've ever been. Dr. Gabriel has been to Europe." Though the circle of faces had frozen, I wasn't finished. "You think you know everything, but none of you has ever been to college."

My mother's words snapped off like icicles. "And none of us has ever made their family ashamed."

"That's what you think," I said and flounced out the door, but I had to wait in the car for Ben, who shook hands with my brother and thanked Marie again.

"You see what I mean?" I raged when he finally joined me, but he didn't answer, and neither of us spoke until we reached the Skyway. The lights of South Chicago were an open jewel box below us, though in daylight those gems were just factories and slum.

He kept his eyes on the traffic. "Your family seems very nice to me."

"Oh, well, what do we want to go to the Symphony for? We could have just stayed and listened to Lawrence Welk with them." I looked out the window, but I was on the wrong side of the car to see, somewhere to the south and west, the Pullman Hotel, where my grandfather had lived when he worked for Pullman-Standard, years before he met my grandmother.

"I'd rather spend the evening with you."

They had built a whole town for the Pullman employees, and to me it was a fairyland, with its ginger-colored brick and white spun-sugar towers. But it had deteriorated, and Pullman had closed, and the city sprawled its ugly way around it, and it was now only a pink blot near the bottom of Chicago maps, a charming and ramshackle historical district. My grandparents died, and my father met my mother under the shadow of the El tracks in Merritt's Sixty-third Street Cafeteria, and he quit the Merchant Marine to work at Inland, and everything that was anything had been over and done with before I was born.

"Why didn't you tell your mother we were dating?"

I'd never even seen the Pullman district except through the window of the South Shore on the way to the Loop. To the east somewhere was the South Shore Hospital, where my mother had labored for thirty-six hours to bring me into the world. "Your eyes," she said, "were the most beautiful sky-blue, and when I saw you again, they had already turned gray." It figured. I couldn't remember Chicago, but I knew it from my mother's photograph album, and I never saw those old pictures without feeling that a cloud had since passed over the sun.

"Janie." He reached behind the gearshift to pat my knee. "I know how you feel."

"No, you don't." He didn't say another word until we were inside Orchestra Hall. We had come to hear Byron Janis play Rachmaninoff's Piano Concerto in C Minor. It was the first classical record I'd bought, but when I told Ben which performance I had, he said, "You're in for a treat then. It's meant to be a hammy piece, and Brailowsky hasn't got a pound of bacon in him."

"Did you ever play it?" I asked as we found our seats in the balcony. Onstage, the orchestra was squawking and tuning. Once Sidney told me, when she came to hear the Phil, that it seemed unprofessional to her, the way the instruments warmed up right out where everyone could hear them, and I'd explained that a violin tuned in a back room might be flat in the auditorium, but I really didn't care about the wherefores. To me, the sudden hush when the conductor appeared was the most magical moment in the ritual.

"Not well. Rachmaninoff was a big man—like Brahms—and he wrote music he could play. You need quite a pair of hands for his concertos."

He squeezed my elbow. "Did you know that Rachmaninoff very nearly didn't write it? He was so depressed that his doctor had to tell him every day, 'You will begin to write your concerto . . . You will work with great facility . . . You *will* write your concerto.' "

"I know." We stood to let two men pass by us.

"Well, I seem to be out with quite a knowledgeable young lady, don't I?"

He often said this, and I could never tell if he was teasing. I giggled. "It says so on my album cover."

The lights dimmed, and the maestro took the stage. It was Jean Martinon. "Watch him," Ben whispered. "He's much more flamboyant than Reiner." I had seen Fritz Reiner twice. He had hardly moved his hands, but he could do more with his eyebrows than most conductors can with a baton. He could make the brass come in with a flash of his belt buckle; he could give the quarternote beat with a wink of his eye.

But Martinon cajoled the orchestra with his fingertips. And Janis. He was powerful, he was sensitive, he was every romantic cliché you've ever heard, and I mean them, because when he leaped from the piano and bolted offstage, my toes were still tingling and uncertain as to whether they'd touched the cool cumulus of Heaven or the dark, hot lava of Hell.

The hall tilted when I stood, and Ben grabbed my arm again. I wasn't sure if it was the height that made me giddy or the gasp I let out.

"Well." We both exhaled again and gave each other a starry look of congratulation, as if we had performed brilliantly just by being there. When our feet were firmly in the lobby, he spoke. "I don't want to keep you out late, but would you like to go up to Rush Street for a drink? Surely"—he smiled—"we should celebrate."

"I don't have to be home."

"I think you do," he said as we strolled up and down the splendor of Michigan Avenue, past the crowned and lighted bays of Alitalia, the Chicago branch of Saks Fifth Avenue, the plate-glass views to the sleek interiors of the travel agencies, and a window full of custom-made shirts silky enough to have made Daisy Buchanan cry. Across the street, stone lions slumbered on the steps of the Art Institute; ahead of us, the Wrigley Building raised its ghostly peak against the satin sky. All Chicago seemed to be a chandelier, there to illuminate the ballroom of my imagination, which was a dazzle of rouge and jewels and tasseled dancing cards.

"Well, I won't go."

He smiled. "One drink," he promised. "Come on—Ravel was right. This wind's enough to blow your kisser off." Wisps of my hair were stinging my eyes. We got the car from the underground garage and headed up the Outer Drive. The black lake fell away to our right; to our left the glitter sharpened now that my cold tears had dried. It was not the shortest route, but I had requested it, and it seemed as if I had only to ask for all the dark world to come light.

"Have you ever been to a discotheque?"

I shook my head, so he paid the cover, and we went down a flight of stairs to the Pussycat-a-Go-Go, where we sat at a table hardly bigger than my lap and watched the twisting throng on the aurora of the dance floor. The waitress wore a black satin cat suit with fishnet stockings, and her breasts fairly rolled across our table as she deposited our drinks. Ben looked more interested than embarrassed; I was the one who felt stiff here. Away from Bloomington, from the dark rows of Orchestra Hall, from the pageant of the Magnificent Mile, he was no longer a teacher, not even a friend. Sitting so close that our knees touched under the table, he was my date, and I wondered what I was doing in a discotheque with an old man, until the faces rocked into focus and I realized that, in my prim white blouse and jumper, I was the one out of time. It wasn't a crowd of schoolgirls and boys. When I think now about having skipped my generation—about how just a few years later the middle-aged women I worked with muttered through the office window at a parade of students with anti-war placards while I sat at my desk and tried to keep my feet still (they wanted to march, against wars or for football teams; my fingers wanted to play John Philip Sousa)—I see the Pussycat. It was not my baccalaureate or the human be-in that I missed. It was the beginning of the ultimate revolution, more successful than any of the ROTC bombings, more successful than civil rights. Look around, if you don't believe me. Mine was the first generation to be victorious in its refusal to act its age. But, by that time, the Pussycat had closed, having failed to attract any adolescents beyond the balding businessmen who thought they could twist their tummies away, and I had married a man whose *daughter* marched up Michigan Avenue with Abbie Hoffman and Jerry Rubin to protest maturity in 1968. I didn't care about politics any more than she did, but I resented my absence all the same.

"Would you like to dance?" Ben was in an ecstasy after hearing Janis. He couldn't wait until next week, when we would get to compare him to Sviatoslav Richter.

"I can't."

He was already standing behind my chair. "Oh, come on—you sound like a lazy student, and, besides, you can't tell me you have no sense of rhythm."

We bumped our way to the dance floor. He was right, of course. Kelly had already whirled me around the basement of the Phi Delt house. It was fun. All you did was find the beat and wiggle your body. Not to stiffen in his embrace when the tempo slowed was harder. He seemed to want me to tuck my head against his jacket, which was scratchy and smelled of mothballs.

We made a dizzy circle and jostled another couple. The light show made me feel like an artificial Christmas tree. "Why didn't you tell your mother we'd been dating?"

"Oh, that old subject."

"Is it because you're my student or because I'm divorced or"—he hesitated—"because you think she wouldn't approve of the difference in our ages? I wouldn't want her to think I was taking advantage of you."

"What do you care? She's not going to yell at you."

As the number ended, he dipped and released me. "I have my reasons." The waitress had taken our glasses, and another couple had taken our seats. "It's just as well. I ought to be getting you home."

"She doesn't care what I do."

He steered me to the stairs. "I prefer not to get in Dutch with your mother."

Outside, a small dark girl in a circle skirt that matched her red lipstick pursued us past the Café Bellini and around the corner where couples were lined up to see the Limelighters at Mister Kelly's. "Señor, señor," she called, making a ballet of her hand and her skirt and a paper poppy. "Only twenty-five cents for the beautiful señorita to be happy."

Ben gave her a dollar. "Here," he said, "a souvenir."

I folded the flower into my purse. "Boy, are you a sucker. You can get these things for ten cents from the veterans."

He shook his head and looked over his shoulder as the girl danced down the block, crying, "Señor, señor, only one dollar for the beautiful"—she scarcely paused—"señor to be happy."

"Why don't you want my mother to be mad at you?" I asked when we were back on the Outer Drive, with the lake and city reversed, as if a day had passed and the sun had switched sides of the sky.

"It's my secret. Why do you think I go out with you?"

I took a minute to consider. "I don't know."

"Why do you go out with me?"

"Oh, well . . ." I said quickly, then stopped, because I'd been about to blurt that, having broken up with my boyfriend, the apple of my eye and the darling of my heart plus a few other organs, I had nothing better to do. "Well, we go nice places. And we know about the same things, except you know more. And you're nice to me." I listed my reasons slowly as I thought of them. "And you tell me I'm pretty, and"—it was too late; I couldn't think of anything except what I had started to say—"you're there."

He didn't comment, and the car was too dark for me to read his face. So maybe he wasn't disappointed, and anyway,

I told myself, he wouldn't have wanted me to lie. After all, it was understood that we were just friends. Wasn't it? It was a mutually convenient arrangement. I had a distraction from my depression, and he had his peepshow as my dorm sisters and their dates spooned goodbyes. So. But there was something about him—something nice and dull and repressed and naïve—that made me feel as if I were the one who was forty, and it made me feel guilty, and it made me feel mean.

"You never told me your family was Catholic," he said.

"Huh?" Then I realized that he was referring to the papal paraphernalia in Dick's living room—the angel who blessed a pair of children on the plastic switchplate, the medallion of Paul VI above the TV, where votives burned before a plastic Virgin Mary. "Oh, that's just my sister-in-law. My brother converted when they got married, but he didn't have to, and anyway they're both excommunicated until Dick's first wife dies. Do you think that's right?"

"Well : . ."

"They never did anything." I took a peek at him. "Do you believe in God?" He nodded. I shrugged. "Yeah."

"You don't?"

"I don't believe in anything." A muscle at the corner of his mouth flickered. "Oh, I would say that you believe in yourself."

"Huh," I said. "Well, anyway, I believe in music. Hey." We were coming out of the velvet darkness of Jackson Park, where the masts of the sailboats anchored in the lagoon were as pale and slender as the tapers on Ruth's polished table, into the neon scraggle of package stores and pawnshops on Stony Island. "Did I ever tell you I used to live in Chicago? Right near here—in Woodlawn—when I was a baby, and my mother used to take me to Jackson Park in my buggy. I don't really remember that—we moved to Hammond before I was two. Woodlawn was going colored—I mean Negro—and my dad got a job with Inland Steel so he could stay home. He was a wheelman in the Merchant Marine, but what I remember is when I was a kid and he used to drive us up to the Aquarium and the Planetarium and the Museum of Science and Industry, where they've got a submarine and a coal mine and Colleen

Moore's dollhouse and everything." I took a breath. Talking in the tiny space beneath the Volkswagen's dome made me feel almost intimate with him.

"I know. My kids dragged me through the coal mine so many times, I thought I was going to have to join the union."

Wax papers were blowing beneath us in the cave that the Skyway ramps made as they swept over Stony Island. It wasn't fair. He had never lived in Chicago.

"Anyway, when my dad drove into Jackson Park, I remember how it was like going into an enchanted forest, passing that last gas station and then everything was pale and cool and green, and when you saw the lake, it was just like diamonds, and when you looked the other way, above the trees, all the buildings—they were diamonds too. And if it was night and you went all the way up to the bandshell in Grant Park, you got to see Buckingham Fountain with the colored lights." I took another breath. "Do you ever remember stuff like that?" Meaning, I suppose, had he too stored memories that outlasted detail—like coming home to Hammond, your brother mad because he missed the baseball scores, and your mom and dad in the middle of a fight.

I don't think I had ever before asked him a personal question. Nor, I think, had I ever paid conscious tribute to the fact that the world had begun before 1945.

He cleared his throat. "Of course. Central Park is like that, and in a snowstorm there's no prettier place than the walk between the Plaza and the Metropolitan."

Which wasn't what I meant. "I thought you were from Pennsyl*vania*." I gave the state an unreasonable accent to distinguish it from New York, which was childish, but why would I remember my childhood if I didn't want to be *allowed?*

"But I went to Juilliard, don't forget."

"Well, you didn't graduate," I said, and, feeling sorry, added, "It's not the *same*." I sat up straight as we came down from the Skyway into the acrid air near Lever Brothers. "P.U." My mother didn't miss Chicago at all. "Oh, at one time . . ." she would say, and her eyes would travel there, but she would finish with a flip of her wrist that meant crime

221

and overcrowding and the way our old neighborhood had changed. "You can have it now." My brother didn't either, and Marie—if she'd ever been there, she had not found it worth the mentioning. Why was I, who could not even re-member when I'd lived there, the one who missed it most? "You know what I wish? I wish I was normal."

He had a funny smile. His tongue kept darting around in his mouth. "I think everyone wishes that."

"Huh," I said and guessed I *didn't* want to be normal, if it meant that what I wished was just the same old thing every-body else wished, too. It was just my luck that thinking you weren't normal meant you were. It made me mad at him, because he'd let me tell him that dull stuff about my dull life in dull Chicago, and my dull wishes, too. He was all those years older, and he'd been to Europe, and he'd been to New York, and he was a teacher, and I was a student, and he knew everything, when all I knew was that I wanted to be too young for him to think he could kiss me good night.

He was saying something about what he wished, but I didn't hear what it was because I was busy feeling bad. Then he looked at me, and the way he looked made me feel scared. He didn't think I was dumb or dull at all.

"I don't want to know what you wish," I said.

He was still looking when the light changed, and he had to slam the brakes. "Sorry. Are you okay?" I nodded. "Jane. What I was going to say . . ."

"I don't want you to."

"Why not?"

My voice squeaked into its upper register. "Because." The car had not moved. "Hey, you've got the green."

He shifted gears. "I don't think you understand."

"Yes, I do." I pressed my face against the window. "Oh!"

"What?"

"Nothing. Just a gas station. My brother worked there when he was still in school." For a minute I saw my brother, standing in the arch between his kitchen and living room, holding his coffee cup with his middle finger as he waited for us to go, and I bit my lip as I turned back to the window.

"Tell me what you understand."

There was nothing I understood. "But why?" I'd said to Kelly. "Have you ever considered that maybe I'm just a bastard?" was his reply. I blinked to keep from crying. "I had a boyfriend. But he broke up with me."

Ben sighed.

"Oh what do you know? You don't know anything about love."

"I don't?" Now his voice squeaked, and the way he was looking at me did make me feel dumb.

"No." I tossed my head. "How could you? You're an old man."

After a while he laughed, but his voice was tinny. "Well, life begins at forty. Isn't that what they say?"

He didn't kiss me good night. On Monday morning I drank five cups of coffee in the Chatterbox, but he never showed. It was just as well, I guessed. Because Kelly was waiting on the steps with his pin when I came in from spring vacation, and what I had to tell Ben was that my boyfriend had come back.

15

*B*ut I didn't say anything about my boyfriend now as I sat in the Fireside explaining, even though I knew he would infer that I'd tried to kill myself simply because I'd been expelled.

"How did you do it?" he asked, and I said, "Took a long walk on a short cliff," because it seemed that stupid.

He nodded at my sling. "I'm sure that hurts, but thank God your injuries weren't more serious. You could have been crippled for life."

"Yeah," I said.

"It's my fault."

"Huh?" The waiter brought us fresh drinks, and I dripped patterns on the tablecloth with my swizzle stick.

"I should have kept in closer contact."

I felt my face flush. "So I don't know what I'm going to do. I'm not going home, but I don't know where else I can go. I don't have any money, and I can't do anything, unless you want to count selling goldfish. I don't even have a high school diploma." I sighed. "This summer I was going to wait tables in Central City, but I never got around to applying, and now it's too late."

"It'll work out," he promised.

"I doubt it." I held my left hand over the glass mouth of the candle. "When you were a kid, did anybody ever dare you to pass your finger through the flame? There's this place—it's not even hot—but anyway I couldn't ever find it." A yellow heat seeped between my fingers, and I dropped my hand to the table, where he trapped it beneath his own. Like Marie, he had little dimples where he should have had knuckles.

"Just listen a minute." I listened. "You don't need a degree, unless you want to teach, which is not the only—and not even necessarily the best—occupation for a musician. And I'm sure that Feltner would be willing to keep you on as a private student. If you wanted to stay in Bloomington, that is."

"How am I going to live?"

"I'd like it if you stayed in Bloomington."

"I wanted to finish school," I said. "It was important to me."

He gave my hand a little squeeze and didn't release it when the waiter brought us another round. I wondered if the waiter thought he was comforting a distraught daughter. Ben caught the side of my face so that I had to look him in the eye. "I would be very distressed if you were to leave Bloomington."

"Well, you're in luck," I said. "Because I don't even have enough money to buy a bus ticket to Hammond."

"I can give you money." I shook my head. "All right, loan it to you, then."

"I don't even know where I'd want to go." The world seemed, suddenly, too small—all that great wide space, and there was no place for me. I lowered my eyes. "My boyfriend left me. He wanted to get married."

He kneaded my hand. The arm that connected me to it felt spaghetti-limp, and the stripes of his tie revolved like a barber pole. I suppose that he thought I was rehashing my leftover sorrows, that I should explain it wasn't the same grief preserved from spring vacation. But it was, and I was sorry I had left my feelings lying out, like a pot of rotten meat that daily grew more distasteful to dispose of. I should have given up then instead of prolonging a misery that was—finally—boring. "You know that I'm in love with you, don't you?" When I didn't answer, he tipped my face up, straining my stitches. "Do you mind?"

"It doesn't matter," I said and looked away.

"You *did* know?"

"I guess so." I inched my hand from under his and took a drink, examining the lip print I left on the glass. "I just wasn't thinking about it. Don't you see? I wasn't thinking about *you*."

"But now?"

I closed my eyes. "Now I don't think about anything."

After an appropriate interval he said, "Will you have a steak, then? They have an excellent filet mignon."

I drifted on in the dorm through the weekend, although Ruth and Martin assured me I was welcome to stay with them until I did whatever it was that I was going to do. They were furious about my expulsion. Martin had even gone to see the Dean of Student Life. Afterward, he slammed into the house, raging at Jake for not emptying the garbage, which was only half-full, and at Josh for no reason at all. At dinner he found a hair in his soup and sent the bowl skidding across the table. He slapped his spoon on his plate and stood. "Is it too much to ask? . . ." My mouth gaped, and Ruth pushed her own plate away. "I don't feel like eating either. No dice, huh?" Martin sat. "No dice. The son-of-a-bitch told me he didn't care if she was Maria Callas. That's how much he knows about music. He thinks Maria Callas plays the clarinet. I'm sorry, Jane."

There was an opening for a typist in the office of the Music School, but I couldn't type, and there was no use trying to learn until the sling came off my arm. I hadn't heard from my mother, and, though Sidney nagged me, I couldn't seem to make myself call. Otherwise Sid left me alone. She was cramming for chem and trying not to let me see her studying the china in *Modern Bride*. After a few days I mailed Kelly his pin. I couldn't think of anything to write in a farewell note except "I will always love you" or some such tripe, so in the end I simply dropped it in an envelope.

Ben did not ask me to keep coming to his class, which I missed. Every now and then, when I would think of something he had said and laugh, Sid would look up to smile and ask, "What's so funny?" And I would say, "Oh, I was just thinking about Ben—Dr. Gabriel—and one time in class when we were singing. He said, 'Don't pronounce the *r*'s before a pause. It goes back to Italian. How many Italian words end with consonants?' And we said, 'I don't know. I don't know any Italian words.' And he said, 'Sure you do: *tutti frutti.*' " And Sid would say, before she bent her head back to her book, "I think he really likes you, Hurdle." And then suddenly it wouldn't seem so funny. I slept late and read Sid's copy of *Madame Bovary*, which was very depressing. I took long walks around the campus, which was also depressing now that the woods were twittering, all lush and green. I let a girl down the hall pierce my ears, though I didn't particularly want to, and Sid had to buy me a pair of gold earrings to replace the black threads strung through my lobes. When I pulled my hair back to show him, Ben pronounced them *"très charmantes"* and presented me with a tiny pair of ivory roses. He was *très charmant* himself, very sweet, and I didn't know why, but that depressed me, too. For the first time, I thought I understood my mother. When my father died—well, now I knew. I wished that she'd call me.

Ben took me to the Philharmonic concert. Already I'd been replaced—by a grad student who couldn't play the Stravinsky half as well as I could. He had no feeling, which was all that I had left as I looked down and saw my fingers working the air. I could still hear the voice of the conductor: "Woodwinds, we need more color from you coming in at AA, especially the low parts. Brass, we need less from you. Trumpets, I tell you in rehearsal, and at the concert you're going to wipe it all out. Never give it one hundred percent." Fifteen years later I hear that concert in my head, as I stand at the edge of the Grand Canyon, gasping one last time at the way the earth seems to have cracked open to reveal an interior more astonishing than the crystal landscape of a magnificent geode, saying, again and again, "This is my last look" in a mnemonic effort so intense, it is futile, for what I want is not merely to remember but to carry the entire canyon away inside me, just as I always carry music. I should have been the second clarinet, and as the applause faded and the seats slapped up, I thought it was the saddest thing in the world that I would never be first. By the time I got backstage, the orchestra was snapping instruments into cases and exchanging addresses for the parties. "Hey, Jane," the oboist called. "Too bad about your arm. You want to ride with us to Myron's?" I shook my head.

And so I sat alone with Ben in a turquoise plastic booth at the Dandale, nodding as he remarked that the trumpets had been too loud throughout *Petrouchka*. "You couldn't hear the woodwinds." "I didn't want to hear them," I said. I had seen him every night, but he hadn't bothered me about himself again, and our conversations had resumed the dispassionate tone of our past mornings in the Chatterbox. That was fine with me, so I said quickly, when he said, "My poor dear," "Kozma warned them. He knew they were going to wipe it out." He creased the scallops on his napkin. "You wanted to play, didn't you?"

"Of course," I said, but I wasn't thinking about playing. I was thinking about the nightly moment to come, when we would stand on the Morrison steps to exchange our now extended goodnight kiss, the one acknowledgment of the words that had passed between us, when his mouth would open so wide that my lips scraped against his teeth and I was afraid I would be sucked into the hole inside. I was thinking how, the night before, when he embraced me, beneath our thin summer clothes the thickness of his cock had pressed such a hard suit into my groin that I jumped back and he blushed, but he hadn't mentioned it, and that—not the billy club of his affection—so he had one, so what, so did everybody—I hadn't thought so, but now I knew—so why did he have to pretend he didn't while he leered at the slobbering couples all around us? *That* was what repelled me now. I wished we'd just fuck and get it over with.

"What would you say if I told you I wished I were playing, too?"

And there it was: a wall of common interests between us.

I moved to the Solomons' to give him a toehold, allowing

him to help me with the boxes—I filled them with my books and clothes and put the frilliest pair of pettipants I owned on top of one, but when my lacy, deep-plunge bra floated off the surface of another, he found a piece of chewing gum stuck to his shoe, and, while he scraped his heel against the curb, I had to hurry my unmentionables clumsily up Ruth's front steps without him. That did it. For a week I had walked as a person with a bad head cold ghosts through a room, feverish, lethargic, faraway. My senses unclogged. He was a hundred years older than I was, but his equipment was intact. The man was normal. He just needed a little help to know it.

But I don't think I knew what kind until I talked to Sid, and maybe even then I didn't really understand. I faked it. Which sounds real tough. I wasn't tough. And so I shouldn't be facetious. What comes next was very sad.

It was Tuesday afternoon, and I was waiting for Sid in the Commons. She had called me from the Kappa house, and, as I stirred my Coke with my straw, I thought how glad I'd be to see her. I'd moved out two days ago, telling her that Blackmon's evil eye made me edgy, but in fact I'd been relieved to get away from her. She was *worried* about me, but she hadn't asked any questions, and that's what drove me bats. All that silent concern. Obviously, my condition was serious. It was up to me to act. So I moved my clothes from one closet to another, and it was with the confidence of a captain that I waited for her now.

"What a mess." It was raining, and she squeezed water from her braids before she sat. A dreary mist of daylight fogged the room. Against the wall a boy was studying. I'd lost track of time, and Sid had to remind me that exams began next week. "I'm going to flunk chem," she said. "There are no two ways about it." Which meant she'd gotten a B on one of her five hundred daily quizzes. "I *studied*."

"You don't have to tell me," I said.

"Oh, why do you always have to be so *clever?* Have you been outside? It's raining silver shit from an angel's asshole." She lit two cigarettes and passed one to me, her eyes darting around her head like dogs to windows.

I tamped the cigarette in the ashtray. "I don't smoke. What's the matter with you?"

"You will," she said. I blinked. "I don't want to tell you this."

"Then don't. You want to play the jukebox?"

"No."

"Oh, come on. 'She loves you, yeh, yeh, yeh.' " I went fishing in the pocket of my red jacket. It *was* mine. Kelly had *given* it to me. "I've got a quarter."

"Put it in your brain. I'm sure you'll find an empty slot somewhere. Did you know Jim Morgan called me?"

I rubbed the coins in my pocket between my fingers and sat, gazing off the length of the room. "Yeah. You told me."

"He called me again. Jesus Christ, Hurdle, how dumb do you think I am? I never asked. I thought if you wanted to tell me you would."

"It was an accident," I said, so furious that I reached for a cigarette, and she tossed me the pack. I banged my empty Coke glass. "It was an accident, I told you. I tripped on a beer can. And Kelly and I did not have a fight."

"I didn't say anything."

I sighed. "Anyway, I didn't tell Ruth either, so you don't have to be hurt."

"I'm not hurt." Now she sighed. "Oh, Hurdle."

A couple had put money in the jukebox, and we both started as the Beatles began singing "I Want to Hold Your Hand."

"He asked me to marry him."

She raised her head sharply. "I don't believe you."

"Well, he did, but I wanted to wait, and he got mad, and now I just want to—it doesn't matter when. Do you think, if I called him? . . ."

She shook her head. "Could I have a cigarette?"

"Oh, sure." I looked down. I'd been shredding the pack with my good hand.

She tried to laugh. "Well it was always a bad match anyway. You could do a lot better than him. By the way, how's Ben?"

"It was a *perfect* match. At least, it's the only match I want."

"Oh, shit." She leaned her head into her hand and stared at where the edge of the table dropped away to her lap. When she looked up, there was a film of tears on her eyes. "Hurdle, Kelly and Marianne got married this weekend."

I had nothing to say. I mean—I should have expected—it was obvious, wasn't it?

"Jim Morgan wanted me to tell you so you wouldn't be alone when you found out."

"He's a nice guy." My own tears had begun to crawl down my nose. "Maybe I should marry him."

Sid put her hand out. "I'm sorry."

I held my left hand above the table, turning it very slowly to examine it in detail. The little bags of skin at the knuckles seemed absurd, and it was more absurd to think so. It was absurd to be sitting in the student snack bar with a puddle of warm ice in the bottom of a glass, to know that if I held it underneath my chin, every tear that ran off would not raise its level an inch. But then life was absurd. There was no purpose at all, except to survive.

"You want to talk?" I shook my head. "You want to go to a movie or something? We could see *Tom Jones* again."

I shook my head and lifted my chin. "I got my stitches out, and next week the sling comes off."

She nodded. "Did you look for a job?" I shook my head again. "Well, then, I have an idea." She leaned into the table. "Why don't you come to Columbus with us? You could get a job there, or, hell, Ohio State has music—you could go to school and live with us, and we could all take care of the baby. It'd be fun." I shook my head. "Why not? Riggs wouldn't mind." Riggs didn't mind anything, and, though it made me like him more, in a way it made me like her less. Which is to say that I loved her, but people without problems make other people sick. "Well, damnit then, what are you going to do? You can't just walk around like a zombie and shake your head all your life." I smiled. "Are you going to be okay?" She touched my hand.

I nodded. "Maybe I'll marry Ben."

231

Her eyes widened. "Are you joking?"

"No," I said. I was, but it's a funny thing about marriage: once the idea has, in whatever terms, been spoken, nothing else can follow but the act. It was not then and is not now surprising that Kelly left the quarry already on his way to marry someone else.

Less than two weeks later Sid married Riggs. In a dress the color of the cornflowers in my nosegay, I preceded her up the aisle of Beck Chapel. Her parents had come up from Greensburg, and Riggs's uncle had flown in from Colorado. A few Kappas and Ben filled out the congregation. Perhaps I imagined it, but I thought the Kappas gave me nasty looks. I supposed they thought I had given Marianne a hard time, even though, as far as I was still concerned, it had been the other way around. We had met once, by accident, and Sid introduced us. I was wearing Kelly's pin, a golden shield above a breast that he had nibbled nearly all night long, and my blouse felt so thin it seemed transparent, as my bright victory tarnished and Marianne turned away. We had too much in common to be friends, though I had known her so well in that one moment we might have been twins. But the feeling wasn't strong enough to make me offer to trade places, and it had passed, for, as I moved my lips to say Sid's vows beneath my breath, dedicating them like a posthumous award to Kelly, I hated Marianne McCullehey every bit as much as she had hated me.

At the airport Sid hugged me. "What a year, huh?" she whispered and hugged me again. "Keep in touch, you hear? I don't want excuses, I want letters." She lowered her voice and glanced at Ben. "Let me know what happens."

Here it is. The Solomons had gone away for the weekend, leaving their cats in my care, and the house felt strangely neat and abandoned when Ben and I went back to feed them. It seemed strange, too, that it should be so quiet, for all night long, when I had been unable to sleep, it had sighed and groaned and mumbled and sung. While I rattled kibble in the kitchen, he knelt to choose a record. I filled the bowls and found two stemmed glasses and a bottle of sherry.

"What a wonderful idea." He was seated in Martin's

232

Morris recliner, his legs crossed like a woman's, a pennant of bluish-white skin between his black sock and cord pant leg. Boccherini was bobbing happily in the background. "Weddings make me feel baroque," he explained. "I thought Sidney and her new husband looked very happy. In spite of . . ."

"They are," I said, not adding that inside me their happiness turned malignant. He had been so interested in Sid, always steering conversations subtly toward her: Did I plan on rooming with her next year? Oh, she was getting married. Had she known her future husband long? Once, in exasperation, I snapped, "About five minutes before he knocked her up." "Oh, I didn't know," he lied and blushed. It made me all the more irritable to know that Sid was so happy she wouldn't mind. I tucked my legs beneath me and began to pick the cashews out of the nut bowl. "Want some?"

"No, thank you." From the mantel the bright streamers of Sid's bouquet hung like the tentacles of an iridescent jellyfish. "You look very pretty," he said, though he'd said it before.

"How about some Bach?" he asked when the Boccherini was finished. "I think Martin has the Landowska *Goldberg Variations*. If you haven't yet, you really should hear them on the harpsichord." He knelt again, pulling out several albums. "Hmm. You'd think Martin would have them in some kind of order."

"Nothing's in order around here."

"Ah, here we go." He removed the disc from its jacket and placed it on the turntable.

I drained my glass. The Variations were jangling in my ear. It wasn't Bach or Landowska or the set, but they seemed too loud, too fast, too tinny. I was very tired. "Could you turn it off, please? I didn't get much sleep last night."

"Excited about the wedding?" He switched off the hi-fi. "You know, of course, Bach wrote them to put an insomniac to sleep. His star student played them for the Count Kayserling all night."

"You're always telling me *things*," I said. "I'm tired."

"Have you been sleeping badly?" I nodded. "Why don't you lie on the couch and put your head on my lap?"

"I'm afraid of the dark," I admitted. "I wasn't sleeping so

hot anyway, and now, with Ruth and Martin gone, when I close my eyes I hear things."

"Have you tried sleeping with a light on?"

"If I have a light on, it reminds me I'm afraid." He tugged at my arm, and I allowed him to carry me to the settee. "I'll wrinkle my dress," I said.

"I would never hurt you."

I was too sleepy to think that it was precisely that which kept him from appealing to me. His lasciviousness was strictly academic. "You mean you want me to take it off?"

"I would never hurt you," he repeated.

I yawned and turned around.

He unzipped the back and helped me struggle out. When I woke, my face pressed to the warm pillow of fat cased in shirt, I was lying in the shadow of my home course in touch typing. He closed the book, and I sat up, sliding my slip back to my knees. The evening light had thickened to honey.

"Feel better?" The arm along the back of the settee touched my shoulder. A muscle in my neck had cramped, and I slowly swiveled it.

"Umhm," I said, surprised it was true. "You should have turned a light on if you wanted to read."

"I didn't want to disturb you. Would you like another glass of sherry?"

I nodded. The wine was the same amber color as the light, and as I sipped, I felt as if it were the light that filled me. "Do you know," I said, "except in class I've never heard you play?"

"Ah, but I've heard you play. I used to stand outside the door while you were having your lessons."

"That's not fair." I took a big gulp of wine because sometime during that year I had learned what all musicians find out sooner or later: both that I was good and that I was hopelessly horrible. It's the point that comes after you have known that you're good and just before you know that you will never be good enough. "Did I make mistakes?"

"Some. You have an amazing range of tone. Hey," he added as I felt myself wilt. "I make mistakes. Rubinstein makes mistakes. Sometimes after he's given a concert and the audience has given him a standing ovation, he says his daughter comes backstage and says, 'Oh, Daddy, what happened?' ''

"I wanted to be better than Rubinstein."

"So did I." He shrugged. "And when I knew that I wouldn't be, I left Juilliard and got my doctorate in musicology. What does that look mean?"

I was staring, through the golden aureoles that fell between us from the window. It was a moment of perfect balance, the light and us on either side, and what I felt in that illuminated instant was either love or three glasses of sherry. I chose love, and it took me longer than you might think to understand that it had, after all, been the sherry.

"I'd like to play for you, but my ex-wife has the piano."

"We could go to the Music Building."

"Do you want to? I have a key to Recital Hall." If it had been a practice room, the sweet blur of affection and sleep and wine might have cleared. But it was not.

"Could we walk?" I asked as he zipped me into my blue dress. Outside, he tucked a sprig of Ruth's honeysuckle in my hair and kissed me. "You are very lovely," he said, and for the first time in weeks I felt lovely instead of broken.

He played the "Moonlight." "Would you like something outrageously romantic?" he inquired, "a little ragtime, or some Shostakovitch?" "Outrageously romantic," I said, choosing from all the rows of empty wooden seats the center aisle of the last row and stretching my head back with the sensual delight of extending my body to fit my tall emotions. "On account of I feel outrageously romantic tonight." He smiled, then spent a moment with his head bowed above the keys. I moved to the front on the first dark sway of notes. I have never heard Beethoven played better, with more feeling, though it may be that all the feeling was in the way I heard. But that's not fair. He played beautifully, I swear he did, and his hands, those small and pudgy hands that would later tap against my nipples while his head bent between my legs, as if my breasts were two bells that he was ringing for my attention— those same hands stalked the keys like tarantulas, and for a minute my modest clarinetist's hands were jealous of his, accustomed as they were to nothing more dramatic than fastening the rimmed holes that I wore down the front of my black concert dress like buttons.

He took a formal moment to hang his head. When he looked up, I said, "Would you want to marry me, then?"

He gazed over my head to the empty auditorium and dropped one hand to pick notes. It was an awful moment.

"Well, you don't *have* to," I said.

"I've had a vasectomy."

"What does that mean?"

He was still picking notes. "It means that we could—you could—never have children."

"Maybe I don't want them." I turned my head to the rising arcs of varnished seats. "Anyway, it's not important. I just thought you might want to, that's all."

He took the stage steps so fast, I didn't see him until he banged the bottom of the adjoining seat and grabbed my hand. "Jane—my dear—you don't understand. I pay two hundred and fifty dollars a month in child support."

I stood. "Well, I guess I'd better be going. Ruth and Martin have a lot of closets to check out."

"Let me take you to dinner."

"I'm not hungry."

"I won't let you be alone."

I shrugged.

"I'll sleep on the sofa. Wait," he called as I started up the aisle, and I paused. "At least let me walk you home."

We marched to the Solomons' in silence, and when we got there, he opened every closet, raised every spread. We finished our tour in the tiny room where I'd been sleeping. It was David's room, but he'd run off with his waitress from the Royal Oaks, to Mexico I thought, or maybe it was to paradise. You couldn't prove by me where other couples went. I missed him, and I was mad at him too. What was I supposed to do? Eat banana splits at the Dairy Queen all alone till I burst? Ben held up a disc from David's unruly stack of 45s. His nose looked grotesque through the hole. "Same junk Bridget plays."

I shrugged. I was crying off and on. He gave me a little squeeze and sat beside me on the bed.

"David used to like me. Maybe I should have run off to Mexico with him."

He swung my legs up. "Try to get some sleep."

"Except he never asked me and now he's gone with what's-her-name." Ben doused the light. "Well, you can't win 'em all, huh?"

"I'll be downstairs. Do you want me to help you with your dress?"

"The thing is . . ." I was crying harder. "I don't know why I can't win any."

He found me in the dark. His arms felt like cats on my shoulders. "Honey," he purred. "Honey."

I sat up. "Did you ever think about just screwing?"

"Of course not."

"I was afraid of that," I said.

He patted my hand. "With someone else, perhaps—after all, I am normal. But I wouldn't compromise you. I love you."

"Oh boy," I said.

"And there's nothing in the world that I would like more than to marry you. But it isn't the right time for you to be making that kind of commitment. I'm forty years old, I have three children, I have an ex-wife, I have bills, and I don't have tenure. To tell you the truth, and I hope I haven't advertised myself falsely, my life is a mess."

"So is mine." I sobbed. "I don't know what you *want* from me."

He parted my bangs with his hands. "I don't want anything but the pleasure of your company."

"Shit," I said. "What you want is to *think* dirty things about me.

"Is it necessary to want something? What do you want from me?"

"I want to fuck," I said.

Very gently he pushed my shoulders into the pillow. "You're overwrought."

I sat up again. "Look, if it's my virtue you're worried about, I haven't had any since I was twelve years old. What do you think they kicked me out of school for?"

For a moment he said nothing, and I had the feeling that if it had not been dark, I would have seen two buds of color open on his cheeks. Then he got up, and his murky figure crossed the faint dusk of light in the room. "You shouldn't have told me that." He paused. "I *forgive* you," he said.

"For *what?*"

"For hurting me." It was my mother's voice, wounded, defenseless, and dignified, an accusation that couldn't be answered because it promised that I could have no excuse, acknowledged that I would be loved not because I was worthy but because the people who loved me were generous. How could I have thought honesty a virtue if I had no virtues to be honest about? I saw my brother again, the lead-colored eyes that would not look at me, the stump where his index finger had been, poking out as he gripped his coffee cup and I flounced out the door. In an odd way Ben reminded me of him, but perhaps I only wanted to be reminded because I wanted my brother's forgiveness instead, even when I knew that, to pay them both back for their love, I would wound them again and again and again. Because I was shameless and tacky to boot, the sort of person who would pull down her pants in public to show the scar where her heart had been ripped out, never dreaming that what embarrassed people most was the fact that her heart should have been under her blouse. That place where imagination meets sex meets heart was a secret region, and I was no longer sure where it had been. Because I had lost imagination, lost heart, and what I had left was just an undignified spot in the gut. He was *old*. I had to assume that he'd survived love, too. I thought of my mother again. And I thought, if forgiveness was offered, maybe I ought to accept.

"Ben." I followed him to the stairs. "I'm sorry."

"And?"

I held my breath while I thought what to say next. I love you? He'd been nice; I owed him that. I looked down. "I appreciate—I mean, you've been very kind to me." I sat on the top step. "Especially now. School meant so much to me, and my family—well, they just didn't ever understand, you know?'' We were going nowhere. ''Would you still want to marry me?''

''Do you love me?'' he asked.

When I looked up, he was leaning over me, his face thrust into mine. ''You love me,'' he said and licked his lips and squeezed his knuckles, his breath coming in triumphant, hot bursts through his nose.

So we got married. Against his better judgment, and he did have better judgment; I give him that. I give him a lot of things. He was a great teacher, a conscientious father, and, much to my amazement, he wasn't even bad in bed.

But he did spend that night on the sofa. Every night until Ruth and Martin returned.

(Do you really think he was normal? I kind of wondered, but then, when we got married, he became real normal, I mean exceedingly normal, and I had to wonder about myself.)

We had been married three days when my mother called. I was watching a roach lay eggs on a bookcase when I picked up the phone. It's quite interesting if you've never seen it. The mahogany mama drops a white ellipsoid of babies from her tail, and if you've already given up, you suck your beer and think how, for a while, they'll still be small. Ben was in the bathroom, dripping shampoo downstairs. We had moved into his apartment above the music store on the square. The oven door wouldn't close, and the shower leaked. The manager of the music store was suing our landlord. Preparing for one of his rants, I held the phone between my shoulder and my chin while I sank the spike of the can opener that was my trousseau into a Hudepohl and kicked my bare foot against the bookcase. By the time those nasty little mothers were big, Ben had promised, we'd be gone.

''Where have you been?'' my mother screamed. ''I've been trying to call you for hours. First I get this notice from the school, and you don't come home, you don't write, you don't call. I don't know what's happened to you.''

''That was a month ago, Mama,'' I said, thinking if she had known how to reach me, she must know I was too big for her to yell at now. "Anyway, it's no big deal. Everything's all right now."

"You have to come home," she said.

"Did you call Ruth? You know, Mr. Schunk's daughter? To get my number, I mean. Did she tell you? Anyway, all I did was spend a night over there. I didn't know you couldn't do that—but this school—it's nothing but rules, rules, rules."

"Listen to me," she said.

"Listen to me," I said. "Mama, I got married. Well, you always wanted me to, didn't you? Don't even worry about school—I'm a musician, you know? What do I need a degree for? Anyway, I'm sorry I didn't call, and I know I did a bad thing, and I'm sorry I didn't tell you about getting married, but everything happened so fast, and guess what. I've got three kids. Like Dick. I mean they're sort of stepkids, really, and Bridget, well, she's almost as old as me, but they could be like your grandkids, too, you know? I mean, you're really going to love them." The fact was I didn't yet know if I was going to love them myself; I'd exchanged scarcely a dozen words with them, and not all of those had been nice, but given time I figured . . . "You remember Ben. Dr. Gabriel? From spring vacation? Well, my name's Gabriel now, and my husband's a professor. Isn't that neat?"

"Shut up," she said.

"Mama, I'm just trying to tell you . . ."

"Listen to me. You have to come home." Her voice collapsed; I think I held on a long time before it came back. I think I said, "Oh, we will. Ben's not teaching this summer, so . . . just a minute, here he is, let me ask him when." I remember him coming out of the shower in the all-too-pudgy-gether, though the neat thing about bodies is that almost all of them look good without clothes. I remember he blew me a kiss before he picked up a shoe to start crushing roaches; I remember the way he parted his lips and raised his eyebrows to mouth "Sid?"

And I remember I kicked over the bookcase and got stitches in the wrist that was just out of my sling because I put it through a window—it was the same window, I remember, that I looked through while I waited for her voice. It was dusk, the sky was the color of bruises, and I watched the starlings circle the courthouse, then settle like soot.

I had a concussion—that is, I remember the way the green ceiling of the emergency room spiraled, and I remember being dizzy that whole summer and never eating and always throwing up. And I remember the roaches spinning on the walls while Ben held me.

And I think I remember telling him again and again how much I had always wanted to love everyone.

But all that was later. My mother's voice shuddered. "You have to come home," she said again. "Janie, your brother's been killed."

Part III

16

I knew a woman who told her husband she was leaving him. He said "Good but before you take that fat ass out the door, I want my credit cards." He made a list and as she stood in the front hall in a tattered Mexican sombrero she'd saved from their honeymoon ("Because how else could I pack it?"), he checked them off: Sears, Master Charge, Texaco, Miller and Rhoads. ("That son-of-a-bitch was always too cheap to join Diners Club," she said. "Screw him. I got my own cards now, you know?")

I knew another woman who left her husband. Four days later he shot her to death. What intrigues me about this is the possibility that both men felt the same.

Ben bowed his head and wrung his hands in his lap. His bald spot beamed lamplight; his shoulders shook. "They guaranteed sickness and health, but I don't remember anything about boredom," I said, though, if he had looked up, he might have seen that I was crying, too. "This is most unfortunate," he said and wept.

Of course, he is fifty-five, and I am thirty-three, but I cannot imagine that I will ever be able to say, simply, "This is most unfortunate." I couldn't say it when my mother died;

245

I couldn't say it when my brother was killed. Because, though I sometimes suspect that all life is just one of those unfortunate things, throughout the misfortunes of mine I have been, intermittently, the man who coolly takes back his credit cards and the man who can take back so little he shoots his ex-wife, or, failing that, himself.

They said Marie said, when the man from Inland asked did mortgage insurance take care of the house, "I don't care about the damn house. Just give me back my husband." They said he said, scuffing first one foot and then the other against the gray rug, "I'm sorry, ma'am. I wish we could do that." They said she said, when he asked was there anything else the company could do, "Get the hell out of my house." I wasn't there, so of course I don't know, but I never heard her swear in my life.

We lived in Ben's apartment above the square until September that first summer we wed, and I learned to cook, equipped with a Teflon-lined frying pan that was warped on the bottom and an aluminum saucepan from the grocery store. Our oven door latched with a padlock, and its one temperature, 500, was regulated by the degree to which the door was closed. The refrigerator we bought for $15, and we shot two cans of Raid at the roaches who lived inside the motor when we moved. I remember how they crackled when I swept them up, a cloud of poison like a fist in my lungs, and I sat down and cried until he said, "Well, here's two dollars if it means that much. We can afford to leave a broom behind." Not that it made much difference; the half-house we had rented on Lincoln Avenue had roaches of its own. Also it had rats, and when I called the landlady, she said, "Honey, can't your man set a trap?" The rim around my man's mouth went white. We called an exterminator, and Bridget's dog ate the strychnine and died.

But it doesn't matter, really, about the roaches or the rats, though if you had asked me any midnight in the bathroom I'd just flushed with light, I don't suppose I would have said it did not. I didn't leave him until long after, and when I did, it was not for circumstance.

My brother was born in June of 1938. He went to grade

school on the south side of Chicago; later he went to Hammond Tech, but he dropped out to work in the open hearth of a steel mill, then the sheet mill, where he lost his right index finger on a coil. In his twenty-fifth year he went back to open hearth. At eighteen he got married, and when his first wife left him, he married again. He paid attention to his three children, was considerate of his wives. He gave them money to play bingo; he taught them to drive. He kept his 1959 Chevrolet Bel-Air in top condition, and, though he never went anywhere in it, he never complained. On his days off he would clean out his mother's gutters, rake her leaves, or mow her lawn. In his garage he stacked the insulation he intended to install in his attic as soon as his next vacation came around. Three days before his twenty-sixth birthday an overhead crane knocked him off a catwalk into a vat of molten steel, and a public relations man drove out from Inland to tell his widow they were sorry—it was most unfortunate.

My fortunes advanced as Ben's declined. In 1963, when we met, he had just been promoted to assistant professor of music. After I came back from my brother's funeral, I went to work as a typist in the Department of Urban Transportation at the I.U. Business School. Once I assisted Ben at a recital; that was in the fall of 1966. In 1969, after Ben's tenure was turned down, we moved to Richmond, Virginia, where he taught college for seven more years, and, against his wishes, I quit typing to audition for the Richmond Symphony. Ben taught high school after college, but that was discouraging. Now he plays accompaniment for a Richmond ballet school, and he gives private lessons. I went to music festivals, first the Eastern, then the Aspen, as principal clarinet. I've made one recording, have a contract for one more. Four months ago I left the Richmond Symphony; next season I will play with the New York Philharmonic. ("You'll be back," Ben promised, "with your tail between your legs. You have to be good to make it in New York.")

My brother was buried as a Catholic; rather, he wasn't buried at all. Because, when they die like that, there is nothing left, and the corporation scrapes down the vat to present the family with a billet of prime steel. So the casket was closed, with a crucifix on top. "Don't say anything to her," my mother begged. "They're giving her Librium, poor thing." Her voice quivered as she dabbed a balled handkerchief at her eyes. "I don't know how she got it arranged with the church. You know, Dickie thinks we're going to Hell because we don't belong."

"Did he say that?" I asked.

She wiped again at her eyes. "No, but that's what they teach them over there. Well, Marie's a sweet girl, and I love her, but I just would of thought she'd ask me how I wanted it done."

I whimpered and put my head in my hands. "Mama, for God's sake, who gives a shit how they bury a hunk of metal?"

I don't know why Ben lost his jobs. I don't know why his cars broke down. The Volkswagen he drove when I met him developed carburetor trouble later that year. Then he had the clutch replaced, and when the transmission went, he traded the car for an Opel, which had to have a valve job the day after the warranty expired. He sold it and bought a Renault, which also had transmission and carburetor troubles, though he kept it until the drive axle broke. Then he got a Datsun, which ran a stop sign into a truck. ("This one *might* have been my fault," he told the cop.) Now he drives a Toyota. The last I heard, it needed a brake job, though it isn't two years old. He had such bad luck, and of course he didn't deserve it—not with his jobs, with his cars, with his wives, both of whom divorced him, although he considered that was their mistake.

Men die in the mills all the time. You can't blame the management. It's hazardous work. The floors are slippery with the animal fat used to keep the steel from corroding, and there are great vats of hydrochloric acid used to pickle the steel. Then there are so many cables that can become faulty, and in the tandem mill the rollers are capable of chopping a man right in half. Some men get killed for not being careful; for others it's only bad luck.

It wasn't the best time to begin a marriage. Ben spent most of his days at the Music Building while I looked out at the square through a film of dirt on the window, took hours just to put on my sandals, went out and then remembered I hadn't brushed my teeth, went back in and forgot what I'd gone in for, looked out the window, took naps, applied for jobs. In the evenings we walked, down Kirkwood Avenue to the campus, past the red-tile roofs of the libraries, the stone tower and gargoyles of Maxwell Hall, down the brick path that went by the Wellhouse into the buzz of tree frogs in Bryan Woods, and back up Kirkwood to gaze into the lighted store windows on the square.

The campus was empty. All the students seemed to be on the sidewalk in front of Nick's English Hut, where they loitered barefoot and in cut-offs, talking to other students who sat on the hoods of parked cars. The conversation hummed to the steady beat of business in and out of Nick's screen door. I hated to walk by them. Though they seemed to be in their early twenties, they made me feel old. Still, when my headaches stopped and we tried to go in, I was too young to be served a beer. So we browsed in the Book Nook and admired the house plants in the window of Ellis Florist while the time and temp flashed on the sign in front of the Monroe County Bank, and when the sunset turned the square rosy, we returned to our hot apartment, which was always stale with our sweat and the spray we used to kill bugs. I don't remember if we ever talked on those walks.

We did not go as far as the Music Building. I hadn't been there since Ben played the "Moonlight" Sonata and I asked if he wouldn't like to marry me.

"Why don't you practive anymore?" he would ask, and I would say, "What for?," looking beyond the baggy white boxer shorts that fluttered around his hairless thighs in the breeze from the fan to the line of my reach on the green wall.

"Well then, you'd better come here," he would say, and so I'd crawl into his lap while he sat by our window and, as he petted my hair and blew kisses across the top, watch the couples straggling past the storefronts toward the brilliant red and white marquees of the Princess Theater and the old Harris-Grand. He was happy. It didn't matter about our apartment or the chicken I served bloody around the bone. When I celebrated my job at the Business School with six yards of hopsacking, I had to point out our new curtains, and, though he praised my clumsy hemming, I realized he had never noticed that we hadn't had curtains before. He hadn't noticed that I was unhappy. "I know what you want," he would whisper, and then we'd make love while the fan blew my juices dry just as fast as they flowed, or if I was crying, he would say, "Don't be so melodramatic. It's not as if you and your brother were close."

Which was true, but he hadn't noticed it wasn't my brother I was crying for.

What hurt me most about my brother was the way he died, with his insulation still stacked in his garage as if it were a great work interrupted by death, that old badly timed luck, a pathetic parody of an unfinished symphony. Ben sighed. "It must be rough, a young woman like that, left with three children to raise." And I would shut up because it made me feel guilty to feel such sorrow for myself.

"We're all alone," my mother cried. *"Why did God have to take my boy away?"*

I cried too. "You don't believe in God. Why do you always have to say that you do?"

I felt dizzy again. Ben had driven me to the bus station. "You don't have to go," he begged. "You're sick." "I'm not sick enough," I said. "My mother called me. I have to go home." But we hadn't mentioned my marriage since I'd arrived, when my mother said, "Marie's at the funeral parlor. I think she's in shock, poor thing. Well, get yourself something to eat. There's all kinds of food." "I'm not hungry. I have a concussion," I added as she gave me an odd, stricken look, as if my brother had died just to raise the moral issue of whether, at funerals, one did or did not waste food. "What happened to your hand?" she asked, and I held out my mitten of gauze. "Oh. It went through a window." She nodded in the same absent way she always had, and it made me so nervous I lifted my other one too, a shaft of light striking my ring through the window like a comic-strip gun. "And this one got married." It was such a stupid thing to say, but she only nodded again.

I took her hand and tried once more. "You're not alone. You have Marie. You have Dickie and the twins."

She shook her head. "She's a young woman. I can't blame her. She'll want to get married again." She clutched at my bandage. "I want Dickie back."

I shifted in my chair, feeling very sorry for my mother, who had lost both her husband and her son but had kept her daughter, who wanted to be a comfort but didn't know how. "Mama, he's dead."

"I want little Dickie." She was kneading my fingers through the gauze. "Janie, we can get him. She's not his natural mother. Don't you remember how we used to take care of him? He was such a dear little guy, and we raised him like he was our own."

"Sure, of course I remember, but we couldn't do that to Marie."

"I want my boy back," She sobbed. "Marie can have the twins."

I put my head on the table and held up a handful of hair. "Mama, you have to stop it."

Now, I'm not saying I didn't like Ben's children. They were just kids who happened not to be mine. I met them on his Monday night the week before we got married. I waited in the car outside the house while Ben went to get his sons, two dark-haired boys, aged twelve and eight, both thin, one already taller than I, the other, in cowboy boots and Bermuda shorts, with the humped back Ben had warned me about and the palest thin legs, like one of those albino house spiders. Halfway down the sidewalk Reese, the younger one, who also had asthma, bolted for the car. "Move," he said to me. "It's my turn to sit up front."

Ben put a hand on his shoulder. "This is Jane. She sits up front from now on."

"I don't mind," I said.

"Well, I do," Edward said, adding, "You're a turd," and I thought he meant me until Reese replied, "Oh yeah? Well, you're a turdbird." Edward said, "You can't ever think up anything by yourself. You always have to call me the same thing I just called you."

251

"Okay, boys," Ben said. "Now we have to get Bridget, so somebody is going to have to sit on somebody else's lap."

"I'll hold Reese," I offered, but he said, "Are you kidding?" and scrambled into the back. Ben hadn't told me that he was claustrophobic, and for what seemed like the rest of my life he screamed whenever anyone even brushed against him in a car. He might have been my favorite since he was the baby, but I swear he got sick on purpose whenever we had plans. I turned my head. "Reese, I have a nephew just a year younger than you. I bet you'd like him."

"I don't like anybody," he said. "And especially I don't like you."

"Oh," I said, and we went to get Bridget at cheerleading camp.

She cartwheeled to the car. "How'd I do, huh, Dad?" She was a head taller than I, quite pretty, with dark curly hair and a little pucker of a mouth. Her voice was a soprano whine.

"Just beautiful," Ben said. "Bridget, this is Jane."

"Oh, hi," she said as I got out and she ducked in back, taking Reese, who hollered, on her lap. And that was the last thing she said to me until after we had played miniature golf and eaten dinner, and then, as Ben walked them to the door, she turned around and said, "Bye."

"They're neat," I said hopefully when he came back to the car. "When are you going to tell them?"

"I already did. Last night."

"Oh." I paused. "Well, I hope they liked me."

"They loved you."

"Oh," I said.

Mama, you have to get hold of yourself," I pleaded as she sobbed face down on the kitchen table and I toyed with my uneaten pie. We had just come from the funeral parlor, where Marie's ghost-white face was a mask clipped to her dress. It was a look that I remembered from my father's funeral, as if the bodies of the mourners had also departed and what was left was only their clothes. "Now you know Dick wouldn't want us to cry." I was crying myself, and I felt like a fool. Because I hadn't the faintest idea what Dick* *would want, except that I was quite certain he wouldn't have wanted to die.*

She raised her swollen face and sniffled. "I know. You're right."

It was because of Bridget that Ben had assumed our courtship was only a matter of biding his time. That first night she pranced around the Putt-Putt while Reese tripped over his club, kicking the plaster pygmy that straddled the hole, and Edward scuffed along behind us. At Howard Johnson's she chanted the menu like a fight song, shaking her fingertips like pom-poms and yelling "Ya-a-ay" when the food arrived. She told her father about her new boyfriend in the same singsong. "She goes through boyfriends," Ben confided, "the way Reese goes through shoes." And so, of course, when I'd told him I had a boyfriend, he knew right away not to press me; it was some pimply adolescent and we would break up. "I couldn't take it seriously," he said.

"Well, I took it seriously."

He smiled. "Of course you did. You were only eighteen years old."

"I'm *still* eighteen."

His tongue darted over his lips. "I know. But now you're *my* little girl." With a finger he circled one of my nipples. "Does my little girl want it?"

My lip curled. I swatted his hand and turned away. I'd never heard him say "fuck" or "screw"; he didn't have to, he could make *it* sound so obscene. My voice hollowed. "His name was Kelly, and he's an Olympic swimmer. He didn't have pimples."

"She wants it," he whispered, and his hand crept around.

Later I would have sins to make up for, and he would learn how to remind me of them. I was too angry now. "Go to hell," I said, and, six weeks into our marriage, we had our first, best fight.

It was because of Bridget, too, that we got the dog and moved. We were at Ben's parents' house in Pennsylvania, and, although she had a Cairn terrier in Bloomington, she wanted to take one of their Labrador's puppies home. "Ask your mother," Ben said, so she called, then said, "Mom wants to talk to you," and passed him the phone.

"I know," he said as I curled into the window seat of his parents' bedroom, watching the faint blush of evening sky turn milky. ("We don't get sunsets," his mother had said that afternoon as we sipped May wine on the patio, letting her hand fly toward the mountain horizon. "Not up *here*." She said it as though she wished they lived anywhere else, and I felt guilty because I thought I had never seen anything quite so beautiful as their nineteenth-century stone house, its twelve wooded acres, duck pond, and very own swimming pool.) "I *didn't* encourage her. I *know* you're the one who feeds George. My parents are *not* trying to foist those dogs off on you. I am *not* irresponsible. Carla—well, I'm sorry. Carla." He put the phone down. "She hung up on me."

"Well, honey," I said and rubbed his back, still listening to the pure flute of stream that fed the duck pond, embarrassed to have overheard.

"I could give it to you right now," he said and turned to twiddle my top button.

My hand slipped under his. "Don't you think you ought to report to Bridget? Poor kid, she's going to be so disappointed."

"That's not my fault." He stood to tuck in his shirt tail, and I suppressed a relieved sigh. I couldn't understand it. He did all kinds of nice, licky things Kelly had never thought of, but there was something so nasty about the way he had saved himself for our marriage and then taken me into a bed under which he had stacked a year of magazines detailing methods and positions. In his drawer, not yet removed from their cardboards, were at least a year of juices for my guaranteed orgasms. "You're going to like this," he promised and cocked the button on a big, black rubber phallus. "No?" He strapped a wedge of stainless steel and plastic to his hand. He licked my knees, and his fingers shivered. "Little Janie—open." I sat up, and he held his hand out, palm jittering beneath a soiled elastic band. "It's just me. What's the matter?" He snapped the apparatus off. "Sweetheart, we're married, *Nothing* is weird." "I just thought it would be more personal," I said. So he gave me the personal touch, which was lovely and every bit as efficient—I thought he should have played the clarinet, he was so good at flutter-tonguing—but his eyes glittered, his lips parted like the doors to a dungeon crammed with shrieking virgins, and I had the queasy feeling that he would have preferred to watch me writhe while he applied his novelty collection. He liked his fucking gothic.

But that's not fair. Maybe he was really hearing string quartets while my imagination gnashed and howled. So I whimpered and moaned, and we sucked and stroked our way to his delayed *crise de quarantaine*, which he had the year his tenure was turned down. He was afraid that his member would age so that it couldn't keep up our twice-daily union, and I felt like a hypocrite as I reached for his cock and thought, Jesus, I hope so.

And still later, when I had my first (and only) fling (with the second trombone of the Richmond Symphony—it's not necessarily true, by the way, what they say about the brass being better kissers), I knew he would never forgive me if he found out, because I was still young and his drive had dwindled to every other day.

If I loved him, then I hated myself.

I gave him a meaningful smile and promised, "Later," and, with his arm around me, we bumped down the back stairs to the library, where his father sat watching TV with the children.

(It never stopped seeming unfair to me that Ben's mother should consider me an adult and Bridget one of the children, although she was a very gracious woman, who never once remarked about my age, never once asked about my background. I felt as if they'd found me, full-grown, beneath a cabbage leaf, and any past I had had served no purpose. The proof of Ben's past slammed doors and shook the stairs, calling, "Grandpa, have you seen my tennis racquet? Grandma, where's my fins?" Mine was a dark secret, and, as Ben's history was illuminated with information over the years, mine grew blacker, and, like shadows on the wall at night, it grew larger, too. I took slow walks with Ben and my in-laws while the children tore through the woods; I weeded the flowerbeds while the children swam; I helped load the dishwasher while the children played old maid and watched television. Christmas after Christmas, I held my finger on the knots while Ben's mother tied bows around Bridget's loud bellbottoms, zippy little miniskirts, and patchwork vests. Once, when we went shopping, she held up an embroidered Mexican blouse. "Do you suppose something like this would be 'far-out' enough for Bridget?" "I think it's neat," I replied, hoping that just once she would give something far-out to me instead of another beige Dacron blouse or white cardigan sweater. Most all of my wardrobe came from them or Ben, who always bought me ruffles, and throughout my marriage I felt schizophrenic, on one day a five-year-old princess, on the next a forty-two-year-old matron.)

"Well, what did she say, Dad, huh?" Bridget was knitting a scarf to give her boyfriend next Christmas—she didn't know who that would be, but the thing about scarves is, they fit anyone—and she punched Edward to move so that she could retrieve a needle from beneath the cushion of the red leather sofa. I had never been in a house with a library before, certainly not one with leather furniture, Oriental rugs, and bookcases built into the cherry paneling that rose to the ceiling and crossed it as beams. (Ben had such fond memories of the books in that room, from Beatrix Potter to the "trumpets sterne" in *The Faerie Queene*, that he still allowed his mother to call him "Benjamin Bunny.") "Can I keep Turnkey?"

Edward scowled. "What do you call him Turnkey for? I don't want a dog named Turnkey."

"Because that's his name," she said and jabbed him with her knitting needle.

"They're killer dogs," Edward said. "Last year Blackie got all of Grandma's ducks."

"They are not," Bridget said.

"I don't want a killer dog," Reese announced. "I want a parakeet."

I glanced at Ben, sorry that he had to break the news. I felt, at that moment, very tender and protective, irked with Bridget for making Ben humiliate himself before her mother and then (as I expected) crying and carrying on until he felt that he'd failed her. He looked unperturbed. "Well . . ." He smiled. "Okay."

"Huh?" I said.

"Ya-a-ay." Bridget shimmied her fingertips, and her boyfriend's scarf dropped half a dozen stitches as it slid from the sofa to the floor.

Ben was still smiling as she hugged him. "I talked her into it. But he has to live with Jane and me."

Edward kicked her in the shins. "How come she always gets what she wants?"

I didn't think I could have said it better myself.

"My daddy died," Dickie told me. "He went to Heaven to live with Jesus."

My mother turned away. "You see what I mean?" she whispered. "Marie taught him that. He thinks I'll go to Hell."

Dickie tugged at my dress. "When I die, I'm going to go live in Heaven with my daddy."

I was guilty. I wanted to suffer. But Bridget was still a bitch.

Edward was morose; Reese's temperament was predictable. He spent so much time in the hospital, I could hardly blame him for being spoiled. Ben borrowed the money for the back operations from his father. Once, in a tight month, I suggested he borrow his child support, too. "It's not my father's responsibility," he said, and I felt awful and didn't say, "But they have all that money," because they did have all that money and I didn't want him to know I was so petty to notice that, after growing up with every advantage, he had a tendency to see himself as mine while I typed forty hours a week to make sure that his children also had every advantage.

In college Bridget traded in her cheerleading sweater for a blue work shirt and faded jeans. (I was still wearing A-line dresses and stockings to work, where all day I typed and Ko-Rec-Typed urban transportation reports. I hated the dresses as much as I hated the job.) She went to the University of Wisconsin to study elementary education; by the end of her sophomore year she had changed her major to art. "Art?" I said to Ben when she wrote. "Does she paint?" Not that he knew of, so she clarified: she was learning photography; she needed $500 for a Nikon; she wanted to spend the summer in Arizona with her boyfriend, an anthropology senior who had a job with a dig; and didn't we think the war was a waste? "Where did she hear about the war?" I sniffed. "They must have done a spread on it in *Seventeen*." The next year, outside the Democratic convention on Michigan Avenue, she got hit on the head with a billy club by the Chicago police. In her senior year she dropped out and split for San Francisco to live in the Haight.

We were sitting at the dinner table in Pennsylvania when Ben gave his parents the news. His father put his hand to his heart. He looked as if he were saying the Pledge of Allegiance or having a coronary or both. The watery shadow of his mother's raised glass of Beaujolais trembled on her cheek like an enormous ruby-hued tear.

"Can't you talk to her?" he asked Ben.

"No," Ben said sadly, "I can't."

His mother dropped her face to her hands as she began repeating, "Oh God, oh God," and I tasted the *carbonnade de boeuf.*

"One of those hippies will give her LSD, and she'll jump off the Golden Gate Bridge. Does she know what happened to Art Linkletter's daughter?"

"I don't know," Ben said, and I said, "U-um, that marinade is great."

"It'll rearrange her chromosomes. She'll wind up on heroin."

"Oh God, oh God," Ben's mother bleated.

"I know," Ben said, and I said, "Honey, try some of this stew."

"What about Jane then?" Ben's father said, and I started, thinking he meant that Ben had better start worrying about me, lest I too split for San Francisco.

"What about her?" Ben said.

"Well, she's younger and she's sensible and if Bridget won't listen to you, maybe she'll listen to Jane." As they all looked at me, I swallowed a whole chunk of meat.

Ben's mother dialed, and they seated me on a stool at the

kitchen counter while each took a chair at the table beyond. I didn't want to be sensible. I wanted to split for San Francisco.

"Hi, Jane; how's Virginia?" Bridget said. We had moved to Richmond only last month, and I had quit typing. I'd intended to go back to school, but Ben got his job there so late, I couldn't file my application in time.

"Great. We found this terrific apartment in a brownstone right near the campus in this neighborhood called the Fan. We live right across the street from the Little Sisters of the Poor, and we've got a fireplace in every room, except none of them work, and we've got a stained-glass window in our bedroom . . ." Ben and his parents frowned.

"Yeah, it sounds far-out. Well, Robert and I were like on our way to get a pizza, but it was good talking to you." Robert was her boyfriend, and we had first met him via her letters when he was just Bob. All spring I had thought she would confide to me that she was living with him, but I suppose she was afraid I'd tell her father, who was no longer Dad but Benjamin.

"Anyway, we want you to see it." I panned my eyes around the solemn circle of faces.

"Tell her not to take any drugs." They nodded. "Ask her if her apartment is safe."

"How's San Francisco?"

"Oh wow." The line crackled. "San Francisco's far-out."

"Well, look. Your grandparents were kind of wondering when you're coming home."

"Tell her we'll send plane fare." The nods grew more vigorous. "Ask her if she's eating right."

"Like out of sight. We went to a rally in Golden Gate Park. Two hundred thousand beautiful people united against the capitalist war machine." She said it in exactly the same tone she had used to gush about pep rallies.

"Oh. It sounds—far-out." But her words had changed, and the more I tried to use them, the more unfamiliar my own perfect pitch became. She was two years younger than I, but I had married her father, and we were a generation apart. "Bridget, your dad misses you. He's worried half to death."

"Tell her we love her," my mother-in-law mouthed.

When I defected, no one ever called to say that my mother still loved me.

I didn't dislike my stepdaughter. I hated her.

"And you wouldn't believe—I've heard the Dead. I've heard Joplin—like *Janis Joplin* right in the same room with me—and later on tonight we're going down to the Fillmore to hear Credence Clearwater Revival."

"What's she saying?" my mother-in-law asked.

I covered the mouthpiece. "I don't know. Something about hearing the dead and going to a revival."

"Oh my God." She put her face in her hands.

"Look," I said. "Your grandmother wants to know if you're eating right, and your grandfather says to say he'll send plane fare, and they—I mean we—all send our love."

"Yeah," she said. "Weird."

"They're right here," I pleaded, begging her to imagine the ring of constituents and me, their elected official, just doing my job. "They want you to come home."

"I know—it's a bummer. Well, tell them I love them too—and, oh, I forgot, tell Benjamin thanks for the bread. But this is like my bag, you know? I'm taking pictures, and I think I shot some really groovy stuff at this march."

"Yeah."

"And like I know Benjamin's uptight, but school was nowhere—just a lot of boring stuff about a lot of boring artists that're dead. This is where it's happening, and photography is where it's at."

"Yeah," I said.

"So, explain it to them, would you? And take care. It was good rapping with you."

"Sure," I said. "Well, peace."

She giggled. "Oh, Jane, you're so funny."

Three years later Bridget was back in school. She got a license to teach kindergarten, "because like when they're small it can be a real creative thing," and she taught for two years, then married the president of one of those centers for creative leadership and had a baby, "because like what's more creative than having a kid?" And when I came home last summer to announce that I was leaving Ben, she called me on the Center's WATS line to say, "I don't understand it. Why would you want to do something like that to my dad?"

"I wish I could drive," my mother said as we sat one last time at the kitchen table, which was littered with the paper plates neither of us had the heart to clean up. The funeral had been that afternoon. She started to cry again. "If your brother was here, he could have helped you bring back your things."

"Mama?" I touched her hand. "You want me to stay for a while?"

"You know, you can ship boxes by bus." For a minute she just sat there. "Well, can you manage?"

I frowned, thinking for a minute that she meant our lives. I had managed mine, I guessed, but I had no idea what to do with hers. "Why don't you ever go out?" I asked abruptly. "There must be lots of widowers or"—I looked away—"divorced men your age."

"You'll have to remember to use mothballs when you pack your wool skirts. Well, you didn't have that much when you went down there, but I suppose you've collected a lot."

The fluorescent light overhead had developed a flicker, and it gave her the appearance of a small nervous tic. "Mama, I'll be glad to stay for a week or two if you want, but you know I have to go back."

"What for?" Her tone was suspicious, then bitter. "It's not like you're going back to school." So we would, after all, have to discuss that. "We respected that when we needed you during the year—don't call Jane, I said, whatever you do, don't call Jane. Oh, I've had enough grief—I don't want to talk about this."

"When did you need me?" I said.

"When I was in the hospital. I had a hysterectomy. You didn't even send a card."

"Mama, I didn't know." I was angry, and I was sorry. I didn't see why I had to be so confused. "No one told me."

"I asked them not to." She sighed and wiped her face. "I'm sorry."

"I'm sorry too," I said, wondering if there would ever be a time when we could stop the endless recitation of the same poor words. "Was it painful? Why didn't you tell me?"

"Painful enough." She shrugged. *"I had a tumor. It was benign."* She looked up. *"Oh, Janie. I couldn't expect that you'd know, but I wanted you to send a card. Do you understand?"*

"Yes." In my whole life I had never felt closer to my mother, and I wanted to go around the table to hug her, but instead I just grabbed her hand. *"I really do."* The skin was so unexpectedly loose around that fan of little bones that I was frightened. *"Mama, do you have anything to drink?"*

But I would have told her I loved her if she hadn't said, *"There's milk in the refrigerator. Or you can make coffee."*

"No, I mean like whiskey."

She took back her hand. *"Are you an alcoholic?"*

"Don't be silly," I said, and the moment was lost.

"I suppose that's why you had to leave school. Do you know how ashamed I am?"

"I'm sorry," I said.

"How could you do this to me now of all times?"

"I'm sorry."

"If you loved me . . ." She choked and looked up.

I didn't know her face. I had never seen it before, not even when my father died. Her features were swollen, and her eyes were the color of a new bruise. *"Mama, I can't come live with you. Don't you remember? I'm married."* She didn't answer. *"I married Ben Gabriel, remember? He came to dinner at Marie's."* I took a breath. *"I have to go back to my husband, but I can stay a little while if you want."*

"How could you get married at a time like this?"

"I didn't know it was a time like this."

"Don't lie to me, Jane. You've caused enough heartache." I bit my lip and began tearing at the gauze threads that straggled above my bracelet of tape. *"Are you pregnant?"*

"No. I just got married, that's all. I married my teacher. You met him this spring."

She stacked one paper plate on top of another and then pushed them aside. *"Janie, that man must have been twenty years older than you."*

"Twenty-two," I admitted, *"but . . ."*

"Yes, and look where it got me," she said, though neither

262

of us had mentioned my dad. "How are you going to feel when he dies and leaves you with children to raise?"

"We're not going to have children."

"And didn't he say that he had children of his own? Janie, when a woman gets married she wants her own family. She doesn't want to be a nursemaid to another woman's children."

"Marie was."

"But Dickie was a baby, and even so, the circumstances weren't the best. Well, she's done a wonderful job. I certainly give her credit for that." She sighed.

"Anyway, they live with their mother."

"So you'll have an interfering ex-wife poking her nose in you marriage, too."

"I don't even know her. I met his kids." I looked away. "They're all right." I scraped a paper plate back and forth across the table. "I thought you liked him when he came to Marie's."

"You told me he was your teacher. What kind of a man would sit there and let your family think—what kind of a man would take advantage of a girl not half his age and lie like that to her mother? What kind of a man would sneak around doing God-knows-what till she's thrown out of school and then? . . ."

I had begun twisting my wedding ring. It was slightly too big, and it pinged against the table. I inserted my little finger and spun it, watching the gold play with the bluish flicker of light.

"You can't answer, can you?"

I hung my head. "It's not his fault. He wanted me to tell you."

"He didn't have the guts to do it himself?" I didn't answer. "Why were you kicked out of school? I want to know."

I didn't raise my head. "It wasn't because of him. He's my husband. I can't let you say all those things."

"Oh? And where is he? A man who loved his wife, who cared about her"—her voice caught—"at a time like this. And you come flouncing into your own brother's funeral just to give us the glad news. Well, I wish I could say I was happy for you."

"That's not why I came, and you know it." I put my head

263

on the table, and my hair spilled into a smear of mayonnaise on a paper plate. "It was because of this other boy." *I began weeping, harder, I think, than I had wept in the last three days.* "I loved him so much, and I love him now."

My mother regarded me with her chin at a sharp, cold angle below the red, puffed blotch of her face. "So you married a man you didn't love," *she said flatly.*

I sat up. "He—this other boy—wanted to get married, and he wanted me to quit school, and I knew—I mean, he didn't say it, but I knew I'd never do anything in my life but raise babies."

"What's wrong with that?"

I couldn't answer. What else had she done? What else had my brother done, except get himself killed in the mill and leave a big, fat insurance check for his wife?

"So you got married anyway, to a man you don't even love."

"I do too. He's very nice." *I dropped my eyes.* "Anyway, I will in a while."

"What do you want?"

"I loved my brother," *I said.*

"What is so goddamn important to you that what's good enough for everyone else just isn't good enough for you?"

For a minute I smarted because I had never heard her damn anything before. And then, when I thought of my father and my brother, the truth was so clear, I had always known it. I gave her a sheepish smile. "I think I want to be immortal," *I admitted.*

Her mouth twisted. "Your brother was so proud of you because you were smart. He always sold himself short. It was my sister this, my sister that. My sister makes good grades. My sister plays a musical instrument. My sister is going to college. I was so ashamed I didn't even show him that letter. And I'm glad he's dead so he doesn't have to see his sister now."

I was crying again, and I'd begun hiccuping, but the dizziness was gone. "Mama, I didn't kill him. Don't take it out on me."

The chair toppled, and my head hit the wall. For a moment I didn't understand that she could have slapped me that hard. The dizziness came rushing back. If it hadn't, perhaps I might have remembered that, while I had lost my only brother, she had lost her only son. My stomach turned over, but I gasped and sat up. "Mama, I'm married, that's how it is. But I can stay for a while if you want."

"I don't want you here." She glanced at the clock and began picking up paper plates. "It's late. I'm going to bed. Not that I'll sleep."

"Please." My elbow had jammed against the floor, and it sent a sharp pain up my arm as I tried to get up. "Please, Mama, I don't know what to do, I didn't mean to hurt you, I'm sorry . . ." I was crawling, tangling my knees in the hem of my dress.

She threw the last of the paper plates in the garbage. "You've never meant anything but to hurt me."

"That's not so, it's not." I began hiccuping again, and I took a breath. "I love you."

"You've never loved anyone in your life," she said.

I cried for a while; then I called Ben. I took a taxi and spent the night in the bus station on State Street. At 6:55 the next morning I left Hammond for the last time. I never saw my mother again.

I left Ben fourteen years later, the day after Marie called to tell me my mother had died.

17

*B*ut I see I've told this all wrong. It isn't the story of why I left Ben at all.

"No," I insisted when Ben suggested I apply for readmission as a special student. "They kicked me out. I'm not crawling back."

"One class a semester—it would get you out among people who share your interests." He looked away, pretending that he hadn't referred to my constant complaints about the three fretful women I typed forty hours a week with in the basement of the School of Business. It wasn't the job so much—or even them, though I disliked them. It was being shut up in an office all day.

"No," I repeated, but after a year had gone by and my depression became so dark that it scared me, I made an appointment with the office manager. I wanted permission to make up time in order to take the Literature and Structure of Seventeenth and Eighteenth Century Music. She frowned. She was pregnant. All of the younger women at the Business School were pregnant that year. They didn't want their husbands to go to Viet Nam, and the coffee lounge was buzzing with the rumor that their student deferments would be canceled.

I was a faculty wife; my husband was too old to go. So I was better off, though they would quit and move when their husbands graduated, whereas I expected I would have to stay until Ben's children finished college. It made me lonely as they gossiped in the lounge. "My old roommate had her baby," I informed them. "It's a boy. Her husband called me from Ohio." One of the women from my office turned to a girl from the staff of *Business Horizons*. "Did you hear Marcia Gallagher is pregnant? I'm so happy for her." "We went to *Madame Butterfly* Saturday night. You ought to go. It's really good." No one answered. "Anyway, you'll all have to come when my husband gives his recital." They looked away, and the receptionist from the dean's office said, "Nobody gives a la-de-da that your husband's a professor."

The office manager hadn't said a word. I took a breath. "Helen Schuyler works through her lunch hour so she can take shorthand."

There was a small cactus on her desk with a plastic rose stuck in the soil. She blew dust from its petals. "I'm afraid I don't see what literature has to do with your work."

"Music," I said. "I could come in on my lunch or an hour early in the morning, or I could stay after at five, whatever would be most convenient for you." My palms were sweaty. I didn't see why she had to act so big. I bet there were times when she got up and there wasn't a glob of toothpaste in the house, just like everybody.

She was still frowning. "It's not our policy to let staff in the building without supervision. There's been a problem with supplies disappearing."

"I don't steal," I said, careful to sound trustworthy instead of indignant. I didn't want to blow my second chance at school just because someone had pilfered a few paper clips. "Lunch hour's fine with me."

"We have let a few gals work through their lunch," she admitted. "If you wanted to take shorthand . . ."

"I'm a music major."

"As I was saying. Your present rating is class two, and you need shorthand for a class three."

"It only meets an hour three days a week."

267

"Or bookkeeping. With bookkeeping and shorthand, you could apply for a class four."

"Well, the thing is, I want to take classes so I don't always have to do office work." I was tearing at my thumbnail, and the more I tried not to, the more I split off.

She lit a cigarette. She was a class six, which gave her the right to smoke at her desk. Everyone else had to wait for coffee break. I imagined a lifetime of lunches spent typing while I completed the courses in bookkeeping and shorthand required for a Bachelor of Bureaucracy, all for the privilege of lighting up whenever I chose. It didn't seem worth it, since I didn't smoke. "You might want to start with advanced typing. Dr. Duke tells me your speed could be improved."

"Yeah." I rose.

"Also, I understand you're not always on time."

"I was late once. Three minutes." Error. I lowered my voice. "We went to a party after a recital, and we overslept, and then we caught the traffic lights wrong."

"See that it doesn't happen again," she said in a voice that seemed nastier for its breezy pleasantness. She swiveled her chair toward her assistant, who had been working on the payroll while she listened in. "Remind me that I have a doctor's appointment at two."

I locked myself in a stall in the ladies' room and cried. Later I thought about mutilating her baby—I could sneak out to her house on my lunch hour, drug the baby sitter, and one by one pull all its little fingernails off. If we saw her on the street with a stroller, I could get Ben to run over the baby in our car, back up on the mangled metal to roll the window down and say, "Oh, I'm sorry—I didn't see you," while I bounced on the front seat and laughed. That made me cry even harder. I was sick.

I *was* sick. I was sick all the time. I had headaches and stayed home from work; my stomach acted up and I went home at noon. Ben ferried me back and forth to the doctor. He was very considerate, so much so that I began to suspect he considered me a chronic psycho, someone whose many illnesses were all in her mind but who had to be coddled since she obviously could not be cured. He had teased me into resuming the clarinet by bringing home the score to Poulenc's Sonata for Clarinet and Piano, which we practiced together, and I decided to audition for the Indianapolis Symphony.

He shook his head. "Janie, that's over fifty miles from here. If you could drive it might be different."

"Well?"

"The gearshift sticks. There's no protection up front if you were in an accident. I don't want you on the highway in that car." I sniffed. "Anyplace you want to go, I'll be happy to take you. Why don't you just apply for readmission and take a class part time?"

"Because," I said, and that was that. In many respects Ben was an incredibly uncomplicated man. He thought he could kiss my problems and make them well, and he simply refused to believe he had any of his own. "You're too high-strung," he said whenever I came home from work complaining about something one of my co-workers had done. "Don't be so sensitive."

I caught the intestinal flu and felt guilty. I had to have two impacted wisdom teeth pulled and couldn't sleep because the Darvon gave me hallucinations. I fell down our front steps on the way to work one morning after an ice storm and cried with humiliation when the x ray showed only a badly bruised bone. "I didn't fall on purpose," I insisted to Ben, who looked away. My body had become my enemy; its motivation could not be trusted. Once a month I cramped while other women bled blithely.

"I want you to ask the doctor to give you something for your bad periods," Ben said when he drove me to the clinic to see about a lingering cold.

I came out with a prescription for Tylenol plus codeine: take four times a day for menstrual discomfort. Ben frowned. "That isn't what I meant," he said, tapping his temple.

"Why didn't you say so?" I let the prescription fly out the window, and the wind swept it behind us like an energetic hausfrau. I felt feverish, and my cough wouldn't quit clattering around in my chest. At home I drank Robitussin and climbed into bed, doodling in an old music notebook to pass the time.

> *There once was a woman named Jane,*
> *Who experienced a whole lot of pain.*
> *"It's all in your head,*
> *Take Valium," Ben said,*
> *Although he was really insane.*

He gave a disgusted little snort when he found it, and after a minute he crumpled the page. "Janie, you can't let these things bother you."

"I didn't know it bothered you that much," he said three months later as he held my hand. I was in the hospital because my legs had stopped working. They wouldn't walk. I heard the doctor whispering with Ben in the corridor. "Nerves," the doctor said, and I thought I heard the creak of Ben's neck as he nodded. I was a ninny, so ashamed to be sick for no reason that I turned my face to the clutter of Dixie cups on the night stand and cried. Why didn't my mother send me a card? "I'm sorry I didn't take it seriously. Janie, I want you to quit that job."

"We need the money."

"There are other jobs."

What had I wanted him to say? That I didn't have to work, that I could go to New York and study with Russianoff, that I could live on a plane above the petty world of survival, given special dispensation because I couldn't make it down there? "All jobs are alike."

"How do you know? Someplace else you might work with people you liked better, and I'd get to see a few more of those pretty smiles." I didn't answer. "Well, how about this then?" He was going to give the recital he'd put off from last year. He was going to play Chopin's *Scherzo No. 2*, Beethoven's "Moonlight," the Gershwin *Preludes*, and—he turned my face toward him—"I thought maybe we could do the Poulenc."

"You mean you want me to play with you?" I sat up. "They wouldn't let me."

"It's my recital."

He was trying so hard that it made me cry again. "I'm here for no reason, and it's costing money. There's nothing wrong with me."

"No," he said, "there isn't. They've got all the tests back, and they couldn't find anything."

Years later I told my trombone player about my breakdown on our one afternoon in his bed. His name was Christopher. He was four years younger than I, and he had fallen in love with me one afternoon on a fifteen-minute break from rehearsal of the Richmond Symphony. He fell out again one morning on the campus of Virginia Commonwealth University while we were having coffee and I said dreamily, "What if I'm pregnant?" "Then I'll marry you," he promised, and we both put our cups down. "Christopher, I'm already married," I said, and, in the moment before he tipped back his chair and rubbed a hand inside his ribbed T-shirt and said, "In that case, there's no problem," he fell out of love.

But before he did, he wooed me with such determination, I think I was touched, although perhaps I was only flattered. For three weeks he ghosted up and down Floyd Avenue at night, hoping for a glimpse of me through the bamboo blinds at our living room window. "That's ridiculous," I said when he told me, thinking it was terribly adolescent but charming. A rose bush rambled up the wooden fence around his back yard, and he dropped blossoms on my music stand. "It won't get you anywhere," I said, hoping it wouldn't but knowing it might. During rehearsal I covered my smile with my hand when the conductor waved the orchestra to a halt, complaining, "As much as I hate to say this, I can't hear the trombones." "What?" Christopher said, and I giggled. The conductor glared at the woodwinds. "I didn't say anything about wanting to hear *clarinets*." He leaned toward the brass. "Trombones, I can't hear you. Bom-bom-de-bom, bom-bom-de-bom. Okay, same place. Two before twenty-two."

In his apartment Christopher had a collection of antique scores that he wanted to show me. "I won't come," I said, knowing I would. But he believed me, so he took me on a tour of Richmond instead. We had been there a year, but Ben and I had seen only the tourist attractions. We had been through the capitol building, the Virginia Museum, the Poe house, and Saint John's Episcopal Church on Church Hill,

271

where Patrick Henry had risen to say "Give me liberty or give me death." When I think back on my marriage, I remember official pleasures, historical houses, and the hush as the music begins. Save for the dark secrets of my character and his skin magazines, I always felt legitimate with Ben, and I felt wonderfully illegitimate as I crossed the Marshall Street Viaduct in Christopher's MG, the top down, the radio blaring "Me and Bobby McGee." I remembered listening to Elvis in the front seat of Dick's old Chrysler, and for a minute I was sad. It had been such a long time ago, and I had been old for so many years, it seemed impossible that I could still be young. I had just turned twenty-five. He flexed his shoulders, and the wind caught a blond ringlet. "Ah, Janis." I thought he meant another girlfriend and was surprised to feel jealous. "Janis who?" "*Joplin,*" he said. "Don't you know anything?" I smiled. "Well my stepdaughter saw her live." He winced. "Anyway, do me a favor. Don't talk about your stepdaughter, huh?" Ben was growing balder, and I thought I was very wicked to be so enchanted by Christopher's mop of golden curls. "Well, I'm *married,*" I said. "I *know* that," he said.

We stood on a bluff in Chimborazo Park, overlooking the James River and Fulton Bottom, the neighborhood of vacant lots and boarded-up buildings where old black ladies couldn't get cabs to the hospital where their sons lay bleeding in the middle of the night because no white drivers would go in there after dark. "I know your husband," he said. "I had a course with him. He's very good." The river was pale beneath the bright autumn sun. I tried to imagine how it must have looked over a century before, reflecting flames the night that all Richmond had fled, setting fire to the city so that the Union soldiers would get nothing when they took it the next day. I couldn't see it—that wide gray band was too calm beneath its patina of light—but my imagination marched to the music. I heard the red-hot roar like a crescendo in the orchestra; I heard the rattle of cartwheels against the cobble-stones. The bells of Saint John's were ringing, and a faint chorus of doomed Confederates whistled as they went by. I had fallen in love with the city the day I'd arrived, coming from up North to claim what was left like a carpetbagger, knowing that it did not belong to me and would not ever, for I had been born with a Northerner's prejudice and would always lack the Southerner's sense of tradition, of honor and family. And quite suddenly I felt ashamed to be standing in that park on Church Hill, where there had once been a hospital in which the Civil War wounded had died for their hopelessly flawed dream, on the brink of nothing more fatal than adultery. "Yes, he is," I said. "Listen, to tell you the truth, I've already seen Richmond. I think I ought to go home."

We got back in the car and drove around for a while. "I know a good place to swim up above the Huguenot Bridge," he said. "I can't swim," I said, thinking with a sudden pang that I should have had Kelly teach me. He parked in front of his apartment in the Fan, our wonderful old neighborhood of narrow brick houses set close to the street. Most of them seemed not to have roofs, though a few had little visors of copper or octagonal shingles, an occasional tiara of ironwork on top. It was in the same block as the Grove Avenue Republic, a three-story house occupied by a band of post-hippies who had proclaimed their independence from the war machine otherwise known as the United States and celebrated their secession by blocking off Grove Avenue at night, opening their windows so that the whole Fan could hear "The Lonesome Death of Hattie Carroll" while they cavorted in the street, exploding beer bottles and passing joints. It was early afternoon, and I presumed the Republic was sleeping. The brick walk was littered with leaves, and the air smelled of tobacco and vanilla. There is no place in the world as fragrant as Richmond in Indian summer, when the air is still so warm that the scents from the spice factory and curing sheds seem to linger like the weather. "It's up to you," he said, stretching his beautiful body against the seat of the MG like a lazy cat.

I studied the white knees of my faded blue Jeans. They were new, but I had spent an entire afternoon washing and rewashing them. In a voice as nasai and absurd as a bassoon, my conscience said, "Are you going to break your marriage vows, risk the ruin of your relationship, and hurt the only man who's never done anything deliberate to hurt you for the sake of one *cheap* afternoon?" But my imagination, in a voice as brassy and cheerful as a trumpet, replied, "You most certainly are."

Later, on his bed, in that naked time that is as strange and slow as the waking moments in a recovery room, when you find life as unfamiliar, sweet, and queer as if, when they cut you, you had really died, I told him about the hospital, the Business School, and Ben. "I think your husband was horrible," Christopher said. "He should have let you quit."

"It wasn't his fault. I could have, if I'd found another job. I was too proud." He didn't understand. I shrugged. "I quit my family, and I might as well have quit school. I didn't want to quit anything else."

"Did they give you shock?"

"They didn't give me anything. I got well because I had to."

"So was the job okay after that?"

"No. But I stopped complaining." I dropped back into the pillows and, without reason or context, said, "I was in love once."

His shadow crossed my face, and he kissed me. "Be in love twice," he said. "Be in love with me."

It had been a long time since Kelly, and if love was what I had with Ben, who said it was, then I had only been in lust with him. Love was nothing but a system of debts. Lust was something else, to the body what the imagination was to the mind, a lucky bandit, dangerous without doubt; but that death-defying nerve was also all its charm. That something shivered as I kissed him back, and I thought, to a long, reasoned blamelessness with Ben, I'd much prefer crime.

It was Ben's fault that I joined the Richmond Symphony. As he promised when I was in the hospital, we played the Poulenc at his recital, the only one he gave in Bloomington, and if I had once thought I would never play again, from that night on I knew that I would always play, and play to perform.

He couldn't perform in public. I didn't know that until I sat in the front row of Recital Hall, waiting for the intermission, after which I was to come in. "I don't understand," I had said at our kitchen table just the night before. "You know the music; you *feel* it. What difference can an audience make?" A lot, my own flip-flopping stomach replied.

"I *feel* the audience."

"Well, you ought to." But the way he felt the audience was all wrong. If he had a rest, he grew ulcers waiting to come in. His hands sweated until the keys were slippery, and his fingers skated to the nearest wrong note. His forehead dripped; his vision blurred. He got stomach cramps in the middle of the andantes and speeded up the tempo to make it to the bathroom. He had no showmanship. Instead of flourishing his tux, he slunk to the piano, and when he bowed, he would not meet the eye of the audience, as if he were a child who expected a scolding instead of applause. The girl who had played principal clarinet to my last chair in the I.U. Philharmonic had suffered the same syndrome. "You're so tiny," she'd said bitterly to me. "Audiences love to see you. When you're fifty, they'll still think you're a precocious little girl. They never like women musicians. I'm better than you are, but I'll never make it. I'll end up teaching at Podunk U. and giving a poorly attended recital every other year." She was right, but, like Ben, she didn't know what her real problem was. She performed flawlessly, but she was stiff. The audience wants to see the clarinet sway. It wants to read the pianist's lips as he sings the orchestra part.

"But you play so beautifully," I'd protested to Ben.

His fingers trembled, drawn up like little spiders too timid to bite. "I can't do it."

And I felt terrible because, even with my stomach skidding inside me, my throat constricting with a necktie of nerves, I knew that I could.

I love the audience. I didn't much care, when I recorded, for the studio, and I like giving lessons even less. I think often of the things Mr. Schunk never told me about Schönberg: what a tyrannical teacher he was, and how it must have been in those early days in Vienna, when the tickets he printed to his concerts entitled the listeners only to listen quietly and not to make their views known aloud by applauding or hissing. For him the concert hall was always a classroom and the audience a discipline problem. He might have been happier had he been like Ravel, who suffered great depressions, to be sure, but who also dressed Toscanini down in public for taking *Bolero* twice too fast, not because he was angry, but because he delighted in the audience's consternation at the scene. All of which makes me suspect that Ravel had a showman's ego, Schönberg the pique of a misunderstood *artiste*. And I think how, when I was younger, I never quite comprehended that Mr. Schunk was envious of his friend the composer, though perhaps not until the years when I knew him and he could no longer play. Because surely he understood what I hope I never have to forget: that when a performer takes to the stage, the audience enables him to transform into art what in the practice room was technique. Every time I play I am Richard Mühlfeld, my instrument singing like Euterpe in the ear of Brahms.

His face was grim. "I never told you—the reason I left Juilliard—I couldn't face my juries."

Ben was an only child, born with the proverbial sterling silver spoon caught in his throat. I didn't understand how choking that could be. He grew up at the keyboard of the Steinway in the west end of his living room, sunlight slashing a staff across his face as his parents drank coffee from Dresden cups and approved. He never stuffed shit in anyone's mailbox, gave a pink belly, played softball, or de-pantsed a girl. What he did was practice, with no sense of having missed out—because his parents told him that he was brilliant, and he believed that meant important too, in that strange and insular way of aristocrats, not at all aggressive, just presumptuous and matter-of-fact. He believed until he left Juilliard. All of a sudden, instead of all along, he had discovered the world.

It is not a kind place, although he won't admit that. Experience doesn't really have to change you, if you refuse to have experience. He still believes he is brilliant, though he has given up all hope of making his brilliance known. He is a man who is quite happy as long as he does not have to leave the little room lit by the glow of his inner lamp.

Abruptly he got up from the table, teeth clenched so tight that he looked like a man straining against the sizzle of an electric shock. He seized my hand and wrung it. "You'll do fine," he promised, as if he had sat down just to tell me that.

And, in the corridor outside Recital Hall, when I saw his raw face and eyes so intense that they looked as if they'd been skinned, I might still have thought he would do fine, too, but it wasn't nerves or excitement; it was terror. I gripped the arm of my seat as he approached the Baldwin visibly perspiring and relaxed only slightly in the polite titter of applause that followed the final notes of the *Preludes* and the *Scherzo*. I couldn't find him in the hall at intermission. "Nervous, Jane?" Martin Solomon called, and I shook my head as I hurried by, still looking. Ben didn't speak when he found me backstage, and he only nodded when I stood up to begin the Poulenc. Though he rushed me, we got a standing ovation, and my face prickled with a pleasurable heat when we bowed, but as soon as I left the stage, I went cold, kneading my hands and pacing the hallway while the wreckage of the "Moonlight" floated out. Afterward, in the car on the way to the Solomons' party, he said, "Well, it went fine, didn't it? I was a little nervous on the Gershwin, but I don't think anyone noticed, do you? I think I played the Chopin well. I don't think I've ever played it better. The audience liked it, don't you think? I should have slowed the 'Moonlight' down. I don't know why I took it so fast. It wasn't too fast, was it? Do you think it was okay?"

"It was wonderful," I said, aching. He could play so well. I had brought an audience to its feet, and I felt like crying.

"Do you think so?" He wasn't stupid; he just wanted to believe me.

"Sure." I closed my eyes and put my hand against the dashboard. "Ben, this is a one-way street."

"I know it," he said and kept driving. "Jane, would you mind terribly if we didn't go to this party?"

I didn't answer.

"I mean . . ."

"I know," I said. "But you can't do that to the Solomons. They're giving it for you." He had to go. It would have been worse if he'd shown he couldn't face them. But maybe I am only rationalizing, an executioner with too much conscience and no stomach. "If you don't want to go right away, I suppose we could stop off for a drink."

"A capital idea," he said cheerily, and so we had a drink at the Dandale while he reviewed the Gershwin, the Chopin, and the Beethoven until the performance was rescored so well that he was the one who said, "Ready?" I nodded and looked down at the pile of confetti that had been my napkin. He had not mentioned the Poulenc.

Ruth and Martin kissed me and congratulated us. Ben rubbed his hands together and said, "Well, it went well, didn't it?" I closed my eyes and let Howard Feltner take my arm to lead me through the downstairs. I said hi to the violinist from the Phil who had, before my last concert, pulled her collar away from her neck to show me the knot the violin had left in spite of the double toweling on her shoulder. "Also," she had confessed in a hushed tone, "I think it's lowering my left breast." She complimented me on the Poulenc and said, "Lucky dog. You have to marry a teacher to rate a recital."

"That's not true," I answered. "Anyway, it was Ben's recital."

"Maybe, but you were the star of the show." As we moved on, Feltner's arm wrapped around my shoulder, she called, "I like your dress." It was the same one I'd worn to marry Ben.

"I wish people wouldn't say that," I whispered to Feltner, who displayed me as he munched olives wrapped in bacon, announcing to anyone who would listen, "She plays like an angel." At my lessons, which I had resumed on a private basis, he complained I would never master the Jeanjean Etudes and scolded me for being lazy, although he knew very well I was not. What he really wanted was to make a French clarinetist of me, and sometimes he would interrupt me to say "When you are playing, the clarinet becomes your voice. Try to sound a little less like an Episcopal minister, mmm? Otherwise, I will have to take a nap." And, as he yawned and curled up on the couch in his office, I would concentrate on making my instrument sound like a fundamentalist spouting fire and brimstone. Which was not at all the Huguenot he wanted. But I had to take him seriously. He had studied with Bellison.

"Congratulations." David Solomon appeared at my elbow, and Feltner drifted off. After a year in Mexico, where he had discovered irreconcilable differences with his waitress, and another year in Brazil, he was living at home again, playing rhythm guitar in a rock band at fraternity parties, signing up for and dropping out of classes.

"Did you come?" I was delighted. I hardly ever saw him now.

"Nah. I just hear everybody buzzing. What's the matter with your husband? I said hello to him, and he looked straight through me."

"Oh, he just gets nervous after a performance. He probably didn't even hear you. Where is he?" I added, looking.

"Around. I saw him in the kitchen. You want another drink? I'll get you some Johnny Walker. The folks serve Inver House to the rabble."

"I'll get it," I said. I needed to find Ben and make sure he felt all right. "Anyway, I drink bourbon."

"Well, see you around." He seemed relieved as he moved off. He never knew what to say to me now that I was married, and it made me sad. I wanted to tell him I was still miserable and laugh about it, but I never knew what to say to him either. I was married, and I should be ashamed.

I didn't see Ben in the kitchen, but Feltner was leaning against the counter, gesticulating to a small circle of people. "So then Starker said . . ." He grabbed my waist. "You all know Jane Gabriel?"

"Oh, yes—you're the little girl who plays so well."

"Congratulations—a fine performance."

"Thank you," I said.

"Tell me, how would you compare the difficulty of the Poulenc with the Bartók Sonatine?"

"I don't know," I said. "I've never played it."

"Jane, you were marvelous. Of course, Howard's always told us that . . ."

"Do you find glissandos effective for warming up when you're playing a piece with such wide skips?"

"Sure." My face felt warm, and in the confusion my attention strayed to a dark-haired man at the end of the counter. He was very short and slender, with a complexion as swarthy as I pictured the one that had earned Beethoven the nickname *"der Spagnol"* in his childhood and the sort of eyes the author of Nancy Drew books had always described as "piercing." A pair of metal crutches with cups for his forearms rested against the counter beside him.

"Did you have an accident?" I asked, feeling the attention I was getting from Feltner's friends diffuse into a pleasant glow. "When do you get off your crutches?"

"Never," he said, seeming to enjoy my loss of composure. "So you're Gabriel's wife." His eyes were so dark, I couldn't find the pupils. I thought he looked like a Gypsy or a jewel thief. Or maybe an assassin. "They told me he had a child bride."

"Jane, Eric Yarber. Eric's the new instructor in piano."

I smiled. "I think I've heard Ben mention you."

"You're not bad," he said.

"Not bad? She's stupendous. And you should taste her chocolate mousse." Elaine Ghent leaned over to kiss me. "We'll have to have you and Ben over for dinner soon."

He ignored Elaine. "What does Herr Doktor Gabriel have to say about me?"

I hesitated. Ben had said that the new piano instructor had a chip on his shoulder and that he was not half as good as he thought he was. "I don't remember."

"Your husband's a jerk," Eric said quietly. Elaine had gone to look for the bathroom, and he nodded in the direction she had taken. "Friend of yours? She's a silly bitch."

"He is not," I said. "He's a kind and generous person."

"And he can't play worth a shit."

"He can too. He plays beautifully." I lowered my voice. "He just gets so nervous when he gives a recital."

"That's a hell of a problem for a musician." He moved his crutches to make room for me at the counter, but I ignored the invitation.

"Furthermore, he's a wonderful teacher."

Eric laughed. "Don't tell me. You were his student. Well, looks like you have carte blanche for the rest of your schooldays." He turned his head as if he'd dismissed me.

"I'm not in school," I said. "I—quit."

"Oh? A devoted little wife. Hubby comes first. She only gives brilliant recitals when she can take time out from baking chocolate mousse." He jerked his head toward the back door and picked up his crutches. "If you'll open that for me, I'll take my rudeness elsewhere. I don't much care for parties."

"You don't bake a mousse." As I held the door for him, he thumped through, and I closed the screen between us. "Anyway, it wasn't my recital."

"That's what you think." He tapped the bottom of the door with a crutch. "It's a nice night. If you get tired of all the attention, I'll be in the back yard thinking up insults."

"Thank you, but I just came in the kitchen to find my husband." I glanced around. "I think I'll go look for him in another room."

Ben was sitting in the living room, having a heated discussion of theory textbooks with two of the teaching assistants. He gave me a little kiss when I sat on the arm of his chair, but did not stop talking. One of the grad students leaned forward. "Mrs. Gabriel, I thought your performance was just excellent."

"The ideal," Ben continued, "would be a worksheet format." He smiled at me and held up his glass. "Darling, if you're going in the kitchen, would you bring me another drink?"

Feltner was still at the bar, and he put his arm around me. "An infant virtuoso," he proclaimed, "or, in the case of ladies, do we say virtuosa?"

Ruth, on her way from the oven with a tray of cheese puffs, said, "It looks like the same plain Jane to me. Howard, you're making a fool of yourself."

"Can't you let my wife tell me that *after* the party? I'll take it," he said when I excused myself to bring Ben his drink. "I haven't told him yet how much we enjoyed the Poulenc."

"Enjoy all the accolades tonight," Ruth admonished as she too squeezed toward the hallway. "I haven't forgotten that you promised to help me paper the upstairs bathroom this weekend. By the way"—she leaned close and whispered— "whatever happened to Ben? He completely blew the 'Moonlight' and nearly destroyed you on the Poulenc."

I spilled my drink. "I don't know."

Eric Yarber had been fumbling at the back door, and now he was giving me an evil grin as I brushed at my skirt.

"I haven't done anything to you." I chunked a handful of ice into my glass and poured it full of bourbon.

"Careful. You don't want to lose your head." Still grinning, he took the half-gallon jug from my hand. "You're quite right. My deepest apologies, Mrs. Gabriel."

I turned my back on him as Margie Geller, the Philharmonic's second flutist, rushed toward me. We had been in Ben's theory class together over two years ago. "Oh, Jane, there you are. You were so *good*, and we all thought you'd just disappeared when you didn't come back. I didn't even know—I can't believe it. Somebody had to tell me when I saw you together at Guiomar Novaes last spring." She looked overjoyed as she caught the hand of a tall, freckled boy and reeled him toward us. "This is my boyfriend, Greg. This is Jane. We had classes together."

Greg looked at his feet. "Pleased to meet you," he mumbled, adding, "You were real good," as if he wished I'd been lousy so that he wouldn't have had to say more than hi.

"We have to go," Margie said. "Can you believe it—I still have hours. Oh." She had collided with Eric, but instead of apologizing, she said, "It's *you*. Bye-bye, Jane. I'll call you sometime." She never did, though I really hoped she would. I suppose that she thought I would no longer be interested in anything an undergraduate might have to say.

"I thought you were coming outside," Eric said.

I studied my wedding ring. "I'm married," I said, and he laughed. "I don't see what's so funny."

"Everything's funny to me. I'm very cynical." He grinned. "You're no Little Mary Sunshine yourself—in spite of the act. Also, you're bored with your husband, who is, I grant you, a bore. No?'' He lifted an eyebrow. ''Mrs. Gabriel, I never make a mistake about character. It's an instinct. Well, since you won't come outside, perhaps you could do me the favor of moving to where I can sit down.'' He flapped a crutch. ''I'm not at my best on my feet.''

''Do you improve sitting down?'' I asked, investigating the other rooms and adding, ''What happened to your legs?'' as he dragged himself behind me. All the seats were taken, and he looked as if he might spit on anyone polite enough to offer him one.

''Polio.'' We were back in the kitchen. ''There is a bench out back.'' I hesitated. ''Don't worry. I'm not going to molest you. Your performance aroused my professional interest, and I'd like to talk.''

Embarrassed to have been so obvious, I held the door. He took the back steps slowly but with skill, and I sloshed through the unraked leaves behind him to the bench.

After a few minutes, I giggled. ''I guess you didn't want to talk after all.'' He didn't answer. ''You're a pianist—what do you think of Bernstein?''

''I think Leonard Bernstein is the Norman Mailer of American music.'' As he paused, I looked back at the house. The bright windows were hung like Lautrec's scenes from the Moulin Rouge against a dark gallery wall. ''So you're a newlywed.''

''I've been married over two years.''

''I was married for six. You played the Poulenc all wrong.''

''I did not.''

''Oh yes you did. You've got the technique, but you're sentimental. You slop it up with feeling. That's okay for Tchaikovsky, but it doesn't do for Poulenc.''

''Music *is* feeling.'' I stood. ''I'm cold, so if you'll excuse me . . .''

''You're not cold—you're hurt. You know, I used to teach at Vassar. I think you might have liked it there. They appreciate sensitive young girls. Finish them off with just a big enough dose of the arts for them to marry insensitive rich boys and feel misunderstood for the rest of their lives.'' He grabbed my arm. "You're damn good, but you're a silly little girl, and you're not ever going to get any better."

"What business is that of yours? Let go of me."

He dropped my arm. "Sorry."

I was too furious to stalk off. "Just because you're crippled— and divorced—and ugly . . ."

"Anything else?" he said.

". . . doesn't mean people are going to think it's neat when you're rude." I was wrong, of course. There were a number of people, primarily silly little girls, who did think so. Maybe I did, too. I hadn't gone in.

"You ought to go to New York and study with Russian-off."

"My career is none of your business."

"You don't have a career. You ought to be going to festivals and international competitions. You're not good enough to win, but you just might be good enough to get a little attention." He looked down. "And my legs and my divorce and my looks are none of yours."

"How do you know I don't?"

"Your husband wouldn't let you." He looked up. "He's jealous of you."

"That's ridiculous." I thought it was. I hoped so still when Ben tried to talk me out of the Richmond Symphony. ("Oh, Janie," he said, "look what a hard time you had just working for the School of Business. You couldn't handle the pressure of performing." *I* couldn't? I thought but didn't say because I hoped he was less jealous than just wrong. I hoped, in spite of the fact that never once did he tell me he thought I'd played well the night we'd performed the Poulenc.)

"Is it? I told you, Mrs. Gabriel, I never make a mistake on character."

"Yes, I know. It's an instinct." I stood stiffly just out of his reach. I hated the way he said Mrs. Gabriel, as if it were some sort of nasty joke, but I didn't want to tell him to call me Jane. "Well, I think you've made a mistake on mine. I'm not at all interested in your opinions."

Behind him the house was still humming, and there was an

occasional burst of high-pitched laughter from one of the three figures left in the kitchen windows.

"No? What about this one? You don't love your husband."

"Wrong," I said coolly and took three steps toward the porch. "Why did you say that?"

"Because it's as plain as the pretty little nose on your face. Take it easy. Believe me, he'll be the last one to know." He patted the bench. "Sit down. Relax. Why should you feel guilty? Take my advice and dump him. You've got a lot to learn, but, like I said, you're damn good, and he's going to do everything he can to get in your way. Well." He paused. "I seem to have hit a raw nerve."

"Not at all. I told you. I'm not interested in your opinions."

"Oh? Then why did you come out here?" He tilted his head as if to hear my answer, but he didn't wait. "Because you think I want to fuck you?"

I had an attack of giggles as brittle as a flurry of staccato high notes. "No, well, I wouldn't think that," I squeaked, feeling very much the fool as I stomped to the porch. The crowd in the kitchen was gone. He bumped in while I was still looking for a clean glass in the rubble of lipstick-stained plastic cups and citrus rinds.

"Why are you so offended? That's what you wanted me to say."

"It most certainly is not." I chose one of the dirty cups and poured myself a big drink.

"You said music is feeling? Well, you played, and that's what I felt." I sipped my drink. "By the way, that dress is dumb. If you don't want to be a musician, you ought to at least look like a woman instead of a flower girl." I didn't answer. "When Beethoven was your age, he was sitting at the piano with a slop bucket at his feet so he wouldn't have to leave it."

I took a big gulp of bourbon. "I'm interested in Beethoven's music. I don't care what he did with his slop."

"She wants to be a musician." David stood in the cellar doorway, a cigarette in his hand. "And as far as the rest of it goes, I don't think you know a woman from shit."

Eric's eyes narrowed as he jerked his chin in David's direction. "Your boyfriend?"

I was too mortified to look at David. "I don't have a boyfriend. I'm happily married, I told you."

Eric sneered at David. "Well, looks like you're out of luck, too."

"She's a friend of the family," David said. "This is my parents' house. I'm asking you to leave."

"Oh? Your parents know you smoke dope in their basement?" Eric turned his attention back to me. "It's a lucky thing you're pretty and make such good chocolate mousse. Because you're going nowhere with the clarinet. When *I* play a piece I get inside the composer."

"Leave her alone," David said.

I set the drink on the table, and put my hands over my ears. Ben was standing in the doorway. "There you are," he said. "We should be going. You have to get up in the morning, and it's getting late."

"I'm ready." I downed the rest of my drink. David shook his head at Ben and retreated to the basement, slamming the door behind him.

"As for you," Eric said, "well, can you type?"

I whirled, but there was nothing left in my glass to throw in his face. I was drunk, due at my desk in the Business Building in less than seven hours. No one would say a word when I came in late, breathless with excuses I wouldn't finish as my co-workers all glanced up at the clock. I snatched one of his crutches and dashed it to the floor.

"Well." He listed to one side, leaning on the other. "I'll bet you're a lively little lay."

"Shall we go?" Ben said, and just as I was about to snatch the other crutch, Ben picked up the first and handed it to Eric.

He was quiet as we got in the car. When we turned the corner, he said, "I didn't expect to enjoy that, but I'm glad I let you talk me into going."

I was crying, and as he reached out to pat my knee, I jerked it toward the door. "Did you *hear* what he said to me?"

"I had an interesting talk with Brian Grasso, that new T.A.

286

He had some good ideas about the theory course. I might just . . ."

"He said I didn't have a career."

". . . adapt one of them when we get to modulations." Ben sighed. "Now, Janie, you can't let these little professional jealousies get you down—although I admit it was cowardly of him to take whatever he has against me out on my wife."

"Cowardly of *him?*" Amazement dried my tears, so I burst into a fresh set.

"Don't be sad," Ben coaxed. "Come on, let's have a smile. You looked very pretty tonight."

"My dress is dumb."

"You know, I didn't realize there was so much confusion among the staff on testing, but Bishop seemed to be under the impression—anyway, I think I got him straightened out. It seems to me . . ."

"He said I played Poulenc all wrong."

". . . that . . ."

"He wants"—I sniffed—"to fuck me."

". . . we should ask students to apply their learning in practical situations." The cords in Ben's neck stood out as big as pencils. "That skinny little kike. I take that as an insult."

He didn't ask how I took it, although he might have guessed years later, when I asked whatever happened to Eric Yarber. Because he did call, and I went to lunch with him, though it was always more or less the same: he was hostile; I was uncooperative. "Why do you want to relate everything to sex?" I said the last time I saw him, and Eric said, "Because that's what most of life comes down to in the end; oh, not the act itself, but the identity, and maybe not for everyone, but it does for you and me. And, though I bet he doesn't know it, your stupid husband, too." He smiled. "You think he loves you so much? I'd like to be around when you finally cut him loose. That man's going to learn a lot about life from you." He leaned across the table. "Would I seem more sensitive if I said 'make love'?"

"What's the difference?" I said. "The answer's still no."

He rescued his crutches as they caught the black skirt of a waitress who was scurrying by. "What if I told you I was in love with you?"

"Then I'd say you're a liar."

As I picked up my purse to go for the last time, he held his beer aloft. "To your outstanding and screwed-up character, Mrs. Gabriel. And, by the way, I am in love with you."

The faculty at the Music School didn't much care for his manner, although I heard some of their wives did, enough that his stay wasn't all that unpleasant. He left when his contract wasn't renewed, and perhaps he is teaching silly young girls at Sweet Briar or Hollins or, like Ben, playing piano at a ballet school and dreaming of what lies beneath those little leotards. He was right after all. I did want to fuck him and didn't have the courage, and, though I don't for one minute believe that he was in love with me, I *am* sentimental—it would have made a difference if I had. I heard him play once, shortly before he left Bloomington. Ben was wrong. He was every bit as good as he thought he was, and he thumped his crutches down beside the piano in the most wonderfully contemptuous manner, as if, like Beethoven, he had nothing but scorn for his body. The world loves a crippled musician.

Because he's the most obvious of all metaphors for the triumph of imagination. He had no conscience, and I followed him into the yard because I was sick to death of mine. The truth is always unrepentant. It is sentiment that is contrite, so my conscience nagged me through the long, subliminal wars of our luncheons. It was such a petty betrayal. I felt no guilt at all for that little treachery to my marriage, but I felt a culpability beyond all reasoned weight for my disloyalty to David. And so I learned that we are not simply what we would have imagination make us; instead, we are what that unwilled truce between imagination and conscience decides.

Ben was fuming. "And Mr. Eric Yarber has got another think coming . . ."

"He said I was silly." I tried to prolong the tears to postpone the rage.

". . . if he thinks he can get away with making passes at

my wife just because he's got his nose out of joint over *my* recital.''

I sat up perfectly straight, wiped my face, and aimed my anger where I meant it, spacing my words as evenly as quarter notes between quarter rests. ''Why didn't you defend me?''

18

When I think of Ruth, I often see her harumphing around her kitchen, a dust of flour on her bosom as she rolls pie crusts, banging tins and muttering, just loud enough for Martin to hear, "Why are we having these people over? I don't want to see them." "I don't want to see them, either, Ruthie," he shouts. "*You* invited them." But she loved to entertain.

And in those long last years in Bloomington after my debut, when I was once again an amateur musician, playing to an empty room I loved being entertained, as if the long days spent setting tabs and staring at the walls of the Business School were a bad dream and my waking hours began when I climbed out of the tub and dusted my body with Chantilly. It didn't matter whom I talked to or if Ben kept me out so late I would feel like quitting everything when the alarm went off tomorrow. My real life was there, with an audience. There were men who made that for me, and I began to play to them with the exaggerated innocence of one who has no interest in delivering a finale. Ben professed to hate parties, but we went, usually early, and were often the last to leave. The way he said "I know you enjoy them" made me feel ashamed, as if my public self were the result of some deep deficiency, but in fact he loved parties, too. If I charmed myself with flirting, he charmed himself with pedagogy, and when we got home, he would continue whatever monologue the departure of guests had interrupted while I buttoned my nightgown and tried to look too tired for the act that he was warming up to with his fervent talk-talk-talking. Then, his eyes blazing with the image of himself that his academic words made, my own vague with listening and drink, we made what passed for love, coming in a frenzy of convicted, solitary egos.

I wouldn't say that Ben and I were popular, but after concerts and recitals there are always celebrations, and often Ruth's dinners were feasts I helped prepare. We were sisters in the kitchen, cursing eggs that broke their yolks into the whites we were whipping for soufflés, sipping sherry while we stirred, passing a spoon to taste for spices. It should have been that way at work, four women in an office, but it wasn't. Men at menial jobs talk about women. Women at menial jobs talk about their children. Having no children of my own, I never really felt like a woman there, not even much like one when Ben undressed me. But sitting in the freckled sunlight that came through Ruth's kitchen windows as she said "You can stuff the mushrooms," I felt wonderful.

It was a feeling I lost when we moved to Richmond, two women in the kitchen doing women's things, because not too long after that I auditioned and turned professional, and Ben made sure I knew that meant unfeminine. "If you have time," he would say, pausing to make sure I caught every nasty nuance, "I have three shirts that could use ironing." In fact, his shirts were Perma-Press, and I was careful to snatch and hang them hot from the drier. In fact, I had never ironed shirts and had more time then than when I'd been typing, but shirts were not the issue, not really.

"Why don't you just say it?" I said once. "You don't want me to have a career." He didn't say it. "What should I have then? I don't have children, I don't have a house, I can clean this apartment in half an hour. It's not your fault," I added, slamming the lasagne into the oven. "It's not your fault," I repeated, looking out the window to the alley where one of the alcoholics who lived next door in the halfway house was cracking a bullwhip against a garbage can. Ben got up to get a beer, discarding the pop top on the table. "I like it here," I insisted. "I *like* this city, I like the apartment, I like everything. But you can't expect me to sit in the ladies' lounge at Miller and Rhoads all day. I have to do something," I pleaded, feeling guilty because I hadn't said that something must be music, the very thing he didn't want me to—no matter that I had once been his best student. He got up from the table. "I thought we were very happy in Bloomington," he said. "What if we had a baby?"

"Well . . ." I hedged because it was one of those things I'd agreed with myself I couldn't have before I'd ever learned to want. He'd had a vasectomy, and I had, just recently, bled for the first time since Christopher.

"It can be reversed," he begged. "You said so. I know I wouldn't listen to you then, but I can check into it. Tomorrow."

I had said no. I had read it in some waiting room magazine.

"Say you want it," he said. "Say you want it more than anything."

"I don't. Not more than anything. Not more than playing."

"I'll make an appointment," he promised.

It had been at a party that I conceived my wish for a child and, failing that, the inevitability of Christopher. It was shortly after we moved to Richmond and before I auditioned for the Symphony. Ben had promised I wouldn't have to work, although the bills were coming in from Reese's last operation. Ben stacked them beneath his Princeton mug on top of the refrigerator, where he also stacked the second and third notices from Sears and BankAmericard so high that eventually the foundation for his mug toppled and it split in two neat pieces on the floor. He was like that about money. We slept on a mattress from Goodwill, but he brought home the same imported wines his parents drank, and we ate artichoke hearts, shrimp, and caviar. If I walked to the store alone and we had bean soup, he smacked his lips just as loudly, but turn him loose in Safeway, he came home with fancy little jars again. When the stack of bills reached the ceiling, I knew I would have to suggest I go to work, and Ben would pretend not to be relieved as he insisted, "Only if you want to." I wouldn't want to, but I would have to all the same, and it made me angry. He lost his job, his cars broke down, he couldn't seem to comprehend that artichokes cost more than carrots, and it was never his fault, but it wasn't mine. So why did I have to be the one to bail us out?

I knew the answer. I had missed the deadline for applying to Virginia Commonwealth University. I felt like a nomad, wandering from the lounge of Miller and Rhoads, where I chatted with the blue-haired widows from Monument Avenue, to Shafer Street Court, where the students tossed Frisbees in wide-legged, unhemmed jeans washed nearly white, the boys in the same multicolored T-shirts as the bra-less girls, their hair grown out so long, you would have thought that it had taken more than just five years. When they got dressed up, the girls wore skirts so short they did not have to bend over for you to see their underpants. At night they gathered on the front stoops of Floyd Avenue and smoked marijuana. They had become the younger generation, and I had no more in common with them than with the blue-haired widows. In my wardrobe of prissy dresses left from the Business School, I belonged in an office with other housewives whose husbands couldn't pay their bills. More than anything, I wanted Ben to give me a pair of jeans for my birthday, but he gave me another dress in what he assumed was my favorite style.

The party was one of those cocktail affairs, supposed to end at seven, that leaves you out at nine, drunk, tired, and hungry, wondering if there are enough eggs in your refrigerator to pass an omelette off as the evening meal. It was given by a musicologist and his interior decorator wife, who had redone two or three town houses in the Fan and then moved out to the West End, where all the tobacco executives lived overlooking the James River. "Wow," I said, peering through a screen of magnificent magnolias as we drove along Cary Street Road. "Did you see that place? It's bigger than the Phi Delt house at Indiana." Ben turned into the driveway of a slightly smaller structure.

We were early. Margot, the wife, escorted me through the house, chatting about Italy, where they had lived for a year while her husband finished a book on the Italian Ars Nova. "Have you been to Firenze?" she asked. I hadn't, but my husband had spent time in Germany and France. She made a little face. Paris was crowded and "becoming so commercial, so Americanized." She didn't care for Germany, "although the Black Forest is lovely. I thoroughly enjoyed seeing that." We had ended our tour in the music room, which was painted a rich burgundy, the grand piano and an Italian writing table enameled a brilliant white. A series of etchings in borderless frames climbed the wall, and, like a triptych, the uncurtained bay window held a view of the riverbank unrolling down a slope of lawn in the late afternoon light. "We feel very fortunate to have found this house," Margot was saying, holding her glass so that its shadow was printed like a topaz brooch on her dress. "Clay wanted to buy into the Fan again, but we've done that."

She was quite beautiful, though Ben didn't think so, her dark hair curved over her ears like a pair of swag drapes into a simple bun, the sort of woman who could carry a suitcase through international airports as lightly as if it contained nothing but a black lace nightgown. I felt like the sort of woman who would have her handle break, her latch fly open, who would leave a trail of ragged underwear down the concourse. I had set an unfortunate curl in my shoulder-length brown hair, and Ben had trimmed my bangs too short. Her five-year-old daughter came in, bearing a tray of crab-stuffed mushrooms, her extraordinarily round, china-blue eyes shyly averted. From the other side of the house there was a faint melody of arriving guests. Margot stooped to straighten the bow of her daughter's pinafore. "Take them around the living room, Genevieve," she said. It was at that moment I conceived. I thought everything would come with a baby—the house, the travel, the fascinating life. Ben would pick up his shorts and socks, the refrigerator would never need defrosting, and I could devote myself to a creative motherhood, my temper growing as smooth as Margot's creamy crêpe dress.

In the living room Ben was absorbed in a discussion of Francesco Landini with the host. I talked with a violist from the Richmond Symphony who taught at V.C.U. He seemed surprised to hear I played the clarinet.

"I'm surprised Ben's never mentioned it," I said.

He introduced me to his son, who had wandered from the terrace to the house. "Donald is just back from Paris," the violist explained before he left to refill his drink. "He's been writing there."

"Oh, Paris," I said, feeling my eyes become brighter with the bourbon. "Paris is so crowded. It's getting so commercial and Americanized."

He was tall, with a sullen, pockmarked face. "Ah, you've been there."

"No," I mumbled, looking away.

"You do speak French, of course?"

On the sofa two music professors were discussing real estate in the Fan. "You snap one up for ten thousand, put another ten into renovations, and it's a guaranteed fifty on resale."

"No." I smiled. "Do you write music?"

"Fiction."

I kept smiling. "Oh. Stories. I read a lot," I added. "I just finished the whole *Forsyte Saga*. It was even better than on TV. Did you read it?"

"Galsworthy was a hack."

"Oh." I bit my lip. "What kind of stories do you write?"

"Experimental. Have you read Robbe-Grillet?" I hadn't. "Actually my work is more like Stein, but contemporary, and it's completely original, of course. Nothing like that crap by Barth and Mailer. After all, they're just precocious traditionalists left fumbling in a time when the traditional narrative is dead, don't you think?" He puffed furiously on a cigarette and spilled ashes down his denim shirt. "Have you read Barthelme?"

I shook my head. "I've never heard of him. Her? I like Charles Dickens."

"Narrative." He blew smoke in my face. "Barthelme writes for *The New Yorker*."

"Oh," I said, and added, "Let me get you an ashtray." I found a crystal quadrangle on a Parsons table covered with vinyl in a snakeskin print. The table was exactly the height of my mother's kitchen counter; a few years before, I would have been reaching for a cup of coffee to bring her after she got home from work, and in that moment I went home, as I reluctantly did all too often, reminded by this gesture, that sensation. I supposed my mother might, at that very moment, be unbuckling her shoes to take the load off her feet. I wondered if Dickie would be playing Little League by now. The twins were nearly five, almost old enough to pass trays at parties. It was six o'clock. Marie would be burping her Tupperware as she stored the scraps from dinner. Had he lived, my brother might have been replacing a washer on the bathroom faucet or, if he was tired, drinking a beer as he watched the news. Or maybe he would be at the mill, working afternoons. Had I been there, I would have been studying the blank white sky of my bedroom ceiling, thinking about leaving. It was not without irony that I felt these pangs of nostalgia. "Where do you write for?"

He tapped his cigarette into the crystal bowl disdainfully. "My work is much too advanced for publication."

At the other end of the room a knot of men in gray suits and women in vibrant jersey dresses were debating the significance of a few dribbles of paint across a canvas hung above the fireplace. It resembled a Jackson Pollock, but the hand that had splashed it performed much more cheaply, since it was attached for the nonce to a graduate student at V.C.U. I'd seen his work for sale in the loan/own gallery of the Virginia Museum, but it had not occurred to me that anyone would buy it.

Donald had lit another cigarette and was sucking it frantically. "You see, what I've done is to take the new objective one step further and liberate it from the last of the senses. Robbe-Grillet tried to do it, but he was hung up on sight. Stein understood that the only object for the writer was language, the pure resistance of the surfaces of words, but unfortunately she was a woman and so incapable of objectivity."

"Oh." I was too bored to take issue, and, anyway, maybe he was right. I didn't feel objective. I never felt objective. I had a feeling that one of us sounded stupid, and I was too subjective to be sure who, I with my faint *oh's* and *haven't read's*, or he with all his theories. "What are they about? Your stories, I mean."

"I call them *fictions*. They aren't *about* anything."

I frowned. "What kind of people are in them?"

He missed the ashtray. "I don't write about character."

I held the crystal dish closer. "Well, what is in them then?"

"My *style*." He gave me a contemptuous look as he stubbed his cigarette. "I take it you don't write."

"I play the clarinet."

"Music is the most decadent of the arts. Entertainment for the bourgeoisie." He swept the room with his arm, and his new cigarette went flying. "Look at these drunken fools."

I rescued it from the rug and ground it out. "I don't think the bourgeoisie finds Cage so entertaining. I don't think they've come to terms with anything but the *idea* of Schönberg yet." I paused and realized I was angry. "Personally, I don't like John Cage. I think he's all theory and very little art. I'm not so sure anyone really likes him, but I know a lot of people who think they should. I know a lot of people who like to *talk* about art." I drained my bourbon.

"What makes you think people are supposed to *like* art?"

I shrugged. "What makes you think they're supposed *not* to? Speaking of drunks, I think I'm ready for another. You?"

"I never drink. I'm too fond of my inhibitions." He lit another cigarette. "Where did you graduate?"

"Woodrow Wilson Junior High School. And I happen to hate my inhibitions, so . . ."

"Wait. I think it's necessary for artists to opinionate. Look." He tapped my shoulder and pointed. "There's a man who loses all his inhibitions when he drinks and becomes his true, rigid, Puritanical self."

I turned my head. "Oh," I said, stung. Ben *was* drunk, and his shoulders had grown squarer. He never stumbled or slurred words; he merely found issues he didn't see when he was sober.

Before I could excuse myself again, the violist joined us, ticking a fingernail against his watchface. "We should be going, Donald. We're due at Zoe Washburn's for dinner now." He smiled at me. "It was a pleasure meeting you, Jane. Perhaps we'll see you again at some gathering."

"Sure," I said faintly and watched them go, thinking okay then, some people are charmed, they have dinner parties to go to when the cocktail parties are through. They have children and careers; they have big houses. It doesn't matter if they're snobs or fools. I wanted those things too, and I meant to get them now. I crossed the room and touched Ben's sleeve. "Whenever you're ready . . ."

"In a minute," he promised and for another hour continued to discuss the significance of Marenzio, Gesualdo, Peri, and Caccini with the host. I sat on the rose-colored sofa and got drunk.

I was so drunk when I stood before the stove at ten that scrambling five eggs seemed as overwhelming as preparing a seven-course dinner for twenty. "I want to have a baby," I said when Ben finished explaining the role of the theorist Vicentino in the development of chromaticism.

"I find that very unfunny."

"I didn't mean it to be funny."

"In fact, I find it rather cruel, although that doesn't surprise me, it doesn't surprise me at all from *you*. You knew before you married me—and, in any case, I already have three children whom I can scarcely afford to support now."

"I know."

He tweaked the lace hem of my slip as I put his plate before him. "Now don't be sad. *You're* my little girl."

"You are *not* my father." I got my own plate, slapping it down so hard that the toast jumped to the table. "I don't have a father, and if you think I married you because I needed one, you're nuts."

"It's nothing to be ashamed of," he said, scooping up eggs with his toast. "As a matter of fact, it's natural. Haven't you read about Electra? She had a feeling for her father that was"—he smiled—"electric."

"You're drunk."

He kept smiling. "If you want a family, why don't you call your mother?"

"Why doesn't my mother call me? I didn't walk out on her. She *kicked* me out."

"If you say so."

"You weren't there. What do you know?" But he'd been there that spring vacation when I'd told my mother and brother that I was ashamed of them, and, because I remembered . . .

I had another memory. Once, when I was in third grade, my teacher sent me to the office with the attendance report. The office had large windows that looked out on the hall, and through them, as I came around the corner, I saw a woman in a black coat laughing at something the secretary must have said from the other side of the counter, where a pocketbook sat open, a pair of gloves beside it, their limp fingers awry. There was nothing remarkable about the scene, except that the woman was my mother, who had come to pay the text-book rental she forgot to send with me, and it made me feel strange to watch her fold the receipt into her wallet, that soiled flap of turquoise leather whose frayed corners and smudged picture windows seemed more intimate than her lingerie. In the washing machine, those undergarments lost their little folds and stains and came out purged of personality, but that wallet wore my mother, and I saw her in it each time she sent me to her purse. Yet, seen from that new and accidental distance, it might have been any wallet and she any woman, fitting her gloves on finger by finger while I dawdled, the smile on her face as unfamiliar as my own caught unawares. I turned my back, willing her to leave before we recognized each other, because, for the first time, I did not want her— her coat was shabby, her laugh too loud—to be my mother; not at school, where I was on my own. Whose fault was it that she was lost?

I cleared the table. "Did you have enough to eat? There are some chocolate chip cookies in the cabinet."

"Ummm." He got the tin. "My little wife makes the best chocolate chip cookies in the world."

"I bought them at Safeway."

"Did I tell you," he said, chewing—"ummm, well you bought wisely then because Safeway makes the second-best chocolate chip cookies in the world—did I tell you I had an interesting discussion with Clay Cromwell? They're lucky to have him at V.C.U. By the way, I noticed you haven't filled out your application."

"I don't want to go to school." I began washing dishes when I saw his expression, turning my back to the table. "Well, I did, but now I don't."

"Everyone has to start somewhere," he said as I jerked my hand from the hot water. "You know, it takes a musicologist to admit that a theorist might have more influence than a composer. Not Gesualdo or de Rore, not even the harpsichord at Ferrara, but that textbook by Niccolò Vicentino."

"Ouch." I turned off the hot water and faced him. "I'm sick of *talking* about music. I'm going to audition for the Richmond Symphony."

"Without Vicentino no one would have known how to adapt the chromatic intervals of the Greeks." He gave me a triumphant look.

"You didn't hear me."

"I heard you. You're making a mistake." His fingers fumbled at my slip. "Let's do it in the kitchen," he whispered.

I slapped at his hands. "Let's not."

But his penis was already pointing at me through his pants.

When I'd been accepted, his response was more direct. Rehearsals were inconvenient; the music business was too competitive. Not to mention my delicate condition, my moods, my nervousness, which he not-mentioned so often that I felt like an invalid whose return to health was a dangerous relapse.

"Jane, I know I wasn't as sympathetic as I should have been when you were in trouble in Bloomington. I can find the money. I want you to see a psychiatrist."

"I want to play the clarinet. What's to analyze?"

"Obsession. Obviously you are crying out for help with this insane compulsion for success."

I left the room in fury. Later I came back. "I am playing last chair with a minor symphony, and I absolutely fail to see how that can be construed as an insane compulsion for success."

"You see what I mean?" he said. "You're overly aware of

rank and feel paranoid because it's not one of the country's best orchestras, which it certainly is not.''

"I give up," I said.

"That's your decision. I haven't asked you to."

"I didn't mean the Symphony." I wept. "Why should I give up that?"

"Why don't you talk to a psychiatrist and find out?"

"I don't *need* a psychiatrist."

"Why are you crying then?"

I swallowed a sob. "I'm crying because I'm *pissed*."

"That's exactly what I mean," he said. "You're not angry; you're disturbed."

We played *Prélude à l'après-midi d'un faune* at my first concert. "What did you think?" I asked. "The oboe was flat," Ben said. He was right, but I'd hoped he wouldn't notice. At our last rehearsal the conductor had said, "Oboe, if you get any flatter, you're going to have to transpose it a half step up." It was after the concert that Ben decided he had never enjoyed parties, in which case it made no sense for him to go. "You go if you want," he said. "I know you always have a good time." "That's okay," I said, feeling guilty and not quite certain what I was guilty of. I skipped every postconcert party that year.

Of course, I could have quit the Symphony, but I didn't. Maybe I had figured out that as long as we were married, one of us was bound to be miserable, and I had had my turn, so it might as well be Ben.

But I doubt it. And I doubt I knew then that, having borne guilt vaguely, one eventually prefers to pin it down.

Christopher was shopping for a lover.

I think maybe I was, too.

19

With the stubbornness of hope, for a few days I believed it perverse luck that I couldn't seem to catch Christopher alone. He was preoccupied at rehearsals, flashing smiles as bright and meaningless as neon signs, making casual conversation when I stopped by his stand and he continued to pencil notes on his score. "What's on your mind?" he said when he met me in a back hallway, summoned by a note I had dropped on the tray of his music stand.

I shrugged, playing with the strap of my purse. He'd *asked* me to be in love with him, and now—when maybe I was, maybe, I didn't know, but he was young, and when I was with him the world seemed so possible, I wanted him, that was sure—now he wouldn't even look at me. "Nothing special. Listen, this weekend"—I twisted the strap—"well, I mean if you were free, I could tell Ben I was going shopping or something, I mean he wouldn't think twice about that."

"I was thinking about heading up to the mountains."

"Oh, sure," I said. "Well, it was just an idea. I thought maybe . . ."

He gave me the briefest flicker of a glance. "You want to go camping?"

I scuffed one toe of my new boots against the suede instep of the other. "Well, I couldn't stay out all night or anything. I mean"—I laughed—"you know."

"Sure," he said and without another look started to walk back to the auditorium. Loss went through my body like a palsy as the stitching on the back pockets of his Levi's curved with his muscled stride, and it was all I could do not to say "Yes, I'll leave Ben," but he hadn't asked.

"Maybe next weekend when you're in town then." I caught up to him. "Or, well, whenever." I took a deep breath. "Have I done something? Are you mad at me?"

"No."

"Well, that's good. I mean . . ." My laugh was breathy. "I thought maybe you were avoiding me."

"Don't be paranoid."

He didn't want me. And I hadn't done anything except be the sort of sap who might fall in love with her lover because he was her lover. He'd even reminded me of Kelly, but too late I realized that what they had in common was simply my response. We were opposite the ladies' room, and I put my hand on the door, waiting for him to say something to keep me in the hall. He shrugged.

"Well, you son-of-a-bitch," I said and waited until the door snapped shut behind me to cry.

I shook my head at the pathetic, splotched face in the mirror. Now there was a real asshole for you. She'd waited six years to have an affair, and when she did, it didn't even last a week. And there she was, crying in the bathroom as if she'd just lost the love of her life. Whining that she couldn't go back to rehearsal; she couldn't ever face him again. I glared at her. "Where's your pride?" I demanded. She blubbered.

At home I suffered attacks of guilt like fainting spells. Sid wrote from Colorado. Riggs was back safe from Viet Nam; their son was in first grade; they hoped he'd have a new little brother or sister soon. I imagined how she'd waited for Riggs faithfully, tucking her son into bed each night, then eating potato chips and watching TV all alone. I remembered how my mother had kept faith with my father, the thin gold band still on her finger years after he'd died. I supposed Marie might yet be true to my brother, even though no one could blame her if she was not. My life had been one disloyalty after another; it was no wonder I felt so alone. It didn't matter that I had lost him, that he hadn't been worth it. I had meant him to be, and so I was guilty just the same.

For months I was an insomniac, and when I did sleep, I woke sweating, searching Ben's face to see if I'd confessed in my dreams. *If* he forgave me, it would be, I knew, just as he'd forgiven me Kelly, dismissing my passion as mere indiscretion, although he remembered it all of his life. I thought it was the worst of both worlds: my crime was reduced while my sentence remained. Soon after we married, he had mentioned that his father was aware of my "past." "My what?" Ben averted his eyes. "Your little adventure with that pimply kid." "He *didn't have pimples.* How *could* you?" I demanded, but Ben said, "Don't get upset. I told him I'd forgiven you." No, as criminal as I felt after Christopher, Ben's was a kind of forgiveness I was better off without.

At least Ben loved me, so I tried to make it up. I ironed his shirts, I baked cookies, I left sweet little notes in his pockets, I asked him questions and thanked him for all his advice. When his vasectomy proved irreversible, I curled up in his lap and confessed that I didn't care, and for days he whistled in the bathtub while I scrubbed his back. He began to refer to my job with the Symphony as my hobby, although I know he had difficult moments whenever a guest pianist performed. I think that until his Bloomington recital, he had still hoped that the man seated at the Steinway before the orchestra would one day be himself. Like me, Ben had trained to perform. I saw how his hands tensed in his lap each time he listened to a pianist, and I felt very close to him then. But for all his righteousness, Ben was not an honest man. Everything he said with his mouth, his hands denied, and I never knew which to address at those times.

So for a few years we were happier, until Ben lost his job at V.C.U. Two months later I found one with the Eastern Music Festival in North Carolina.

For three days I didn't tell him. I thought about turning it down and never telling him. I thought about how, a long time ago, I could have turned down all my ambitions, stayed in my own bed at night, majored in music education, and gone home to live in my mother's house and teach band. This was different, but that's the thing about choices: you think that making one leaves others, only to find that with that one you've really made them all. I told him.

We were strolling down Boulevard beneath a gaudy December sunset. To the east the second-story windows of the avenue's apartments had turned to gifts wrapped in pastel foil. "It's only six weeks " I said my voice splintery. "And Greensboro's not that far."

"My piano is here," he said.

I chewed my lip. After a while I said, "Well, I don't *have* to go."

"You needn't stay home on my account."

"I know."

"Contrary to what you think, I am perfectly capable of living alone. I did quite well before I met you, in case you've forgotten. You're not indispensable."

"I'm coming back," I said.

As the sky darkened, we sat on the ledge of the empty fountain in front of the old entrance to the Virginia Museum and the double row of flagpoles whose banners had been taken in for the night. The pulleys were ringing like wind chimes. The street lights had come on, old-fashioned globes on top of green iron posts. On summer evenings I thought Boulevard must look like Paris, with those lampposts and tiered porches and lacy trees in the pearl-gray light, the scent of the flowers that were sold all day at the open-air stands on the corners still mingling with the smell of warm sidewalks. In December the sky flared and died as quickly as an oven match. Ben bent to pat a dog sniffing at the base of the fountain. "I was good at teaching, I swear I was."

"I know you were. You were the best teacher I ever had. You'll get another job, you'll see."

His shoulders straightened as the dog trotted off. "You don't have to patronize me. I knew when I let you join the

Symphony this would happen. You can't handle success, Janie. You never could."

My throat clenched with rage, and I nearly snapped, "You mean you can't handle failure," but maybe he was right—I should have known better than to bring my success up in the middle of his failure. Maybe I should have known better than to succeed when he was failing. But when could I be successful then? "Well, maybe if you came to North Carolina you'd make some contacts."

"You're too ambitious," he said. "That's one thing I never liked about you."

"But what *reason* do you have to stay here?"

He shook his head.

"Well, I guess there must be a whole list of things you don't like about me," I said, hating myself for sounding small. For over eleven years I had wondered if I loved Ben: on Monday I didn't; on Tuesday I might; when we had drinks in the garden of Poor Richard's to celebrate a special concert, I thought I must; when he licked his lips and undressed me, I knew I never had. And when I thought of my mother, I knew that if I didn't, everything that had ever been wrong was my fault. It had never occurred to me that he might have days when he did not love me. It had never occurred to me that love always has reservations. But it occurred to me now. And it occurred to me that, like my mother, I had been very foolish to put everything in the name of love. I loved the dark museum behind me. I loved its Fabergé eggs, its miniatures of the czars, and red carpet so rich it might have been dyed with the blood of peasants. I loved my block of Richmond, brick sidewalks broken up by the roots of the old Norway maples. I loved our apartment with its high ceilings and long hall, its pillared mantels and stained glass. I loved its view of the Little Sisters of the Poor behind its brick wall and iron railings. I loved the fourth movement of Brahms's Fourth Symphony, the chorale of Beethoven's Ninth. One could love things like that, never people. In order to love people, you had first at least to like yourself.

"You're too aggressive. You want what you want, and you don't care how you get it."

"Well, I want to be good at what I do, if that's what you mean. Who doesn't?"

"I don't," he said. "I don't care anymore."

A skeleton of shadows on his face scared me, as if the baggy skin beneath his eyes had already begun to tear away from the bones. He was too old to have to find the heart to start over, and it wasn't his fault, but I was only thirty, and that wasn't mine.

"I'm going," I said. "I'm sorry it makes you unhappy, but I'm not going to watch my life pass by just to make you feel better about yours."

His voice rose. "You're selfish, Janie. I took you in when you didn't have anyplace to go, not a dime to your name, but were you ever grateful?"

"Oh, I see. You didn't marry me; you got martyred to me."

"Very clever. You never had a thought so big it wouldn't fit in your mouth. I should have known when your own mother turned her back on you, but, no, I felt sorry for you."

"Well, I don't know why you didn't know better. You were certainly old enough." I stormed away, but halfway down the block my anger dissolved into tears. I walked back. "I'd be ashamed to sit there and say I let an eighteen-year-old girl who hadn't even graduated from high school take advantage of me."

"You don't have any shame. You didn't have any more shame than to whine and cry about how petty the women at the School of Business were and the professors didn't respect you and your stomach hurt and you were bored, until I let you play at my recital just to get some peace, and then you took all the credit."

I sat and put my head in my hands. "Ben, that was almost ten years ago, I was fucked up, but I never . . ."

"Oh yes you did. You acted like a prima donna."

"No," I said with a quiet certainty that came rarely in our quarrels. "I went back to work and paid your child support and never played again in public for years."

"I hate you," he said suddenly. "I hate you." And before I could recover from the shock of knowing that it was the

307

only honest thing he'd ever said to me, he had dodged a car and crossed the street.

My heart exploded. "I don't hate you because I don't love you enough to hate you," I screamed. "I whined about my job because I didn't know it was you that made me unhappy." I sat on the sidewalk and wiped my nose, confused again because if I didn't hate and didn't love and didn't leave, what was I crying about? "You didn't marry me because you felt sorry for me; we got married because you were in love." I beat my palm against the pavement as I sobbed. "Ow."

"You want a ride?"

I looked up. The car Ben had dodged was at the curb, the driver leaning across the seat to crack the door.

"Go to hell," I said, not sure if I was speaking to him or to Ben.

"Have a fight with your boyfriend?"

"Husband." I wiped my face.

He nudged the door, and I thought, well, all right, I should leave.

He took me to a bar across the river. "This is Janet," he said to two men playing pinball. "Jane," I said, but they didn't tell me their names, and he hadn't answered when I asked him his. He was balding, his face was cleft like a dish-faced dog, he wore black-rimmed glasses and black work shoes run over at the heels. There was something young, not youthful, about him and his friends one of whom wore a waist-length ponytail, although that sixties' look had long been out of style. I drank beer after beer that no one seemed to order, and as the pinball machine rattled and rang, the other two cursed Captain Fantastic, and he complained, "Elton John, man, he's a fag." After an hour or so, he glanced at me and said, "You want to play?" I shook my head. Another hour passed before he jerked his chin in my direction. "What do you want to do then?" I shrugged. "What do you do? You," his long-haired friend added when I didn't answer. "She's married," my driver said, drumming his finger on the glass. "Oh yeah? You and your husband got one of those liberated relationships?" I shook my head. "She doesn't say much, does she?" "I play in the Richmond Symphony," I said. "Oh yeah?" Ponytail said. "Weird."

When the bar closed, the other men took off, and we went to a Toddle House. I wanted to go home, but didn't think I had a home to go to; and I didn't have my purse, so I couldn't ask him to drop me at a motel. Stomach swimming, I drank coffee while he sopped up egg yolks with his hash browns.

"You got a name?" he asked, then said, "Oh, yeah, Janet; you told me. So tell me, what did you and your old man fight about?"

"Nothing."

"You always fight about nothing?"

I shrugged. "I don't know. My career."

He polished his glasses with a napkin. His eyes looked weak without them, a red parenthesis indented on each side of his nose. "You some kind of ballbuster or something?"

I laughed. "Yeah, that's what he thinks."

"I'm a musician too," he said, putting his glasses on. "I can play 'Yankee Doodle' on my balls." I smiled politely. "You ever meet a guy that could play 'Yankee Doodle' knocking his dick against his balls?"

"No," I said.

After he paid the check, I said, "I really ought to go home. My husband's probably getting worried."

"I thought you said your husband didn't like you." He pressed his fingers into my arm so hard they hurt, and I was almost frightened, but if Ben didn't care where I went, why should I?

His apartment was in a row of new brick town houses of the sort that spring up near shopping centers once the trees have been torn down. Other than a heap of beer cans, the downstairs was bare. In the bedroom upstairs there were three cartons of records, a stereo, a filthy mattress, and a pile of dirty clothes. Above the mattress, where I might have expected Brando in *The Wild Bunch* or James Dean taped to the wall, there was a dimestore picture of the Crucifixion made of some peculiar plastic that gave the obscene illusion that Christ's eyes opened and closed. "You want to hear some music?"

"Sure." I frowned at a framed portrait on the windowsill. "Is that your mother?"

"I got the Stones, the Allman Brothers, the Who, Fleetwood Mac, Rod Stewart, you name it. You don't like rock, I got jazz. Grover Washington, Jr.—you like Grover Washington? You don't like jazz, I got blues. Bessie Smith—you like Bessie Smith? I got Billie Holiday, Lightnin' Hopkins, Mississippi Fred McDowell, Mississippi John Hurt. I got John Lee Hooker, Howling Wolf, Robert Johnson. You don't like niggers, I got white boys. Koerner, Ray, and Glover, you ever hear of them?" He touched the portrait, and it fell with a loud clap. "I'm not a fag."

"I didn't mean you were." I glanced at the blinking Christ again. "Where did you get that?"

"Jesus loves me," he explained and crouched beside the stereo. "You don't like blues, I got country. Willie Nelson, Waylon Jennings, Dolly Parton—you like Dolly? Little voice, big tits. You don't like tits, I got Emmy Lou Harris. So what do you want to hear?"

"Whatever you like."

He gave me a sharp look. After a minute he said, "You want a beer?"

"No thanks." While he went downstairs, I flipped through his records and frowned. He didn't have one of the albums he said he had. They were all show tunes, Mantovani, Ray Conniff, Engelbert Humperdinck, Tom Jones. The other box was full of devotional music, Pat Boone's Favorite Hymns, Songs of Inspiration by the Living Strings, the Mormon Tabernacle Choir. When I heard the exhaust fan go on in the bathroom, I tiptoed to the closet and slid the door open slowly to muffle the sound, but it was empty, three bare wire hangers on the rod. The toilet flushed, and I caught my finger as I jerked the door closed.

"What do you think you're looking for? You afraid I dress up in women's clothes?"

I took my injured finger from my mouth and turned around. "No."

"Oh yes, you did," he said, and I looked guiltily away.

My gaze wandered to the picture that had fallen on the windowsill. "Is that your mother?" I asked again.

"Who?" he said.

"The lady in the picture." I resumed my stance before the closet, wanting the distance of the room between us.

"None of your business." He got up and began pacing. "What's it to you?"

"Nothing. I was just curious, that's all."

"Curiosity killed the cat," he said, and I swallowed. "You want to hear a record?"

"Sure."

He paced faster. "Make up your mind," he said.

"Yes, sure, I want to hear a record."

"I can't do it for you." He had stopped pacing, but his hands were shaking, and his face looked as if the features wanted to fly off but his glasses held them there. "You have to tell me what you want to hear."

"Why don't you play some Mantovani?"

He resumed pacing. "I got Willie Nelson, Nelson Algren, Lord Admiral Nelson, Earle Nelson, Ricky Nelson. I got Nelson Eddy. I got Duane Eddy. I got Eddie Fisher, Elizabeth Taylor, Richard Burton." He stopped. "I also got the biggest cock you ever saw."

I flattened against the closet, and the door jumped back against its track. He sat again. The blower to the furnace came on. It was hot, and I hadn't taken off my coat.

"It's not my mother," he said.

"Who?"

"In the picture. It's not my mother." He drummed his middle finger on his chest. "I was in Viet Nam. Did I tell you?"

"No."

He stretched his left arm and cocked his right hand, a human rifle aimed at me, and my heart shot into my throat. So he was a vet whose mind had come unhinged. The war was over. It had not affected me. I thought of Sidney waiting for Riggs, of Ruth when she got the news that David, the only one of her sons to go, had had an eye shot out. Were Riggs and David crazy now? I couldn't think so, and foreboding had a strange, wet taste in the dry cotton of my mouth. I did not believe that he had been in Viet Nam. I just believed that he was nuts.

He dropped his arm. "I was a pilot. I got shot down over the D.M.V."

The inside of my cheek was bleeding where I'd pinched it with my teeth.

"It's D.M.Z.," he said. "The D.M.V.'s the Division of Motor Vehicles. Why don't you listen when I talk to you?" I closed my eyes as he took off his shirt. "I wasn't in Viet Nam." His belt buckle rang against the floor. "What do you think?"

I began to shake. My fingernails were cutting into my palms. "I don't know."

"Well, you got to have an opinion."

"It's very big," I whispered.

"Was I in Viet Nam or wasn't I?"

I opened my eyes. He was standing a foot in front of me in a pair of women's bikini pants printed with yellow happy faces. I didn't laugh.

"Well?"

"Okay, yes," I said, "you were."

"Ha, I fooled you. I want you to suck me off."

I didn't move.

"I want you to suck me off," he repeated.

I shook my head.

"Janet . . ."

"Jane," I said, and for another minute we just stood.

"I want you to suck me off." He whimpered, his head listing to one side as my chin pointed up. It was my mistake. I thought, for a second, that I could just walk out.

I was beating and pulling at the night lock when his hand closed on my throat. "Please," I sobbed, "please," but the sound was just a rattle as the chain slid from my grasp.

"Jesus loves me," he said. "He wants me to do this to you."

*　　*　　*

312

Ben came to get me in the hospital.

"Who called you?" I said, my mouth straining to make words.

"I called you. I was worried. You don't look too good."

I had two black eyes, a broken nose, three missing teeth, a gash above my temple, four crushed ribs, a new terror of the world, and eighteen shallow stab wounds in my gut. "Little girl," the doctor had said when my eyes first fluttered, "you were lucky. He must have got that steak knife at a gas station giveaway." His voice was stern. It said that he had better never catch me half-dead in his emergency room again.

"I don't feel too good, if you want to know the truth."

"No questions asked," Ben said in a voice that meant he didn't. It was the same injured, pontifical tone he used to forgive me all my crimes.

"That's okay; I wouldn't answer," I whispered, trying to be jaunty in my victimhood, but the words were blurry. I had taken a ride from a stranger, it was my fault, and I cried instead.

Later he would say to the police with the most outraged emphasis, "My *wife* was beaten, my *wife* was savagely attacked, she was left for dead beside the highway while I sat home and *worried*, what do you *mean* you have no clues?"

They meant that I would give them none.

Now he said, without the faintest trace of guilt, "I didn't mean it. I *love* you, and I'm going to take better care of you from now on." And then he added, "I'm sorry. You'll never play again."

I raised my head and cracked a bandage. "Bullshit," I said.

20

*T*he marriage could have ended then, but it was a habit of such neutral value that it did not seem worth the trouble to break it. Marriage protected me from passion and from terror, and that was all I required of it. My life had lost interest for me, and, in an odd echo, Ben's seemed to have lost interest for him too. We lived in the remote courtesy of our unspoken, private visions.

What his were, I couldn't say. Mine were all music, and in the long months before I could play again, my mind filled with such lucid tones that I could *see* their colors—hues so acute, so delicate and heavenly, they could never have been composed. My nerves sang beneath my skin. I touched my coffee cup and felt its music; I lay my cheek against my hand and listened. My imagination was iridescent with the genius of pure spirit. One morning at the breakfast table, as Ben sat repeating, "Janie? I said I think I'll take the car in for a tune-up if you don't need me to drive you anywhere," I watched his lips move with incandescent harmonies, and I knew that I was mad.

I did not go to North Carolina the next summer. I had barely begun to play again, and my clarinet felt unfamiliar in my refurnished mouth. I did not hurry my recovery. Perhaps I understood that the palette of exquisite sound would fade once the instrument for realizing it was back in my hand. With the leisure of one who enjoys his own delirium, I savored it in anticipation of my return to the dull necessity of art. And when I did return, it was with an unaccountable patience of ambition, a gentle irony for our clumsy mocking of the muse's synesthetic song.

But I returned, and when I did go to the music festival the summer after, Ben and I exchanged six weeks of letters that chatted of two ordinary lives. He met me at the bus station in August and took me to dinner, and for a while our conversation became as animated as those letters, but by the time we reached our apartment, we had discovered it was only a repetition. We had nothing else to say. When we went to bed, he hadn't touched me, and I lay awake half the night, aware of the Fan's night noises and of him, after all those weeks of sleeping solo on a quiet college campus. I wondered why we had been so faithful. I assumed he had. I had, in spite of a persistent French horn who was really not unattractive. By the time we did make love, Ben had picked up a summer cold, and he sniffled at my breasts as he sucked the nipples. He came inside me with as much enthusiasm as I'd gone into the I.U. Business Building. All winter we did the job like that: he didn't quit; I didn't fire him.

The next summer I went to Aspen, and again we found a great deal to fill our letters. I had never been west of Chicago, and I wrote him long descriptions of the landscape, the green geometry of spruce and ski runs on the fertile mountain shouldering one side of the town, the tangles of gray sage that grew like wiry tufts of hair from the red-rock skull above the other, the enormous stars. The town itself was a carnival, benches along the red-brick malls full of college kids who seemed to have nothing to do but watch the tourists who paraded in and out of the funky shops and restaurants in T-shirts that said SNOWMASS or BUTTERMILK or ASPEN ASPEN ASPEN, sporting cameras, Visa cards, and bags of popcorn from the circus-wagon vendor. On back streets the Victorian frame houses were painted amusement-park colors, and in the meadow just below Red Mountain, the tent where we played our concerts promised to send into the streets a company of lion-tamers, clowns, and tutued bareback riders, while the Flying Wallendas did trapeze tricks on the chairlifts that pointed the way to the horizon. Giddy with the altitude, I sat in Farfunkel's beer garden and thought, so money does grow on trees, as I watched the coin-sized aspen leaves twirling on those beautiful white branches. The fourteen years since I'd left college had simply never happened, and the letter I was on my way to mail to Ben might have been a girl's epistle to her mother: full of *did*'s and *saw*'s, with stars as big as polka dots dressing up the dream that the sky was mine for touching. I had left him, just as I had always had to leave home one way or another, although my mother would have to die before I knew it.

She died late that August, just a few days after my thirty-third birthday, a week and a half after I'd returned to Richmond, and I flew into O'Hare for the third time that summer, having twice glimpsed the Chicago skyline in the distance as my plane descended from the clouds that looked as soft and white as angel hair from above, and then seen the airport, as dreary as a steel mill. While I'd waited to change planes, watching the baggage trains scuttle across the stained cement, I understood that I was fifty miles from Hammond but might as well be thousands. This time I was going home, and I took a limo-service bus that traveled the expressway past the suburbs of yellow-brick ranch houses. I think there is nothing sadder than those flat Chicago suburbs, with their hip roofs and sooty eaves, their treeless back yards just big enough for a garage and a tiny, aboveground swimming pool. On the left, just before the green exit sign for Calumet Avenue, a bright blue water tank spelled HAMMOND. and I had that cold shock of recognition that comes not so much from recollection as from the shattered disbelief that what you left behind went on without you.

Marie picked me up at the K-Mart, where the bus stopped. She was heavier, her features less prominent, hair lacquered in an unstylish little helmet so thin that the teasing showed. She had new glasses with orange frames and wore a blouse in a green and tan print that looked like Iowa seen from an airplane. I wouldn't have recognized her.

"My gosh, you haven't aged one day." She gave me a self-conscious hug, then backed off, gazing across the parking lot as if it pained her to see me. I had always looked a great deal like my brother, although neither of us had seemed to look much like our parents. We took after our father, my mother said, but I was only nine years old, and I refused to accept the diagnosis. His eyes leaked; disease had made excavations in his flesh; his skin looked like a suit of clothes he had slept in. Marie squinted through her glasses. I was wrong. What hurt her was the sun, which had just come out, flaring off the cars. She caught the hand of a little girl in a bandanna-printed halter. She had told me on the phone that she'd remarried. She was Mrs. Stanley Plotski now; her husband was a plumber. "This is Rick and the twins' aunt Jane," she said. "Say hello, Marlene."

Rick. So he had finally convinced her. He was twenty-one now. Dickie wouldn't do.

"The lawyer has the key to your mother's house," she explained as we drove to her new home in Munster. "But you're welcome to stay with us tonight."

I nodded. My allergies were beginning to itch inside my nose, and I breathed through a Kleenex as we passed the Wicker Park Pool, where I had clinched my lifelong fear of water by walking off the edge of the deep end when I was four. The water had smacked in my ears, but when I opened my eyes, the world was as slow and fluid as if I had nine months to explore it before I would scream with my first air. I couldn't have been down a minute, yet I remember that water-world as clearly as if my gestation had been there. It was veined with a tremble of light. A swimmer kicked off the wall, trailing bubbles like galaxies. When I exhaled, the sound was like a drain being pulled in a tub. I inhaled, and a lifeguard fished me out. He handed me, screaming and sputtering, to my brother, who had been practicing cannonballs off the high dive and hadn't missed me. Then he turned to another guard and said, "Well, that woke me up. The little brat nearly gouged my eye out."

Marie turned the corner at Ridge Road. "The cross is still there," I noticed, referring to the crucifix put up by the Knights of Columbus just beyond the bathhouse. Coming out from the pool that day, I thought Christ was the lifeguard, had imagined him storing his baby oil and whistle in the elbow of that lofty perch. Oh, he was my savior, all right, but the son-of-a-bitch had begrudged my saving. "I forgot to ask how it happened."

"Heart attack. One minute she was fine, and the next she just keeled over." Marie reached her hand out but returned it to the wheel without touching me. "She always kept things to herself, well, you know how she was, and, what with Rick and the twins being older—they're in high school now, time sure flies, I'll tell you. I don't suppose I'd seen her in a month. It was a real shock when the hospital called." She parked in front of a yellow-brick ranch house with a plaster madonna in the front yard and a station wagon in the driveway. "Okay, Marlene. You can go on and play at Linda's, but I don't want to have to call you home for dinner."

Her husband was eating a sandwich in the kitchen, and he wiped his hand on his shirt as he stood to shake my hand. He looked average, his voice was average, his house was average, with vinyl-covered pedestal chairs around the table in the kitchen, a plaid Herculon sofa in the living room between two end tables that held matching lamps, and carpeting the color of dead winter grass.

"You want some coffee? Make yourself at home." Marie measured grounds into the percolator. "Stash, honey, how come you're home so early?"

"Why do you think?" her husband said. "I got to reorder that commode. She waits till I get it all hooked up and *then* she decides it isn't the right color. She didn't think it would look so orange. Orange. It says right on the goddamn carton that it's pink." He shook his head and glanced at me. "You ask a man what he wants, he tells you. You ask a woman, it's 'I don't know, well maybe . . . on the other hand.' " He snorted.

"Where's the twins?" Marie asked.

He shrugged. "I ain't their baby sitter."

I blew on the coffee Marie poured me. "I can't wait to see them. And Dickie."

"They probably went to the pool. Were their bikes in the garage?" Mr. Plotski shrugged again. "Oh, you won't recognize them," Marie said to me, as if I might have thought I would. "They'll be sophomores at Munster High this fall. They went to Hammond for freshman."

Hammond High. I had an image of the concrete-floored halls as dark as caves, where I had banged my locker shut for the last time over fifteen years ago, and looked up, surprised to hear those halls still filled with students every hour, my nieces among them. Were they in band? Scratchy uniforms hung in mothballs in the storage room behind the auditorium stage, the metallic clanging of the doors to the instrument bins. I thought I'd forgotten, but the images were as vivid as if it had been yesterday. Friday nights before the football games, trying to knot my black tie in the makeshift girls' dressing room with its pull-down maps of the Roman Empire, my uniform jacket flung over a desk on which someone had carved *veni, vidi, vici,* while the boys tried to peer around the drawn shades of the classroom. Sitting on the concrete steps outside the bandroom two years in a row as I explained to the drummer who had asked me to the prom that I just didn't plan on going, and afterward the bassoonist said, "You nut. What are you, queer or something?"

"You wouldn't recognize the school," Marie said. "They had a fire and remodeled. It's got air conditioning and carpet now." She shrugged. "It was arson. Kids. It's not like when we were young."

"No, I guess not," I said, feeling odd to hear myself included in an older generation just after the summer when I'd finally learned to feel young.

Marie smiled at her husband and took his hand. "I guess we'll be grandparents one of these days now. It doesn't seem possible, does it?"

"Has Dickie gotten married?" I asked. Twenty-one. Dick and I both married when we were eighteen. I had never thought about that before. Neither of us had graduated from high school. Both of us had married young. And unhappily. I winced. My mother had married a man twenty years her senior. Coincidence. These things meant nothing unless I chose to see them. I pushed my chair out from the table and fanned myself with my paper napkin.

"Are you hot?" Marie said. "Stash, why don't you close the windows and turn on the a.c. ?"

"Because it eats money faster than I can make it. She's from the South. She's used to being hot." He poured himself another cup of coffee, stirred in milk from the carton on the table. It struck me then how all my life I had been sitting around tables, just like my mother. The people changed—first your family, then your roommate, then your husband—and no matter whom you left, someone else would be there, you too, knees tucked under, hands fidgeting, wishing you had thought to do anything with your life except just sit. "Me, I've never been south. Too many damn mosquitoes."

I wanted to get up, but I couldn't just wander around without permission. In a minute I would ask to use the bathroom, and Marie would blushingly direct me, apologizing for the soggy towels and dirty basin, and I would feel obliged to go and come back so quickly that she would be relieved to know I hadn't poked my head inside a room with unmade beds or underwear wadded in a corner. I swung my knees back beneath the table. "I'm fine. It's just the coffee."

"Would you rather have ice tea?" Marie asked. "We got some instant."

"Coffee's fine," I said and watched her husband beat a bongo rhythm against the table. I wondered if she loved him as much as she had loved my brother. Did he resent the twins, Dickie, her first marriage? Would he come to her late husband's mother's funeral? My husband was in Richmond; he'd been in Bloomington when my brother's steel carcass was buried. "A man who loved his wife . . ." my mother had said, trailing off to imply he would have been there with her, at her brother's funeral. Also she had said, "You don't love me. If you loved me, you wouldn't do that." But I had done it. Talked too loud, wised off, whatever. Quit high school against her wishes, gotten myself expelled from college against mine. Married without asking who might give my hand. Left home and never written, never mind she didn't write me either. I had never wanted to be like her; I had never wanted to be left sitting around a kitchen table while the chairs emptied one by one. I braced my hands against this kitchen table as if a grip on things would keep my tears from sloshing over. I had not admired my mother, never mind that I should have, surviving to raise me. I had meant to leave her behind, but, like a frog in the throat, she had stuck in my imagination, and I knew with the unexpectedness of bereavement that I had loved her all the same.

"A little later, if you feel ready, we can go on up to the funeral home. Rick phoned—he'll be there." Marie gave my hand a sympathetic pat, then touched her husband's. "He's got an apartment in Calumet City with a couple of fellows from the mill." She shrugged apologetically. "Well, you know how it is. He's a young man now, coming and going like they do. Living at home . . ."

Stash gripped the edge of the table. "This is *my* house, I told him. You want to live in *my* house, you follow *my* rules. Otherwise get out."

Marie leaned toward me. "He drinks a little bit and stays out late—you know how it is—but he's got himself a real nice girlfriend, and he makes good money. He'll want to settle down."

Stash frowned. "I wanted to teach him plumbing. But no, you got to be an apprentice. He wants those big bucks right away."

"Well, he's young," Marie said.

"He hasn't got a skill," Stash told her. "The way things are now, you got to plan ahead. I told him, you don't know what's going to happen, but one thing you can count on: people are always going to have to shit." Marie tried to scowl, but she laughed, and Stash jerked his chin at me. "Isn't that right?" He looked at Marie. "See there? She's a smart girl. I may be a dumb shitski Polack, but at least I know the score. That right, huh, kiddo?" I gave him a weak nod, and he rose. "Well, if you ladies will excuse me, I got to take a shower."

"Don't pay any attention to Stash. His bark's worse than

his bite. He and Rick didn't get along so good. Well, Rick's got a temper, and anyway he's of age now—it was time for him to get out on his own." Marie's look asked my approval. "Rick works at Inland." She looked away. "Well, you can't blame them. What happened happened. It wasn't Inland's fault."

My mouth was open.

"It wasn't anybody's fault." Her hand curled on the table, knuckles turning white. "He should of listened to Stash. I raised that boy. I raised him to remember his father. The twins, well, that's different. They were just babies; they never had any daddy but Stash." Her jaw quivered. "I didn't raise him to make his father's mistakes."

"My brother didn't make mistakes."

Her look was sharp, but she said, "Your brother was a wonderful man. I loved him. I raised his son." She got up. "You want any more coffee?" I shook my head, and she pulled the plug. "Stash is a good man too."

"I'm sure he is," I said coolly.

She plunged the cups into a sinkful of soapy water. "Well, what would you of had me do? Live out my life in mourning, like your mother? You can love somebody enough to die yourself, but that don't bring 'em back, you know. You went off to live your life. You think the rest of us were supposed to have better memories than you?"

"No," I whispered and bowed my head.

"When your brother lost his finger, I wanted him to get out of the mill. But no, we had house payments, the twins were on the way, he had to be the great provider. It was his fault, he said; he shouldn't of been horsing around. You tell me—did you ever know your brother to horse around?" She sighed and began rinsing the cups. "It wasn't his fault, and he knew it, but he transferred back to the open hearth. He told me that was safer. What kind of fool did he think I am? The work's dangerous, that's all, and your brother was nobody's fool but his own." She turned the water off and wiped the soapsuds from her arms. "I don't blame him, understand. He was human. Well, I am too."

I nodded, my eyes heating up with tears. She sat down at

322

the yellow table. "Your mother never forgave me for getting married again. Oh, she didn't say that, but you know how it is. I went by every few weeks to make sure she got to see plenty of Rick and the twins. Well, Stash didn't much care for her. It was hard for me to have her over here. She didn't really want to come anyway."

I closed my eyes, meaning to tell her it wasn't her responsibility, it wasn't her fault I had been too proud to accept mine, I understood, I didn't blame her and didn't want her to blame me—but the words came so fast they stuck.

"I'm sorry. This was hardly the time—whatever happened between us is done with, and whatever happened between you is no concern of mine." She returned to the sink and tightened the faucets, though I hadn't heard them drip. "No use in dragging up the past. Well. It's five o'clock." She smiled brightly. "If they know what's good for them, Dawn and Mimi ought to be home soon."

I swallowed. "I can't wait to see them."

"Oh yeah, they're big girls now," she said, and when Stash came in, ruddy from the shower, we were sitting, not talking, the table like a banquet spread between us, a feast of grief and love and guilt that we consumed as silently as if we were sisters at a family repast, plates heaped with our portions.

21

*T*hat was the summer of 1978, and now it's the summer of 1979, and I have been back in Aspen, more amused this year than enchanted by the illusion that the stars sit just beyond my shoulder, waiting to be plucked from the sky. I have traveled from the flatlands ever so slightly closer, but the earth still pulls me, and the stars remain an unimaginable distance, clustered like a Morse code of signals in the breath of a voiceless god. Like everything born, I am dying—even the sun's going to go in about five billion years. It was David Solomon who told me that, and when he did, I lost my own voice for a minute, as upset as if I were going to be left here in the dark. He laughed. "Jane, don't you have any idea how many other suns there are?" It is difficult for me to accept that I live in a world ruled by science, that the Heaven I refuse to believe in does not exist, that there is another whose space is calculated in terms as mysterious and unreasonable as the mind of Job's petulant god. And yet, no matter whose time I mock with rhythm, ticking is still ticking, whether it's a clock or metronome. I thought immortality had these chances—art, love, good deeds—but they are only metaphors. There is a world we cannot measure. It is not the miracle itself, but the belief in miracles. The imagination is nothing but the will to argue for the soul.

I was sorry. But I couldn't explain to Ben what I was sorry for.

"What did I do?" he said over and over. "Is there someone else?" he asked. "Then why?"

I rented two rooms overlooking the new Business Building at Virginia Commonwealth University, with its parched and treeless lawn, brick walls the angry purple color of a burn. I was sorry that I missed him less than my view of the Home of the Aged run by the Little Sisters of the Poor. I'd thought it was a convent at first, topped by a peeling wooden cross, on its hill behind a brick wall crowned by an iron fence, a froth of greenery spilling over like a weathered copper halo falling down, but later I noticed that the snowcapped men and women I saw shuffling across its grounds seemed to have no sense of mission. Or perhaps what I noticed was that God's mission had no sense of them. The youngest were no more than ten years older than Ben, and it hurt me now to see him, aging not so much in fact as aging in my eyes. Without a young wife on his arm—but, to tell the truth, he looked younger, slimmer too. He had new wire-rimmed glasses. There was a week when he seemed to be turning into a seedy old man and I ached, but then his unkempt jowls turned into a beard.

He gave me money, and when I refused, he took to hiding it until, reaching for a coffee cup or my underwear, I was startled by a twenty-dollar bill as often as by a skulking roach.

"I wish you wouldn't," I protested. "The rent here is very cheap."

"I don't doubt it," he said, but I would not admit that the place gave me the creeps too, lath showing through one jagged hole in the wall where at night I imagined rats. A previous tenant had slathered the apartment with a dubious brand of poison. "What's that smell?" Ben demanded, gagging on the sickeningly sweet stench. "Help me move the refrigerator," I answered, gasping. "My God," he said when we pulled it out. "How can you live in such filth?" I heaved a great sigh and smarted tears of relief. "Oh." I wept. "Oh. Oh, Ben, it's only a mouse." He gagged again, and I sobbed, "Take it away, take it *away*."

He invited me to dinner. I was losing weight, he said. I was gaining weight, I argued, but it wasn't true. I had shed five pounds, most of them from the effort of retalking everything we ought to be sorry about. He was determined that if we could not be lovers, we must be friends, and the image of his smiling farewells lingered like a bad taste in my mouth. I cursed him, but he wasn't there, so I ended by cursing myself.

I resigned from the Richmond Symphony, effective the next season, and began to look for another orchestra.

He gave me a cashmere sweater.

"I *really* wish you wouldn't."

A Persian kitten.

"Ben, I don't even like animals. What am I going to do with a cat?"

"Use it to catch mice," he suggested, but I gave it to the pound and took the sweater back.

"No," I complained as he came by with one more tissue-wrapped package that spring. He perched on a windowsill while I unwrapped a gold neckchain. "Ben, it's lovely, *but . . .*"

"Fourteen carat. Well, you have such a pretty neck. Next time maybe I'll bring you a chair."

My apartment was furnished with a mattress, a music stand, a trunk on which half a dozen new reeds were soaking in a dish, and one straight chair. I didn't want another. I was leaving for Aspen in three weeks.

How was I, he wanted to know. Was I seeing anyone?

"Sort of, I guess so." I shrugged. I was sleeping with a filmmaker from V.C.U., but it was all very casual.

He cleared his throat. He had something to tell me: he'd met someone. Her name was Heather, and he was sorry, but he wanted me to know—he was *not*—that is, what he meant was, and of course . . . After all, we were still married.

"Separated," I said. "Ben, don't you think you're a little old for blue balls?"

And then . . .

"How old is Heather?"

He scratched his groin. What difference did it make? She was very mature for her age. "By the way, she'd like to meet you—well, I've told her so much about you. I thought maybe you and your new fellow would want to go to dinner with us sometime." I shook my head in disbelief. "Why not? We can still be friends, can't we? My treat," he promised. "What's his name?"

"Who?"

"Your new fellow."

"Oh. Tom."

"Well, I'd like to meet him. I have to make sure that he takes good care of my little girl."

"Are you nuts?" I snapped, then slammed into the next room because I thought that I might kill him if I stayed.

When my temper cooled, I came back. I had something to tell him, too. The New York Philharmonic needed a clarinet.

His face darkened. "You'll never get in. Frankly, I've always thought it was a mistake, the way people catered to your talent. You aren't that good."

"I will get in." I raised my chin. "I am that good, Ben."

"I see," he said after a minute. "Is this Tom, Dick, and Harry going with you?"

"You don't have to be snide."

"Are you going to marry him?"

"Of course not."

"Well, naturally I wondered. Are you having relations with him?"

"I don't have to report my sex life to you." I started to leave again, but stopped. "Although I think you'd really get off on it if I would."

His face had resettled into its familiar bland popishness. "I knew there was someone else. That's the way you operate."

"You don't know shit." When he started to speak, I cut him off. "You think I need somebody else? You think I needed you? Wake up, Ben—I'm through with that. I should have known it when a fucking psycho bashed my face in so bad I couldn't get a clarinet in my mouth for six months, because I wouldn't suck him off. And you know why I wouldn't do it? Because that's exactly what I'd been doing all those years for you. Blowing your puny little ego like it was some great big cock.''

''That's right, blame me.''

''No, I don't blame you,'' I admitted in a voice gone tired. It does not make you feel better to say these things; it just wears you out.

''I suppose you had a lot of affairs.''

If I didn't admit to Christopher, I was a liar just saving my skin; if I did, what was the point? Would it make him feel better to be angry? Or worse to have been deceived? It had been so long ago. Surely the statute of limitations had run out.

I was going to audition for the New York Philharmonic. It didn't matter what he thought.

''I'll sue you for adultery.''

But it did matter what he thought, because now it was just another victory in our long war. I didn't hate him enough, so the victories spoiled.

''Sue me for whatever you want.''

He gave the doorknob a vicious wrench, but it was loose and just wobbled in his hand. ''When are you leaving?''

''The first of May. I want to visit Sid on the way to Aspen, and I should stop off in Bloomington first. Ruth might have to have another operation. Martin didn't say, but I think it's serious this time.'' He was looking at me so steadily, I dropped my eyes. ''Well, she's not going to die. Ruth's the only person I know who's going to live forever.''

He moved toward me. ''Janie, I'd take you back. In spite of everything. What's the matter?'' His hand hesitated, then settled on my shoulder. I shuddered. If I let him touch my shoulder, did I have to kiss him? If I kissed, did I have to screw? I knew a woman in the Symphony who slept regularly with her ex-husband. ''Greatest sex I ever had,'' she confided. ''It's the best of both worlds, now that his fucking lordship knows he has to knock if he wants in.'' ''Why not?'' Ben asked. ''I love you and you love me. Don't you?'' I turned my head. ''Don't you, well don't you?''

''Stop it,'' I said. ''You're choking me.''

He dropped his hands. "Well, I know you do."

I glanced at my reeds. They needed to be sanded and played. He always did this, came over just after I set them to soak, and here he was again, spilling love like a soiled handkerchief from his breast pocket. I gathered the reeds and crushed their tips in my hand.

"You and my mother," I said. "You both use love as a weapon. You want to use it to flog me to death."

"Your mother's dead," he said flatly.

I tossed the reeds in the garbage. "Do you know she still had my picture in her wallet? The last one I had taken at Hammond High."

He sighed and went through a little ceremony of smoothing himself out and hesitating, planning to leave but not leaving, waiting to announce.

"If she didn't love me, she should have torn up my picture. If she loved me, why didn't she let me know?"

"Janie . . ."

"It's over, Ben. You can make it go on when someone dies, but when they leave, you have to know. I don't love you."

"But I love you," he insisted his face puffing, his new glasses beginning to steam. "You're my *wife*. I know, I know, I wasn't sympathetic about your family problems; I was too hard on you about your career. I was *hurt*. It seemed so unfair; everything you touched turned gold."

"Ben, don't."

"I admit it—I *tried* to make you feel bad, but that's all over now, you'll see. We'll go to New York."

"Please."

"I know I did things, but I did them because I loved you, I was afraid I'd lose you, don't you see? Even that letter . . ."

"I don't know what you're talking about," I said, embarrassed into anger. "Ben, I've told you before—I've asked you not to come over, I've asked you not to give me anything. Now I mean it."

He looked down. "They asked me to write a letter when you were expelled."

"Who?"

329

"Martin, the Dean of Music. They thought, since I was your teacher . . ."

"And you didn't write it, did you?" I said slowly.

He didn't answer, and, with a sickness beyond anger, I understood everything.

"You did. You told them that, in your opinion . . ."

"Because I loved you. Don't you see?"

I turned away.

"And it didn't make any difference. Look how well you've done, and now you're going to New York. Well, that's something to be proud of, isn't it? Janie? Janie? Jane!"

I turned around. "It made *all* the difference, Ben."

He whimpered. His face was as wrenched with need as a squalling infant's.

He wanted me to forgive him.

I saw him last at the airport in Richmond, where I'd gulped a Manhattan and picked up my tote bag as lightly as if it contained nothing, ready to board the jet to Chicago, where I'd catch the commuter flight to Bloomington. He was standing in front of the metal detector, behind a dozen red roses, and I nearly screamed with impatience while very tenderly he kissed me goodbye. "Step through, please," a security guard repeated. "Step through or please step aside." "I'd better go," I said. "I'm holding up the line." They made me lay the roses on the conveyer belt; he lifted his hand in a final gesture; I was free, but all the way to Chicago I cried.

Ruth's hair had thinned since her first operation; her flesh had caved in. She had cancer. They'd removed both her breasts a year ago; this time they'd taken her uterus, and I hovered around her hospital bed so solicitously that she finally sat straight up and said, "For your information, Miss Nightingale, I have no intention of dying. So you can just take those blasted petunias back to the florist and bring me a martini if you want to do something useful. They won't even let me have a glass of wine in here."

"They're roses." I laughed. So she wouldn't die after all. For a minute, when I first saw her, her hair spilled in gray tangles around her gaunt face, I'd been afraid she would. "And, as a matter of fact, I didn't buy them. My ex-husband gave them to me."

"On second thought, make that a pitcher." She flailed in the sheets, looking for the button that raised the bed. "Blasted bed jacket," she muttered, untangling her arm from the gown sleeve. "It hardly comes down to my navel, and they haul me down for radiation with my fat old butt hanging out for all those pimply young doctors to see. You tell Martin I want out of here. He won't listen to me, and he hangs around with such a long face you'd think he was the one who'd been butchered." She glared. "Imagine what those doctors would want with my old puss. I should have asked for a sex change. At least I'd have something to show."

I shook my head.

"Oh, what do you know?" she said. "You never had anything but your appendix removed. Wait until they take away your sex."

My smile trembled, but I held it. "I never even had my appendix out. Anyway, I thought"—I blushed—"I mean . . ."

"You bet," she said. "They're going to give me hormones." She turned her face so that all I could see were the snarls of her hair. "They smell like death. Can't you please just get them out of here?"

"Sure." I picked up the plastic pitcher I'd stuffed Ben's roses in.

"And, Jane, you tell that nurse—I want a martini," she said. Without its old robustness her voice sounded querulous.

When I got back to the room, she had the bed adjusted and was resting against its elevated head, her face the color of paraffin, with purple caves beneath her eyes. "You didn't tell me you and Ben got divorced."

I sat in the bedside chair. "Well, it's not final yet. And I would have, but Ben didn't want me to."

"Don't tell me he's ashamed. Good grief, these days you have to apologize if you're married. I told Martin we ought to get a divorce and just live together to keep up with the times."

I laughed. "Oh Ruth."

331

"It's true. Did I write you that Sam and his wife are separated?" She shook her head. "You'd think they would have figured out they didn't like each other before they started having puppies." She glared at me. "How come it took you so long?"

I shrugged and studied the steel panel of lights and buttons mounted on the wall, the blood pressure equipment hung like a telephone. The measured rush of air through metal vents was chilly, with a thin and faintly antiseptic smell. It was such a bloodless place. They could cut your sex and your heart out, and all you'd see would be the clean white gauze of bandages.

"I told you not to marry him."

I ran my finger down the seam in my denim skirt, ashamed to concede I knew at last what she and Martin had known all along but could not tell. "It wasn't that bad. And Ben's a wonderful person."

"Phooey," she said. "He's a petty man, Jane, and if it weren't for him, you might really have gone somewhere."

I shrugged again. "Well, I haven't done so badly. Did you get the Lutoslawski? I'm recording Stravinsky's *Three Pieces* next. Do you know they're the first—well, really, the only—thing I ever heard your father play? Anyway, I'm going back to the East Coast next week to audition in New York." I looked out the window. A haze had turned the sky the color of pearls. "I know what he did. It doesn't matter now. I'm not as ambitious as I used to be. Your father expected too much from art."

"Oh, my father " She sighed. "He was disappointed in his life, so he passed the burden on. Well, who isn't disappointed in his life? He wanted *me* to be a research biologist."

I had a sudden image of Mr. Schunk, his copper bracelet sliding into the rolled sleeve of his cardigan as he wiped the dark moons beneath his eyes, saying, "Is horrible life."

"That's not true," I said aloud, surprised by my vehemence. What he had wanted for me I *had* wanted for myself—still did—to so dazzle myself with success that I could believe life miraculous.

"Oh, what do you know?" she said again. "I was so smart

I just wanted to have kids." She rolled her eyes to suggest how that had turned out, and I laughed. She wasn't sorry a bit. "By the way, whatever happened to that old boyfriend of yours? You know, the nice one with the beautiful shoulders—what was his name?"

"Kelly. I don't know. He got married and had a kid."

"He might be divorced now. You ought to look him up."

Smiling, I shook my head. "Ruth, you never change."

"Was I supposed to?" She lifted one hand, her wrist bony beneath a hospital bracelet the sickly color of baby-bottle nipples. "You tell Martin to get me out of here. How am I supposed to sleep with these nurses poking needles and shoving bedpans when the toilet's not ten feet away?"

"I will," I promised.

She leaned forward. "You know, David's never married—I don't know what his problem is—and then there's Sam, now he and Ellen are getting divorced . . ."

I shook my head. "Ruth, I'm almost thirty-four. I can find my own boyfriends now."

"Do you have one?"

"Well, I did, but . . ."

"There," she said. "You see?"

When I got to the house, Martin was sitting barefoot in the living room, listening to Mozart's Twenty-first Piano Concerto as he drank gin from the bottle, a torn pajama top hanging out over his pants. He squinted, an expression on his unshaven face as if he couldn't quite place me. "She looks good, don't you think?" he asked, and I was so shocked I couldn't reply.

Instead, I bustled into the kitchen with a brisk promise of dinner, as if I expected Ruth to be there already chopping onions and banging pots. Two bulbs in the overhead were burned out—the light was dingy, the counter littered. I raised the lid from a saucepan. Creamed corn lay congealed on the bottom. I lifted another lid and gagged as I dropped it. Without Ruth's touch, the polish had worn off the house, and it now seemed as if the polish had held it together, floors tilting and ceilings cracking while dibs and dabs of food grew fur jackets on the stove.

333

The front door slammed. "Where is she?" David's voice hollered, and his boots clopped against the worn-out tile.

"Here," I cried into the refrigerator and whirled. A carton of spoiled milk flew from my hand as I clapped it to my mouth and gasped.

He gave me a goofy grin. "Hey. It's good to see you, Jane."

"You too," I said weakly and lowered my hand. His thick black hair sat on his head like a storm cloud, and a grim black patch covered the hole where his eye had been. In the ten years since I'd last seen him, his face had grown fierce, and he looked exactly like the stranger you don't want to meet on a dark back street. "I'm sorry." We hugged self-consciously.

"It's just the patch," he assured me, picking up the battered carton, which dribbled sour milk down his hand, perhaps guessing that the strange authority of his half-sight would leave me speechless until he acknowledged it. "Kids follow me down the street. You get used to it. They messed up the lid pretty bad. I can't wear a glass eye."

"Does it hurt?" I didn't know what else to ask.

"Nah." He grinned and rinsed his hand. "You look great. I'm sorry about this mess—I just got in last night. Pop said you're cooking dinner. What were you going to make?"

"I don't know." The sight of him put me off balance, so I looked away, feeling his lopsided gaze on the back of my neck like a hand. I had been so eager to see him, and now I had nothing to say.

After a minute he opened a cabinet and took a can of tomatoes out. "Spaghetti?" he inquired. "That's always good for whenever you don't know. I think there's some ground beef in the freezer." He tore a sheet of foil to wrap the garbage. "Listen, it's been a long time—I feel awkward, too." He waited as if he hoped I would respond, then dumped a plastic bag of muck from the refrigerator. "I think this used to be lettuce."

It was exactly the way Ruth would have taken charge, marching right on by the shyness, because if you couldn't overcome it, you could at least clean up the kitchen and eat. I smiled. "You've got a pot on the stove that may have been stew."

He raised the lid and swallowed.

"Pop said you were at the hospital. She looks terrible, doesn't she?"

"Well, not so bad, really." I opened the freezer to hide my face. "She's very alert."

"Well, she's crabby, anyway. Here, I'll chop the onions while you brown the meat." He swabbed out an iron skillet and set it on the stove as casually as if we had spent the last decade cooking together every night. "You know, I've missed you. How have you been, Jane?"

"Oh . . . fine," I said, stricken again. What could I say? I've been terrible, but now I'm okay? What could I ask? How was Viet Nam? "Do you have any sausage? It's not that good if you just use beef."

"Just a minute." He was sharpening the saber-shaped knife he had removed from a leather case strapped to his belt. With a flourish that resembled a karate move, he split two onions and diced them. I shivered. He looked capable of dicing me.

"Are you sure that knife is sanitary?"

"Nope." He smiled. "It's *clean*," he added as he handed me a package. "Sausage. So what have you been up to the last ten years?"

I made an incision in the plastic wrapper, then busied myself peeling the thawed blanket from the cube of beef on the stove. Martin was so drunk he forgot the first two movements of the Mozart each time he played Band 3 with its postscript of Vivaldi on the other side; I didn't know where the others were; and here was David, watching me with his matter-of-fact assurance and blank, Cimmerian eye, asking me to account for the ten long wasted that left me clubbing at the frozen core of beef in the ruins of his mother's kitchen and totally tongue-tied. "Oh, not that much, really. Damnit." The meat slid across the skillet, and he caught the iron pan as I sent that skidding, too. "Well, I'm on my way to Aspen. I play with the festival orchestra out there. I've been playing in Richmond, I made this recording, I won the Denver competition last year. Do you have any mushrooms?'' I spun Ruth's spice rack and pulled out the tins of thyme, marjoram, and oregano. ''How about you?'' I spun the rack again and pounced. ''Aha. I knew she'd have some caraway. Your mother said you were in New York. How did you like it?''

''Didn't.'' The skillet tilted on the edge of the stove and he grabbed it. ''You are the most brutal cook I've ever seen. It's already dead, you know.'' I stood aside as he worked the meat, oddly touched by this small competence in a man I had known mostly as a teen-aged clown. ''That's it? Ten years? No divorces, no affairs?''

I don't know why it made me laugh. ''Actually, I have an audition with the Philharmonic. What's the matter with New York?''

''Nothing, if you like it. If you don't . . .'' His voice thickened as he turned away. ''I spent thirteen months as a door gunner on a chopper squad, and . . .'' He faced me again. You know. ''Trite, huh? Are you still married, Jane?''

''Of course, I'm reading the ads in *International Musician*— in case I don't make it in New York, though I'm not really worried, that is, John Watley told me—he's a cellist, maybe you've heard of him? I mean I have quit my job, and I do''—David was grinning as my words got slower and I felt quite faint—''have to work, now that . . .'' I opened the refrigerator. ''You want a beer?''

''Sure.'' He held his hand out. ''Human interest?'' he pleaded.

I popped a beer for myself and sputtered foam. ''Well, funny you should ask. I'm getting a divorce. I had an affair with a trombone player, that was years ago, I was seeing this filmmaker—his name was Tom, he was married, but I didn't—he *lied* to me, it wasn't even necessary, it was just a casual thing, you know?'' Mortified with the excess of confession, the poverty of human interest my life held, I sat at the table. ''It was just such an insult, and it's none of your business, I don't even know why I would tell you, you can't just ask those kinds of questions after all this time.'' I was startled that the strangeness between us was not only years but anger, an anger so unreasonable it left me babbling, embarrassed by the necessity of a friendship that had never happened but always been implied.

He sat beside me at the table. "Jane . . ."

"Jane." Martin appeared in the doorway, holding the gin bottle by the neck. "Jane, could I fix you a drink, Jane?" He sloshed gin into a mug David had not yet washed. "There you go. A very dry martini. Find her an olive, Davie." He pulled up a chair. "Well, she looks good. Everyone says so. She's got some color. Don't you think she looked good, Jane?"

"Very good." Underneath the table David tried to find my hand, but I stood. "We've got a great dinner coming up here, Martin. I hope you've got an appetite."

"Now, don't you bother about the mess, Jane. I've got it under control. When Ruthie gets home—spotless." He made a lateral gesture and upset the mug.

"Pop, I think the record needs changing," David said, rubbing his hand against his sopped denim thigh. "Why don't you put on something else?"

Martin picked up the bottle. "You know, I was a little worried for a while, but now I can see—she's getting back her color. What would you like to hear? Mozart? Vivaldi? How about some Villa-Lobos? Davie has always had a great interest in Brazil."

"You pick it." David put his arm around me as I puttered at the stove. "Jane, he's just drunk. Ignore him. Ignore me," he added when I shrugged away. "I wasn't making advances. Although . . ." His smile sparked. "Okay, bad joke. I was just—well, fuck it, never mind. You look great, and I'm happy to see you." He knelt in front of a cabinet. "No noodles. You want to go with me to the store?"

I shook my head. "I'm sorry—I didn't mean—I'll make coffee."

"He won't drink it."

"Well, maybe if I make it . . ."

Now he shook his head. "There's nothing you can do, Pollyanna. She's dying. He can't hack it."

"Well, I don't know."

"I do know. I think you can allow him a binge."

"She's your *mother*." I waved him away as I bit my tears back and grabbed the counter.

"What would you do if she were yours?"

"My mother dead," I said. "My father's dead, my brother's dead. I am *not* going to let anyone else die."

"And you think if you love them enough you can stop it?" His hand touched my hair as I turned toward him. He made it sound less stupid than honorably mistaken. I was frightened. I thought he was going to kiss me. "What kind of wine would you like?"

"Any kind," I whispered, my throat so tight I had to swallow it to speak.

She died seven weeks later, in July. "Jane, you had a long-distance phone call," the secretary in the festival office said when I came in from rehearsal. "Martin Solomon. You're supposed to call him back." So David was right, I thought, and closed my eyes and reached my hand out, as if by holding her old number I could still keep Ruth in my grasp.

"Not bad news, I hope. You can use my phone if you want."

"Thanks, Buffie. I can call from the Paragon."

Her eyes widened. "You still seeing that cute guy? Any time you get tired of him . . ."

I smiled. "I'll let you know." So it wasn't the horrible life Mr. Schunk had promised—it was too damn small and predictable for anything that grand. I started to cry.

Buffie's hazel eyes filled. She was the sweetest, most inefficient secretary in the world, late to work every time she saw a prairie dog run over on the Ashcroft Road. "Did someone die, Jane?"

"Yeah, someone died," I said and wiped the tepid tears from my face, astonishing us both by bringing my fist down on her typewriter. The type ball jammed and hissed against the page.

I had just missed the shuttle, so, as I often did, I walked the many blocks to the Hyman Street Mall, where my summer friend Bugs tended bar at the Paragon. He was more than a decade younger than I—a tall and lean, tanned and sun-

338

bleached blond who wore his athletic good looks like a pair of Topsiders. I had selected them just as I might have bought shoes. He caught my eye, he was comfortable, he looked sturdy. I liked him, and if that seems mean, I should say he liked me, too. There are times when you can buy exactly what you've been shopping for. He would fix me a drink and hold my hand, and the banal fact of life would seem very reassuring to me then.

This is the last, I thought as I walked, moving slowly and with effort through the hot, thin air. First my family, one by one; then I left my husband; and now Ruth had left me. Now I was the orphan I had always aped, except that *orphan*'s not the word to use when you're nearly thirty-four. Perhaps the word is *heir*. There was no one left to be an heir to me.

Once, I made a will. It was the year I had rheumatic fever, and for the long months of my recovery I was taken out of school. Though I would have to repeat first grade the next year, no matter what I'd learned, my brother taught me to print, and, with his help, on a Big Chief tablet I misspelled my last will and testament, bequeathing my dolls, my game of Candy Land, and each of my Crayolas to the friends I thought would want them most. My mother was so upset when she found it that she spanked me while she cried. What now seemed odd, as I dodged a red jeep on Hopkins Street, was that I had no memory of having been afraid to die. Instead, I breathed again my mother's strange, metallic scent as she bent to kiss me good night and smooth my hair. I know that alloy now: it is the unyielding odor of a billet of prime steel. That is what terror smells like to me, not the must of aging skin, not the reek of internal parasites, but the simple, stupid possibility: if death can come by accident, then it is probable that life is accidental, too.

At six, I did not understand the formula, though I recognized the fear. I did not believe in God, but I said my prayers: "Now I lay me down to sleep, I pray the Lord my soul to keep. If I should die before I wake, I pray the Lord my soul to take." These were the lines my mother taught, and what I thought they asked for was a picture of my soul. "I hope it takes," she would say each time she snapped the shutter on her Brownie; "I hope they take," to the clerk at Walgreen's when she left the film; "What do you know, they all took," when she brought the packet home. And I would sort through those glossy black-and-whites, frowning at my flash-closed eyes, the dismemberment accomplished by the combination of the view finder and my mother's eye, the top of my head chopped off me this time, a left ear sheared from me next, thinking, oh, so tnat's what my soul looks like—sort of startled, sort of lacking, always unaware, always missing what seemed to me a vital part. I came to my enduring faithlessness without a struggle: to my mother, the camera was always much more mystery than God.

There was a postscript to my prayers: "Please bless Mama and Daddy and Dick. And if you want to make my mama happy, I guess you better go ahead and bless me too. Yours truly, Janie Hurdle, amen."

What I have always believed in is my voice, piped into my black instrument or put into words. I had said the word, one too many words it seems, for, as in fairy tales, you do not ask four wishes when you are granted three. As requested, I got well. And then my father died.

Here is what my father left me: a bag of broken images like a sack of pieces from a china figurine. The blue tattoo of an anchor on his arm. The pockets on his gray work shirt, his black lunchbox, a crumpled pack of Lucky Strikes. A brown spot on one fingernail, the clear green shadow puddled from the oxygen mask above his face. The blue tremor of his lips, which have deepened to the very color of the weight I cannot lift from his sad arm. *Roll your sleeve up, Daddy. I want to show your anchor to my friend.* When I try to mend those pieces, I see, instead of the man I might have known, a Merchant Marine whose boyish soul is printed in my mother's photo album, I see the varnished yellow door to his room closed in my face.

And I see me, tugging at the sleeve of a gray suit I never saw him wear, I see my mother, yanking like a Fury at the collar of my new blue dress. Her lips tremble too, but they are white, pinched with the anger that will shape everything I know of her life. "Jane Catherine," she is saying, "you are plenty old enough to know better than to pull a stunt like this." "But I want to see his tattoo," I am protesting, "I want to know it's him," and she hisses, "Who did you think it was? If you loved me, at your own father's funeral the least that you could do would be behave."

And if I loved my father, the least I could have done was not to shout. My mother paid a teen-aged neighbor fifty cents to keep me quiet while I played; but I had been quiet for too long, and I cracked a piece of clothesline, hollering at a kitchen chair to giddy-up, screaming at the baby sitter when she tried to take my horse and whip away. On her way out of the back yard, she grabbed my shoulders and shook until I thought my head would bobble off. "You little creep. I hope you go to Hell, because if your daddy dies, it's going to be your fault."

A man in running shorts jogged by me, a pair of New-foundlands circling him like satellites, their pink tongues lolling from their mouths. My feet were dusty, and the axis of one rubber sandal ground dirt into a broken blister as my thongs flip-flapped against my heels. I cut up Monarch Street and paused to watch the shortstop collide with the second baseman in a hippie softball game. According to my former stepdaughter, the hippie scene had been over for ten years, but Aspen, for all its chic, all its sprawl of fake chalet motels, was a mountain burg, and news arrived there slow. The shortstop's voice floated past the Crystal Palace. "Cocksucker. That was my play."

Here is what my mother left me: her house, her life insurance, some Kroger's stock, and three stamps stuck inside a stained red leather wallet I'd never seen before. It contains a pair of high school portraits, my brother at seventeen and me. He is smiling with his mouth closed to hide the gap between his teeth. My own smile is as open as a summer house, but the plastic picture window has smeared clouds across my face, as if a storm is brewing and the camera has caught me just before I close up tight. There are other pictures—my nephew, my twin nieces, also my mother's social security, Golden Age, and Kroger's I.D. cards. These were the facts of her long life.

The fact of mine is contained in three obituaries clipped from the *Hammond Times*: survived by . . . surviving are . . . survivors include.

It is a fact that explains nothing; it was my mistake to think it should, for what I alone escaped to tell myself was, simply, I survived. I did not kill my father; I did not let my brother die. But I had believed my mother, believed that if I loved them, I would take no pleasure in my life once theirs had been denied.

What David had tried to tell me was that our wishes are not numbered and our lives are not obliged.

A couple roller-skated by me, awkward on the bricks. Farther down the mall, someone played a tuba; I could hear the faint oompa. I was ready to call Martin. His wife, my friend, was dead, and we had loved her, and I was sorry, very sorry; that was all.

Part IV

22

I'd made it. Years ago I had trained to be a soloist, but
Mr. Schunk was wrong. A clarinet needs an orchestra.
In May I signed my contract with the New York Philharmonic.

"But what good is success if you don't let it spoil you?"
John Watley complained in June, as I refused his daily offer
of a drink to celebrate. He was the principal cellist in the
Philharmonic as well as in the Aspen Festival Orchestra, and
he was my favorite friend in Colorado, but we had already
had our drinks; we had already celebrated.

"Last summer she was married. This summer she hates
men." His look raised ridges on his rubber forehead—he had
a gawky, goofball face straight out of Looney Tunes. "Shorty,
I'm all for liberation. I always did the dishes. You can ask
any one of my ex-wives."

"Maybe she just doesn't like you." The secretary snickered.
Of all the musicians, he was Buffie's favorite too. How could
we help liking him? He behaved as if life were so ridiculous,
it must be parodied.

But I meant to let success spoil me. I meant never to get
distracted again. "John, I have to practice. Besides, chastity
builds strong character."

"Chastity rots the body and ruins the mind. Also," John said, "chastity is boring."

I couldn't argue with that. I gave lessons, I rehearsed, I practiced, I performed. I went to bed with the warmth of professional pleasures, but my dreams were cold. In the sweet, I was loved by the *New York Times*; in the nightmarish, nasty critics stood in for incubi. The town was jammed with young men who sparkled with health and sex appeal—for instance, Bugs, whom I met one night in June after staring for a week, having taken up the habit of sipping a lone Manhattan in the cool dark solitude of bars each afternoon. The Paragon was my favorite, a palace of Victoriana—flocked wallpaper, gilt mirrors, velvet love seats, ferns—and I liked it best on those afternoons, when I sat at the polished bar and watched tourists parade past a window bright with Colorado light, as if I were the single patron at a Loew's matinee, obliged to do no more than sit while the people on that screen participated. I liked that quiet hour, filled as my days and evenings were with tuning, arpeggios and airs, relentless theory. Bugs set the phone book on our table as he distributed our glasses—it was a crowded night, and I was there to celebrate Brahms's Clarinet Quintet with the other chamber players—then nudged the book toward me.

I frowned. "Am I supposed to call someone?"

"Me."

"Forget it." John Watley slipped an arm around my shoulder. "She's auditioned for the angels. The mundane pursuits of mortal men do not interest my friend Shorty."

"John, you're such an ass," the viola said and went on opining on the use of winds in string ensembles.

"Why would I do that?" I said.

A smile lit his face, which was as wholesome as a Sealtest carton. He was exactly what I wanted, a boy whose ordinary handsomeness seemed to be his whole attraction—in other words, some sex to keep my body company while my spirit mingled with the cerebral corps of muses. I smiled back.

John squeezed my shoulder. "Son, what we have here is a genuine reconditioned virgin. A miracle. Fourteen years of marriage and then''—he lifted his voice in oratorio—''she has risen.''

The viola rolled her eyes.

''You're one of the music crowd?'' I nodded. ''I've seen you here in the afternoons.''

''Shorty.'' John snapped his fingers in front of my face. ''Remember me? John Watley, brilliant cellist—I wouldn't say so myself of course but the *New York Times*—Shorty. Did I ever tell you how my second wife used my bow for a rack to dry her pantyhose?''

''You live out by Castle Creek?'' I nodded.

''That's what she got out of assertiveness training. Some women just can't handle liberation.''

''Could I walk you home?''

''Don't bother, we've got a car,'' John said as I said, ''Sure.''

''Bleached.'' John tapped his temple as Bugs left to answer a summons from another table. ''You don't want to get mixed up with a guy who peroxides his hair.'' I exchanged another smile with Bugs as he passed on his way back to the bar. ''That wasn't a good line. Do you think that was a good line?'' John asked the viola when the chamber players finished their second round and I mentioned casually that I thought I'd stay to have another drink, why didn't they go on? ''What's he got that I haven't?''

''Looks, youth, a full head of hair . . .''

''That's what I mean. He's just another pretty face.'' As he got up to go, John whispered in my ear, ''Don't forget, chastity builds strong character.'' But when the bar closed, I walked home with Bugs.

''So how's your character?'' John asked the next morning as we stood in the office to check our mail. ''You giving up New York to take up skiing?''

I tossed an ad for ligatures into the waste can. ''Why are you so nosy?''

''My life is dull.'' He frowned as he skimmed a letter. ''Are you having an intellectual relationship with Blondie, or is it the real thing?''

I tossed another ad and picked up my copy of *The Clarinet-*

ist while he went through a stack of inquiries and invitations of the sort that famous virtuosos get. "I'm having fun."

"Actually, gossip has been proven the most healthy form of recreation. All the titillation, none of the tedious involvements."

"I'm not *involved*."

"Good. Just don't let him talk you into giving up the clarinet." He handed a letter to Buffie. "Could you write these people and tell them that I'm sorry but I'm booked for the season. And if they're interested in next year, they should get in touch with my agent."

"What makes you think I would?" I demanded.

He scanned another letter. "Gad! Here's a woman in Sioux City, Iowa, who wants to know if I'm her long-lost cousin. Hmm?" He glanced at me. "Because you've got more talent than drive."

I tossed my head. "Bullshit."

"Otherwise you would have been in the Big Apple years ago."

"How come she thinks you're her cousin?" Buffie asked.

"I don't know, because she's got spare time to think, I guess. Where the hell is Sioux City, anyway?"

"Out there, with the rest of the world," I said. "You know, there actually is a rest of the world, John? There's a whole middle of the country between New York and Aspen."

"That," he said, "is a dangerous figment of your imagination. Don't get pissed, Shorty." He smiled. "You'll still be a star, if you leave the boys alone."

"You're one to talk. How many times have you been married?"

"Three, but there's a big difference between us," he insisted as he took my arm and steered me toward rehearsal.

"Yeah? What's that?"

"You've got looks and youth. I've got irony."

But John was wrong. I did have drive, I had my heart set firmly on my future, and, because he was so harmless, for the nonce I had Bugs. I also had bad moments, as even in the best of worlds, which was where I considered I now lived, one does. Bugs disliked the music crowd, became sullen at parties, and we fought. He taught me to play tennis; I was lousy. I threw my racquet and stamped my foot. I couldn't get a passage in Prokofiev's Sixth Symphony just right, and the conductor gave me hell. I cracked the bell on the clarinet Mr. Schunk had left me; my students argued with my advice. And when the moments passed and didn't matter, I thought, well, I must have irony. Bugs quit his job and went to Europe. John took up with a student cellist and took on a misty look. "How's *your* character?" I grumbled and was miffed but not upset. I would have liked to moan to him about Manhattan rents according to the *Times;* I would have liked to hear him say it was unlikely that I would be pushed from a subway platform or raped in Central Park. I would have liked, but he was busy, and that was the way the cookie crumbled, the way the apple cored: some days you had it all, and some days you had less, but you always had your future, and as long as you could dedicate your present to it, you had no spare time to think about whatever it was from the long past you might have lost.

I hardly ever thought of Ben.

Then it was August. In two weeks the music festival would be over, and I would be hunting for an apartment in New York. I was glad—the Philharmonic was what I had always worked for, even when I hadn't known it—but it was with a little lurch in confidence that I observed the ritual: students who had been best friends quibbling in the halls, romances begun in June now soured, a worried look on the faces of the married indiscreet, talk at the dinner table shifting from summer gossip and the passion of aesthetic postulates to home and concerns of human size. How it had hurt me just the year before—the carnival not closed yet but already the sense of ticket stubs and soiled wax papers fluttering across the empty lot, I with a home to go to and no desire to go home, wanting to beg another hour of celebration from the weary crowd. But this time I was ready to go too, as eager as the rest to get on with my real life.

And I was cranky with uncertainty. Would I find an apartment? Would I get good notices? Would Zubin Mehta like my style? That morning I knocked over a stand in a diminuendo at rehearsal and received a scorching look from the guest conductor when the orchestra broke and howled. My own practice went badly, the early afternoon of lessons worse. "I don't know what you *want* from me," one of my students complained. "You say staccato, so I play staccato, and then you start bitching about computers like I've committed some great crime." "Staccato means . . ." I sighed and then despaired because I was tired, and, for the moment, I couldn't remember what anything meant. "Look, there is nothing, not a single diacritic . . ." "I don't think that word is in my musical dictionary," she said, and I snapped, "Well, it's in mine, the one I keep in my head, where it also says that, unless you're dealing with something other than traditional forms of music, you had better play with *some* kind of feeling. When you play staccato, you cut that feeling short. It's still there," I begged; "it's just abbreviated. Do you understand what I mean now?" "No," she said. "I paid a lot of money to come out here for some tips on my fingering and embouchure. I didn't come to get a lecture on my soul." I put my head on my desk. "Susan . . ." She held out her clarinet. "This is an instrument. I'm a person." "Susan . . ." "We are not the same thing." I had another student waiting. I raised my head. "You're in the wrong business then."

When I came out of my studio in the late afternoon, just in time to play tennis before dinner if I had had anyone to play tennis with, John was standing in the hall.

"Number four," he said with a sheepish smile. "Well, it won't last, I know. But then, what does, except genius? And you and I both know that's a long haul for solitude. She's got a class right now. Would you come have a drink and help me celebrate?"

I had a headache. I was lonely, not especially for Bugs but for some body, and I was furious with John. "Congratulations," I said sourly. "But I happen to have a piss-poor attitude about student-teacher marriages, my boyfriend left, I'm horny, and I've had a rotten day, if you don't mind."

"Rotten days." He looked morose. "Well, like wives, they come and go. She's moving to New York. It *is* the best thing for her, she'll get good training, good exposure, hell. She'll be okay."

"Yeah? What about you?" I said, gave in, took his arm, and walked. "You look like a lovesick moose."

"What happened to Superman?"

"That shows where you've been all week long. Haven't you noticed Buffie wearing black? He went to Paris, and she was so convinced that when he got tired of me, she could step right in. Hey. It doesn't matter; it wasn't important by design. It's just"—I sighed again—"why do the students have to be so obstinate?"

"Bad lessons, huh?"

"Lousy," I admitted. "They want to ride the ski lifts all day long and drink all night, they want to fuck and fall in love, and then diddle their fingers on the keys a little bit if they get time. And I don't blame them, but . . ." I relented. "Come on, let's go have that drink. You think this engagement will last long enough for me to drop these scores off in my room?"

We turned the corner of my hall, and I glimpsed a man slumped just beyond my door. He stood up, reshouldering an enormous backpack, as I rummaged through my purse, bringing up bits of Kleenex, a leaky ballpoint pen, and the string end of a frayed tampon. "Damn. I know my keys are in here somewhere."

"Jane?"

I turned around. "My God." And as David Solomon adjusted his gear so that he could hug me, I sprayed his khaki shirtfront with astonished words. "I must be blind. What are you doing here?"

He glanced at John and hesitated. "Passing through."

And so I have not gone to New York, although I mean to still. As soon as I see the sun set into the Grand Canyon, where I am sitting with David, who laughs and says "Behind," because he can't be sure that I don't know the sun will not set *into* anywhere. Piñon scents the air. The wind is up; it's cold above this fire that is more brilliant for dying, cliffs the deep color of embers, ragged shadows black as cinders but so much larger they really take my breath away. And for a moment I am not sure the sun won't fall. Why shouldn't it? Everything in this world is so impossible. "Go put some jeans on," David says as I give my shorts another tug.

"I don't want to miss it."

"You're not going to miss it." He checks his watch.

"It might set early."

He laughs again, and his eye patch jerks. "Believe me, it'll set right on time."

But I don't believe him, so I run all the way back to the van we've left parked at Yaki Point, where a line of cars is growing, people huddled with the heaters on until the countdown, as if the sun is just a rocket ship and Houston has scheduled its return. There is a splash of disco from the radios, mingled with an incredulous babble of foreign voices and the canyon's own deep hum. The overlook is sprouting tripods. I dump my suitcase, not bothering to repack, and stumble toward the ledge where David sits apart while I'm still pulling up my pants. To the east the moon has risen, translucent as a fingernail. I glance over my shoulder, but the sun is still there, a little yellow ball bounced against a deep blue heaven scuffed by clouds, its reflection rising from the canyon like a mist. I think it's stuck. I think it will not set at all. I think I will not go to New York. I think I am in love with David Solomon.

I don't know how I let this happen.

Oh, I know how I got here. We left for the Grand Canyon the day after the music festival closed—because I had mentioned in an offhand way that sometime in my life I'd like to see it, and for David sometime in your life is always now. For two weeks David bunked in his down sleeping bag on the floor of my small room, *I* was the one who talked him into staying, just by pointing out the many things he ought to do and see since he was passing through and didn't seem too clear where to or in any special hurry.

"Couldn't get me on one," John said when I told David he would have to ride the ski lifts, as the three of us sat celebrating John's fourth try at marriage. "All that space makes me dizzy. There's something unhealthy about unpolluted air. People are supposed to be knifed in subways; they were meant to breathe exhaust. Take away their paranoia, and what have they got left?"

"You sound so homesick," I complained.

"I am. I like garbage on my sidewalks. I like sidewalks. What can you do with a mountain except look?"

"Climb," David said.

"What is this, a wise guy?" John said to me. "Here's to your new home, Shorty. Seven and a half million people can't be wrong, even if they are all nuts. The *Times* is the only paper in the country that rubs off on your hands, but it's also the only paper in the country, and there you have it—it's filthy, it's not fit for human habitation, but it's the only place to live."

"Not for me," David said.

"You're not a musician." John narrowed his eyes. "Or are you?"

David seemed to think about it. "I'm a carpenter."

John's face was blank. It astonished him that there were people whose profession was not art.

"I'm hungry. Why don't we go to the Mother Lode?" I asked, but John was meeting his fiancée in the dining hall, so David and I went by ourselves. By the time we had finished two plates of spaghetti and a half-liter of red wine, we were laughing at the fact that, as far as Italian cuisine went, John might be right about New York.

The waiter appeared like a ghost, bowed from the waist, and said, "Another carafe, sir?"

I clapped my hands. "Another carafe," I agreed.

"Could I get you some dessert, sir? The tortoni is quite excellent."

I shook my head, suppressed a giggle, and looked away as the waiter twitched. It was the patch. I'd never heard anyone called *sir* in the Mother Lode before. "No thanks," David said. "I think the lady wants to drink."

"Don't you?"

He smiled. "I do," he said and raised his glass.

". . . also Weller Lake and the Maroon Bells." I finished my recommendations for sightseeing as I swallowed the last drop of wine from the carafe. My napkin was balled on the table. "It's just a great place to pass through."

He paused, in a way that suddenly gave me pause too. "Why don't we smoke a joint and sleep out? It's too late to see the Maroon Bells, but I'll bet we could see stars."

"Oh," I said, "well . . . for one thing you have to get a reservation for a campground forever in advance." "Do we need a campground?" "Also, I don't have a sleeping bag. And I really should go to the student piano recital tonight."

"What time?"

"I mean they're not *my* students, but—eight."

He checked his watch. "We'd better hurry then. It's a quarter after nine. Check," he said to the waiter, who leaped to proffer it.

I spilled a clot of bills from my wallet, but he brushed it back. "That's for being a good guide. Jane, I think of you as an old buddy from way back, and since we are old buddies, I hope you won't mind my saying that I think you've gotten paranoid. I've got all I need to dream on and a spare bag in my van. Stars?"

"Stars," I agreed, red-faced but relieved.

We took a jeep trail into the national forest and parked the van in a meadow near a rocky stream that caught the moon-light like mercury.

"Stars," he said as he snuffed the roach that burned my fingers and ogled a sky as black as Halloween but full of silver pinwheels as spectacular as the Fourth of July.

"Stars." I sighed, full of painless throbbing in my bor-rowed bag, plunked next to his beside the stream, which played a cheery baroque air. "We sound like idiots." I was having an idiotic difficulty in emitting words. "I think I must be stoned."

"I'm not only stoned, I'm drunk."

"Yeah, that too." I sighed again feeling as aimless and as happy as if it *were* a holiday. "Are you really a carpenter? I thought you worked in a bookstore in New York." He'd been a rock guitarist, an orderly, a Marine. At one time, his brother Sam had told me, he dealt drugs. Sam was a lawyer,

Jake a reporter. Why, Ruth had lamented, can't David stick to anything?

"There's no money in it. I like to read, but working in a bookstore isn't exactly the same thing."

"I could've told you that."

"You weren't around, Smart Mouth. Anyway, there are some things you know that you still find out. Carpenter's the classy way to put it—I've always done odd jobs. I like working at something where you can *see* results, something that's finished when you're done. It's not hard to make a living doing things that people don't have time to do right for themselves."

"How come you joined the Marines?"

"I was about to get drafted." He laughed. "I don't know. It seemed like a good idea at the time."

"Was it?"

"Are you kidding?"

"I didn't think so." For a while we lay and watched the stars. I thought how pleased Ruth would have been to see us, although she would have been nudging our bags together and whispering lewd instructions in my ear. No wonder I was paranoid. "Did you know your mother was always trying to fix us up?"

He didn't answer.

"Of course, she was always trying to fix everybody up." I propped myself on an elbow. "I can just see her, telling Martin to be sure and get married again, naming every divorcée and widow that she knew." I sat up. "I'm sorry. That was a really thoughtless thing to say."

"Pretty much the truth, though." We had become disembodied voices in the dark. "It wouldn't be such a bad idea if he took her advice. Well, you saw him."

I was sorry. If helplessness was a tribute, it was not the one that Ruth would have wanted. "Well, he can mix a mean martini. At least that's what she always claimed. Did she ever get one? That's what she wanted me to bring her in the hospital."

"No, but she hollered like hell for it till the end."

It was exactly the way I wanted to remember her. "I really loved your mother."

"I really loved her too."

A coyote yapped in the distance. "David, you don't suppose there are bears out here?"

"I don't see why there wouldn't be."

"Oh shit." I pulled the bag up over my face. After a minute, I peeked out. "Maybe we *should* sleep in my room."

"And miss the stars?"

"I've seen them. They're very nice."

He laughed. "You're truly scared? You really want to go back?"

"Well . . ." The stream played a mordent. The air had a wonderful chill, nipping at my cheeks while my body cosied in its thick wrapper of down.

"Not really," he guessed. "You just want to be assured that the wilderness is safe."

I was irritated. He was the sort of man who made you feel he saw through you, and it wasn't just that illusion of an eye behind the patch that was like a trick of one-way glass. I have always hated that feeling, secrets splayed on an examination table like the quilting you've never seen inside your own cunt. "Well, how is everybody in Bloomington? I really didn't see anyone when I stopped off."

"I don't know that many people anymore. I saw Elaine Ghent. Remember her? She's divorced now."

"That's no surprise. She was pathetic. Every time I talked to her I wanted to take a bath, I felt so icky-sticky. She was such a lush even the students used to talk about her." Elaine, I knew, had had an affair with Eric Yarber, and my voice sharpened to such a nasty edge that I felt ashamed. "Of course, they used to talk about all the faculty wives. It pissed me off when I was sick to remember how I'd listened to that tripe." The days in Bloomington when I'd been sick seemed wonderfully remote, and for a minute I felt like one of those students again, whispering about someone I barely knew, the theory teacher Gabriel, who'd married a student not half his age and then had her break down on him. "I never heard anything bad about your mother, though."

"I never heard anything bad about you."

"Why would you? You had to have an inside track."

"I had a track of sorts. Every other man in the Music School wanted inside your lace pants. Nobody could believe it when you married Gabriel."

"He was a nice man." It made me feel terrible to know that I defended Ben not because I believed the best about him, but because I wanted to believe the best about myself. "And I never wore lace pants."

His grin flashed faintly in the darkness. "When I was an eighteen-year-old punk still whacking off over a centerfold of Avis Kimble and copping a few feels at the drive-in, you were sitting in the living room *conversing* with my parents. Not to mention this professor who had your telephone number tattooed on his dick. And that was after you fucking your brains out all night with a hotshot campus hero who goes on to win a gold medal in the Olympics. And *he*'s so nuts about you, he'd spend Sunday afternoon tossing a football to a depressed Clearasil junkie who never made high school varsity just because my parents were your friends. I thought you wore lace pants."

Somehow my past sounded a whole lot better the way he told it than the way I remembered it. "Bronze. And anyway, he ditched me, remember?"

David's voice softened. "You feel bad about your marriage?"

"Well, I was married fourteen years." But there was something about him that made me unwilling to claim sympathy I hadn't earned. "No. I don't even think about it." I didn't intend to think about it, either. What would be the point? I felt like the knight who comes to the chapel to ask questions, but I was so appalled by the answers that I skittered off like a rabbit in the abandoned sanctuary. I meant to skitter off again and was horrified to hear my voice, strange with vigor, blurt, "I couldn't stand him, I just couldn't stand him. He was so weak, he made me sick." So I did hate him after all. I didn't want to, but that inevitability of failed love was precisely why I had resolved never to risk my heart again, that and not, as I had convinced myself, the demands of my career. "Anyway, what about you? You fucked a lot of faculty wives, didn't you?"

"Not very many."

"Elaine Ghent? Well. Did your parents know?" He didn't answer. "No, I guess they wouldn't. Your mother was broadminded, but not that broad. I don't suppose you ever told them what your fascination with Mexico was, either."

After a minute he said, "Her name was Cathy, and she was a remarkable woman."

"Oh, the *waitress*. I thought her name was Mary Jane."

"I would have married her, but she fell in love with a college boy in Acapulco." He hesitated, as if he were trying out a story and hadn't decided whether that was the beginning or the end. "So I ran some drugs, nearly got my ass shot off, *did* get it kicked, and made half a million dollars that's still sitting in a bank in Switzerland. Sam must have told you—he's the only one who knows." I waited with a sense that this too was subject to revision, was disappointed when his tone dropped to a final note. "So we're even. Elaine told a story on you, and my brother told one on me."

"What did Elaine tell you about me?" Inside my sleeping bag, my hand rose in an instinctive gesture. Why did it bother me, not just Elaine, but to know that his life had gone on all those years while I'd kept mine on hold? "She told you about Eric, didn't she? Well, I never slept with him."

"I know."

There are two kinds of personal trespass. A few bruised toes equal misdemeanor. The knot that tightens like a fist inside your chest is felony. The petty guilt that I had felt for my betrayal backed up in my throat. Who was he to know?

"I didn't like Eric Yarber, but I would have rather seen you with him than with that milktoast Gabriel. At least Yarber had some guts. All your husband had was a lot of phony piety."

"Elaine Ghent's no merit badge, you know."

"I wasn't bucking for Eagle Scout. And I'll say this for Yarber—he was in love with you. The only person Gabriel was ever in love with was himself. You ought to hate him, Jane. Because I'd bet my life he made you feel like shit for getting kicked out of school; oh, in his pious way, of course—no doubt he 'saved' you. Didn't you ever wonder about a man who wanted to save you from yourself?''

"You don't know anything about it." There it was again, the one inexplicable anger that made them all unreasonable. *"You weren't even there!"*

"What should I have been there for?" he asked. "After he made you such a *wife* that no one could be your friend, not even my parents, who were there and thought the world of you. If I know more than makes you comfortable, it's not just Elaine, it's them."

Like all people who cannot afford to, I try never to think of wasted time, the years I could have been playing for the Philharmonic, the years I spent married to someone I should never have been married to. That last was a private lie, and, no matter who had told him, he had no right to repeat it. Ben had told me once, and that was enough to know. "Well, that pretty much takes care of me. What have you done that makes you so smart, Mr. Millionaire?"

"Half," he corrected. "But I've never touched that money, and I never will."

"I don't believe you," I said coolly. "I think you watched too much TV."

"Well I wish the TV had told me what to do when I was blind out of my mind with the big T's, sitting on the road outside Cienega at three A.M. with fifty thousand dollars in my pocket and a gun I didn't know how to shoot. When those bushes rustled, I would have been glad to see a bear." I pulled my sleeping bag tight around my neck. The coyote was still barking, and David's voice had changed, as if its faint taste of irony had turned bitter in his mouth. I wanted to hear this story; why, I didn't know. "Because those mountains were crawling with *cabarones* just as mean as the *banditos* you've seen at every crummy drive-in movie in your life. You want to go to a foreign country, run some bigtime drugs. I didn't handle marijuana; just powder, mostly coke." When he turned his face toward me, his skin was luminous, and his voice had the energetic, amazed timbre I associate with truth. "You don't have a family then, you don't have a friend.

Your textbook Spanish isn't spoken. *Dinero*. You don't have it, you can't get it, you might as well be speaking Greek. And when it gets to the point that a nice Jewish boy from Indiana wants to finger rosaries and say Hail Marys, he's got to play cops and robbers with the *federales* all the way to a whore in Mexico City, where he can pay to shake before her votives, hoping she won't notice he can't get it up and hoping to hell the husband in the picture on her dresser has a gun he knows how to shoot and is standing guard outside. I should have told my parents that? You think I should have explained to my mother that I'm such a drifter because I talked so much money I can't find the decimal point on a paycheck? When I got so scared I couldn't drive, I took a plane to Bern with five hundred thousand bucks taped to my thighs and then sat on the Riviera for six months trying to bake the chill out and get excited about nude beaches."

"I thought you went to Brazil."

"Sure. I developed an interest in Latin American culture. What else are you going to tell your parents when you're eighteen and fall in love with a thirty-year-old waitress with two ex-husbands and three kids and run off to Mexico because you hope she's never been with anybody that romantic? I left a note, but by the time I was level-headed enough to follow up with a postcard, I was running highs in the hills and then, the next thing I know, I'm sitting on the patio of a pink hotel counting bank slips while I watch a lot of droopy tits get sunburned. I didn't have a name, let alone an address. All I had was one sincere prayer that 'The Purloined Letter' never got translated into Spanish, because any *federale* that wanted to come looking, there I was, turned inside out and *obvious*."

As clear as if it had been snapped by my mother's Brownie, I had this picture of him: shirtless and barefoot on his parents' stairs, beer foam in the beard he'd long since shaved, the glimmer of a watchface above the banister as he hurried past the room where Ben and I sat sipping cognac, his mother saying, "Did you see David? He got in last night. He's been traveling in Brazil." There was another picture, which I had never seen before: his empty room, creased beer can in the wastebasket, a mouse-colored clot of dust clinging to the needle brush of his broken Motorola, down the hall a slot of light beneath the bathroom door, his beard falling, mute black commas in the sink.

I wanted to hear the story because the space between the pictures was the space where our friendship might finally begin, and I was touched not by the story but by the telling, by the certainty of my intuition that he told it because he wanted to tell *me*.

I ran my finger along the zipper of my bag. "You mean you never did go to Brazil?"

"Listen, I *regret* this—the Latin Americans are wonderful people, and I'm sure they have a beautiful culture. The closest I ever got to it was banging a waitress from Buena Vista, Indiana, five times a day in a cheap Mexico City hotel room, where the bugs in the drawers were as big as my socks and the only way to tell them apart was to shake them. I should have gone to Brazil? I took her to Acapulco so I could get a tan and be less boring. The first day I eat some *puerco perdigado* sunk in *salsa verde*—and while I'm in bed with terminal trots, she falls in love with a blond Yalie on spring vacation. *He* can dive off cliffs; all I can do is moan, and believe me, I'm still moaning when I start getting those postcards from New Haven. By the time I figure I'm in shape to go kill them both, one of her ex-brothers-in-law has shown up—there's no telling how many she has, I'm not even sure she didn't understate the husbands—anyway, he's got big ideas and a connection. Also a very big and stupid mouth, which got blown off with the rest of his head one night in Rosario while I was trying to get my cock back in my pants before the *cucarachas* in the outhouse decided to hold it for ransom. I was at the airport in Guadalajara before I even bothered to zip up."

"You're exaggerating."

"I'm telling you the truth. I celebrated my eighteenth birthday like any other optimistic virgin punk—next year I intended to get laid, this year I was still getting off *thinking* about it. Well, I fell in love and I got laid, and before I was twenty I was a half-millionaire who felt damn lucky just to have my ass left. No,'' he added, "I never got married. That's what you wanted to know about, wasn't it?"

"So you screwed other people's wives instead." I smiled, as if we were wise old adults, talking about our misadventures as impulsive children. I wasn't angry with him after all.

"I got into faculty wives," he said slowly, "because when I came back, every girl I asked out wanted to tell me all about the float her sorority was going to build with the Sammys for Little Five Hundred. I'm not bragging. I was grateful. For a while they made me feel like I'd done something exciting instead of butthole stupid. There are times when you need that kind of illusion."

I felt sorry that he should need to depend on people for illusions. A long time ago, I thought, I had learned to make my own in music. "Well, I take it back about Elaine, then. I was nasty."

He hesitated. "Elaine was a very nice, extremely generous person, and your friend Eric Yarber treated her like shit. I would have punched him out for her if he hadn't been a cripple."

"He wasn't *my* friend. I couldn't stand him."

"Oh?"

"Well, maybe I liked him a little."

"Run that by again."

"I didn't like him at all, but I was dying to fuck him," I said in exasperation. He laughed. "And I never did because I didn't want to hurt my husband." He didn't disagree. "Oh, all right. I never did because I was scared to. I wanted him to think I was wonderful."

David reached out to pat my sleeping bag.

"I mean *I* wanted to think I was wonderful. I never loved my husband. I couldn't sleep with anybody who knew that."

"You're wonderful," David said in a sleepy voice. "But I've been on the road all day, and if I don't get some sleep, I'm going to die."

"I'm not tired." I yawned. In my whole life I had never slept beneath the stars, and it seemed an incredible omission, just as never having swept a racquet with my wrist before had been a sudden bereavement the first time I surprised Bugs's ball in midair and heard it whock against my strings. I wanted to keep talking. "How come you did join the Marines?"

"Good night."

I wanted to tell him about my life, to tell him how I had finally come to live for half a year in the prismatic music of my solitude, how I could no longer hear its exact hues but could feel it in my skin now beneath the black sky or in the sunlight, moving. But it was late, and I did not know how to say it. "Did you kill anyone?"

"Tomorrow." His voice was thick and furry. "Will you talk to me? I was a Marine, and I was in a war. I joined because fucking other men's wives is good only in a very short run for illusions. Lights out."

"You mean killing people is good for longer?" He didn't answer. I touched my hands to my cold face, then felt myself drifting after him. There would be stars again. I didn't have to hold out for these. Because it seemed, if the past had so many surprises tucked like boxes inside boxes, friends wrapped in the fragile tissue of acquaintance, the present and future could hardly fail to be miraculously layered. When I woke, he was smiling, leaning on the neat roll of his bag, a web of gray I hadn't noticed in his hair like a spider's fine netting. We agreed that neither one of us had ever wanted anything so much as breakfast. As I gave my bag a few clumsy lops, he said, "Do you want to tell me now?" And I slid into his van, although I didn't know it, already on my way to Arizona.

We talked for two weeks. We hiked around Maroon and Weller lakes; we rode the ski lifts; while I rehearsed, he toured Ashcroft and swam at the Grottoes; and when the music festival was over, we put John Watley on the white-knuckle flight to Denver. His fiancée had driven his car to Idaho to pack and tell her mother.

"Shorty, it's been nice knowing you."

"My character is intact, John. I'll be there."

He jerked his chin at David, who was reading a flight schedule at the counter. They had already shaken hands and wished each other well, although I knew—even if they wouldn't say so—they did not like each other. "Moshe Dayan coming with you?"

"John, you're a racist."

"Actually, I miss Superman."

"A sexist."

"After all, he was just Clark Kent in disguise. Face it, Lois. We were meant for each other."

"A real asshole. You hear me? You're going to miss your plane."

"Oh well," he said and set his flight bag on the table. "We'll always have Paris."

"You're not funny." I was laughing.

He leaned toward the uniformed attendant who was reassembling his shaving kit. "Maybe not today, maybe not tomorrow, but soon, and for the rest of her life . . ."

"Miss!" the attendant called as I bolted after him. "Security. Ma'am, airline regulations . . ." My arms were pinned behind my back as soon as I reached the airstrip, and when John turned around, I felt so foolish for my impulse I did not know what to say.

"For God's sake," John said. "All she wants is to say goodbye. Oh, maybe in a moment of passion I promised—but you're a family man, surely you can understand. I have to go back to my wife."

I twisted my head to get a look at the man who held my arms. "It's a joke."

"Ma'am, the airlines do not find jokes funny."

"I read the sign," John said. "And, frankly, I have to say I think that's what's the matter with the airlines. Just don't break her fingers, huh? The *New York Times* doesn't know it yet, but she's a brilliant clarinetist. Sweetheart . . ."

The clasp around my wrists tightened.

"He's a *friend*. I'm not even sleeping with him."

"That serious?" John winked and put his hand on the railing. Three steps up he turned around. "Don't be a fool, Jane."

When they finally let me out of the ladies' room—I'd had no idea what such searches entailed—David was still reading schedules. He looked up and smiled. "One thing I've always

liked about you—your flair for drama. Ready? It's a nice day
for the Grand Canyon. How about you?''

"Well, I would, but I have to be in New York." How
could I have neglected to get my ticket? I had to get started
on my apartment search.

He left the brochure on the counter. "I think they have
airports in Arizona."

"You know, I'm actually going to miss that turkey. Well,
I'll see him, of course, but . . ." We walked toward the van.

"Don't get me wrong—I like him, even if he does think
New York is the promised land. But isn't he kind of an
asshole?''

"He's a *nut*." As David turned the key, the radio buzzed,
and I slid the volume lever down. "A genuine Brazil nut. He
thinks I'm in love with you."

"We can't all be Jeane Dixon."

I laughed and rolled the window down. "Okay, why not?
New York will still be there next week."

He read maps while I packed and chattered. Could we take
the Million Dollar Highway? Could we stop at Mesa Verde?
We could. We would. Fifty-seven miles beyond Mesa Verde,
where four states meet on a stone tablet in a landscape of sand
buttes as bizarre as thunderheads seen from an airplane, we
would watch a woman coax her dachshund's stubby legs into
the four angles of the inlaid X while her husband clicked their
Instamatic, and we would laugh so hard that when I leaned
from Colorado into Arizona to kiss David, we would miss,
his lips hovering over Utah while mine puckered above New
Mexico. "A goddamn omen," I would mutter later. "Do you
realize it's already the twenty-third?" "Stop counting," he
would answer.

But that would be after. We would ride the first fifty miles
from Aspen in self-conscious silence while I second-thought.
What had possessed me? Why was I doing this? And I would
glance at him as he glanced away from me, suddenly aware
that our looks had begun to linger and smoke, that they had
been doing so for days. And I would be afraid that he could
feel the flame between my legs until, just outside of Redstone,

he pulled the van to the shoulder beside yet another spectacular stream in yet another spectacular national forest.

"Jane."

"I know."

We left my door flapping as we stumbled and splashed through the stream into the woods, where the sun stabbed me in the eyes as we fell and John became clairvoyant. It took us six days to reach the Grand Canyon.

It will not take six hours to reach New York. In forty-three hours I will sit at a table in the Figaro trying to smile over cappuccino as I say "I told you" to John Watley. I have not told David that I love him. Once the countdown has begun, what's the point?

And so I do not tell him anything as I stand overlooking the spectacle of light and shadow.

"Don't," David says behind me, and I start.

I take a breath, and my heart resumes. "Jesus Christ, you scared me. I very nearly fell in."

"I'm sorry. You scared *me*. You looked like you were going to jump."

"Are you crazy? What would I do that for?" But I know. A grand canyon is like a mountain—up or down, you want to go. Fear of heights is not the fear of falling, but that old terror of the self, the impulse to leap first and then think in that timeless last mile of undistracted space. "I was just looking."

"Well, do me a favor and look from back here." But I am feeling difficult, and so I look from where I am.

To the west, distance is a grainy purple. Its measure is the place where backlight becomes porous, above the molten cliffs, the shadows big as dinosaurs. The sun hangs just below the burning clouds. I see now that it will set, and I am afraid of the dark. All my life I have been, although I have talked myself into believing I was silly, turned on lights to prove that it holds nothing light cannot contain. I never dreamed I was rehearsing, that what I feared was not burglars, rapists, or even murderers, but just the empty, awful shape of the dark itself, this primeval blackness that is already creeping up the walls, waiting to sink its cold teeth into my bones.

Today is my thirty-fourth birthday. If he loved me—but he

hasn't said so, and I am much too old to be the fool who is shivering here, waiting to be asked back beneath his arm for one last night.

"You'll have to remember to wrap up in a blanket in the morning," he is saying. "If you think it's cold now, wait till you feel the wind at dawn."

I love the way his voice does not go with his looks, a sound like dry bread breaking, a casual assurance to the tone that belongs with comeliness. I love the ease with which his words come, the attention of his ear. I love the way he will not let me lie, a silent patience with revision until my story comes out right.

His voice is reasonable; his ear is accurate. I do not believe that he would ever lie to me. I do not think he lies.

I cannot comprehend how a man like him can have so little purpose, how a man who sees the world so clearly with one eye can make his hands and feet wear blinders, doing this and that, but never doing anything with more intent than to get by.

And yet I love the way he divests me of my own plans, as if the future is of no account until the present's done. For him the present is perpetual. For me now is the name of that temporary place between what's finished and what is not begun.

He makes me laugh.

I want him to ask me to go with him. I won't, but I want him to ask.

A car radio is bleeding into the dusk at the point just out of sight. I wonder if, when you die, the senses leave you one by one. Perhaps, when this hot light has cooled, I will hear a fading sound. I would accept that. But not this: of all the ways to die, I think love must be the worst. It makes you think and act like such a dope. "David."

He holds his arm out, and, as I settle inside it, the cold metal button on the pocket of his denim jacket scrapes against my cheek. The hurt that I first felt for him has moved upward from my crotch into my throat. I want to touch his hair and feel it spring back like a fresh-baked cake. I want to slide my hand along the coarse grain of his cheek and underneath his patch, to lay my fingertips against his socket, but I can't lift my hand, I can't speak, and he does not.

This afternoon, when we parked the van between the tour buses at Desert View and finally peeked over the rail crowded with Japanese festooned with Nikons, overcome with vertigo and awe, he was full of geological facts.

Hiking along the Canyon Rim Trail later, I complained. He read too many books on science, and, while I had no argument with science, I didn't want to hear majestic depth reduced to banal circumstance.

"What's so banal about science?"

I sat, dangling my feet off the edge. "It doesn't believe in mystery."

"Of course it does. *Jane.*"

"I'm not scared—unless I look straight down." I gave him a sheepish smile as I scooted back. The sky was as bright blue as the nylon of his backpack. It looked more solid than the shimmering pastels of distant rock.

He sat beside me. "Science believes in the fundamental mystery. Religion leaves all the little ones and takes the big one away."

Once, when I was on a plane, the woman in the window seat turned to me. "Look at that," she said. "Just like a quilt, all those little roads and little fields and little houses. I like to think that's how the world appears to God." I craned my neck. We were over the Midwest, which was parceled out in empty squares like bogus presents beneath an office Christmas tree. "I hope not," I said. "I can't see the people." "That's because they're too small," she said as if she were speaking to a child. I closed my eyes, still clutching my plastic cup of melting ice and bourbon. "I don't find that particularly comforting."

Here is what it always comes back to: I don't believe in God but cannot seem to let him go.

I smiled at David. "Well, I'd speak to the man upstairs with your complaint, but we're not on speaking terms."

Now I gesture toward the canyon's puzzle, gigantic jigsaw pieces of orange fire and black ash. "Go ahead. Explain it."

"What time's your flight?" he asks.

"Ten-something, I don't know. My ticket's in the van."
Say it, I will. He ran off to Mexico once. If he wanted to say
it, he would. "Well, I wish I weren't leaving." In the
distance a car door slams. The radio sounds like shooting
stars. "I love you," I admit, then quick, before he looks, cut
my eyes away. My hands are tucked into fists, prepared to
beat him up, I guess, if he does not love me.

"I wondered when we'd get around to that." After a
minute he checks his watch and then the sky. "Ten more
minutes. What did I tell you? It's going down on time." My
mouth opens, but the words can't get past the clot of rage and
fear. "No, I don't think I will. I'm not taking vows just to
put you on a plane."

"But I have to go." My voice is a small leak of misery. *To
give him up.* "I can't break my contract." I do not add that I
am tempted beyond reason, all the same.

"I wouldn't ask you to." He turns his head, and in the
poor light his eye is the color of cold rain. "I knew where
you were going when I came after you. I don't blame you for
the contract, Jane."

I raise my foot and squint along my pant leg in an effort
not to cry. The corrugated sole of my small hiking boot
appears much larger than the sun. This is present, and soon it
will be past. I will get over it. It's just that I don't want me
to. I put my foot down. "You could come live in New York
with me."

He shakes his head.

"But what's so awful about it?" I protest, remembering
the time I wanted to go to New Orleans—there had been an
opening for a clarinet there, too, and Ben had lost his job, but
I was afraid to point that out, so I simply said, "Don't you
think it would be exciting to live someplace like, oh, say New
Orleans?" "New Orleans has the highest rate of bladder
cancer in the United States," Ben replied, and that was that,
since to have pushed it would have seemed as if I wanted him
to die. "Cancer? Dirty air? Subway crime?"

"I told you. It's not rational. I just can't stand to feel that
crowded—like I'd kill a hundred Viet Cong to move up one

space in line. I don't want to have to feel that ugly about myself. It scares me."

"You didn't feel ugly about yourself when you were machine-gunning Viet Cong down?"

"No."

"Well, then you're right, it isn't rational," I say, wondering why I am not more horrified. He has killed, by his own admission, more than a hundred people, and he does not apologize.

"I want to show you something." He lifts his hand to his forehead, but even before that grim black patch has cleared its hollow, I have winced and closed my eyes. "You wanted to see so bad, now look. It's not going to make you sick."

I slit one eye, but in the dusk I need both. The patch sits like a smudge of mill grease on his forehead, and just below is his scarred lid, shaped by the steel ball that has been sewn into his socket, a broken strip of stubby lashes like a typed-in blank. I don't know why it makes me cry. It's far less horrible than simply, dumbly blind.

"I would rather have kept it," he is saying as he slides the patch back down. "But I can't say I really miss it."

"But why?" I am sobbing.

"Because I don't agonize like you do over things that I can't help. I'll miss you more tomorrow than I will next year. Come on now, quit crying. I love you. What do you think I came to Aspen for?"

I wipe my face on my sleeve. "You said you were passing through."

"And you weren't suspicious when I didn't have a destination? You were afraid of me. What else would I have told you? 'Jane, I've come for you'?"

"No." I have to laugh because he makes it sound absurd and so I wipe my face again, but then it isn't really funny and so I end up crying. "Why does it have to be this way? Why do *I* always come back to the same choices? I can't give up music."

"Why do you have to be so melodramatic? I don't want you to. And if you broke that contract, you would never find another job."

I think it is the casual curve of his shoulders toward the west that brings this old anger back: my brother's shoulders curved toward our brand-new TV, and I am maybe four as I trip over the corner of the rug and burn my arm along its nap. In that stunned second of silence before I begin to scream, Bugs Bunny rips through Elmer Fudd's carrot field and my brother laughs. "What's going on out here?" my mother demands when my brother too begins to wail. "I didn't do anything," he insists and glares. "She kicked me in the shins." And I am much too young to explain that what he did was fail to feel my pain.

"How *can* you sit there? . . ."

"Janie, I don't think we should be corny about this. The setting's bad enough. Now I'll take you to the airport, and then we'll say goodbye."

"You *don't* care. If you loved me . . ." As he turns his head, I hear my mother's echo, and I am terrified.

"Watch the sun. It's almost time."

"Fuck you."

"Fuck you too," he says, but then, as I jerk away, he has me, one hand is closed around my wrist and yanking until I turn around. "It would never occur to you—would it?—to compromise. It would never occur to you that, just because for me careers don't mean that much, I might still understand how yours is more to you. My *father* is a musician—and I learned one thing from him that my grandfather never knew, because his life was so terrible he *had* to hide in art. What's your excuse? You don't have enough imagination to live and be an artist too? You don't have to live in some exalted world. So if it comes back to those same choices, it's because you want it to." He drops my wrist. "Just don't whine to me about what you're going to lose."

"I'm losing *you*."

"Then lose me with your chin up and don't be sentimental."

"But you won't come to New York."

"No, I won't, not for good."

"Well, then? . . ."

"Use your head, why don't you?"

But I want the Philharmonic forever. I don't want another job.

"I would like," he adds, as if it is merely an addendum, "for us to get married and have kids."

"But . . ."

"Janie, that's a proposal. How can you answer it with 'but'?"

And I am in love with this man now. What if being in love is not enough? And what if—don't be silly my heart says, but my brain insists on all sides of the matter—we find that we have been in love but it was only temporary? It is not fair that, in a world where life and death are luck, we have, day by day, to make decisions, to balance on our mortal toes in an eternity of imagination.

Yet we are poised, and all along my skin, we are humming, dancing. It is the same thrill that buzzes down my body during certain passages of music, that miracle of nerves that is the mundane secret of all transubstantiation, and for one gilt moment before it all begins again, the argument of impossibilities, the trivia of exasperations, the sun pauses above the horizon, time wags its tail and waits.

"What do you say?"

I hesitate.

It begins anyway. As his eye widens, I turn my head, and the sun sets behind the canyon just like the ball that drops into Times Square every New Year's Eve.

About the Author

A native of Chicago, Lee Zacharias has taught at Princeton and the University of North Carolina at Greensboro, where she directs the Master of Fine Arts Program in Creative Writing and edits *The Greensboro Review*. Her short stories have appeared in a number of magazines and are collected in her first book, HELPING MURIEL MAKE IT THROUGH THE NIGHT. LESSONS is her first novel.